THE
# Unlikely
# Spy Catchers

THE
# Unlikely
# Spy Catchers

## Carla Kelly

CAVEL
PRESS

Seattle, WA

# CAMEL
# PRESS

Camel Press
6524 NE 181st St
Suite 2
Kenmore WA 98028

For more information go to: www.camelpress.com
www.carlakellyauthor.com

This is a work of fiction. Names, characters, places, brands, media, and incidents are the product of the author's imagination or are used fictitiously.

Cover Design by Dawn Anderson

The Unlikely Spy Catchers
Copyright © 2019 by Carla Kelly

ISBN: 9781603811088 (trade paper)
ISBN: 9781603817004 (ebook)

Printed in the United States of America

*≈*

*To the memory of Robert J. Chandler, Ph.D., historian.*
*And Euclid again, of course.*

*≈*

# Books by Carla Kelly

## FICTION

Daughter of Fortune

Summer Campaign

Miss Chartley's Guided Tour

Marian's Christmas Wish

Mrs. McVinnie's London Season

Libby's London Merchant

Miss Grimsley's Oxford Career

Miss Billings Treads the Boards

Miss Milton Speaks Her Mind

Miss Wittier Makes a List

Mrs. Drew Plays Her Hand

Reforming Lord Ragsdale

The Lady's Companion

With This Ring

One Good Turn

The Wedding Journey

Here's to the Ladies: Stories of the Frontier Army

Beau Crusoe

Marrying the Captain

The Surgeon's Lady

Marrying the Royal Marine

The Admiral's Penniless Bride

Borrowed Light

Enduring Light

Coming Home for Christmas: The Holiday Stories

Regency Christmas Gifts

Season's Regency Greetings

Marriage of Mercy

My Loving Vigil Keeping

Double Cross

Marco and the Devil's Bargain

Paloma and the Horse Traders

Star in the Meadow

Unlikely Master Genius

## NON-FICTION

On the Upper Missouri: The Journal of Rudolph Friedrich Kurz (editor)

Louis Dace Letellier: Adventures on the Upper Missouri (editor)

Fort Buford: Sentinel at the Confluence

BUT LOVE IS A DURABLE FIRE
IN THE MIND EVER BURNING
NEVER SICK, NEVER OLD, NEVER DEAD
FROM ITSELF, NEVER TURNING.

Sir Walter Raleigh, *"Walsinghame"*

# — Preface —

Was it the winter's cold that brought out painful lumps the damned British called carbuncles on his hands? Was it the night he woke up, terrified, because he dreamed he forgot how to chew? Lately they had been given only watery soups. Was it the crazed prisoner who tried to escape by gnawing on the bulkhead until his bloody mouth filled with splinters? Was it the gibberish language and smells of the rafalés, truly insane, who flitted about the three decks of the HMS Captivity, wearing nothing and squatting wherever they chose?

It was all that, and it was none of that, Lieutenant Jean Hubert decided. He had discussed the matter a few days ago with signalman Jacques Rien, fellow prisoner who had served with him in the West Indies aboard the sloop-of-war Calais. They had decided to put away discussions of ratatouille and compliant women and determine what made captivity aboard a prison hulk in Portsmouth Harbor unbearable.

This was scarcely philosophical, but they had to choose topics other than cuisine. Yesterday, two prisoners beat each other to death, arguing whether Languedoc's potage made with cream and truffles was superior to that found along the Rive Loire. Their jailers had laughed as the men bludgeoned each other into insensibility. No, food was, so to speak, off the table for a while.

Jean and Jacques Rien came to no consensus. Later that evening, swinging in his hammock and trying to shut out sounds of men coughing, farting, arguing, dying, Jean decided that the worst thing about being a prisoner of the Royal Navy was lack of solitude. Had he possessed any remaining louis d'or, he would have traded it for a quiet corner on the Captivity. Surely there must be one somewhere.

Officially, solitude meant a few days in the Hole for those who talked back or otherwise irritated their captors. It took little provocation, but not even isolation was quiet. The sound of men weeping in darkness was worse than women in tears. A smart man could cajole a woman, but a man? Hardly ever.

Jacques Rien had admitted to a growing uncertainty that his wife was still faithful to him. Yolande had not heard from him in years and had no idea he was merely a channel away now, and not in the disease-ridden waters off Saint-Domingue. Jacques fretted that she had found someone else.

Jean Hubert had no such worries. He had no wife, no parents, one brother in Canada and a sister who had the misfortune to marry a minor aristocrat and now lay rotting in an unmarked grave, her severed head probably between her legs.

Peace and quiet. Warmth would be nice, but it was optional. Real food would be good, too, but after a while, even a starving man starts to regard meals with some indifference.

And while he was imagining the impossible, Jean Hubert added one thing more: the ability to open a door and walk outside, needing no one's permission. That would be freedom.

# — Chapter One —

## LONDON, LATE FEBRUARY 1804

*A*m I a man or a mouse? Able Six asked himself as he glowered at his poorly tied neckcloth. *I am a husband, and thank God for that.*

His next glance took in his wife Meridee, who sat on their bed in Grace Croker's London townhouse. Meri wore that now-familiar serene expression, directed downward at their son Benjamin Belvedere Six, whose eyelids were at half- mast as he nursed.

Three months should have been long enough for the newness to wear off for Able, considering how nimble his mind, but such had not been the case. There Ben lay, with little fat rolls in abundance, a testimony to good mothering. He was a calm baby with Able's black curly hair and dark eyes.

"I hope he is not a genius," Able had remarked to Meridee not long after his birth, which made her laugh.

"Even if he is, shall we let him be a baby?" she replied.

At this moment, Able was hard put to tell whether the mother or the son appeared more content. Now was the moment to test her.

"Please accompany me to Trinity House," he said, with no preliminary cajoling. "You've filled our laddie to the brim, and he will likely sleep until we return, with Mrs. Perry in charge."

"My love, I have not been invited, nor am I ever likely to be."

He watched as she gently hoisted Ben to her shoulder, where he produced a resounding burp that startled him and jerked his head up. After one owlish look around, their baby returned to his milk-induced coma, nestling into that most pleasant space between his mother's neck and shoulder.

Moving gracefully, Meri deposited their offspring in his cradle. She stuffed herself back into her shimmy, then scrutinized Able and his neckcloth. She turned him toward the end of the bed, where he obediently sat.

"Let's start over." She bent toward him, keeping her voice low, even though Able was certain not even a pack of baying wolves would have roused Ben, not after that feeding.

The expert where he was not, Meri smoothed down the untied ends, flicked them here and there, tugged a bit, then stepped back. "You'll do," she told him. "And no, I will not trespass on the – what is it you call them?"

"The Elder Brothers."

"Such an odd name. Are they all geriatrics?"

"I'll remind you that our boy's namesake can hardly be called ancient." He patted the bed and she sat. "Captain Sir Belvedere St. Anthony is but forty."

"Forty hard years." He saw all the sympathy in her eyes.

"I know. There are times – too many to count – that I loathe and despise Napoleon for what he is doing to us."

She cocked her head to one side. "How many years more will we suffer the Corsican Tyrant?"

"Ten if a minute," he said, well aware that even *he* had no idea. "Let us see if Sir John Moore prevails on land. We will continue to do our part at sea." He smiled. "And at St. Brendan's, which is what brings us to London, when we would all rather be in Portsmouth." He nudged her. "Even you, Meri? Ever think you'd come to like that devil-may-care den of iniquity?"

She gave him her clear-eyed appraisal that he craved because of its honesty. "I decided I can live anyplace where lives the man – well, men now – I adore." She nudged back. "Even Euclid."

When he started to laugh, she put her hand over his mouth. "Hush!"

"Ben is sleeping the sleep of the well-fed," he reminded her.

"I wish I knew why you were asked here."

"So do I."

"I thought you knew everything." She nudged his hip.

"I don't read minds, Meri."

He returned the hip nudge and added a hand on her thigh. "I still don't read minds, but even the most oblivious husband would understand what you're up to."

"Are you grateful?"

What to do but kiss her? His brain emptied out as she kissed back, and messed up the neckcloth she had reconstructed from ruin. She took the dratted thing from his neck and pulled out a new one from the bureau drawer.

"This looks even better," she declared a few minutes later. "No more kissing."

"Not ever? Horrors! I can calculate the number of times we have kissed and done much more, and arrive at a percentage that would make such a threat seem improbable in the extreme."

"I have no doubt you can," she replied. Thank merciful heaven they had been married long enough that such mental nonsense didn't faze her. "You have likely already done it."

"Aye, miss."

"Plead all you want, my love, but I wasn't invited to Trinity House."

Able knew he could win. All he had to do was speak the truth.

"Meridee, I'm fair terrified to go without you," he said and meant every syllable. "Who am I even to be sitting on a bed in Curzon Street? There are still times when I feel like a workhouse bastard. I don't belong in London's most fashionable district."

"Neither do I," she told him, her head against his shoulder now. She touched his face, sighing when he turned his head and kissed her palm.

"Meri, do you ever feel like a feeding machine?"

"Yes!" she replied with good humor. "Would I change that? Never."

As he stood up, Able tried not to think of his own mother, a Dumfries whore. After she birthed him in an alley, she had cared enough to drag herself to the church steps and leave him there, before she crawled away to die alone like a wounded cat.

Trying *not* to think was one of the few things Sailing Master Durable Six couldn't do. He remembered his mother panting and groaning as she gave birth and suddenly how cold he felt as Scottish rain drenched his naked skin and he cried for the first time.

*Think of something else,* he commanded his phenomenal brain.

In a moment, Meri stood beside him, her hand over his eyes. "No, no," she whispered. "Don't."

All he needed was Meri close by. He held her to him until the scroll that was his remarkable mind changed to Euclid's propositions. The feel of his wife's hand covering his rapidly moving eyes soothed him.

"Very well, Able, I will come along. Will they throw me out?"

"They wouldn't dare. I'll corner Grace Croker downstairs. You know how she enjoys a challenge. You'll have a willing accomplice." He sniffed her milk-damp shimmy. "Find something dry to wear, though."

She swatted at him. He laughed and hurried downstairs to the sitting room and found John Mark instead of Grace. Dressed neatly in black, with the St. Brendan the Navigator patch over his heart, John contemplated the globe.

With emotions decidedly mixed, Able watched him, seeing a lad much like himself when he joined the fleet, although John was eleven to his nine. *There was a world at my fingertips, too,* he thought. *There are still days that I miss service in the fleet.*

Eyes bright, John looked up when Able entered the room.

"Where away, Mister Mark?" Able asked.

John pointed to the Mediterranean Sea. "Here, sir, standing the watch."

"In time, in time," Able said. He stood by the globe, his hand on John's shoulder, marveling at the change one year could make in the life of a lad whose origin had been desperately sad.

He knew John Mark still woke himself up with nightmares of the Portsmouth workhouse where he had been taken as an infant. More than once, Able was relieved that he knew no one else with his total recall, especially John Mark. When he came to St. Brendan's, the boy's workhouse matron had filled in the tragic details.

The lad's mother had been a prostitute, like Able's mother. Rags stuffed in her mouth to silence her screams, she had been dragged aboard a ship, hidden, and passed around from sailor to sailor. Nine months later she had been kicked ashore naked in Plymouth. She gave birth on a freezing dock as her prison-frigate sailed with the tide.

The ringleaders had been caught and forced to confess. Before she died, her only words had been, "In all that time, couldn't they have given me back my dress?" Thank God John Mark had no recollection. Better he not know that the monsters had been transferred to other ships, and not hanged. The Navy Board had shrugged at the terrible business. "She was but a whore," had been recorded in the court document. The baby went to the workhouse, remaining there until the age of ten, when the experiment at St. Brendan the Navigator School began.

After John's year in her care, Meri had been firm in her refusal to send him back across the street to St. Brendan's dormitory. She had argued effectively that John would remain under their comforting roof until the nightmares were gone.

"Sir, we look fine as five pence, don't we?" John asked. Despite everything, he was a cheerful child.

"I declare we do," Able agreed.

"Did Mrs. Six fix your neckcloth?"

"She did. Is it so obvious when she does it, versus when I do it?"

John Mark grinned and returned his attention to the Mediterranean.

"Where is Miss Croker?" he asked.

"Sir, I believe she is reading in the library."

He strolled down the hall to the library, and there was Grace Croker, their hostess. The sister of St. Brendan's headmaster, Thaddeus Croker, Grace had invited herself along because she wanted to give her Mayfair rowhouse an airing. She had begun teaching last spring when Master Rodney Blake, English literature and grammar instructor, had come to a fitting end after a pimping career that might have gone unpunished because of his rank and fortune.

Wealthy and bored in London, Grace hadn't been hard to convince and happily came to teach. Possessed of a brain as quick as her brother's, she had proved essential to St. Brendan's. Her continued employment, even minus salary, was not a sure thing, but nothing about St. Brendan's was a sure thing. Perhaps that was why Able had been summoned to Trinity House. Maybe the Admiralty had gotten word of the nearly forgotten, centuries' old monastery near the docks and wondered what was going on. Trinity House's various duties were a mystery to most, even Able, except that sometimes its members were called upon by the crown for work of a discreet and silent nature.

Grace looked up when he came in and closed the book, her finger saving her place.

"Able, are you and John Mark ready?" He couldn't overlook her grin. "I can see Meridee did something wonderful to your neckcloth."

"As ever."

"For a genius, there are times when you are not so smart," she teased. Theirs was the camaraderie of teachers. At times she exasperated him, but he admired her more. Heaven knows he must exasperate her, too.

"I have convinced her to come along with John and me, and sit in the gallery, if there is one."

"I doubt ladies are allowed."

He noticed she had removed her finger from the book. "She took some convincing. I, uh, promised her that you would come along and buttress the argument."

"You know I will." Her expression softened. "You can't do this without her, can you?"

"I would never presume to try."

# — Chapter Two —

"Will I do?"

Meridee wasn't fishing for compliments. Once result of motherhood had meant an impressive bosom. Since dresses didn't grow on trees in the Six household, she had hoped to fit into her last-winter frocks sooner.

"You will always do," her trusty man told her.

"It's too tight."

"It's just right. There is not a man in the Royal Navy who wouldn't like to be in my shoes, Meri."

She came closer and whispered, "I put some padding in, you know, in case I leak." She glared at him when he laughed. "If, and mind you this is if, the Elder Brothers decide I can stay, I wouldn't want them thinking ...oh, I don't know what. You fluster me."

That was an honest assessment. There he was, holding her tight, when any servant could wander by.

"You fluster *me*," Able replied, totally unrepentant. "All the Brothers will see is a charming lady with a magnificent bosom."

"You are impossible to argue with."

"One of my charms."

Meridee already knew that her man always had a ready comment. Generally. After Ben made his noisy entrance in November, Able had stared in silence at the slimy, red-faced infant in his arms. He had no words then.

She knew him. If Master Durable Six wanted her at Trinity House, he would find a way. Meridee spent a moment in Grace Croker's kitchen where Mrs. Perry had assumed undisputed authority merely by her massive presence. "Ben is full to the brim and we shan't be too long. I hope," she added.

"I'll bring his cradle down to the kitchen after you and the master leave," Mrs. Perry said, looking around as if daring any of Miss Croker's servants to object. Meridee pointed to a quiet corner with the warmth of the fireplace to recommend it, and blew a kiss to her more-than-servant.

Grace Croker was putting on her gloves in the hall, her eyes already flashing their militant gleam. The woman did love a challenge. Able had warned her what might lie ahead in attempting admission into an organization nearly as exclusive as the House of Lords.

"If we can't gain admittance?" Meridee asked. The Croker landau bowled along toward Tower Hill with both Sixes and John Mark, who looked with interest on the bustle that was London.

"We will not consider failure," Grace said firmly.

"Please, Master Six, why am I along?" John Mark asked, as they stopped because of a collision between a bread wagon and a poulterer taking geese to market. The squawking easily overbore the sound of the arguing drivers.

"I suspect the Elder Brethren want to know what we are doing at St. Brendan's. Mind you, I am not certain."

"Who are they?"

"It's an old organization, started by King Henry the Eighth in 1514," Able said. He stared out the window at the geese, who were now nipping the driver of the bread wagon. "Noisy London. God help us. Trinity House regulates our island's buoys and lighthouses, and licenses pilots and sailing masters. I never went that route to become a master, although many do."

By now, interested passersby had subdued the geese. To Meridee's amusement, most of the birds were being quickly led away, probably to dinner, while the men fought on. Grace's driver moved ahead after cursing them both.

"I suspect Trinity House has fingers in more pies than we know of," Able said.

"Our school?" John asked. There was nothing slow about the little boy who leaned against Able.

"I've wondered."

"But why am *I* here?"

"Lad, I think they have got wind of the Gunwharf Rats and want to know more. And didn't you tell Captain St. Anthony about Mr. Maudslay's block pulley factory?"

Meridee watched John's face light up. "I could watch machinery all day."

"I know," Able said with a lurking smile, "and you teased and nagged at me to let you volunteer to serve as an office boy there. I can remember your every word."

He could, of course; even John Mark knew that by now.

"A block pulley factory is prodigiously noisy, but I like it," he admitted, then brightened. "Do the Brothers *know* block pulleys?"

"Every tar knows them, laddie."

Meridee smiled inside when Able's arm went around the boy. She watched the two of them, dressed alike in St. Brendan's sober garb, with its distinctive patch. Both had curly hair, but John's skin was tan. She sighed, wondering which of the many men who had tormented his mother was from Africa, or the Caribbean, or somewhere in between.

"Block pulleys aren't exciting, but not a ship would sail without them," John said. "I could tell the Brothers that, if they ask."

"You could."

Able laughed when John Mark said seriously, "Don't tell Nick or any of the other Gunwharf Rats, but I truly love block pulleys."

"That's because you are a mechanist at heart, like Mr. Maudslay who interpreted Marc Brunel's drawings, and Simon Goodrich who is building the factory," Able said.

"Davey Ten is already studying to become an apothecary. Stephen Hoyt is, hopefully, clerking in Australia, although we have yet to hear from him. Should I despair of actually training many sailing masters?"

Meridee watched a shadow cross her husband's face and she knew he was thinking of his prize pupil, Jan Yarmouth, dead these ten months after a shipboard accident in the Mediterranean. She wanted to reach for him, but John Mark was there, and by no means slow. None of the Gunwharf Rats were slow. His voice gentle, John changed the subject.

"Sir, we should have brought along Nick. He can already swim better than all of us and likes to stare at our binnacle hour upon hour." John sighed. "And he doesn't get seasick when we take Sir B's yacht into the sound."

"I would have brought you both, but for Nick's sprained ankle."

Meridee saw Nick's sad face in her mind's eye. Last summer, the boy with no last name had gathered together his courage and his love and asked if he could take on her maiden name of Bonfort, since, as he pointed out, she wasn't using it. They had happily been sharing it ever since, officially since a recent visit to the magistrate.

"I depend upon you to remember everything that happens in Trinity House and record it in your ship's log tonight," Able said. "You might be quizzed by Headmaster Croker, too. Poor man. He was supposed to be with us, but someone gave him the mumps."

"Which is why we are on holiday, so to speak," John said. His eyes on Miss Croker, he whispered to Meridee, "I hear he is not an easy patient."

"I heard that, and you are right," Grace Croker said, from her side of the carriage. "I am happy to get away, too."

"Even if it is to stare down Elder Brothers, Miss Croker?" John asked. "How old *are* they?"

"I think the term has more to do with experience than age," Able said. "They number thirty-one. Captain Sir Belvedere St. Anthony, our Sir B, is one of them, and he is forty."

"Gor, that is old!" John declared.

Grace Croker spoke up. "It won't seem so old when you are forty," she told him, with all the crispness of upper class diction at her command. "I am thirty-five soon. Wretched boy! Don't look so surprised."

"I am eleven. Forty? Ancient."

Grace laughed, probably confirming John's suspicions about her good humor, once away from the classroom, where Miss Croker held forth on penmanship, grammar and decorum.

"Since we are spilling all our secrets, I am twenty-seven and Mrs. Six is a mere twenty-four. And now you're wondering if we have the strength to roll over in bed." Able winked at Meridee. She knew precisely what his agile brain was thinking. Able had no trouble rolling over in bed, or doing anything else there.

"Still... Elder Brothers. Are there younger brothers?"

"There are indeed." Able cleared his throat. "And what's more, the current warden of Trinity House is none other than William Pitt, our recent prime minister."

"Gor! Will *he* be here today?"

"Unlikely. I suspect he is a busy man, for all that he is currently out of office. We'll probably be talking to old merchant mariners and Royal Navy men who will have trouble staying awake."

"I'm a little afraid, Master Six," John admitted.

"I am, too, lad."

"Make that three of us," Meridee added.

"You, too, Meri?"

"I doubt Grace and I will even get through the door," she told him. "Perhaps I have less to worry about than I think."

Fifteen minutes later, Able pointed out the dignified two-story building on a quiet corner street. "Trinity House. Courage, now."

"Blimey, Tower Hill. Isn't this where a lot of gentry coves lost their heads?" John Mark asked, suddenly more interested.

"No cant, John Mark," Grace Croker said, her voice firm in her best educationist's tone.

"A fair number of…let us call them men who made imprudent choices," Able said. "Fifty, if memory serves me."

John Mark leaned across the sailing master, a casual gesture that would never have happened only months ago. The simple, careless act warmed Meridee's heart.

"Mrs. Six, does memory always serve the master?"

"Always," she told him. "Fifty men."

Meridee looked with interest on a modern building, probably the latest word in design, with two small cannon flanking the entrance. Beyond the understated style, what distinguished Trinity House was Neptune and his trident atop a flagpole.

John darted out of the carriage, remembered himself, and held out his hand for Miss Croker. Meridee glanced at Able, who had closed his eyes. She watched his face drain of color. Sometimes he retreated to the Dumfries Workhouse, a little boy who could not explain himself to anyone, and with no advocate who cared.

*I care*, she thought. *I care so deeply*. She put her hand over his eyes. She felt his eyelashes against her hand as he opened his eyes.

"You won't leave me alone here?" he whispered.

"Never," she replied, her lips against his ear. "Euclid is probably lurking about, too, drat the man."

He chuckled, in charge of himself again. "Now, now, my love." He looked around to make sure John Mark was out of the carriage. "Euclid may have been banished from our bedroom, just as you insisted, but I would never deny him the pleasure of a visit to Trinity House. Or you."

"If I can get in," she said. It was her turn for inadequacy.

"You will get in. That I do not doubt."

"I wish I had your confidence."

"You know how that works, dearest," he said. He stepped out of the carriage and held out his hand for her. "What's mine is yours, and apparently mine is Trinity House right now, for better or worse. That really should be in the wedding vows."

"Now you would rewrite our vows?" she teased, anything to calm her nerves.

"Nay, lass. How could anyone improve upon, 'With my body I thee worship?' We'll leave our vows alone."

"Oh, you," Meridee said and felt her face flame.

"Just a few hours and you'll be back in Curzon Street with Ben. All will be right in your world." He helped her from the carriage. "My world, too."

Her courage returned.

# — Chapter Three —

Easy to say. When Able found that his legs were rubber, Grace Croker gave him a kindly glance, took John Mark's hand and marched up the low steps to the entrance.

Meridee's arm through his steadied him. He had no idea who was holding up whom, but that was one of the joys of marriage; it didn't matter.

The door opened upon a one-legged fellow with an eye patch, obviously the veteran of many fleet actions or encounters with pirates.

Able's wife took in stride the sudden retreat of one small boy from the steps. He slowly moved behind her, where it was safer.

"That's the doorman," she whispered to John. "He is no obstacle. You've been invited here, John Mark. Don't forget it."

"I have, haven't I?"

"Yes. Did you come back here to buttress me? Alas, I have not been invited."

"Aye, Mam, that's what I did. Are you feeling better now?"

"Yes, my dear. Thank you."

It was Able's turn. He mentally shoved aside all the theorems, broadsides and propositions clambering about for attention in his brain and took the letter of introduction from his uniform pocket. A few strides, and he held out the invitation.

"Sailing Master Able Six and John Mark, student, are requested and required to attend upon the Elder Brothers of Trinity House," he said.

The doorman glanced at the invitation and nodded. "Come inside, master." He looked at Meridee and then Miss Croker. "But not the ladies. They can wait for you elsewhere."

"I'd rather they were admitted, too."

"Impossible, sir. Trinity House is for seafaring men only. I could lose my situation here, if I allowed them entrance."

Able tried another tack. "I suspect John Mark and I have been invited here to discuss St. Brendan the Navigator School. My wife and Miss Croker are equally important there. If the Elder Brothers really wish to know how we function, they should include the ladies."

The doorman didn't look convinced. "Then they should have been mentioned in the invitation. Will you come in or not, Master, uh, Six?"

"I'd rather not," he said, going against every instinct that obeyed orders. "Ladies, shall we return to Curzon Street?"

"Dearest, it's an order," his wife reminded him.

She was right. "I imagine it is," he said, resigned, but not content. "Very well. John Mark and I will hike home when we are done here."

"I think not. Gervaise, move me closer, if you would. Sutton, kindly move aside and let these people in. *All* of them."

And there he was, Captain Sir Belvedere St. Anthony, godfather to Able's son, managing to look authoritative and magisterial even in a wheeled chair, pushed by his valet, Gervaise Turenne. The doorman stepped aside and Sir B gestured them to follow.

"We won't get you in hot water, Sir B?" Able asked.

"I don't care if you do," Sir B said. "You know my theory on forgiveness versus permission."

"I saw it in full bloom in the occasional fleet action," Able said, remembering well.

"As long as I don't get the sack," the doorman said, but he was grinning now. Sir B had that effect on everyone Able knew.

"That will never happen," said a firm voice, another voice of command.

Able turned toward the street, took a breath and another one. William Pitt himself was coming up the steps, brushing raindrops off his caped overcoat.

"Able, is that..."

"Aye, missy," he whispered. "We're in rare company." He bowed as Meri curtsied and John Mark stared, open mouthed. "Come now, lad. You'll catch flies."

John closed his mouth and managed a remarkable bow, one that made the august man smile and say, "Oh, the navy. How *do* you blokes do it? And Miss Croker, too? How on earth did *you* fall into this den of thieves? I thought you had scruples."

"I was more than fortunate, Billy," Grace said. Able had to resist his own repetition of John Mark's stare as she extended her hand and the former prime minster shook it as he would a man's hand. "I'm delighted to see you."

The illustrious man tipped his low-crowned beaver hat to Grace. "So good of you to summon me, Grace. I don't always have time for these events."

Able turned to Grace, who by now had crooked her arm through the arm William Pitt offered. "Miss Croker, you fair amaze me."

"He's a lifelong friend." Grace patted Meri's cheek. "My dear, your man doesn't know *everything*. And here we are, getting wet."

Too stunned to even look around and enjoy the simple beauty that was Trinity House, Able let the doorman take his boat cloak, bicorn, and Meri's cape, followed by John Mark's smaller boat cloak. William Pitt added his overcoat to the pile, with Grace's cape on top. The doorman didn't even stagger as he stumped away on a good leg and a wooden one.

"There should be introductions," Pitt said, his eyes on Able. "Are you the remarkable man I have heard of?"

*Speak, speak,* Able told himself. *Bastard you may be, but you're no longer a workhouse boy.* He bowed again. "Sailing Master Durable Six, sir. This is my wife, Mrs. Six. John Mark is one of my pupils at St. Brendan's."

"I have heard of your school from Captain St. Anthony," Pitt said, with a slight bow in Sir B's direction. "And from my friend Thaddeus Croker, your headmaster, and Miss Croker, my childhood friends." He directed his attention to John Mark. "Grace Croker can climb trees with amazing speed, Mister Mark."

"Gor, sir!" the boy exclaimed.

"Gor, indeed," William Pitt said, not batting an eyelash.

Able wanted to laugh in the worst way, which would have probably earned him a jab in the ribs from Meri. Instead, he turned his attention to older men in dark suits gathering at the top of the branching staircase.

Pitt cleared his throat. "For some reason known only to God, I do not doubt, I was elected warden of this remarkable collection of old tars, who jealously guard our buoys, navigational markers and coasts." He bowed toward the stairs. "How many years has it been, gentleman?"

"Six at least, Mr. Pitt," said one of the Elder Brothers. "Come aboard, all of you."

Meri's hand tight in his, Able gave her fingers a squeeze then went quickly to Sir B and grasped one side of his wheeled chair. With a pang, he realized how light the man was as he and Gervaise lifted him up the stairs to the first floor.

Able walked beside Sir B, following the formidable phalanx of Elder Brothers in front of them, William Pitt in the middle. "Sir B, why am I here? You've been remarkably coy about this summons," he asked.

"Word gets about, no matter how much Headmaster Croker would wish otherwise," Sir B said, keeping his voice low. He lowered it further. "There was that nasty business last spring with the, ahem, disappearance of that regrettable lump of carbon I will laughingly call Master Blake. His family does have court connections."

"I doubt they miss him," Able whispered back.

"So do I, but everyone keeps up appearances. Here we are. Gervaise, wheel me up with the others. Able, you and John Mark sit in those two chairs." Sir B nodded to Meridee. "Mrs. Six, you and Gracie behave yourselves, Gracie especially." He winked at Grace when she glared at him.

Able didn't know where to seat the ladies. Elder Brothers were finding their places around a long, baize-covered table, u-shaped and connected at the head, but with a narrow aisle, as if to allow for a secretary to distribute documents for comment and perusal.

He felt Meridee press against his shoulder again. She gazed around with wonder in her eyes.

"What in the world are we doing in a place like this?"

"It's a far cry from the steps of the Dumfries Church of Scotland," he said under his breath, his odd mind swooping and darting about in split-second bursts from his birth in that back alley, to cold church steps, to beatings in the workhouse, to life in the fleet, to hunger, cold, heat, and the plunging fire of battle, to the warmth of his wife's body, to the milky smell of his son hopefully asleep in Curzon Street and guarded by a big black woman with a ring in her nose. His thoughts landed him right here, bumping as gently as Sir B's yacht the *Jolly Roger* bumped against the dock after a training sail to the Isle of Wight and back.

Without a word, he found Meridee and Grace seats away from the table, but not too far. He squeezed his wife's hand, then gazed into her lovely eyes, so kind.

He knew she was as frightened as he was, so he allowed himself the unspeakable luxury of another bursting thought that blasted through all the fear: Meri Six loved him. He could do anything, be anything, because he knew that. At the end of the day, she would go home with him, no matter what happened in this place.

# — Chapter Four —

## HMS CAPTIVITY – PORTSMOUTH
## FEBRUARY, 1804

Even Jean Hubert's dreams gave him little pleasure. Here they were, captive in the stinking hold of a prison hulk, anchored in Portsmouth's harbor, where every day the ship's foul waste buckets were dumped out of portholes. The *Captivity* rolled in a brown stew of feces and bloody stools, depending on the tides. Jean shook his head to clear it. Why could he not remember the simplest things? Oh yes, something about organizing an escape club. Surely not. "Escape club" sounded almost festive, as though this whole ordeal were a lark.

*Eh bien*, a meeting, and a select one at that. Claude Pascal, the hulk's self-appointed judge and chief officer below deck, had tapped some of them on the shoulder that afternoon and whispered, "Deck three, near the Hole, after lights doused."

Why he had been chosen, only God knew. It was anyone's guess. All Jean wanted to do was sit at his rickety desk and draw pictures of *la belle France*. A shady deal with a guard meant he could hand off two sketches a week, for a paltry ten sou. They were worth more, but who was the prisoner here? the guard regularly reminded him.

All the same, it was enough to buy someone's meat ration, or stockings probably taken off a dead man, more sketching paper, and colored pencils. He was better off than some.

Dark came early. The daily count of prisoners began at two in the afternoon, which meant standing in one place too long, and complete purgatory for those among them with dysentery. To counter the boredom at first, Jean imagined walking along the beach at Trouville, or ducking into a favorite bookshop in Caen. Lately, he thought of nothing, because it was easier.

The evening swill followed. It was a meatless day. No one ate Thursday's dried herring, at least no one in his right mind, which meant that probably quite a few ate it. Friday's cod was a mushy stew, but there was bread, now and then.

After the guards threatened them and shut down the hatches, little pinpoints of light bloomed here and there. The air was so poor in the winter, and oxygen so scarce, that the light was hard to see. He joined the other men moving toward the back of deck one, his deck. The damned English had no idea their prisoners could move from deck to deck other than by the companionway. Last year while everyone sang "La Marseillaise" really loud, a carpenter cut a small square in their own dark corner. Another one in the deck below, and *voilá*, nothing was off limits.

One man could squeeze down at a time, down through the next deck, and then in the bowels of the hulk near the Hole, where, thank God, no one was confined currently.

Claude Pascal called them to order. "*Mes amis*, we need to coordinate any escape attempts. Do you know what happened to François du Lac yesterday?"

They all knew. No one wanted to talk about it. Brave François, or maybe foolish François, had cut a square in the side of the ship about midway between deck two and the waterline, covered himself in bilge slime and squeezed out through the impossible opening. No one warned him about the nails studding the outside of the hulk. He had caught his canvas bag with clothes and a few coins and dangled there as the sky lightened and sentries saw him.

They had used François for target practice, and they weren't good shots. François dangled there still, and probably would until he finally melted into the harbor, a potent reminder of the folly of escape.

"We must know is who is planning what," Claude said.

*Me? Never*, Jean thought. Perhaps it wasn't a thing to be proud of, the honor of France and all that, but he hadn't cared much for the aristocrats, and he wasn't particularly enamored of the Jacobins and republicans who had followed. What he wanted was to be left alone.

With fierce eyes, Claude waited. A hand went up, and another.

"Stand, Citizen Remillard," Claude said. "You are a gunner, are you not?"

"I am, Citizen Pascal." He gestured beside him, and a small boy stood up. "And this is Pierre Deschamps, my powder monkey."

The boy ducked his head and would have sat down again on the deck, but Remillard fixed him with a glare.

Jean stirred uneasily. Already he did not care for this scheme. *Let the boy alone*, he wanted to say, but that would have called attention to himself.

"Citizen, we have been watching the water hoys," Remillard the gunner said. "It appears to me that we could each climb inside a keg. One of you in the know could mark the two kegs, maybe a knick with a knife. That way, whoever is to sling the keg into the hoy for the return trip to the harbor would be one of us here, informed of the escape." He shrugged. "Otherwise, poof! Someone might complain to the damned English that the keg was too heavy and all would be over."

No one said anything, which cheered Jean. It was a foolhardy scheme. But as he looked around, he saw too many thoughtful gazes, as if their owners were considering the idea. *Mon dieu*, he thought. *Don't listen to Remillard, Claude.*

Claude evidently was not susceptible to thought waves. "What would happen then, or do you know?"

"I casually asked one of the guards about the kegs," Remillard said.

*Brilliant, brilliant,* Jean thought in disgust. *And he probably casually told Captain Faulke, goddamn him.*

"He said they are stacked in one of the harbor inlets by the factories. A day or two passes, and then they are filled, taken back to the water hoys and over to us. I think it would be entirely feasible to stick a small man like me in one keg, and the lad in another. When the kegs are returned to the wharf, we wait until dark and climb out." He drew his fingers together and kissed them. "Then home somehow to *la belle France,* to fight another day."

"Aren't the kegs offloaded to the dock? Wouldn't the Englishmen on the other end of this process notice heavier kegs?"

*Lord help us, I have spoken out loud,* Jean thought, horrified with himself. *Well, someone has to set these ninnies straight.*

Remillard, damn him, seemed to have an answer for everything. "The water hoys usually arrive back in port near dusk, what with winter limiting daylight. I would wager that the dock workers are in such a hurry to quit that they leave the offloading until morning, when we are long gone." He shrugged. "Besides, we are so thin now. We weigh nearly nothing."

More silence. Jean Hubert, sensible man, closed his eyes. He knew what was next.

"What say you, men?" Claude asked. He turned to Remillard. "When are the next water hoys due?"

"In two days, Citizen."

Claude Pascal looked around again. "Are we in?"

# — Chapter Five —

## TRINITY HOUSE - LONDON

"I hope we're not in anyone's way," Meridee whispered to Grace. "Able should have seated us farther back."

"Then you would be out of his line of sight," Grace said simply.

Grace was right. Funny how a man so capable, brilliant and wise as Master Six required her presence. Meridee smiled to herself, thinking of the times she had been working on some mundane project in the kitchen or in the little room off the pantry he had dubbed her office, only to find him on the prowl for her.

She grew a little warm at the thought of that room with its shabby desk and thoroughly comfortable daybed, where they occasionally ended up, once he found her. Good thing the door had a stout lock. For all she knew, Ben had got his start on that daybed.

She asked him once why he felt the need to search the house for her, considering that she was generally available within calling distance. "It's not a mansion, my love," she had reminded him.

He turned serious. "I think there is a part of me that will always wonder if I am worth loving," he said. "Some maggot gets inside my head – along with all the others – that tells me I should look for you."

She smiled even now to think how that conversation concluded. "And here you are, already down to your shimmy, and it is only eleven o'clock in the morning. Maybe it was a good thing I came along. You could freeze like this."

Why was she thinking about that now, of all times? Easy. It was a comforting thought and she was currently terrified. Better to take one deep breath and another, and look around.

As imposing as were the current monarchs whose paintings flanked the fireplace, with its massive mirror reflecting sunlight from opposite windows, more impressive was the almost-life-sized portrait of twenty-three gentlemen, positioned on the wall behind the curiously shaped table. Powdered and wigged, the subjects were dressed in elegant black suits with red stand-up collars. She looked around the room at the men assembling and saw the same uniform.

William Pitt moved to that center place of the U, and the Elder Brothers joined him. It must have been the signal for everyone to rise. Meridee and Grace rose, too.

"Brothers and guests, let us pray," said an Elder Brother. "Almighty God, who calms the tempests and bids us find safe harbor through the grace of thy son, Lord Jesus, attend us this day in our assembly. Guard and guide this mighty nation, is our prayer. Bless our sovereign king and his queen. Protect all ships at sea and those who command them, and our lighthouses. Smite the French wherever possible. Amen."

"What a militant prayer," Grace whispered. "The poor French."

More interested now than frightened, Meridee watched a man without a red collar handed around papers to the men at the table. Perhaps he was a secretary. She heard the low buzz of conversation.

She looked at her man and John Mark, seated at the open-ended foot of the table, wondering if the lad was ready to start fidgeting. What she saw humbled her.

Both Able Six and John Mark sat absolutely still, eyes ahead, hands in laps. As she watched them, she knew they had both reverted to workhouse days, where inmates who moved about or otherwise caused a disturbance could find themselves struck or denied a meal. Able had told her as much one night when he felt like reminiscing, which was seldom.

The business of the meeting seemed to conclude then, with the secretary gathering up the papers, some of which, as Trinity House warden, Mr. Pitt took a moment to sign. What looked like claret came around next, and glasses, brought in by two servants. She glanced at Able, who still sat like a statue.

"Brothers, we are here at the urging of Captain Sir Belvedere St Anthony," Mr. Pitt said finally. He looked around the hall, and nodded toward Grace and Meridee. "This has come with a first for us, as well. Hoorah for the ladies."

The men chuckled. No one seemed irritated. They were navy men, after all, with a certain reputation, or so Meridee reasoned. Thank goodness she saw no pointed stares or ogles. She knew an ogle was one thing that would have lifted Able out of his chair immediately. He tended to be proprietary about her.

But Mr. Pitt was speaking. "A singular school has come to our attention, one that we might wish to have a hand in. It is…" He looked down at his notes. "St. Brendan the Navigator School in Portsmouth, located close to Gunwharf." He looked again. "In fact, it appears that the lads have taken to calling themselves Gunwharf Rats."

After the laughter died down, one of the Elder Brothers spoke up. "Gentlemen of St. Brendan's, surely you can relax a bit. We're not in formal session."

Able's shoulders lowered and he leaned back. He rested his arm on the top of John Mark's chair and the boy shifted toward him. They exchanged glances.

"Indeed, you put us to shame," the same man said. "Have you been studying Greek statuary?"

"No, sir," Able said. He gave Meridee a glance, almost one of validation. "John Mark and I are both alumni of workhouses, where a fidget can get you a lash. We're well trained. That is all."

Meridee didn't mistake the intake of breaths in the room.

"You, too, Master Six?" someone asked.

"Aye, sir. I'm a workhouse bastard from Dumfries, Scotland," Able replied with no hesitation. He looked at John Mark with real affection. "John is one of my Rats."

Mr. Pitt appeared unflappable. "Perhaps you should explain Gunwharf Rats."

"Aye, sir. While cleaning out a stone inlet, we found a long-expired *rattus norvegicus*." Meridee could tell Able was in his element now. He rubbed his hands together. "With the somewhat reluctant assistance of my wife, the boys cleaned the bones and mounted them on a wooden plaque." He turned to John Mark. "Correct me if I'm wrong, but didn't *you* dub all of us Gunwharf Rats?"

"Aye, sir." John seemed to swallow his fear. "We hung the plaque in our classroom. We...we even touch it for good luck before examinations."

Mr. Pitt nodded. "I could have used a good luck talisman any number times in the last seventeen years, leading this unruly nation." When the laughter died down, he glanced toward Sir B. "I am getting ahead of the story. Sir B, tell us more."

"With pleasure, Mr. Pitt. Move me a little closer, Gervaise."

Sir B's valet did as requested. "Better. Thank you. The tall fellow with the curly hair is Sailing Master Durable Six. He teaches the calculus to brave students, instructs all our mathematical courses, plus a hodge-podge course we call seamanship. Our goal is to train lads to become sailing masters, is it not, Able?"

"Aye, captain."

"Introduce your lad, please," said Mr. Pitt, who was leaning forward and listening with some interest.

Meridee noticed other men doing the same. She also took note of the ones who leaned back and folded their arms. One of them, a florid fellow in a too-tight uniform, had a positive sneer on his face.

Able nodded to Mr. Pitt. "Brethren, this is John Mark." He glanced at Meridee again. "John is one of two remaining students who have been boarding with my wife and me, practically since we arrived at St. Brendan's ourselves, and newly married."

"We began this lodging experiment with four students," Sir B explained. "These students our headmaster felt needed more nurturing than some of the other lads who live in St. Brendan's dormitory. One student is now in Australia, clerking for a secretary in Sydney Cove. We're waiting for our first letter from him, are we not? Another is serving as a loblolly boy at Haslar Hospital."

"Not a sailing master's apprentice among *that* lot, eh?" commented Mr. Florid Face, and he didn't sound accommodating to Meridee. "So much for good ideas."

"We're a young school, sir," Able said promptly. "Four of our older students went to sea as sailing apprentices only last May, when the treaty broke. Three are serving in the fleet now as such. One died...died in a shipboard accident."

Meridee heard all the pain. So did Sir B, who spoke up quickly. "We have six in advanced training now, don't we, Able?"

"Aye, sir." Able looked at Sir B, and then Mr. Pitt. "Sirs, if I may..."

"By all means, Master Six."

"I reiterate that we are an experiment. We are discovering that not every lad is suited to the duties of sailing master."

"Send them back to the workhouse then!" said that same disagreeable brother, even as the man seated next to him frowned. Meridee's hands knotted into fists. She relaxed when Grace gently put her hand over them.

"Never!" Able declared, taking a step forward. "That loblolly boy is very soon to be examined for apothecary apprentice. And as for Stephen… if mail were not so slow, we would have a good report from Australia, I have no doubt. You see, sirs, what we have discovered at St. Brendan's is that even bastards deserve a chance."

"You would know," came the dry comment.

"I would," Able agreed, his voice calm. "Believe me, I do."

He sat down and John Mark moved closer. Meridee yearned to stand next to both of her Gunwharf Rats. For all his forthrightness, John still trembled at loud voices. She looked at Sir B, giving him the full wattage of her glance. To her gratitude, he nodded.

And then to her dismay, he cleared his throat and looked about the suddenly quiet room. "Brothers, you need to hear from another person in this room. You need to hear from…what should we call her, Able? St. Brendan's house mother?"

Her man turned and grinned at her. She saw the relief on his face, even as hers drained of all color.

"The lads call her Mam. I prefer to think of her as my sheer delight and St. Brendan's secret weapon."

"Very well, then," Mr. Pitt said. "Sheer delight, is it? She'll make you pay for that! Mrs. Six, front and center, please."

# — Chapter Six —

Even a genius doesn't get the facts right all the time. Perhaps he had finally asked too much of this gentle lady who wed him willingly, had no objection to loving him generously, and gave him a son gladly. As he had admitted last spring, he didn't always comprehend social nuances, no matter how prodigious his brain. His palms didn't usually sweat, but they were sweating now.

"Oh, really…no," Meri said. "What can I possibly say?"

"Volumes," Sir B replied. "You know Master Six better than any of us, and the Gunwharf Rats, too, I would wager."

Did he dare ask this of her? Certainly, he did. They were partners in everything. Just the mental reminder of that simple fact put the heart back into his body.

"I need you, Meri," he said and held out his hand.

She was on her feet and by his side in no time. He indicated the chair he had vacated, but she shook her head. John Mark took that as a signal to stand beside them. When Meri pulled him close to her, there was no mistaking the little fellow's sigh of relief.

Considering that he had no idea why he had been summoned to Trinity House, and where the questions would come from, Able needed to know something first, before he would subject his wife to questions. That wasn't too much to ask of a careful husband.

"Sirs, before there is any interrogation of my wife, I would like to know why I was directed here," he said, taking in the men at the table, and the others seated against the wall. "I know your business is licensing sailing masters and pilots who bring ships over the bar and up the Thames. I know you of Trinity are the men who see to the regulations of buoys and markers and lighthouses and their maintenance. Why are you interested in St. Brendan's?"

"Captain Rose here," said the Elder Brother seated next to Mr. Pitt. "I can answer your questions, for they are valid ones."

Able sketched a creditable bow. He knew of Hector Rose. Who didn't?

"Master Six, we at Trinity do all that you mentioned. You are likely aware that we provide almshouses for poor and infirm seamen and their widows and orphans."

"I am. It does Trinity House credit."

"We do more." Captain Rose said it firmly, then paused, which gave the simple statement a certain heft and weight. "During this time of national emergency, we do things that no one in England is aware of."

The silence following that statement was so loud that Able consciously asked the typical cacophony in his brain to settle down. Sometimes genius was a noisy burden.

Captain Rose stood up and walked around the long table until he stood before them. He smiled at John Mark, who leaned closer to Meridee. Her hand went to his head.

"What I say here, anything you hear… is between us. John Mark, is it?"

The boy nodded. When Meri patted his cheek, he gulped and said, "Aye, sir."

"Absolute silence is a requirement of the service, at times," Captain Rose said. "Do not disappoint me."

"N…no, sir."

"Mrs. Six?"

"I understand, captain," she told him. "Complete and total amnesia," which made the Brethren chuckle.

"I needn't ask you, Master Six," he said. "Or any of the rest of you? Very well. Captain St. Anthony has requested that we consider St. Brendan not only as a noble experiment in meeting the growing needs of the fleet, but also in relation to Portsmouth Harbor and the prison hulks."

"How is that, sir?" Able asked.

Captain Rose was silent a long moment. He looked down at John Mark. "Lad, you're partly the reason we called your master here."

"Me, sir? Gor!"

Captain Rose smiled, suggesting to Able that the august man knew more than a little about small boys. "Master Six, you gave some of John's drawings from the block pulley construction to Sir B, along with other work from your students."

"Aye, captain. Sir B requested it when I came bounding in one afternoon, ready to show off what we were learning in that hodge-podge, after-school class I teach. John's sketches were among the material."

"A seamanship course?"

"It started that way, sir, but everything seems to catch our attention." Able glanced at his wife. "Well, mine, at any rate. Meri started calling our class the Gunwharf Rat Symposium, and the name stuck. Now the class is in addition to our formal seamanship."

"I assume you have a full day of classwork," another captain said, one of those who had originally sat back with his arms folded. He was leaning forward now. "Where did you stick in this class?" The Brother grinned at Meridee. "Gunwharf Rat Symposium, Mrs. Six? Are you as singular as your husband?"

"I wouldn't have thought so," she said, then turned kindly eyes on Able. "But who else would marry such a man?"

"Hear, hear," said the irrepressible Sir B.

Able shook his head at the humor, and suddenly realized that Meridee was humanizing them all. Bless her. "We took a vote between early in the morning or later at night, you know, after Mess Call and before Dowse Lights. Later won out. We meet from eight bells to two bells. Our only rule is that we can discuss anything we want. No subject is off limits, which means John Mark dragged all of us to the block pulley factory. You tell them, John."

"I went to the butcher's with Mrs. Perry one day and we walked by," he said. Able watched the light in his eyes grow. "I heard steam whistles and banging and I was curious. I stood on a box and looked in the window. Gor! There were machines moving and wood turning on lathes! I never saw the like."

"And...?" prompted Captain Rose, by all appearance equally captivated.

"Here, sir." The boy ran to Grace and picked up his sketchpad. He handed it to the dignified captain and flipped through earlier pages. "I drew what I could. A nice man inside the building showed me everything." His face fell. "Mrs. Perry wanted me to hurry along because the dead chicken in her basket wasn't getting a minute younger."

All the brethren laughed at that. Meri put her hand to her mouth and laughed, leaning against Able. He put his arm around her.

"It was Mr. Marc Brunel's invention, sir," Able said, when the merriment subsided. "Mr. Maudslay refined it and Mr. Goodrich is assembling the machines to Brunel's specifications. We, uh, managed to gain entrance a few days later and walked through the whole factory, or what is completed now."

"And wouldn't you know, sir? Master Six had a suggestion to fix a pulley-making part to run smoother." John was nearly jumping up and down in his enthusiasm. "He does that."

"So I have heard," Captain Rose said. "May I borrow your sketches, Mister Mark?"

"You may," the boy said. He flipped a few pages. "I should take out this one."

"What is it? My stars, this is lovely." Captain Rose looked at Meridee. "Is this little Ben?" He bowed toward Sir B. "Named, I am told, after that Yankee captain Hallowell and our own Belvedere."

Meridee left Able's side and approached the end of the table. Able watched her eyes grow soft. "I didn't know you sketched him, John."

"Master Six said you are going to be twenty-five soon. I wanted to give you a drawing of something I know you like," he said, then looked around when the men – probably husbands – laughed some more. He hung his head. "I shouldn't have said you were that old, should I?"

Meridee pulled him close. "I'm younger than Master Six, and he doesn't mind! I want to frame this, but only after you sign your name in the lower right corner like all true artists."

"This lady, sirs, is my secret weapon," Able said. "Mrs. Six scolds the Rats when they need it, reads to them, tucks them in bed each night and holds them close when there are night terrors." He took a deep breath. "We all have those, upon occasion."

"You are not along there, master, workhouse or not," someone else said. "But don't you fear molly-coddling the lads, Mrs. Six? Both the merchant marine and Royal Navy are hard services, never more than in wartime."

"Oh, no," she assured him. Her hand went to her heart. "No one in St. Brendan's has a mother, do they? Who is there to teach such boys manners and kindness?" She clasped her hands together and looked at Able for reassurance. "I treat them as I would my own.

And probably as your wives treat your children. They are no different, no matter the circumstances of their birth."

Captain Rose nodded and returned his attention to John Mark. "I'll borrow your sketches, if I may, and return them soon. Tell me, lad: what would you like to become when you grow up a little more? Your master here would probably tell you that any answer will be a good one, as long as it is your idea."

The boy nodded. Able knew he was a thoughtful child, one prone to silent consideration before he spoke, unless enthusiasm carried the day, as it often did.

"I would make block pulleys in the mill," he said. "Maybe I would find a way to improve upon the mechanicals, then keep them running day and night, if need be."

"Not for you the glamor of a fleet action?" This question came from Mr. Pitt himself. "Pretty ladies strewing flowers on the water when you return? Ceremonial swords presented?"

"Puking is never glamorous," John Mark said, startled at the laughter that followed. "It isn't! Master Six says I will get my sea legs eventually, but it hasn't happened yet, no matter how many times I sail in the harbor."

"Yes, but making block pulleys?" Mr. Pitt asked.

"Sir, do you know that some nine-hundred-plus pulleys are required on the average frigate? If they are not there, the ship does not sail. We cannot *all* be admirals, especially if there is no ship to sail."

"No, we cannot, Master Mark," Captain Rose said. He turned his attention to Able. "Carry on, Master Six." He gave a nod to Meridee. "And Mrs. Six. Carry on with your excellent work. Let me add one thing more." He looked around, as if the walls had ears.

"Watch the harbor. I believe you have a vantage point in your home, with chambers that overlook the bay, and St. Brendan's below you."

"Captain, do you fear mischief?" Able asked.

"Every day and night," Captain Rose replied, his voice heavy now, his words weighty. "Let me quote the illustrious Admiral Horatio Nelson: 'You must hate a Frenchman as you hate the devil.'"

He bent down from his great height to address John Mark alone. "You, too, lad, and your fellows at St. Brendan's. Be alert there in your school by the harbor."

Able wondered, as he had wondered since his youth, if his father was one of those Frenchman to be loathed and despised. It was a disquieting thought. Thank God no one except Euclid, William Harvey, Nicholas Copernicus, Anthony van Leuwenhoek, Isaac Newton, Galen, Aristotle, and if he was supremely lucky, his very own keeper, Meridee Six, could read his mind. In her case, she read the portion that mattered: his whole heart.

# — Chapter Seven —

M r. Pitt broke the silence. "There we have it, gentlemen," he said, keeping his voice soft. "Upon request, we have learned a little about St. Brendan's, and admonished even the very young to be alert for mischance."

He returned to his seat, folding his hands in front of him. "Brethren, I would propose that we add a reasonable sum to help in the running of such a school. Do I hear any objections?"

Meridee's eyes went to the Brethren who had earlier looked resistant. Beyond that one captain who still stared hard at Able, she saw others who appeared more receptive.

"Master Able, how many courses do you teach?" a Brother asked suddenly.

"Two mathematics courses, and the calculus to two students before breakfast," Able replied. "That was all the time we had available. Seamanship fills the afternoon, and our Gunwharf Rat Symposium after dinner, sir."

"Could you add more classes?"

"No, sir. I have a wife who likes to see me now and then, and a son, who unlike me, has a father."

"War demands sacrifice, Master Six," another man said, his tone milder.

"What more would you have me do, sirs?"

"What more can he do?" Meridee asked, speaking entirely out of turn. "The sea already has his whole heart, sirs. My son and I get what's left. We don't begrudge his long hours, but sirs, he's a better man and teacher because of us. Only ask him."

"She is right, Brethren," Able said. "Scoff if you will, but I have a mind that never stops. It does slow somewhat in the comforting association of those I love the best. I need them. Meri sends me back to duty with peace in my heart."

"We ask enough of you, then," Mr. Pitt said with all the finality in his voice from years of serving as the nation's prime minister. "Gentlemen? This is a small school, and an experimental one, if you will. And we have not even mentioned the fact that Miss Croker over there is one of the instructors, as well."

Heads swiveled. Meridee heard a gasp or two.

"Miss Croker, what do you teach?"

"I teach English grammar and penmanship," Grace said, her right and privilege to speak as firm as Mr. Pitt's. She rose and stood beside Meridee. "Heaven knows they need it. Perhaps you did, too, sirs, earlier in your careers."

She had them and she knew it. *I could never do that,* Meridee thought, enchanted.

Mr. Pitt surprised Meridee. "What else could you teach, Miss Croker?"

She could see even Grace was surprised. The elegant woman pursed her lips and looked at the ceiling, as if expecting something to appear. Perhaps it did, because she did not falter.

"Sir, I could teach rudimentary medical treatment," she said, then nodded, as though the new idea struck a welcome chord. "I could also manage the elementary mathematics, which would free Master Six to even more advanced effort."

"Excellent," Mr. Pitt said. "Master Six? What would her help allow you to do?"

"We could move that calc course *after* breakfast," he said, which made some of the Brethren chuckle. He turned toward Grace. "Grace, I could devote more time to actual navigation if you did take that lower mathematics class. Seamanship is so vast a course. Headmaster Croker could probably add more charting and intermediate reading to his plate."

Mr. Pitt nodded. "Do you need more instructors?"

"Someone to teach French conversation," Able said promptly. "If we're going to keep fighting the blokes, we'd better understand them, wouldn't you agree? I would like..."

He looked down. John Mark was tugging at his sleeve. "Aye, lad?"

"Something mechanical, if you please," John said earnestly. "Something with gears and bolts and wheels."

"I heartily concur, John Mark," Able said. "I could teach that, but there is still only one of me. Perhaps we can encourage Marc Brunel himself to drop by, or Henry Maudslay."

John's eyes grew wide. "Gor!"

"We can ask, can't we?" Able said, as if only the two of them stood there, master and student, workhouse boy to workhouse boy.

Captain Rose raised his hand, as if he sat in a classroom. "Master, would St. Brendan's ever consider taking on regular lads from good homes?"

"No, sir, I would not," Able said promptly.

"Why not? St. Brendan's could benefit everyone, as far as I can tell."

Able reached for Meridee's hand again. She clasped both hands around his.

"It has been my experience – ask any Gunwharf Rat – that as soon as someone of even the smallest privilege is thrown in with workhouse lads, these privileged newcomers try to exert superiority. St. Brendan's is a tender flower, a social experiment, if you will. Let these boys be."

Meridee watched her man's old eyes as he surveyed the room, taking his time to observe each face. "They come to us expecting nothing. No one wants or needs them. They discover skills in demand in our wartime naval service and they apply themselves. They find out who they are – not merely castoffs and byblows, but lads of worth and intelligence. They are already making their mark in the Royal Navy. Let us continue our work with them alone."

Mr. Pitt took his time. "I know you Brethren well," he said finally. "There is nothing you would not do to further our skill in this time of national emergency."

"St. Brendan's is so unorthodox!" one of the Brethren burst out.

"A woman teaching? A workhouse bastard himself in a position of authority?" exclaimed the red-faced man, his face even redder. "Unheard of."

Meridee thought of Ben and the many times in his short life she had seen his father kneeling by his cradle, as if amazed at his good fortune to have a son. Tender flowers, indeed. Who was more tender?

"Gentlemen, gentlemen," Mr. Pitt said. "Our new age of...of..." He smiled at John Mark, "...of mechanism and scholarship demands more of us than we have given before. Add unrelenting war to that. Mix it all together. We must be willing to innovate. We could do as we always do and expect different results, but that is the surest sign of failure."

He looked at the sheet of paper before him, picked up his pen, dipped it in ink and crossed out something. He substituted other words or numbers – he sat too far away for Meridee to tell – blew on the page gently, then started it around.

"Add your initials and a yea or nay, Brethren," he said simply. "We have entered a new age."

Meridee held her breath as the paper went around the u-shaped table. She heard the scratch of pen on paper. The secretary walked to the middle and took the paper over to the other side of the gap.

Able stared at his shoes, unable to watch. Meridee noted each man, as it dawned on her that this summons to Trinity House was a test. Someone was determined to help it succeed or let it fail. Thank the Lord God Almighty that Sir B had never stated precisely what this whole visit was about. Or maybe even Sir B hadn't known. That thought took hold of her and she wondered.

But here they were and the paper was going around. It stopped with Mr. Pitt, who looked it over for such a lengthy time that Meridee felt her head begin to ache. Her fingers tingled because Able's grip had grown stronger. He had probably known all along what was happening.

Mr. Pitt showed the paper to Captain Rose, who nodded, his expression unreadable. Meridee glanced at Sir B, ordinarily a charming fellow with a certain studied indifference about him, probably a product of his aristocratic upbringing. She had never seen him so serious.

"Well then, sirs, and lovely ladies," Mr. Pitt said finally. "You have our permission to breathe, Master Six. The marks on this paper indicate that we of Trinity House are taking St. Brendan's under our wing. Do you think Headmaster Croker's illness will cure more quickly when you assure him that we are happy to funnel three hundred pounds annually into your school to help it grow? I insist that you start paying Miss Croker and find a French instructor, too."

The normally poised Miss Croker gasped. It was Able's turn to look at the ceiling with its cherubs and their navigational instruments. He raised Meridee's hand to his lips and kissed it. She saw tears in his eyes.

"I think Headmaster Croker will recover instantly, Brethren," Able said finally. "Thank you, sirs. You will never regret this."

"We had better not," Mr. Pitt said. "Continue your work, and while you're at it, keep an eye on those prison hulks in the harbor. Stand a watch and keep it. "

# — Chapter Eight —

## PRISONER OF WAR HULK – HMS CAPTIVITY

Perhaps he had been too skeptical of Claude Pascal's decision to support the gunner's mate and the powder monkey in their audacious bid for freedom. Like the rest of the prisoners who had hoisted the two kegs containing Gunner Remillard and Pierre Deschamps into the empty water hoy, Jean Hubert waited for the other shoe to drop.

Nothing. Perhaps they had succeeded in their bolt to freedom. Even with no method of communication, there were ways to learn if an escape was successful. Many an escape had been fouled immediately, when roll call turned up a missing prisoner or two. When that happened, Captain Faulke ordered all prisoners to stand at attention by their rolled up hammocks while all three levels were searched. And if the mood was on him, the captain made them stand there for hours after.

Buying time for escapees mattered. For a few *sou*, the *rafalés* would flit about from deck to deck and answer for the missing persons. If the escapee made it as far as the Portsmouth dock, only to be apprehended, the result was usually torture until the poor rascal divulged the name of his prison ship, upon which time the guards descended again on the hulk for more torment. One punishment for the men on board was to cut already scanty rations for a week or more until some died, and others grew even more determined to escape.

This time, two days passed, then three. By the fourth day, the prisoners on Deck One decided perhaps the water keg scheme was worth another try by two more men. Another meeting was called. Jean went with no more enthusiasm than before, except that even planning an escape he didn't believe in was a diversion from the stultifying monotony of the daily grind.

Two more prisoners volunteered to be crammed into empty kegs and hoisted into the next water hoy, due tomorrow. "You know, before I lose my nerve," said one nearly toothless fellow.

Claude Pascal objected. "No, not tomorrow."

"Why should I wait?" the prisoner asked.

"It is a simple matter, *mon amie*," Clause replied, his voice so placating, so soothing. "Let other water hoy sailings pass. We don't want to press our luck. Maybe in a week, maybe, two. Trust me."

Before the man could object – even Jean wondered why waiting mattered, since the first attempt had obviously succeeded – Claude moved on to other business, the sort of news that concerned them all.

"Some of you with top deck privileges may have noticed an increased number of bodies brought above deck," he said.

The men looked at each other, the barely breathable air somehow thicker with such news.

"It's typhus," Claude said, then held up his hands in a placating gesture. "I know, I know! Who dies of typhus?" He looked around. "We do, my friends, because we have no reserves of strength to fight it. Besides, who can stop the fleas and lice on this dreadful hulk?"

"This would be an excellent time for First Consul Napoleon to invade England, wouldn't it?" someone said from deeper in the gloom.

"Perhaps he is even poised in Caen or Calais, ready to do precisely that," someone else said, to hoots of derision. Prisoners were a skeptical lot.

"Very well, late next week for another hoy," said the hopeful escapee. "If we are still alive."

*If we are still alive,* Jean thought as he returned to Deck One. He scratched his neck, and then his arm, and was that an itch on his thigh? Was he imagining it? A man could worry himself into hypochondria, with or without lice.

All Jean wanted to do was complete his latest sketch, this one of the countryside around Rouen, with the cathedral in the distance. He hadn't been there in years, but he added rolling hills anyway, reasoning that the English who bought his sketches probably had no idea, either, and he was good at drawing hills. He would draw what he wanted, pocket the few pathetic *sou* that each picture earned him, buy what food he could, and try to stay healthy enough that if he did come down with typhus, it wouldn't kill him. A prisoner probably couldn't hope for any more than that. He sat down to work.

His methodical, orderly day – much like the one before – was upended immediately by a guard.

"Jean Hubert," the guard said, resting the butt of his musket on Rouen's imaginary mountains. He moved the butt around until the color smeared. "Come with me."

"I'd rather usher you into hell and slam the door," he declared pleasantly in French, counting on the general ignorance of English guards to keep him safe. Of course, he could have said it in English, too, but the guard needn't know that. Nearly two years ago when his incarceration began, Jean Hubert pledged himself to keeping as small a profile as possible. He suspected that survivors were those who didn't stand out.

Topside, it was nice to breathe the far better air, even if the bright sunlight made him put up his hands in defense. A look around reminded him that even for the guards, life on a prison hulk wasn't good. Such a notion might have bothered him, had he cared even slightly for his captors.

The guard took him to a closed door in the stern of the hulk and nodded to the sentry, who knocked, stuck his head in, exchanged a few words and opened the door wider.

*What is this?* Jean thought, surprised. Sometimes prisoners were ordered topside to clean up messes. Only a month ago, two prisoners told him about hauling food on board that they never saw: cheese and soft bread and good wine. "Not even a bite?" he had asked. "No, no," one prisoner from Breton said with a shake of his head. "It was almost enough, just to sniff the wax around the cheese."

He entered the cabin of Captain Tobias Faulke, with its comfortable chairs grouped near the stern windows. The only view was the next hulk anchored in line, but *eh bien*, it was better than suffering belowdecks in poisonous air. Standing there in broken shoes, the yellow shirt with TO painted in fading black on that space between his shoulders, the too-short yellow trousers, he faced the captain.

Captain Faulke leaned back in his chair and regarded him. His expression inscrutable, he pushed a sheet of paper across the desk toward Jean.

Jean looked down at one of his earlier drawings of Rive Seine, with Notre Dame in the distance, surrounded by fog. He had spent more time than usual on that sketch, trying to get the correct mood. Even if it was intended for a *petit bourgeois* English clerk or rent collector who probably had no idea how exquisite it really was, the artist inside that yellow shirt still sought to do his best.

Of course, there was the small matter of smuggling out a sketch for money, an illegal act. Never mind that most prisoners were engaged in making something to sell on the outside, anything for a few *sou* to keep food in the stomach and breath in the body for one more day. As in most ventures of a susceptible nature in life, the trick was avoiding detection.

*Why me?* he thought, perplexed more than frightened. *Why have I been singled out?*

"Prisoner Number One Dash Eighty-Seven, is this your work?"

Jean knew full well what Captain Faulke said, but he looked around for an interpreter. One had to maintain the charade. No one else in the cabin. Now what? He remained silent, because that seemed prudent.

"Jean Hubert, I know you can speak English," the captain said, with a sigh that bordered on the theatrical. "Others have informed me." He turned the drawing around. "It's rather well done, especially considering the obstacles you work under. But never mind that. Have a seat. Tell me something about yourself."

He remained standing. Captain Faulke seemed willing to wait him out, but for how long? At what point would a man in power summon the sentry and send him to the Hole to think about his sins, or take away more of his pathetic rations? And who had informed on him?

"Lord, but you're stubborn, Lieutenant Hubert."

*He knows my rank, too? Next he will tell me I am from Cherbourg.*

"And your father was a *bourgeois* from Cherbourg, was he not? Owned a small hotel, I believe. Speak to me, lieutenant, because I have a proposition for you."

Jean folded. Why not? "Very well, sir."

"Wise of you not to be stubborn on a prisoner of war hulk," Captain Faulke said. "Sit down. Let me serve you some excellent sherry."

Jean sat. He tried to maintain a casual air when the captain went to a sideboard and returned with a bottle, glasses, and macarons, *O Dieu*, macarons. Faulke poured the sherry and passed the plate of macarons.

Jean wiped the saliva from his lips and took a macaron. He had never eaten a better one, and followed it with three more before he bothered with sherry. But what exquisite sherry! He closed his eyes. He imagined himself anywhere but where he sat, then wondered what he would have to do in return for this.

"What do you want from me, *capitain*? he asked.

He had to credit Faulke for not acting coy. "You will enjoy this. Did you know that my family is on board with me?"

*I neither know nor care*, Jean thought. No matter what happened in the next few minutes, he couldn't give back the macarons or the sherry. "I did not know."

"I have a daughter aged ten who shows some artistic talent. I would like you to give her daily lessons," the captain said. "For this I will pay you one meal eaten here when the lesson is done, and one shilling a week."

Of course he should not agree to this, but had he a choice? A meal? Perhaps, but a man shouldn't surrender too easily. "What sort of meal?"

"You'll note the irony of this, because you are a smart man, but I have an excellent French cook. Whatever you like. Yes or no?"

"If I say no?" One shouldn't spread one's legs wide like a common whore, after all, and succumb, should one?

Captain Faulke shrugged. He was English; he didn't know how to shrug properly and have it mean something. "Back where you were."

"No punishment?"

And then the captain reeled him in. He leaned across the desk and his eyes turned into slits. "Isn't belowdecks punishment enough, you fool?"

Lulled by the sherry, Jean hadn't expected that much malevolence. He leaned back involuntarily, then cursed himself for his weakness. "Very well," he said, in a voice not his own. "I will do it."

The captain's eyes stayed slitted for another moment, just long enough to convince Jean that he was capable of playing a deep game. He sat back and resumed his captain face. "Tomorrow at nine of the clock I will expect you here in this cabin. I have papers and pencils. Go now."

Jean Hubert couldn't leave fast enough. His heart racing, he forced himself to saunter casually to the door, as if he visited with the captain of a prison hulk every day. Where this would lead he had no idea. All he wanted now was out.

He opened the door, where the sentry and his guard stood chatting.

The guard took out his cord and bound Jean's wrists again. "Back we go," he said. "Lucky you."

*Outside that cabin I still do not speak English*, he told himself. He gave the guard a blank stare and was rewarded with a cuff to his head for his pains. It wasn't much of an effort.

He ducked and dodged the next blow, wondering if everyone on board already knew his business.

As he looked up, Jean saw Claude Pascal standing in the shadow by the bulkhead. He stared, certain his eyes were playing tricks on him. Was that how the captain knew he was from Cherbourg and spoke English? Surely not from Claude Pascal. He blamed his suspicion on the sherry.

# — Chapter Nine —

## TRINITY HOUSE, LONDON

Theirs was a walk of quiet, unexpected triumph from Trinity House to the street. Able noticed John Mark's frown, and knew him to take orders seriously, especially orders from a former prime minister and a tableful of men of power.

"Are the Rats up to standing a nighttime watch?" Able asked the boy who preferred noisy machines to silent sail.

"Aye," John replied. "All of us." He stopped. "Master, do you love England?"

*Do I love England?* he asked himself. He glanced at Meri, who walked with Grace Croker, their heads together in conversation, Meri who loved him and slept in safety because the wooden walls of the Royal Navy — his navy — protected her, and now their son, too.

"I am fond of England," he said, *but I love my wife and son more.*

"Even if England hasn't exactly treated us well, master?"

"Even so," he replied simply. "We Rats will do our best to change that."

John Mark was satisfied. "We will stand the watch."

Able knew he was too cynical to feel the tug of tears at John's earnest answer, but he did. He stood by John until Sir B came closer, and the two of them helped Gervaise take the wheeled chair down the three steps to the sidewalk. It was time to relax now, and ask his mentor something that had been on his mind during the entire interrogation — what else could he call it? — inside the stately building.

"You knew what this was, didn't you, Sir B?" Able asked. "What sparked it in the first place? We have been doing our best to set an insignificant course to attract no attention."

"We have, indeed. Come closer. Gervaise, wheel me nearer and go stand over there," Sir B said, every inch the captain, even though he had not stood on his feet in four years and was far from a quarterdeck. "Kneel down, Able, and listen." Able did as he commanded. "Did you think the disappearance of that...that rancid instructor would go unnoticed?" Sir B asked, his face as stern as Able had ever seen it.

Able's agile brain shot through the whole list of that former teacher's felonies in seconds and left him shaken as though the matter had happened only moments ago. Gambler, cheat, abuser of students, pimp for aristocrats who wanted to prey on the helpless — all of that was Rodney Blake. Good riddance to the man.

"Too bad he had a family of some prominence," was all Able could muster, because he did understand. "I will go to my grave wondering what happened to those earlier students who ran afoul of him."

"I, too." Sir B sat back. "Blake's family has made inquiries, asked some pointed questions about St. Brendan's. Although he may not be prime minister at the moment – I predict that will change soon – Mr. Pitt has forwarded me letters from Blake's father." He gave a weak smile. "I'll likely never know, but the tug of fatherhood must compel a man..." His voice trailed away.

Able thought of Ben, his short life already so unlike his father's. "Yes. I understand that. A father would never want to give up, even when hope is gone. So Mr. Pitt summoned us to check St. Brendan's for soundness," Able asked, "because Blake's father harbors some suspicions?"

"I think that is so," Sir B said. "And yet...Mr. Pitt didn't inform me ahead of time, or ask my opinion about this meeting, something he usually does. Odd, that."

Able knew he was quite capable of forging the late and unlamented Blake's handwriting. *I could send the family a letter from the interior of Canada from their son, and they would believe it*, he thought. *I could follow it a year later with a letter from the provincial governor of Quebec, expressing his condolences that Sir Mallory Blake's son had been eaten by a polar bear.* The idea had some merit, but he didn't think Sir B in the mood for such a solution.

"What is so damned amusing to you in this situation?" Sir B exclaimed. "Out with it."

Able leaned closer and told Sir B about easy forgery and polar bears. He was rewarded with a crack of laughter that cleared the air between them.

"Pitt did want to know enough to satisfy the Blakes, but our Trinity House warden also has a genuine interest in St. Brendan's," Sir B said, resuming *his* thoughts. "I've told Mr. Pitt a few things, and he knows Thaddeus Croker well. Our headmaster should have been here, but alas, mumps." He grimaced. "And so we thrust you upon the stage, with little John Mark. I knew both of you would acquit yourselves well, and then you were smart enough to insist upon Meridee's presence."

"She does have a disarming way about her," Able said, after a glance at his nearest and dearest, who was starting to fidget. He knew what she was like when her milk started to flow and there was no Ben around to do his duty. Time to move this conversation along handsomely.

"She does." Sir B lowered his voice still farther. "Now the Brethren know what we are about, and have set us the task of watching the hulks for signs of trouble. They seem to have wind of something, although I do not know what. Can we do it?"

"We can," Able said. "We'll organize a watch."

"Hurrah for St. Brendan's. I put you in the hot seat and you didn't scorch yourself." The captain glanced at Meridee. "Neither did she. You two were obviously made for each other."

"Without a doubt." Able interpreted the current darts his dear wife was throwing his way. "Even now, I know precisely what she is thinking."

"Surely not."

"I do. She is tugging at her bodice most discreetly, but I know she wants to skedaddle home to our heir and offspring, and nurse him."

"Take her home before she bursts."

Able laughed and stood up.

There was scarcely time to analyze what happened next, but it probably hadn't taken a minute: a startling exchange on a busy London boulevard, followed by a sudden curse and a shove that sent Able sprawling toward the street. Meri shrieked as she reached for him. He flailed and struck her by accident, dragging her down with him. His utter humiliation in front of the people he most admired. The look of distress on John Mark's face. The realization that his world would never be fine, fair or easy.

Chatting there with Sir B, Able caught only a glimpse of the red-faced Elder Brother who had never changed his expression from one of active dislike. If anything, the look of extreme dislike had only intensified, after Mr. Pitt announced the annual stipend to St. Brendan's. The man had flung himself out of the assembly room and made a great clatter on the stairs. *Good riddance*, Able had thought.

But here he was, barreling down the shallow steps, the loathing on his face probably visible to ships at sea, like one of Trinity's famous lighthouses.

Able's first instinct was to step in front of Meri. For once in his life he wasn't fast enough. With a grunt, the Elder Brother slammed into him and pushed him and Meridee into the street. She crumpled under Able's weight and landed in the gutter.

All attention turned to his wife as he slid away and swiveled to help her, then cover her with his body as the enraged man kicked at them.

"Sir! Stop!" he gasped, grabbing for Meridee, who tried to crawl under him again for protection, her hand to her face where Able had accidentally struck her as he fell.

"Get out, you bastard!" the man roared. "How dare you think to come into a place so far above your station? You have less standing than a garden slug! I think my Brethren have lost their senses!"

The man looked around wildly, as if seeking another target. He found it in Sir B, and pointed a shaking finger at him. "If you were not a cripple I would call you out. This was probably all your idea! Can't you leave dregs like this in workhouses where they belong?"

"You, Captain Ogilvie, are either drunk or mad. Leave now and nothing will be said about this."

Sir B spoke in a low voice, a dangerous voice that Able had heard before, once in an Asiatic port full of cutpurses and assassins and another time from the quarterdeck at a minor South Pacific fleet engagement when matters were at their worst. Able turned to help Meridee to her feet. She grabbed him, then pushed him toward the man in the wheeled chair. "I am fine," she quavered, even though he knew she was anything but fine. "Stand by Sir B."

"Help the cripple, help the cripple," the captain mimicked. "You, Mrs. Six – what a stupid name – may pretend to be a lady, but no lady would come within a barge pole of a workhouse bastard putting on airs! You are no better than he is!"

"That's enough," Able said, his brain absolutely silent now, as if all the polymaths and geniuses inside were wondering what he would do, too. He looked around for a weapon, anything, to beat the man senseless for his rudeness to the dearest wife a man could possess. Nothing.

His face registering shock, William Pitt hurried over. The captain threw off Mr. Pitt's hand on his shoulder, glared at the former prime minister as if he wanted to thrash him, too, then took off at a fast walk down the side street, turning back once to glare at them all and mutter, "Bastards all. So ye shall remain. Ye can't put a bonnet on a pig."

"Should I summon the watch?" Grace Croker asked. Her arms were tight around John Mark, who had turned his face into her skirt. "Steady now, Mister Mark."

"I will kill him," the boy said. "Only let me go."

"He is not worth anything that dignified, John," she said in her firmest teacher voice. "I am not turning loose of you until you promise me you will not go after him."

"John Mark, as you were," Able snapped. "This is not your fight."

"Yes, it is," the boy argued, his voice scarcely audible from the depths of Grace's skirt. "You're a Gunwharf Rat, too."

"So I am," Able said, humiliated and wondering where to turn. He couldn't bring himself to look at anyone but his wife, who held her arms out to him. He walked into them and let her hold him.

"Meri, you love me, don't you?" he whispered, for her ears alone.

"My goodness, such a question," she whispered back. "I love no one else. Well, I love Ben, too, and Able, I'd better get to him quickly."

"Able, come here a moment," Sir B commanded.

He shook his head. "Not now, sir. Maybe later. We're going to Curzon Street and home tomorrow."

"Gervaise, wheel me to that stubborn man over there, the one St. Brendan's cannot manage without."

*Leave me alone.* Able wanted to shout the words, but Meri was smoothing his hair now and murmuring something that sounded like her conversations with Ben. His celestial mentors crowded back into his head, but he didn't want them. "Tell them to go away, Meri," he said.

Bless her, she understood. She put her hand over his eyes. "Just leave him alone for now," she said softly into his ear. "He's busy, can't you see?"

Apparently they could. All he was conscious of was Meri's heart beating too rapidly against his chest and it felt wonderful. He sighed and relaxed.

"You know, it's within my capacity to prosecute the man," he heard Mr. Pitt say to Sir B. "What could he have been thinking?"

"Change is hard for some," Sir B replied. "We can probably arrange for Captain Ogilvie to return to sea sooner than he anticipated. In fact, I would recommend it."

"It could not happen too soon for me, Sir B."

"Yes, dreadful business," his captain said. He shook his head as though he couldn't believe what had happened. "I know Ogilvie well enough. He can be impetuous and thoughtless, but I never knew him to be cruel. I wonder what else is afoot." He managed a smile that didn't reach his eyes. "Master Six, in this case, all's well that ends."

Able turned around then, able to face the others because Meri held his hand. "I can resign my appointment at St. Brendan's and return to the fleet, if I am an embarrassment, Sir B."

"That's the last thing I want right now, with the possible exception of dysentery," Sir B said. "No one said this …this…whatever it is we are engaged in was going to be easy. Mrs. Six, do you need a poultice for your eye?"

Able took a good look at his darling. "Oh horror, I did that when I landed on you," he muttered. "Seriously, are you all right?"

"My dress is a bit of a ruin, but it was too tight anyway," she said, and took him by the arm. "And look – here is our carriage."

When the coachman, a quizzical expression on his face, let down the step, Able helped her in. When John Mark started to follow, Grace took his arm.

"I have a much better idea," she said. "I think that without too much effort, you and I could talk Sir B into escorting us to Astley's Royal Amphitheatre tonight. We will even invite Mr. Pitt, if he doesn't mind low company."

"I don't, as it turns out," the statesman said. "Sir B, I believe we are going to crowd into your carriage and eat at your table before we set out for the circus. Don't wait up for us, you Sixes."

# — Chapter Ten —

Their ride home was a silent one, Able's expression set in stone, except for the muscle working in his jaw. Meridee leaned against his shoulder and he finally put his arm around her, which relieved her heart as nothing else could.

"I don't understand what happened," he said.

"It was obvious he wasn't in agreement with anything Mr. Pitt or Captain Rose said," she replied. "Able, has something like this occurred before?"

"Oh, now and then."

She watched his expressive face, seeing and hearing the bitterness that startled her, because her husband was a realistic, cheerful man, most days. But not all days.

He visibly gathered himself together. "I don't mean to be sharp, my love," he told her. "I need a thicker skin, perhaps."

She took his hand and kissed it, then pressed it against her heart, so he could feel the constant beat. He smiled after a long moment. "Do I ever mutter in my sleep about Harvey's treatise on the circulation of blood and how the heart pumps?"

"Oh, now and then," she teased in turn, without the bitterness.

He leaned back and closed his eyes, looking old and weary until he dozed, to her relief. She knew him. When he opened his eyes again, he would be more his usual self.

He was, but it took longer. The humiliation lingered in his eyes. Still, he made an effort, helping her from the vehicle. He started to chuckle when the butler, looking a bit fine drawn around the eyes, ushered them into a townhouse filled with indignation from a small set of lungs.

"I sense a career in the Royal Navy," Able said. "He'll be heard above all storms at sea."

Meridee rushed directly to the kitchen, unbuttoning her bodice as she went, because Ben's peremptory summons waited for no one.

"Not a moment too soon," her housekeeper said. "He did enjoy his cream pudding, but that only lasts so long. Mrs. Six! What happened to your eye?"

"It's a long story I don't have time for right now," she said. "It will keep." Meridee gave her housekeeper a meaningful glance which she knew would suffice, because Mrs. Perry was swift to understand.

Meridee sank into the comfortable chair Mrs. Perry had vacated. Able propped a hassock under her feet and held their squalling son while she undid her corset in record time, and held out her arms for her baby. Silence reigned, as Benjamin Belvedere Six nursed and patted her breast. All was right in his world. If only things were right in Able's world.

She concentrated on the relief to her body as Ben did his duty. Able sat beside her for mere moments, too restless to remain still. Mrs. Perry watched him as he paced the floor, opening her mouth once with a question, then closing it when Meridee shook her head.

"I'm going for a walk," he said finally.

"Not too late, I hope?" she asked, trying to keep her voice light, even though she knew he could see through that façade and spot the worry underneath.

"No. Trust me." He blew a kiss to her and left the kitchen.

As soon as the door closed, she told Mrs. Perry everything that had happened. She watched the housekeeper's eyes narrow into malevolent slits until she began to fear for the odious Captain Ogilvie, should he ever dare venture near St. Brendan's.

"I wish I could protect my husband from ogres like the captain," she said. "Why should a man's birth dictate how he is treated all his life?"

"I asked myself that same question once, Mrs. Six, when I stood naked on an auction block and felt men's hands all over me," Mrs. Perry said quietly.

"Oh, dear, I have fumbled, haven't I?" Meridee asked.

"Not really," her servant replied. "You told me once how awful it felt when you realized that without a dowry, you would never marry."

"It doesn't equate," Meridee argued.

"It does." Mrs. Perry touched Ben's hand and smiled when his white fingers curled around her black one. "*This* will be the lad who knows better fortune than all of us. Wouldn't you agree?"

Meridee nodded, too ready for tears to speak. She sighed with relief when Mrs. Perry applied a cool, damp pad to her throbbing eye, then prepared a sandwich so she could keep up her strength.

"All I want to do is take care of my baby and my husband," she said, when Mrs. Perry handed her a glass of milk to accompany it. "Mrs. Perry, is there something wrong with me?"

Meridee handed Ben over for a final burp and pulled herself together, but looser this time. Tight corsets were no longer her friend.

"Wrong with you? Hardly," Mrs. Perry said. She cradled Ben's head in her large hand and put him in his crib. They both watched as he settled himself into sleep. "You're doing precisely what you want to do, aren't you?"

"It's so ordinary. A husband and children are all I ever want." Meridee leaned closer. "Do you think Able will get bored with me? My aims and goals aren't exactly lofty, are they? I know I can never even approach his brain power. Do you think he will wish for someone more like him? I worry sometimes."

"No one can approach that mind." Mrs. Perry gave her a gentle look, the sort of regard that Portsmouth's butchers, bakers and hangabouts would never credit from such a formidable mountain of a woman. "Mrs. Six, you are exactly the woman such a man needs and craves, and he knows it," she said. "I doubt he wasted a single second in courting you, back when he was poorer than a church mouse and had no expectations whatsoever."

It wasn't that long ago and she couldn't deny it. "Not a moment," she said. Meridee drank the milk dutifully. Mrs. Perry handed her a sliced apple next, which she polished off. "I think I am eating more than both Nick and John combined," she protested, and shook her head at a chocolate biscuit. All *that* earned her was a glare of no trifling size, so she ate it, too.

"Of course you are eating more!" Mrs. Perry said. "You're feeding a future sailing master in the Royal Navy."

"Or maybe a surgeon or a mechanist," she teased, then regarded the woman who meant far more to her than a servant. "Ben will be anything he wants to be. I suppose you're right. I am happiest when Master Six and Ben are close to me."

"And so is Master Six. Even a blind man could see his regard for you."

"I hope he will not walk too long tonight. I want him here."

Able returned long after Grace and John Mark came home from the circus, the boy bursting with enthusiasm and anxious to tell her everything, even as he scrubbed at his eyes and yawned.

"John, it will keep until you ride home with us tomorrow," Meridee said.

The boy yawned again. "P'raps."

"I am afraid you will be without John Mark for another day," Grace Croker said, as she sat on the sofa beside Meridee. "Wouldn't you know it, but there is a balloon ascension tomorrow morning in Hyde Park and Sir B insists we attend with him. You and the Six men will take my carriage back to Portsmouth, and we will ride with Sir B the day after." She patted John's shoulder. "Right, John? John?"

A quiet summons to the butler found the sleeping lad in capable arms and on his way up the stairs. Grace leaned back, a smile on her face.

"I had the most delightful time of my life, just watching one child's enjoyment," she said. She held her hand out to her friend. "Meridee, you and Able are going to have so much fun taking your little ones to circuses and balloon ascensions and picnics." She stopped, her expression contemplative bordering on regretful. "And here I thought Grace Croker should enjoy being a spinster with a fortune of her own, and no one to control her or dictate her life in any way."

"Don't you?" Meridee asked, surprised. This Grace seemed different from the Grace who was quite prepared to brazen her way into Trinity House, should it have proved necessary, or had no qualms about teaching workhouse children in a private academy. This Grace even looked a little wistful.

"I'm not certain anymore," Grace said. "Forgive me for silently laughing at you because your dresses don't quite fit now, or teasing about your fidgets because you are ready to nurse and there is not a baby nearby."

Meridee smiled at that. "It would never do for me to snatch up someone else's infant on the street and relieve the strain, now, would it? And as for my dresses, Able told me to be patient."

They laughed together, but Grace sobered quickly. "I almost think I envy you." She kissed Meridee's forehead and started for the door. She turned back. "Where is Able?"

"He went for a walk. Hours ago." Meridee rose and followed her, unwilling to let an ally and friend out of her sight, not when she felt so alone. "I think it is one thing for my husband to be called up short for felonies he has no control over. It is vastly another for it to happen when I am there as witness."

"Poor man. Should we worry? Should we search the grog shops and gaming hells?"

"No. He'll return when he has worn himself out sufficiently," Meridee replied, hoping it was true. "I cannot deny that I am grateful for you to keep John Mark here another day so he and I can ride home almost by ourselves."

Grace blew a kiss to her. "You can credit Sir B. He knows your husband well, doesn't he?"

"He does. I know him better," Meridee said quietly. "Please thank Sir B for me." Her good humor righted itself. "And have a lovely time yourself, with one of the Royal Navy's notable heroes."

"My dear, what woman wouldn't want to attend a balloon ascension with the dashing Captain Sir Belvedere St. Anthony, and an equally enthusiastic student who loves gears and pulleys?"

"Fair enough. Good night. And thank you both again."

After telling the butler not to wait up, Meridee took herself upstairs a few minutes later. She stood for a long moment by the window, gazing down on a street vacant of pedestrians and horses, wondering where her man was, wanting him with all her heart.

Ben slept peacefully in his crib, not even stirring when she touched his black curls and raised the blanket a bit higher. She didn't bother with her nightgown. The room was warm. Her cheek throbbed and she wanted to cry. She pulled the unused pillow close to her and surprised herself by closing her eyes immediately.

She opened them hours later when someone equally bare moved the pillow and lay down beside her, pulling her close. Without words, they made love. She doubted it was a dream.

# — Chapter Eleven —

Meridee woke early, even before Ben had a chance to start cooing and looking around – such a pleasant way to greet the day. She raised up on one elbow, the better to see her sleeping husband. She had hoped to see him still relaxed and at peace with himself after what even a veteran of General Merrymaking would have called a prodigious spell of lovemaking, but no.

His hands were knotted into tight fists and his breathing seemed labored, as it had that dreadful time last spring. When he had recovered from his admittedly strange brush with death, he had told her in some detail of the polymaths from other ages who seemed to be waiting for him in a cosmic antechamber. If another man had spoken that way, she would have put it down to too much acquaintance with rum. She knew Able was never a man to linger in his cups. She believed him.

She put her hand gently over his eyes, cuddled close to him and breathed evenly and steadily until his respirations matched hers. She watched his shoulders relax and his hands open. Soon they were running down her back in a lazy way that told her she could take away her hand from his eyes.

He knew she wanted some detail he had not provided last night, otherwise occupied. "I walked and walked," he said. "Over to the Palace of Westminster, then through some park or other. I wore myself out."

"Not too badly, it would seem," she said. "Unless I gave myself rather willingly to some stranger in my bed last night, I don't know when I've been so thoroughly rogered."

"Language, language," he scolded, but she saw the smile back in his eyes. "And it was actually at two fifteen this morning."

"Two fifteen? Rogered? I could have said something more colorful," she teased. "After all, I live in Portsmouth, close to the docks."

"Meri, you should never listen to smooth-talking sailors," he teased. He stretched and got up, wandering over to their son's crib. He brought Ben back to their bed and changed his diaper like the expert in [nearly] all things that he was. "Ready for him, my lovely human spigot?"

"Someday I will thrash you for that," she said as she quickly cured Ben's imminent starvation. "Or perhaps not. I doubt there are many fathers in England who don't whinge about changing diapers."

"Especially standing in the altogether," Able added. "I've caught you sneaking peeks."

"For all that I know you quite well, of course I look," she teased in turn. "I have no particular experience to state this, except my earlier sneaking peeks in Father's book of bare naked Greeks, but you compare favorably."

He laughed, a welcome sound. After a good scratch that made Meridee roll her eyes, he went into the dressing room and came back wearing his ratty dressing gown. He lounged beside her, running his foot down her bare leg.

"I've been thinking…" he began, which made Meridee whoop with laughter. "You have no respect for genius."

"And what have you thought about?"

"When we return home, I am thinking of asking Mr. Maudslay if he would lecture my older class once or twice on mechanics. Provided he has the time, of course. I know Mr. Brunel doesn't."

"You should ask him," she said. "Better yet, Mr. Goodrich is the builder. I think John Mark is his most fervent admirer. Try him."

"Touché, Mrs. Six," Able said. "Perfect. I know St. Brendan's doesn't pay you enough."

"You do," she replied, trying to look demure while wearing nothing but Ben and a smile.

Here came the reward: he blushed.

They left London without a backward glance, after a surprising visit from a breakfast guest.

Grace Croker announced to John Mark over bacon and eggs that in one hour she was taking him to a balloon ascension in Hyde Park. "John and I will return tomorrow or the next day to Portsmouth. You Sixes can go ahead today." She turned to John Mark, whose mouth was open in amazement. "That is, if you're interested in seeing such a spectacle. I want to see it, and I need a boy as a shield."

Never slow, John Mark was her match. "If I must," he said in a droll way that to Meridee sounded like years ahead of genuine, sparkling wit. *And to think you were born on a bare wharf in the rain*, she thought.

"You must, John," Grace declared. "Sir B insisted upon such an expedition." She leaned toward her co-conspirator. "Don't tell Mrs. Six, who is a stickler about proper eating, but I believe there will be eclairs and macaroons afterword."

"Blimey, Miss Croker!"

"I will assume that is a yes," Grace said. She nodded to Able. "Tell my brother I have every hope he will make an uneventful recovery from the mumps. Better not tell him that none of his St. Brendan charges are regretting a few more days of idleness until he is fully on the mend."

An under footman came into the breakfast room, holding out a silver tray to her husband. Able read the note in his usual blink. He handed it to Meridee, and quickly left the room.

"What in the world…" Grace began. She made to rise, but Meridee put her hand on her friend's sleeve.

"Don't, even if it is your house. If he had wanted an audience, he would have asked for one," she said. "We'll wait."

In a moment she heard Able's footsteps, and others. Able opened the breakfast room door and ushered in William Pitt.

"Goodness," Grace said under her breath. "A prime minister at breakfast?"

Mr. Pitt bowed over her hand and then Grace Croker's, and gave a nod to John Mark, who was busy with bacon. Mr. Pitt turned to Grace with the wry humor of a long-time friend. "I'll wager you never thought to see me for breakfast, Grace."

"Do join us, Will," Grace said, as calmly as if England's former prime minister dropped in every day.

Mr. Pitt selected baked eggs and toast from the sideboard. He stood a moment by the empty platter that had held bacon, as if waiting for more to materialize.

"I can share my bacon," Able offered. "I did take rather a lot."

Grace tried monumentally hard not to laugh, which earned her one raised eyebrow from her childhood friend.

"I would like a few pieces," Mr. Pitt said. "Pardon my reach." He reached over and selected two slices from Able's plate. Grace had to turn her head and practice great forbearance, to Meridee's amusement.

Mr. Pitt dug in, but politely. He sat back after he downed his eggs and nodded to Grace. "You should ask me to breakfast more often."

"Will, really," she said with a laugh. "Did I? Come any time. We hardly stand on ceremony, do we?"

"We do not."

*Why, Mr. Pitt, are you here?* Meridee wanted to ask.

At ease, Mr. Pitt looked around the table. "I debated about this. Tossed and turned a bit, even. Possibly I am overreaching."

"Everything I have heard about you, sir, would suggest that is not possible," Able said. He put another piece of bacon on the former prime minister's plate. "Here, sir. When you return to power someday, as I know you will, I want you to remember me as a fine fellow who shares bacon, and not the bastard who doesn't know his place in society, and blacks his own wife's eye."

"Bacon is not required," Mr. Pitt said, then chuckled. "Nor is it ever turned down." He nodded in Meridee's direction. "Mrs. Six, if everyone looked as fetching as you do with a shiner, it would become fashionable. No, Master Six, you were surprised and assaulted by someone who ought to be relieved of his title of Elder Brother."

"That won't happen," Able said.

"No, it won't. However regrettable his behavior was, Captain Ogilvie is a well-connected, powerful man. That, I am certain, is a reality you understand."

"I do, sir. Better than most."

Mr. Pitt spread marmalade on his toast and ate a small corner before speaking. Meridee suspected he knew at least as much about drama and building suspense as

Edmund Keene, Drury Lane's favorite actor. William Pitt must have been a wonder, when addressing the House of Commons.

"I won't drag you around Robin Hood's barn," Mr. Pitt said at last. "I noticed something odd during that regrettable scene in front of Trinity House."

Able winced. "The oddity to me is why didn't Captain Ogilvie spill his budget *inside* Trinity House? He had ample opportunity there, plus a ready-made audience."

"I believe he wanted to make a scene exactly where he did," Mr. Pitt said.

Meridee thought about the moment – the angry words, the shove, Able falling backward onto her, his elbow against her cheek, everyone gathering around them, opening her eyes, only to close them when Able covered her with his body as Captain Ogilvie kicked him.

"He certainly succeeded," she said.

Mr. Pitt nodded. "Master Six, all eyes were on you and your lady."

"I hardly need reminding," Able said, in a tone so dry that Meridee could have brushed sand off it.

Mr. Pitt forged ahead, gesturing with the bacon. "I came up behind Captain Ogilvie and had a different view. I watched him slip a folded piece of paper into Gervaise Turenne's hand." He popped the bacon in his mouth.

"Gervaise?" Meridee asked. "It would be hard to imagine two more unlikely confederates."

"Ordinarily I would agree with you, Mrs. Six, but these are not ordinary times." He shrugged. "Am I too suspicious? Possibly, but Sir B's valet has French connections, has he not?"

"His parents are *émigres* since the Reign of Terror," Able said. "They live quietly in Kent on heaven knows what."

"We should find out what they live on, heavenly or otherwise. I will drop a word to a friend at Horse Guards."

"That's it?" Grace asked. "Someone odious passes a note. Have you said anything to Captain St. Anthony?"

"You know Sir B well, madam," Mr. Pitt said. "Should I?"

"I don't know," she said. "I will see him this morning. He is taking John Mark and me to a balloon ascension in Hyde Park."

"Use your discretion," Mr. Pitt told Grace. "After all, Gervaise will be there, won't he?"

"Always. They are seldom apart. But…but… *Gervaise?*"

"Who can say? We live in dangerous times."

After a few more pleasantries, Mr. Pitt rose to take his leave, Able accompanying him.

"Grace, I would say nothing about this to Sir B," Meridee said in a low voice out of John Mark's hearing.

"Your reason?"

"It's early days in … in this investigation or observation or whatever we wish to call it. Let's let sleeping dogs lie for now."

# — Chapter Twelve —

With Ben in Meri's arms, Able happily shook the dust of London off his feet and handed his wife into the Croker carriage.

Able watched as Mrs. Perry took her place, smoothing down her dress and giving Meri The Look that said, *Now he is mine*. No fool, Meri handed over their child, who settled at once into the roomy comfort that was the formidable African's lap. Soon Meri was tucked close to Able.

"Just so you know, Master Six, when we stop for the night, I'm in charge of Ben once he is fed."

Meri attempted a remonstrance, but it sounded feeble to Able's ears. Heaven knows *he* never had any intention of arguing with the woman who outweighed him and who probably could outfight him, if it came to that.

"Mrs. Perry, he might wake up in the night." It was a pathetic argument and they all knew it. Mrs. Perry smiled, sensing victory in the air.

"Now when has Ben done that recently, Mrs. Six?"

"Well, perhaps this time you may have him," Meri said. She cuddled closer to Able.

That night in Haslemere, once their little one was fed and bedded in Mrs. Perry's room, Able enjoyed the unbelievable luxury of strolling along Charter Walk with a beautiful woman, enjoying the one person he needed. He was a man with no illusions. Likely there would be more children, but their little ones would eventually grow up and create lives of their own, precious lives, to be sure, but other lives. Meri was his forever.

"What say you, missy: should we go for another year and term at St. Brendan's?" he teased.

She leaned against his shoulder, a partner in repartee. "Let's try it out and see how we like it, shall we?"

"Aye, lass. I must say, though, how thoughtful it was of Master Croker to come down with the mumps and declare a week's holiday."

"Wasn't it?" She turned her forehead into his shoulder and he stopped. They stood that way because they could, with no one needing either of them. "London was no holiday, though, what with your grilling in Trinity House, and the unfortunate business in the street."

"We secured significant funding for St. Brendan, and I *have* encountered bullies in grog shops and gaming hells before." He kissed her forehead. "Part of my misspent years with the Fleet, dearest."

They walked on, Able savoring the presence of his wife and no one else.

She thrilled him to the depths of his heart. What a woman.

"Able, you haven't heard a word I have said."

No, he hadn't. Better admit it. "You have me there, Meri."

"Turn off Euclid for the night, and that is an order."

He stopped their stroll that had been moving slower and slower anyway and put his hands on her shoulders, drawing her close. "I was only thinking of you, Mrs. Six."

"No one else?"

He heard the humor in her voice and wondered how any sane woman could cope with his brain. "Cross my heart," he replied. She felt good so close. "I was sort of wondering if you might enjoy a romp in a quiet inn with a well-endowed sailing master."

She did, starting immediately in the direction of the inn at such a clip that he laughed and grabbed her hand to slow her down. She shed her clothes in record time and so did he, two heaps of winter clothes on the floor. They were lodged at the back of the inn, so there was no pressing need for silence. There was even occasion later for talk, the mundane, idle sort of chat of husband and wife with time on their hands.

"Best conversational setting I know," Able said. His eyelids were drooping, but his wife's weren't. He knew her well, though, and knew she would sink like a stone in about fifteen minutes.

"We need another student-lodger," she said, drawing little circles in his chest hairs. "I'm ready for another one."

"After we get home tomorrow, I'll see how Master Croker is doing and get his approval," Able said. He ran his hand down her bare arm, wondering how women were so soft. "Now that St. Brendan's is buttressed with more cash, I'll ask him to look for a cartographer – maybe an artist - and a French speaker."

"It would be advantageous if we could find one person who did both," Meri added. "That way Grace Croker could be paid."

"You're a shrewd lass. I don't think that whatever pittance she is paid will make a difference to a woman of wealth."

"Able, you're just a man," Meri began.

"A few minutes ago, you were intensely grateful."

"Oh, my. Words fail me," his irrepressible wife acknowledged. "No, it is this, my love: The idea of a woman being paid for work." He heard her chuckle as she burrowed close to him, a familiar movement to him because he knew she was composing herself for sleep. "I receive two pounds a month as …as… what am I?"

*Completely indispensable to me*, he thought. "I believe the Gunwharf Rats decided to call you Mam."

"Yes. Mam. I use that money to buy extra food and yarn for stockings for them and what all."

"You do."

"I also put a little by for myself, because I earn it," she said, and he did understand. "It isn't much, but I can do with it as I please."

"If you were paid what you are worth to me, there wouldn't be enough money in the entire world," he said. "I hope that two pounds a month goes far enough."

"It does," she said. "My sisters aren't paid for what they do. I am, and I like it. This is a modern age." She sighed. "But why war? We all fight, in our own way."

It touched his heart to hear her include herself in the titanic struggle against Napoleon that had begun again, after the half-hearted Treaty of Amiens that had brought them together.

"It frightens me, too, as you know better than anyone."

That led to both of her arms around him, as if she could hold him tight against all the evil and hurt in the world.

"You'll be teaching everything, taking care of me and our young lodgers, and now keeping an eye on the harbor and its hulks."

He kissed her hair. "I might add that you still need to learn to swim."

"I can float," she reminded him.

"I'd rather you could swim, too."

"Like John Mark?" she asked, and laughed into his chest.

"I fear he will never learn well, which reminds me: I will see that John becomes more involved at the block factory, in the office and on the floor. We wouldn't have to worry about him leaping into the water from a sinking ship. The sea isn't for everyone is it, Meri? Meri?"

Asleep. Content, Able lay back into her warmth. For a moment, the inn seemed so distant from the Channel, which he knew was precisely one hundred nine kilometers, plus one thousand, one hundred and thirty five in small change on the other side of the decimal point. For a moment, he wanted to plop his family down in the North American interior, where no one probably thought much about war.

They could live and never give a thought to Napoleon. For all Able knew, the recently crowned emperor of France was probably in his shirt sleeves right now, holding a candle over a map and measuring the distance from Calais to Dover, not a great leap.

In his mind's eye, he saw all the Elder Brothers seated at the u-shaped table in Trinity House, playing their somewhat mysterious role in the war. The scroll that was his brain opened next upon Mr. Pitt, undoubtedly returning to power as prime minister and first lord of the treasury again, a man who knew how to finance and wage war. It opened next on the Red, Blue and White fleets, patrolling Channel waters and the Mediterranean, pitting themselves against the continental menace and saying, "No farther."

Now it was time to sleep and regroup. Tides rolled in and out, seamen stood the watch, and soon he would be back in his classroom with his Gunwharf Rats. Until then, he could savor the richness of his life with Meri Six, and now Ben.

He ordered his nimble brain to shut down. He concentrated on matching his breathing to his wife's. He kissed her head, and let himself go.

# — Chapter Thirteen —

A fter dropping off Meri and Ben and dumping their dirty laundry downstairs, Able's next stop was across the street to St. Brendan's, and up the broad stairs.

Able paused a moment, pleased to see students sweeping the halls, shining doorknobs and scrubbing tile and battling cobwebs. Amazing how an old place like St. Brendan the Navigator School seemed to produce spider webs at will.

He nodded to the formidable old biddy, widow of a bosun's mate, who presided in the hall, making sure the work was done to Royal Navy specifications, or so some of his students had complained.

"Shipshape and Bristol fashion, Master Six," she said as he walked by. "The idle brain is the devil's playmate."

He nodded and watched the lads a moment. "Back to lessons next week?"

"Aye, master," one little fellow piped up.

"Did someone dust our Gunwharf Rat?"

"Aye, master," said another. "We're ready for class again."

"As you were, men," he said, and continued down the hall, pleased when someone started to sing "Heart of Oak."

They were a far cry from the quiet, cowed children who came to St. Brendan's, bruised by hard times they had no control over. Or the defiant, noisy lads ready to brawl for the smallest morsel or warmest corner by the fireplace until they learned no one needed to fight for anything at St. Brendan's except good grades.

*We are working miracles*, he thought, as gratitude filled all the spare places in his mind not already occupied. He glanced out the window at his home across the street, where Meri was probably rushing about, unpacking, or maybe just chatting with Nick or Betsy. *And miracles are working on me, too, lads.*

Able knocked on the door with the discreet metal scroll proclaiming the apartment of Thaddeus Croker, headmaster and man currently recovering from a wicked case of the mumps.

Thaddeus's servant, a morose fellow, ushered him in. Whispered questions about the state of St. Brendan's headmaster led to a sorrowful shake of the head, and the comment, "He's been dwindling, sir, dwindling, I vow." His lip jutted out. "He threw a bowl of gruel at me this morning."

"He sounds more like a man on the mend, Bertram."

"Sir!"

"Bertram, I trust I may visit the headmaster," Able asked, as the two of them stood there in the apartment's foyer, the servant making no move and the mental clock in Able's head ticking louder and louder.

*Patience,* Able thought, with diminishing patience. He knew Bertram had an affinity toward the dramatic. At the moment, he appeared unwilling to budge or offer anything remotely resembling information. He would not yield, and Able had neither the time nor the inclination to wait him out.

"Thaddeus! Thaddeus!" he called. "Where away?"

"Able, do come to me," he heard mostly distinctly, even above Bertram's sucked-in breath and noisy exhalation, sounding like the most put-upon servant on their foggy, damp island. "I don't know why I never have visitors."

"I do," Able said under his breath. He tapped lightly on the door and entered. "Bertram is both intimidating and quite capable of keeping out the faint of heart. How are you, sir?"

"Bored," the headmaster croaked, and waved him toward a chair by the bed. "I stink from Bertram's poultices. Able, you're a reasonably intelligent man." (It was joke between them.) "Will a mixture of iodine, saltpeter, wax, asafoetida and God knows what else cure *anything?*"

How to keep a straight face? "Headmaster, I have heard asafoetida is used as a defense against pregnancy in some primitive societies."

The narrow-eyed glare the headmaster threw his way suggested to Able that Thaddeus Croker was probably on the mend.

"That's the best you can offer me?" he grumbled.

Or perhaps the headmaster was still ill, Able reasoned. He tried to tamp down the laughter rising inside him. He *had* to be ill. Why else would the invalid offer such low-hanging fruit? *Resist the urge,* Able thought, then failed.

"Your poultice is one of the great triumphs of medicine. You reek. I doubt you could tempt any nubile female to get within a barge pole of you – perfect contraception, asafoetida or not." Able laughed out loud, even as he unwound the eye-watering bandage. "There, sir. I should toss this in the fireplace, but it might explode, I would die, and Meri would be so disappointed."

Thaddeus held his neck and laughed.

"I recommend a clean cloth instead. When the swelling is gone, any physician will pronounce you no longer a menace to society. Give it a few more days."

"I told you I was bored," Thaddeus repeated.

"Let me tell you what transpired in London. That should divert you."

By the time Able left, the headmaster had resigned himself to three more days of quarantine. Even better than the dangled carrot of no more wretched poultices and better food from the kitchen was the promise of three hundred pounds a year from Trinity House. Able saw no point in mentioning his own shabby treatment by one of the Elder Brothers, or Mr. Pitt's breakfast commentary about Gervaise Turenne.

"Trinity's warden, Mr. Pitt himself, was most specific that you start paying your sister for her work, and that we find a French teacher and a draftsman or artist," Able told him. "Someone to add some polish to our students' lives."

"It will be my pleasure," Thaddeus said.

When Able returned to his own house, he could nearly feel the order and love within, beginning as soon as he opened the door. Betsy greeted him with a curtsy and took his boat cloak and hat. She said Mrs. Six was in the sitting room with Nick Bonfort, their other young lodger.

"He's hobbling about pretty well now, master," Betsy said, beaming at him. This Betsy was far cry from the thin and wary child who had made her way to Portsmouth from a workhouse in the north, looking for her twin. She touched her apron pocket. "And I have a letter from Jamie." She held it out to Able. "Would you like to read it?"

"Very much, but let us wait until dinner, for all to hear," he said.

She put the letter back in her pocket and patted it with something approaching tenderness. "He's safe, sir." She hesitated. "He always begins his letters that way, as if he knows I worry. Sir, did you begin letters home that way, too?"

"I would have, had there been anyone for me to write," he said, and watched the concern build on her face. That would never do. He touched her shoulder. "Betsy, only think how lucky your twin must feel, to know there are always letters waiting for him."

Appearing considerably more sanguine than the convalescing headmaster across the street, Nick Bonfort glanced up from the book on his lap. His face split into a wide, welcoming grin. "Hullo, sir! Ezekiel Bartleby made me some crutches so I can get about."

"Talented man. May I join you?"

Meri indicated the chair beside her. Able scooped her up instead, which made Nick laugh out loud when she shrieked. He sat down in the chair and deposited her on his lap in a froth of petticoats. He gave Meri a smacking great kiss on her cheek.

It was all nonsense, but Able had learned early in his tenure as quasi-father to some of St. Brendan's young pupils that nonsense was what workhouse boys needed. Even better than good food, blankets and a bed was the knowledge that mothers were for teasing and caring about, and fathers could be firm and loving, too. Most had known neither.

Nick Bonfort, the boy with no last name at first, was a serious child, earnest in his studies. He was quietly devoted to the woman who had happily shared her maiden name with him. Able told Nick about the visit to Trinity House and the pledge for more funds, which might mean more instructors.

He told Nick of the need to be ever watchful, over their own house and St. Brendan's itself. Serious child that he was, Nick nodded. He glanced at Meri and chuckled.

"Master, I think she fell asleep," he whispered to Able.

"Meri Six? Never," Able said. He had felt her regular, deep breathing against his uniform sleeve. Someday when Nick had a lady of his own, he would appreciate the tenderness of such a moment. "She's just resting her eyes."

"Am not," Meri muttered, then returned to sleep. Able and Nick grinned at each other.

"Sir, I have an idea," Nick whispered. "I think we Gunwharf rats here at home and over at St. Brendan's should start standing a nightly watch over our part of the harbor. You know, keeping an eye on the hulks in case a Frenchman tries to escape and do mischief. What do you think, Master?"

"That, Nick Bonfort, is precisely the injunction we were given in London. How did you know?"

"It seemed logical, sir."

*You will command a frigate someday*, Able thought, with admiration. *Maybe serve as Trinity House's warden*. He frowned. *Provided nasty cases like Captain Ogilvie die out.*

"It *is* logical," he agreed. "This nation will see our worth, won't she?"

"We Gunwharf Rats can stand a watch for England," Nick said quietly, "whether she knows she needs us or not."

# — Chapter Fourteen —

There was nothing like the comfort of her own bed. Meridee came awake slowly, which suited her nature, fully aware that Able was probably already up, sitting in a chair by the window, his long legs propped on the window seat, actively thinking about something

They had spent a quiet evening in the sitting room, with Nick demonstrating his prowess with crutches and then taking a tentative step. "Not so bad," he had announced. "The surgeon told me sprains hurt worse than breaks. What do you think, Mam?"

"I've never had either, so I couldn't tell you."

Her answer didn't seem to satisfy Nick. "What about you, Da?"

She held her breath with the loveliness of the moment. Nick seemed not to notice what he had said. Able's head went back against the sofa in surprise, then down against his chest as he struggled with an emotion she knew deep in her soul was foreign to him. Certainly someday Ben would call him Da, but this was Nick Bonfort, unaware.

"I think I would trust your surgeon, son," Able answered, his voice cracking like a schoolboy's.

And that was that. Matter-of-fact, solemn Nick Bonfort became their own. The three of them looked at each other in quiet agreement. She waited for Able to speak again. What he said did not disappoint.

"Nick, when it's the three of us, please do call me Da," he said when he could talk. "With others in company, I must remain Master Six."

"I understand," Nick replied. "Da." He said it again, trying out the word. "Da."

"What are you thinking of, my love?" she asked her man that morning as he sat so still, gazing out the window. "Euclid?"

He turned to look at her, surprised. "Well, no, actually." He held out his hand to her. She slid to his side of the bed where she could reach him from where he sat. "I was thinking about my father. I wish I could have known him."

"Dearest, what is your earliest memory? Think a bit."

He gave her a strange look. "I've already told you about my birth. Wasn't that odd enough?"

"Is there more?" Meridee knew no other couple in the world was having such a conversation on a cold February morning.

"I remember two heartbeats, you know, suck and swish over and over." He chuckled as he changed the mood. "You'll have to agree that is a long way back, Meri. That's it."

54

His expression grew thoughtful. "No Euclid. I haven't thought of him in several hours. Should I worry?"

"*I'm* not worried," she said, and got out of bed, tugging at her nightgown. "He's your best friend."

"Next to you," he told her, grabbing her for a kiss. "Oops. You have a second sense about Ben. Quick kiss then."

And here was Ben, getting creases on his fat rolls now, staying awake to coo and smile. After breakfast no one had to rush off to class. She savored the unbelievable luxury of turning her baby over to his father, who flopped on the sofa, propped his knees up, and chatted with Ben about Nikolas Copernicus and the earth's rotation while she finished kitchen duties with Mrs. Perry and Betsy. Nick made his way downstairs cautiously, trying out his sprained ankle without a crutch.

He limped into the sitting room, where he made himself comfortable on the floor by the sofa. Meridee stood in the doorway and listened. She thought they weren't aware, but Able tipped his head back to almost see her.

"Meri, what do you think of this? Tell her, Nick."

"Mam, remember I mentioned Mr. Bartleby?"

"I do."

"He might like to watch the harbor with us."

"He has a bakery to run," she reminded Nick.

"Da tells me that once a sailor, always a sailor. And he is tough."

Meridee could see any number of demerits to this idea, but knew better than to shoot it down. Life with her nephews in their father's parish in Devon had taught her things she was putting into practice now. "It has possibilities."

"We should consider them."

"Nick, you sound like a captain I once served under," Able said. "Let me suggest your idea to Headmaster Croker. Right now, I want to look in at the block pulley factory."

"I wish I could come, Da."

"So do I, son. When school resumes next week, I believe we will be making class visits. We need to know more about this modern age we live in, of factories that turn out parts quickly in mere days, instead of weeks. You'll be there, then."

Nick yielded graciously enough, especially since he had no choice. After breakfast, they left him in the sitting room with Betsy and Ben, who had trained his eyes on the maid with the flaming red hair.

"Does he know his own name yet, Master Six?" Nick asked, formal now because Betsy was there.

"Possibly, but I don't think Ben will come when you call him," Able joked.

"When he starts tugging at his eyelids, please put him in his bed, Betsy," Meridee said.

"And what about Ben?" Betsy teased in turn, which meant both young people were laughing as the Sixes left the house, with the baby staring from one to the other.

Able stood a moment on the outside steps. "Hard to believe that is the same

Betsy MacGregor who for six weeks shook like a leaf whenever anyone here slammed a door or raised a voice." He offered her his arm. "And now Mrs. Perry tells me that Betsy bargains with the best of them in the fish market."

Meridee nodded. "And Nick has good ideas."

"I honestly can see him on his own quarterdeck someday." He gave her a tender glance. "Now he is this boy of ours, who has staked his claim on your heart and mine. How did that happen?"

Never mind that a carter was passing, hunched over his reins, and two sailors crossed the street with the rolling gait of men just released from a long voyage. Able held her close.

"We must not have been paying attention," she managed to say.

He cupped his hands around her face. "I don't think this is precisely what Headmaster Croker had in mind when he asked you to take in little lodgers."

"You're certain about that?"

Meridee kissed Able's cheek, and tucked her arm through his. They strolled away from the docks and crossed a footbridge leading to a series of brick buildings, one behind the other.

"Building Twelve. Let's see who is here," her man said as they walked up the steps of the building near the inlet where cutters and hoys were tied, little vessels that darted from ship to shore on whatever business the navy intended.

There was no one in the foyer except a child sweeping. He stopped when they passed. He wore shoes, or what had been shoes at one time, but were now bits of leather held together with twine across his foot. His yellow shirt had one button.

"Good morning," Meridee said, thinking of clothes that Nick and John Mark had outgrown and wondering how soon she could get them to the little fellow's mother. "You're doing a lovely job."

He eyed her solemnly and returned to his task.

"He's so small and it is cold in here," Meridee said.

Able took a step toward the boy, who backed up, his eyes wide with fear, and flattened himself against the wall. He held his broom in front of him as if trying to hide behind it. Able stopped.

"Meri, you ask him where Mr. Maudslay is."

She came toward him slowly, reminded forcefully of a pup her nephews had found one cold morning, shivering next to the front steps of their father's parish church. The little thing had wagged its muddy tail once and then no more, because the effort seemed too great. Not even a warm blanket and milk came soon enough.

"Where might we find Mr. Maudslay?" she asked, keeping her voice low and soft.

He looked at her in disbelief. Meridee's heart seemed to swell in her breast as she wondered if anyone had ever said a kind word to him. She decided to do something Able had suggested once: she didn't look him in the eyes, but turned her head away slightly. "Mr. Maudslay?" she repeated.

Out of the corner of her eye, she saw him shake his head, his own eyes wide with terror, because he knew he had not given her the answer she wanted.

"Never mind, my dear," she whispered. "We'll find him. You can keep sweeping."

Still depending on the puny protection of his broom, the lad edged along the wall until he had distanced himself from them. She noticed that Able had already backed away, his eyed full of sympathy. She wondered what of the million events in his head he was recalling, then returned her attention to the boy.

He had gathered quite a large pile of what looked like sawdust and bits of things, but what she assumed was the receptacle was positioned beyond her. She knew she was in his way and he wanted to work, but she frightened him.

"Able, is that a piece of paper close to you by the wall?" she asked.

He looked around and walked slowly toward where she pointed. "It's a thin sheet of wood."

"Hand it to me, please."

He did as he asked, ignoring the child, who froze, then continued to sweep when Able backed away.

Meridee took the slice of wood and walked slowly toward the child. He swept more furiously, wielding the broom until she sneezed, which made him freeze. She sneezed again and he slowly relaxed.

"So much dust. Here, sweep toward this board and I will dump the sawdust in that ash can." She said it firmly, pantomiming the task.

After a long moment, the boy did as she directed, sweeping the trash onto the board as she held it. When it was full, he stopped and waited.

"Excellent! You did that well."

Meridee took the board to the ash can and dumped it, then came back for more. Quicker now, he swept the debris onto the board and she dumped it again. Two more times and the job was done.

"We did that well," Meridee said.

The boy stared at her as if he did not understand English. Maybe he was a half-wit. She took a step closer and he backed up. She pointed to herself. "Meridee," she said. "Meridee." She waited.

"Peer."

Peer? What sort of name was that? Perhaps he meant Piers. "Piers?" she asked.

He darted down the hall and out of sight. He might never have been there, except the hall was swept clean, or at least as clean as a place with sawdust would ever be.

"Do...do you think Piers belongs to someone here?" Meridee asked, not even sure what she wanted to know.

"I doubt it. Ah, here is someone who might be able to tell us where Mr. Maudslay can be found. Handsomely now, Mrs. Six."

A tall man stood in an open door. He wore a carpenter's apron and had a genial expression.

"Master Six, you were here before, trailed by a little boy who didn't want to leave, if I recall correctly."

"I was, indeed. Simon Goodrich?"

"The very same." Those kind eyes looked Meridee over, but not in a way to make her feel uneasy. "Would this be Mrs. Six? John Mark has spoken of her."

"It would be, Simon. Meri, Mr. Maudslay might be the mechanist, but here is the artificer."

He bowed, she curtsied. "Mr. Goodrich, that little boy…"

"He showed up one or two weeks ago. He's a little ghost, but he is always ready to sweep."

"Showed up?"

The carpenter nodded. "They show up, they work a while, we feed them, and they move on, heaven knows where."

"I think he said his name was Piers."

"Bravo, Mrs. Six! That's more than any of us have ever gotten out of him."

"My wife has a way with little boys."

"Then you are to be congratulated." He indicated the large room beyond. "Come in, please, and pardon our mess."

Meridee followed Able into what was probably the heart of the factory. Before the door closed, she peered into the hall for the little ghost with the broom. She thought she saw him, watching her from an alcove, but she couldn't be certain. *I have a project,* she thought. *My home needs another boy.*

She knew Able's eyes were on her, so she gave him the full force of her own. No words were needed. He nodded slightly, then turned his attention to Simon Goodrich.

*I wonder if people think we are two sillies, wearing our hearts on our sleeves?* she thought. *I wonder if it shows?*

# — Chapter Fifteen —

"Master Six, I took your suggestion from your last visit, and moved that wheel one quarter inch closer to that dial. It runs like a top now. How did you know?" They stood with Simon Goodrich in front of a machine that Able could tell baffled Meridee.

*Anyone else in my shoes would have done the same thing*, he thought. "I watched it a while," he mumbled, embarrassed, his eyes on Meri because he knew she was his golden chance to change the subject.

"What in the world does all this do?" she asked, right on cue. God bless his wife. And even better, she turned to Simon for her answer. Able was promptly, gleefully aware that Simon Goodrich couldn't take his eyes off Meridee Six. All thoughts of more compliments to the man who took a glance and changed the entire efficiency of the machine had fled Simon Goodrich's brain, from the looks of him.

"You'd better explain it to her, Mr. Goodrich," Able said.

Simon explained it in simple terms, not that Meri was simple – far from it – but she needed the workaday description, not some treatise on torque, motion and angles which was the only way Able could manage.

"This is the modern way of making block pulleys?" she asked. "And you do it in mostly metal, instead of wood?"

"Precisely, Mrs. Six," Simon said. Able laughed inside to watch the smitten Mr. Goodrich walk his wife through the whole maze of machines and almost-finished parts, going through each step of the process that, when completed, would no longer require the services and hours of a dozen or more block makers, working at home or in small factories.

"When this is done, the whole manufactory from start to finish will only require four semi-skilled men, and it will be ten times as fast."

Able watched the animation on the artisan's face and heard it in his voice. Less pleased would be the skilled fashioners of block pulleys suddenly thrown out of work by modern times. *Only wait until steam powers all our Royal Navy ships*, he thought as he walked along. *We won't need block pulleys at all because there will be no more sails. And after steam? Something to do with atoms.*

At the end of his impromptu tour, Simon Goodrich handed her a model of a metal pulley, one of what he called a prototypon. "They will look like this, Mrs. Six."

She hefted the thing and handed it back, obviously impressed. "Mr. Goodrich, we lubbers see the sails and hear the guns, but without *these*, no ship would sail in the first place."

Could a man have a better wife to shift the matter back into his lap again? He cleared his throat. "And that brings us to a confidential matter, Simon, if you will indulge me."

"Certainly."

"The Brothers of Trinity House – the lighthouse men – have enjoined all of us at St. Brendan's to be mindful of unfamiliar people skulking about Portsmouth's factories," Able said. "It would be easy enough to set this building on fire and ruin the production of a vital component."

"Mr. Maudslay and I have already discussed this possibility," Simon said. "We will set up guards. There should be enough lame or aging sailors hereabouts to assist. Sooner, rather than later, eh?"

"We can probably add some officers from the local constabulary,' Able said, thinking of Walter Cornwall, who had been threatening enough last year when he terrified an already frightened Betsy MacGregor, searching for her twin. *I need to cultivate that source,* he thought.

"We will be watchful, Master Six," Simon assured him.

"I know you will," Meri said. She touched the artisan's sleeve. "Sir, I am wondering about that little fellow in the hall. Does he...does someone feed him?"

Simon brightened, and snapped his fingers. "Mrs. Six, I should be thanking you. That St. Brendan boy of yours..."

"John Mark?"

Aye." He leaned toward Able. "By the way, I see a future for him doing what I do. With some more tutelage, his drawings will be vastly useful to those manufactories I know are coming."

"What would you call him? A designer?"

"Why not?" Simon shook his head, as if to rearrange the mound of facts and details he was already responsible for. "Aye, we thank you for generously sending John Mark with enough food to feed little ... Piers, you say?... and one of our other lads on my staff who is supporting himself."

"When did we..." Able began, but Meri gave him a discreet thump to the ribs.

"He is a benevolent little fellow, is John," she said, as smoothly as if she knew what was going on. "We trust you'll be wanting him back here."

"As soon as ever," Simon replied. One of the workers called to him from the top of distant scaffolding. He sketched a little bow to Meri, waved to Able and started off at a trot, shouting, "Let John Mark come back soon," over his shoulder. "And any others."

They turned with one accord and started for the entrance. "And here I have been thinking John Mark was experiencing a growth spurt and hungry all the time," Meri said as she hurried along the hall, then out the door into the busy street. She stopped. "Why didn't he tell me he was giving all of his lunch to Piers? Doesn't he trust me yet?" She tried to sniff back tears.

Able held her close. "Meri, Meri, don't be quite so contrary," he crooned in her ear, oblivious to who might be watching them because he really didn't care and never would. "I don't know if I am articulate enough to explain the complex relationship all of us Gunwharf Rats have with food."

He led her to a bench beside the wharf, where empty water kegs carried to and from the prison hulks were stacked. The kegs were tall enough to give them a little privacy. While she fumbled in her reticule for a handkerchief, one of those useless lacy ones, he gave her his more substantial one.

"Blow," he said. She blew, and her sobs turned into hiccups, as they usually did, which made him want to smile. He was smart enough not to. He squeezed onto the bench beside her.

"Have you ever been hungry?" he asked, then answered his own question. "Of course you have. You once mentioned running away from home and pouting in an apple tree for a while."

"Until I got hungry."

"Did your mama feed you when you came home?"

From the depths of his handkerchief, Meri nodded. "She gave me a swat to the backside, then sat me down for dinner. It was cold, but it was still dinner." She leaned against his shoulder. "I knew she would feed me. You didn't have that luxury, did you? You or John Mark or any of the Rats."

"We knew we *wouldn't* be fed," he said. "Oh, don't cry about that. You'll admit I'm an admirable specimen now, won't you?"

"More than adequate," she replied, still watery, but her eyes had their usual zest for life returning.

He could tell she was ready for what he had to say. "I finally quit staring at other officers' plates in the wardroom when I became a sailing master. It took that long. Captain Hallowell pointed that out to me once." He took her by her shoulders. "We have to know that there is food enough. I think...no, I know... that John Mark feared if he told you he was sharing his lunches with a little ghost of a child, you might get angry and cut his own food."

"I would never..."

He stopped her with a kiss. "I know you wouldn't. On some level, John knows it, too, but by all that's holy, it is hard to convince your stomach *and* your brain."

"What should we do?" she asked, after a long pause.

"I'll talk to him. What should we do about the little sweeper? Can we encourage him to come home with John some afternoon?"

"That shouldn't be hard," she said.

"It might be. I doubt he trusts anyone."

Meri digested that fact then nodded. "I'll make certain John has more than he can possibly eat, packed in his daily lunch. And then I let things go? Let the lads work it out?"

"Aye, miss. Let's go home now."

Meri let him pull her to her feet. She looked around at the kegs, as if seeing them for the first time. "What are these for?"

"The water hoys take them out to the prison hulks several times a week."

She ran her hand over one, then tapped on it and listened. "What happens if there is a storm and the hoys can't leave the harbor?"

"The prisoners go thirsty. If there is a long storm, they go hungry. I hate war."

Theirs was a quiet walk home, with Meri looking over her shoulder at the pulley block factory three times, as if calculating how she could storm the thing and snatch out a little sweeper.

"Why would Piers not trust me if I were to tell him about living in a house with beds and food and sturdy clothing? Did you notice how thin his shirt was. Able, it's March!" she burst out as they turned down their quiet street.

He had no difficulty being patient with the rational woman who shared his bed and board and was capable of giving him children, just like normal people did. "Meridee, when you speak of houses and beds and food and clothing, you're talking about things that barely register in Piers's brain," he pointed out. "You could be speaking Martian, as far as it seems to him."

"I could invite him to dinner?"

"That's a thought. Well, look who is here."

A muddy post chaise had pulled up to the Sixes' house across the street from St. Brendan School. John Mark leaped from the carriage like a boy with stories to tell. Able laughed and shooed him toward the house, after reminding him about his duffel, which the post boy held out to him.

Meri walked to the chaise and leaned in. She leaned farther in, then stepped back and nodded to the postilion, who tipped his hat to her and spoke to his horses. Expertly he turned his team and stopped them directly across the street. Meri waved, then walked to Able, holding out a package.

"Grace thinks we aren't too old for candy kisses from Astley's Circus." She popped one in her mouth. "Open up, my love."

He did as directed, happy he wasn't too old. Maybe it would make up for all the times he felt precisely that. He sucked on the sweetness and blamed his celestial mentors, from Euclid to Newton and Leibnitz, and that odd fellow from the future. There were times when his brain didn't know which century it belonged in, but Meri didn't need to know that.

"Grace wants me to visit her soon," Meri said, tucking her arm through his. "She is unhappy about something."

"Any hints?"

"Perhaps," his wife replied. She stopped and watched Grace Croker, dignified and tall, climb the front steps, followed by the post boy, who staggered under a mound of luggage. "I looked like her once before."

"When?"

"When I wasn't precisely certain where I stood in our admittedly odd courtship."

"You must be mistaken, wife. How many times has she declared herself a satisfied spinster?"

"Things change, husband."

# — Chapter Sixteen —

Dinner was lobscouse, everyone's favorite, accompanied by the luxury of white rolls from Ezekiel Bartleby, who lingered long enough in the kitchen to hear about Astley's Circus.

"Elephants, Mr. Bartleby!" John Mark exclaimed. "I was so close I could smell them."

"Methinks that's not much of an endorsement," the baker said.

John shrugged. "No worse than cleaning out the stone inlet last year," he said, with a nod at Able. The nod turned into a grin and a glance at Meridee. "Or boiling the wharf rat."

The baker waved a hand and left the same way he had come, through the kitchen and out the back door. "Johnny, I doubt Mrs. Six will ever allow another rat in her kitchen."

Meridee gave a proper grimace, the one she knew John, and probably Ezekiel, wanted to see. A year and then some with her own Gunwharf Rats had changed her perspective. She saw the inlet and the rat through John's eyes as solid evidence that he had a history now that included more than the bleak misery of the workhouse. With gratitude in her heart, she saw John Mark as a well-scrubbed lad – Mrs. Perry's threats of soap and water promptly heeded – who could reminisce happily now, and count friends, and eat until he was full, and be tucked in at night. She swallowed, determined not to cry.

She mostly succeeded, since dinner was on the table. There was Able already seated with Nick, his eyes on their small son, who waved his arms about in his bassinet, a wicker laundry basket doing double duty. It was Able's turn tonight to have Ben by his chair at the end of the table, so she could eat in peace. In her magnificent husband, she saw another child who could eat until he was full and be tucked in at night any way he liked, which usually involved her.

*I have so much*, she thought, as she passed the peas to Nick Bonfort. "You didn't even need that cane tonight, did you?" she asked.

"No, Mam. I navigated successfully," he replied. Nick did love big words, almost as much as he loved adding up columns of numbers in his head.

They ate in relative silence. Meridee had attempted including conversation in their meals, recalling many a rollicking discussion of everything ranging from polliwogs to how hard the pews were in their father's church: nattering between bites in her brother-in-law's house. But no, the Gunwharf Rats preferred to concentrate on their vittles; as did Able.

If Mrs. Perry concocted a sweet, that was another matter. A seafaring man could lean back in his chair and chat between bites. Tonight's treat had been left on the warming table by Mr. Bartleby, who probably would have denied all knowledge of it, because he disliked compliments.

As it turned out, the Spotted Dick was the perfect accompaniment to Able's extra treat. He waited until John and Nick had dug in, then called for Mrs. Perry and Betsy to join them and bring more bowls and spoons. When everyone was seated, Betsy and Mrs. Perry looking at each other, he pulled a battered letter from his inside pocket.

"I have here our first letter from Stephen Hoyt," he said.

Meridee sat back with a sigh of relief. A year and a few months is a long time to wait between letters. She understood the implication. "My love, that means he found his mother quickly, didn't he?"

"He did. Headmaster Croker and I have already read the letter," he explained. "I didn't want to open it here at the table to find bad news to accompany our Spotted Dick."

The Rats nodded. They understood bad news better than most.

While the boys ate and Meridee assumed charge of Ben, he read the letter from the Gunwharf Rat who kept running away until Meridee took him to London to find out precisely where his parents were, both of them serving sentences on the other side of the world in New South Wales. Sir B had arranged for him to travel with a clerk and his family, bound for colonial offices in Sydney, the voyage a lengthy one.

Meridee cuddled her baby as Able read of crossing the Atlantic and stopping in Rio de Janeiro to take on fresh water and more livestock. Stephen described the long, boring journey from the Atlantic to southern Pacific, to finally land in Sydney in one piece.

"'Mr. Quaiffe found my mother almost at once,'" Able read, pulling the lantern closer now because daylight was gone. ' Ah, this is satisfying, lads. 'Mam is working in the infirmary, tending the sick and delivering babies, when needed. I work for Mr. Quaiffe in his office, copying correspondence intended for other stations, but I live with Mam. We are both paid a wage.'"

Able read in silence for a blink or two, which meant he turned a page rapidly. "'On and on, and this, lads: 'Tell the Rats hello from me.'" He chuckled. "'And tell Mrs. Six that I won't be running away again.'" He sat back. "That's it. I suggest that you write him a letter."

"D'ye think he and his mum will ever return?" Nick asked. "That is, when she satisfies her sentence?"

"No. It's a long way, and the passage expensive." Able's wise eyes took on that faraway look that Meridee saw now and then, and knew he was thinking of the sea and ships, and land nowhere in sight. He sighed, just a small sigh, but it went to her heart. "Mrs. Hoyt has found respectable employment where she is needed, and Stephen is turning into a government employee. I will add a small note to Mr. Quaiffe, and assure him that Stephen is good with his numbers. As you were, men."

After the table was cleared of dishes, he set them to work writing letters to Stephen and adjourned with her and Ben to the sitting room. He found his comfortable spot on the sofa with Ben leaning against his upraised knees and handed Meridee the letter, turning to the page he skipped.

She knew what she would find, and there it was, Stephen writing to assure her that his mother had set him straight on Papa's death at sea. *He wasn't a hero, as you told me, Mrs. Six*, she read, *but you knew I needed that, didn't you? Mum and I had a little cry and then a laugh, so we are fine. Please be fine, too."*

"You knew what he needed, Meri," her husband said. "You have that knack. Give us a kiss and go hurry those boys along."

She thought about the letter long after Able slept, wondering if she would ever understand the pull of the open water. She turned over carefully to watch her husband, to savor his deep breathing, and feel a little envy at the length of his eyelashes. He was her man and she loved him. *Don't ever go to sea again*, she thought.

She heard Ben whimper in the next room – amazing how her hearing had sharpened with her baby's arrival – and knew the problem. She shouldn't have eaten those onions with tonight's roast, considering that somehow everything filtered through to mother's milk.

She left their bed and hurried to Ben. She changed him, then jiggled him in her arms, knowing that he needed to pass gas to feel better. She walked with him in the hall, then opened the door to the empty bed chamber on the seaward side of their home, the better to keep Ben's irritation quieter to the sleepers.

It was also her chance to observe the only challenge she ever felt to Able's loyalty. She knew how much he enjoyed taking Sir B's yacht into Portsmouth sound, a regular event now, designed to soothe him and train the Rats in helmsmanship.

After a few minutes, Ben let out a noisy wind that made Meridee chuckle and think of his father, who didn't do well with onions, either. She could have put Ben back to bed then, but the water beckoned her, too. She held her now-sleeping son and continued her pacing.

She gazed at the dark water and the row of seven brooding prisoner of war hulks. She looked closer. That was odd. A lantern blinked a message from one of the hulks. Who could it be signaling? Two blinks, a pause, two blinks, a pause, one more. She waited. That was all.

Ah well. Her feet were cold, and Ben slumbered now. Why should she waste the perfectly excellent warmth of a sleeping husband's legs?

In the morning after breakfast, Able took his boys across the street to St. Brendan's, dressed in their old clothes. "We have to tackle the dust and grime, so says Mrs. Blackstock." He sweetened the pie. "Then I believe we will visit Building Twelve, better known as the block pulley factory. That is, if it won't bore you."

John Mark practically jumped up and down. Even the more serious Nick Bonfort nodded with considerable enthusiasm, and then frowned. "Suppose I cannot walk the distance yet?"

"We'll hire a carter," Able said.

After Ben was full and entertaining Betsy with coos, Meridee threw her cloak around her shoulders and hurried across the quiet street herself. Up the stairs to the Headmaster's quarters and a rap on the door brought her to Grace Croker, pacing back and forth in the sitting room with some energy.

"Goodness, but you wear me out," she teased. "Of course, Able assures me I was built for comfort and not speed. Grace, whatever is the matter?"

Trust Grace to be forthright. She stopped her relentless pacing and went to the door of the sitting room. Meridee hid her smile as Grace listened to the fierce argument in progress from what was likely the headmaster's chamber.

"My brother and Bertram have been going at it hammer and tongs for inside of half an hour," she said as she closed the door with a decisive click. "Thaddeus is a terrible patient. Someone should shoot him."

She stared at Meridee then burst into tears. Meridee blinked in amazement then did what she did best, or so Able told her: she hurried to her friend, wrapped her arms around her and let her cry.

The tears ended soon enough, as the organized, efficient, practical spinster blew her nose into the handkerchief Meridee gave her and sat down with a plop.

"Meridee, tell me honestly: what does it feel like to be in love?"

*I wondered when you would figure it out,* Meridee thought. She sat beside her friend. "Oh, out of sorts, wondering if the object of your affection has a clue, certain you are barmy to even be thinking naughty thoughts. Will that do?"

Grace nodded, her eyes dry now, almost as if she had run out of tears. She took a deep breath and another. "I have known Belvedere all my life," she began. "Who do you think first dubbed him Sir B?" She stopped and reached for the next handkerchief Meridee offered. She looked at it suspiciously. "Why do you have two handkerchiefs?"

"Because I've been watching you."

"You knew more than I did," Grace said, in her usually frank manner.

"Maybe."

Grace sat a moment in silence, as if wondering how to speak what her heart was telling her.

Meridee squeezed her hand. "You can tell me."

All Grace needed was permission. "W…we were at the circus. Gervaise wheeled Sir B in and John Mark helped. He's a scamp about his studies, but otherwise a dear boy."

"Sir B?" Meridee couldn't help herself and received the glare from Grace she knew she deserved.

"Meridee, at times you try me."

"I know," Meridee replied, all complaisance.

"They were wonderful box seats close to the circus floor. I sometimes wonder how he does it and on such short notice."

*Money helps,* Meridee thought. *It doesn't hurt to be an acclaimed hero, either.*

"I watched Sir B with John, so self-assured, so kind, and I thought to myself, 'Wouldn't he make a wonderful father.'" Grace leaped to her feet, paced the width of the room twice then stopped in front of Meridee. "Merciful heavens, I want to be his wife! Me!" She resumed her track across the carpet. "I have known that man for years. I remember all the teasing at my expense between him and Thaddeus – they're five years older than I am. Why am I thinking like this?"

"Because you love him."

"How can this possibly work?"

Meridee felt her own heart break a little at such a question. Sir B was chair bound, in pain, rail thin, and not even slightly robust. She thought of her own healthy man, full of quirks to be sure, but vigorous in all the ways that a wife craves.

"It will work if you fight hard enough and if you truly want it to," she said finally. "Do you?"

Instead of pacing, Grace sank onto the sofa. Meridee watched an entire range of emotions cross her face, ordinarily a plain-enough face, but one filled with love this time. What a difference it made.

"I do," she said quietly. "I truly do. I'll have to figure it out, won't I?"

# — Chapter Seventeen —

## PRISON HULK HMS CAPTIVITY

To Jean's surprise, Ianthe Faulke proved to be an excellent student of art. She was ten years old, self-assured, well-dressed on this ship of rags and tatters and quite effective at turning a blind eye to the misery around her.

Not that the captain's quarters were miserable; far from it. Someone in the family obviously had money, because the great room across the end of the stern and the smaller dining room – the only rooms he ever saw – sported furniture that didn't come from a supply depot. There were even velvet curtains across that wonderful row of windows, and if he was not mistaken, a Turkish carpet underfoot. He had seen enough of those in Mediterranean ports of call.

He knew Ianthe was allowed nowhere else on the ship, and he marveled at such a hothouse existence. Jean wondered if the child had any idea of the misery on all three decks beneath her, and decided she did not.

Two days into their lessons, he changed his mind about his pupil. Captain Faulke had given him carte blanche to order any art supplies for Ianthe that Jean wished. He had quickly submitted a request for a sketching pad, drawing paper, and a box of soft pastels, which appeared the next day like magic. Jean's tired eyes rejoiced at something as mundane as art supplies on demand.

Ianthe was less enraptured. "I do not like the way the powdery stuff rubs off on my hands," she announced, as she sat down by the stern windows with all their lovely light for drawing that he could only envy.

"You can wipe it off your fingers with a damp cloth," he assured his pupil. "I will teach you how to smudge the colors into something close to clouds or smoke."

"I do not like the feeling, I tell you," she said more emphatically, folding her arms.

He attempted to cajole her. "Miss Faulke, it is what we happen to have right now. You'll appreciate what you can do with pastels, once you try them."

"I never will," she informed him, then turned a sly look on him. "See here, prisoner Number One Dash Eighty Seven, it is this way: if you argue with me, I will tell Papa. He will put you in the Hole and rats will gnaw at your toes. I insist upon wax crayons. Now."

Jean felt his blood run in chunks. Whatever *bonhomie* he felt turned to fear, and even deeper distrust of the English. *Mon dieu*, this child was a monster with a sweet face, and not to be crossed or thwarted.

*This war cannot end soon enough*, he thought, as he forced himself to bow, and promise crayons the next day.

So, it was crayons, a less artistic medium, to Jean Hubert's way of thinking, but at least it would not get him sentenced to the Hole.

Besides the chance to breathe better air and trade his deck's constant twilight fug for the bright light of nature, Jean Hubert enjoyed the pleasure of a clean linen shirt and English-made trousers. He had found them folded on the dining room table on his second day with the note, *Wear these. I do not wish to frighten my daughter by your current appearance. Mrs. Captain Faulke. P.S. Wash if you can. We do not care for prisoner stink.*

*We don't like reeking, either*, he thought in anger. He swallowed his Gallic pride – something he was becoming increasingly good at, to his dismay – and bent to the will of the autocratic Faulke females, anything to be a deck closer to freedom, even though he was as imprisoned as ever.

Far and away the best part about his new employment was one good meal a day, served in the cubby off the dining room, after the lesson was done. It was usually cold, because the steward who served it had no love for the French. At least it was food that could be chewed and not merely spooned down. He loved the fresh bread, even though it was a far cry from what he could find in the average *boulangerie* in an average French village. He nearly cried at the appearance of potatoes and beans all firm and tasty, not boiled down to mush.

Jean knew in his heart that he should save some of this food for certain prisoners he knew were ill and dying. Before God Almighty he tried to think of them as he sat squeezed himself into the alcove and took the tin lid off the dish, but he could not. The Lord would likely beat him with more than a few stripes after he died, but at least he had real food now.

Once he understood how the wind blew with his scheming little student, Jean Hubert knew he could manage this peculiar assignment. And he would have, if he hadn't overheard something that frightened him even more than Ianthe Faulke.

He came to the morning lesson feeling better than usual. Since Ianthe had rejected the lovely box of pastels, he had been granted permission to appropriate it. His two sketches of sunrise on the Loire had earned him slightly more money, which brought with it the relief of knowing that his modest stash of earnings was becoming nearly robust, as least by prison hulk standards.

The lesson had gone well, too. When Ianthe felt like cooperating, she produced her own charming sketches. Her indulgent papa – no prisoner would have recognized *this* man – had procured four oranges, which had led to a humorous scene.

"We must sketch these pretty things," he told his pupil, who nodded. "But there is one problem."

She raised one eyebrow.

"It is this," he began, and gave her a tutorial suited for the ten-year-old mind, about the beauty of asymmetry. "*E voila*," he concluded with a small flourish of his hand because he was after all, French, "three oranges would be more aesthetic than four. What should we do?"

"We should eat one," she informed him. "Peel it for me."

He did, hoping she would share. To his infinite delight, she handed him five segments. Could this day get any better?

"Let us try this," he told her, when the fourth orange was a memory. "Arrange the three remaining oranges, and then let us include the orange peel. How would you do that?"

She did have an eye for arrangement. He nodded. "*Bien joué!* Now, mademoiselle, draw."

They both sketched the oranges, first with the peel, and next more formally grouped around a goblet. "Tomorrow let us fill in with color," he said, and she nodded.

Ianthe bounced off happily, and Jean retired to the dining room cubby, hopeful of a meal perhaps lukewarm this time, since there was a cold wind blowing off the sound and March seemed determined to exact all the punishment it could on a man who preferred the Caribbean, or at least the south of France.

The food was cold, but the memory of those five orange segments warmed his heart. Or would have, if he hadn't found himself eavesdropping on the worst conversation of his imprisonment.

Almost full, he was wiping his mouth on his sleeve when the dining room door opened. Jean wondered later what would have happened if he had popped out of the alcove carrying his used dishes, and apologized for any inconvenience, and left. It didn't happen that way.

Maybe it was his natural reticence, honed to sharpness by war and imprisonment. He decided instead to lean back into the cubby, and that made all the difference.

"You are telling me *what?*"

Captain Faulke's crisp comment sounded no different than his tone of voice with prisoners, except that it was softer. After all, he was in his living quarters, and not dispensing disagreeable information to hundreds of prisoners whose lives were already miserable.

"*Capitain*, as we speak, two potential escapees in empty kegs are waiting to be swung out of the hold and onto the water hoy."

Jean had to clap his hand over his mouth to prevent his gasp of recognition. He took a breath and held it, wanting to doubt his hearing, but knowing he could not. Claude Pascal had an unmistakable lisp. What was he *doing?*

He was betraying the prisoners. Suddenly lightheaded, Jean felt himself start to sway. With real effort, he took a careful, quiet breath, knowing with a sick feeling in his stomach that the time was past where he could bumble out of the alcove and get away. Any movement now meant his death.

"Excellent, Claude, excellent. The two kegs are marked?"

"With a small *cp*." Ah, that lisp. Damn Claude Pascal for fooling all of them that he was their factotum, their liaison with the captain, the man who had pledged his fellow Frenchmen that he would work tirelessly to make their lives easier. Jean closed his eyes.

"I'll dispatch a cutter immediately with that information," Captain Faulke said. "There are dock workers who know what to do." He chuckled. "They are waiting for my orders."

"What will *you* do?"

*Oh Claude, you demon from hell, don't sound so eager*, Jean thought. *How can you do this?* He felt tears on his cheeks. *It's for money, isn't it? No wonder you seem better fed than all of us. No wonder you have four pairs of wool socks, four more than all of us. I have seen them.* He listened in misery as coins clinked from one hand to another hand. *Earning a sou here and there is one thing, but betraying your fellows?*

"Do? It's so fitting! My two men will open those kegs as dusk is coming on, stick the fresh water hose inside, hold it there until it fills, then nail it shut and drown them. They'll be too weak to resist."

Jean wanted to bang his head against the bulkhead, tear his hair, scream, do something. What could he do? The plot was going to move forward no matter if he revealed himself or is he stayed silent. He would be the next man dead, probably even sooner than the poor men in the kegs, who were looking forward to freedom. After all, that earlier attempt must have succeeded. Why not theirs? Claude Pascal had been wise to tell them to wait, hadn't he? Hadn't he?

The captain laughed. "And I will write a report to Admiralty, telling them I foiled an escape plot." More coins changed hands. "Enough of these reports will get me out of this wretched assignment and you will eventually return to France a wealthy man."

The two demons chuckled. "Tell me, Claude, what are you planning to do with all the money you will make, between now and peace?"

"Land, a house, and a fat wife."

They laughed and left the dining room. Head bowed, Jean Hubert, artist, prisoner, man who wanted to do nothing but get along until all this madness was over, sank to his knees in the tiny space and pressed his forehead against the deck. In agony, he heard the command given to hoist up from the main deck ten water kegs, one at a time. He sobbed out loud, then put his hand over his mouth.

When all was silent, he stepped out of the alcove. He stood there a long moment, listening, barely breathing. Silence. He opened the door, his eyes now on the door to the companionway.

There she stood, Ianthe Faulke, eating an orange. Jean sucked in his breath and gave her what he knew was a ghastly smile.

"I just finished my luncheon," he said, hoping it didn't sound as lame as he heard with his own ears.

"You're not supposed to be here now," she said in that flat voice he recognized from her argument over the soft pastels. "I will have to tell my father."

# — Chapter Eighteen —

Meridee smoothed down her dress, then looked at herself in the mirror, turning this way and that. No gaps. The bodice that two weeks ago was uncomfortably tight felt just a little snug, nothing more. *Vanity, thy name is Meridee,* she thought. Equally pleasant was the comfort of a quiet, well-ordered household. Until Able Six came walking to Pomfrey two years ago, she could not have imagined being mistress of her own home, with a family.

Classes had begun again and her home was currently quiet. Ben slept in his small chamber. A militant look on her face, Mrs. Perry had set out for the fish market, determined to find cod, or take a fishmonger or two down in the attempt. In the back yard, Betsy had applied herself to beating the sitting room rug draped over the clothesline that morning by Nick and John before they hurried across the street for class. Able even had a moment to kiss her soundly with no audience before he walked across the street to classroom duties.

She had told Able last night about Grace's admission of love for Captain Sir Belvedere St. Anthony, which left him silent. "No ideas?" she had asked.

"Not really," he said, cuddling her close. "And I thought *my* courting was doomed to destruction."

"It appears not," Meridee said.

He chuckled at that. Silence and then, "You know how I sometimes think I cannot quite follow subtle nuance?"

She nodded, composing herself for sleep.

"I will tell you one thing I have observed about the estimable Sir B."

"Which is…"

"He appears to be a man past hope for himself. This will require a hard cure."

She thought about that as she walked downstairs, wondering how to kindle hope in a man who thinks – who knows, if Able was right – he has no sexual appeal to a potential wife. That Sir B was wrong was beside the point, Meridee reasoned. She understood. She had once resigned herself to a lifetime of antique virginity, tending nephews but never her own babies, because a woman with no dowry could expect nothing. "Things changed," she said softly. "They can for you, Sir B."

She spent a moment looking at the clock, reminding herself with this new term of scholarship who among her charges would show up first, after class. After morning classes and before luncheon, Able had started taking John Mark to Building Twelve, carrying a sketching pad and new pencils, and the admonition to do whatever it was Simon Goodrich required of him, even if that meant sweeping the sawdust-coated floors, or just oiling machinery.

That first day, Meridee had packed John's lunch bucket with an extra sandwich and dried fruit for the little boy in the yellow shirt named Piers. "He's shy, but he's hungry," John told her, which meant another sandwich, because Meridee knew little boys.

Nick Bonfort had been formally invited by Master Six to join a class of young scholars examining the rudiments of algebra. "I'm not too young?" Nick had asked.

"Not at all," Able assured him. "We'll tuck our little class in after seamanship, and before dinner." Those two certainly wouldn't be first to loom over the stewpot in the kitchen.

As the early spring sky mellowed toward dusk, John would likely trail in first, but never in a hurry, because everything at the docks interested him. "He's a born mechanist," Able told her. "I expect that any moment he will dismantle one of your kitchen appliances, probably the apple corer."

"And reassemble it?"

"With any luck. He'll draw all the parts first."

"And how do you know that?"

"Because I told him to."

John had come home yesterday with a drawing of what looked like a jumble to Meridee, but which he proudly proclaimed a drawing of a lignum vitae saw. He sat her down at the dining room table and explained that Mr. Goodrich was making a saw of true size for the pulley factory. "It will be twelve feet tall," he said. "He said I could help him."

*And you will*, she thought, remembering last year's quiet boy, the introspective one who only now was exerting a calm sort of leadership that Able said would suit him well, no matter whether he led on land or sea.

The house was nearly too quiet. Meridee sat down in her favorite chair and reached for her overflowing mending basket. She could think of no excuse to avoid it, especially since Headmaster Croker had raised her salary to three pounds a month. Nowhere had the headmaster specified the darning of little boys' stockings, but Meridee knew her duty.

She had finished darning Nick's pile of stockings when she heard someone running down the street and shouting, "Mam! Mam! Oh Mam, please!"

She threw aside the basket and reached the foyer when John Mark, his eyes wide with terror, slammed open the front door so hard it banged against the wall. He grabbed her around her waist and nearly toppled her.

He held her tight, sobbing into her bodice, his face white, his whole body shaking. He was also soaking wet.

"John, did you fall in the harbor? Let's find you a blanket."

He shook his head and she felt him shudder. Meridee grabbed him by the shoulders and held him away from her, not caring that she was wet now, too. She gave him a little shake. "*What?*"

The shake was enough. "Mam, you have to help them!"

"Who?"

"The men in the kegs! I think they're prisoners, but the watermen are drowning them. Please!" He took her hand and dragged her toward the open door.

"One moment, John." Meridee broke his grip. She ran to the kitchen and out the back door, where Betsy was pounding on the rug. She kept her voice low and calm, even as she felt the rising tide of John's anguish in her own heart. "Run and tell Master Six to hurry to the water hoy dock, then come back here and stay with Ben. Now!"

With no hesitation, Betsy dropped the rug beater. Meridee had already turned to the kitchen again, but she stopped. "Wait! When you've warned him, run to Landport Gate Station and ask for Walter Cornwall."

"Mrs. Six, I can't!" Betsy said, her eyes filled with terror.

Meridee knew her maid of all work was remembering the night Constable Cornwall nabbed her eating out of an ash can and nearly had her removed to the Landport station, before she could find her twin Jamie MacGregor, a St. Brendan student.

"Do it," Meridee demanded, in a voice unlike her own.

Betsy nodded, her face grim. She pulled up her skirts and tore around the side of the house. Meridee took a deep breath and held out her hand to John Mark.

Silent now, and intent, the boy ran up the street with her, past the baker's and onto the busier road. She jerked him back when he nearly darted in front of a cart and horse, then ran faster with him, as the driver yelled something highly uncomplimentary.

John led her through a crowd of sailors to the normally quiet inlet off the Gunwharf, where water kegs from the prison hulks were offloaded, and then filled, for their return to those miserable wrecks that rode at anchor. She pressed her hand against her side, wishing she had not laced her corset strings so tight after Ben's last meal.

"Mam, see?"

Breathing heavily, Meridee saw dock workers grouped around two kegs that had been pulled out from the others. Two men were holding down the lid while another nailed it shut. Meridee gasped to hear gargling sounds and gagging from the inside of the keg.

*Merciful Savior*, she thought, still unable to breathe after her pell mell run from her quiet home to the place Able told her never to go by herself.

"You can't do that," she managed to gasp, which only brought laughter.

Dumbfounded, she turned her attention to the other water keg, where two other men held down a man, pushing him lower and lower, as the third worker trained the water hose down on him. The man in the keg raised his hands then clasped them, pleading in silence as he gargled and began to drown before her eyes. When the hose came out, the lid slammed down. He banged against the side of the keg, a sound Meridee knew she would hear in her heart for the rest of her life.

Beside herself, Meridee grabbed at the man with the hose. "What in God's name are you doing?" she demanded. "Stop this cruelty at once."

He shoved his unwashed face close to hers, uncomfortably close. No one ever invaded her privacy like that except her husband, and that was no invasion. Even worse, he snatched at the front of her dress and pulled down. Frantic, she grabbed at his hand as her bodice came away.

John Mark jumped on the man's back and yanked on his hair, screaming at him. One of the other workers threw the boy against the empty kegs. Meridee shrieked and tried to reach for the little fellow. She tore herself from the worker's grasp. She forgot about the spectacle of her breasts exposed to the gathering group of men and tugged at the keg's lid like a wild woman. Her tears mingled with phlegm as she broke her nails trying to get the lid off. Breathing heavily themselves, several men touched her and started edging her away toward a row of kegs shielded from view of the wharf. She felt a hand under her skirt and sobbed out loud.

Oh no, no, she thought as she struggled. "Don't touch me again," she gasped. "My husband will kill you."

They laughed and crowded closer. "If he can find us," Water Hose Man said. "You're prettier than most whores down here."

Her outrage over the treatment of the two prisoners in the kegs – what else could they be but prisoners? – paled as she thought of John Mark's poor mother, hustled aboard a ship under cover of darkness and passed around a frigate for nine horrible months. And there, John lay now, sitting up and staring in disbelief at blood on his hand. Dusk was approaching fast. She knew she had no friends on that wharf except one small, dazed boy.

A primitive part of her brain commanded her to stay on her feet, no matter what. If she fell, they would be on her in a moment, their blood lust already up by what they had done to two men committing the crime of trying to escape from hell on earth. She backed away and put her hand to her pocket, remembering. She felt the bird-shaped scissors from her darning basket.

His hands digging into her waist and wandering to her exposed breasts, Water Hose Man dragged her to him. She grabbed the scissors and scraped them down his face.

With a roar of pain, he slapped her so hard her jaw seemed to explode, and threw her into the water.

# — Chapter Nineteen —

Down she went, down and down into cold, oily water much deeper than the stone inlet at St. Brendan's where Able had taught her the rudiments of floating last year. She floundered and fought her way to the surface, gasping to breathe as her mouth filled with seawater and whatever else floated in such a toxic place.

Panic filled her entire body and brain as her winter wool dress and warmest petticoat dragged her below the surface again. At least her shoes were gone. She had been wearing felt slippers when John Mark ran into the house. She must have lost those on her run.

*Able* ran through her brain. She resolutely forced herself not to even think of Ben as she went under again, struggled to the top and thrashed, trying to breathe. *Able please.*

How could she ever understand what happened next? Who was that little dark man in her mind now? She had seen him somewhere. Was he in a book she had dusted? A fellow customer in Ezekiel Bartleby's bakery? A bust in Able's classroom?

Euclid. Dear lovely Euclid, the Greek mathematician whose propositions her husband so loved to quote, even when he wasn't aware he was doing it. He had told her once that the propositions calmed him. She had told Able to banish Euclid from their bedchamber, and as far as she knew, Euclid spent his nights elsewhere.

But there he was. Euclid smiled gently and told her, "If a straight line set up on a straight line make angles, it will make either two right angles or angles equal to two right angles. That is Proposition Thirteen, dear one."

There was more, but she saw the picture in her mind and remembered what to do, because the proposition calmed her, too, something she never would have imagined in her life. Down she went again, but this time she reached under her skirt and untied her petticoat. It dropped away and she moved to the surface faster. Her dress went next, with her shimmy the only thing between her and nudity. So be it. She shivered as the cold March waters dug in deeper.

In her calmer frame of mind, she heard Able this time, his Scottish brogue more pronounced than usual because he was teasing her as he put his hand against her backbone and flipped her up in the stone inlet last year. *Lean back as though I am tugging you up by your belly button,* she heard from somewhere inside her brain or heart. *And breathe. Fill those marvelous lungs. Lean back! Show me your tits!* Then, *Pretend you're a starfish.*

*Right angle lines, Mrs. Six. Come now. You want to raise your own baby.* It must be Euclid this time. Shivering, swallowing more water, Meridee turned on her back, spread out her legs and arms at right angles like a starfish and floated. Never mind now that everyone on the dock could see her nearly naked splendor. She breathed, shivered, sank a little, panicked, and righted herself, but she floated.

For how long? She shivered as the cold waters did their best to claim her. The sun went down, bathing the dock in weird twilight. Or maybe it was lanterns now. *Able. Euclid. I can't do this much longer, even though I want to with all my soul.*

She closed her eyes, serene in the face of death, wishing for one more glimpse of the man she adored and the baby she cherished. Did women die with those thoughts foremost, thoughts that went beyond self-preservation? Did her body always belong to others, and she only realized it as death came calling?

It was too much. She sank below the dark water, trying to move her frozen legs and arms and starting not to care. Her eyelids were too heavy to open. All she had to do was breathe in water, which was beginning to sound almost irresistible.

Instead, she heard a splash. It annoyed her for a brief second and then jolted her back to life as someone wrapped his hands in her hair and yanked her to the surface.

"Breathe, Meri, by God, Meri, *breathe.*"

She tried, and coughed instead, but never mind. Able lay on his side, put his arm under her breasts and pulled her onto his body. Using a sidestroke, he swam them both to the dock, where more lanterns glowed now. He held her high as someone else grabbed her under her armpits and unceremoniously hauled her up. Just as quickly, her other rescuer wrapped her in a blanket and held her close.

"You'll be all right now, Mrs. Six."

She opened her eyes to see Walter Cornwall, the Landport Gate constable, holding her as tenderly as she held Ben. In the deepest part of her heart and brain, she saw Betsy MacGregor running to Able, then running to Landport and the constable, a man who terrified her like no other. She owed Betsy MacGregor her life, and would owe her until she died in some distant year, and not mere minutes.

Constable Cornwall rocked back and forth with her, then relinquished her to other arms, Able's arms, as her husband climbed onto the dock and pulled her onto his lap. He sobbed into her neck and she cried, too, both of them wailing like babies. She felt another blanket drape over Able's shoulders and envelop her. Cocooned in the darkness of wet wool, she shivered and shook, and breathed.

She heard murmurs around her, something about going for a surgeon, and Able saying, "Send him to my house across from St. Brendan's," and then, "Have you a carriage or a cart, Walter?"

"John Mark," she managed to say. "Oh, please."

"He's right here, my love," Able whispered in her ear. "A little battered, but more upset."

She grabbed Able's sodden shirt. "What those men were doing! My God, Able, stop them!"

"What men?"

Meridee sat up and looked around, pulling the now-soaking blanket closer. All she saw now on the dock were men dressed like the constable, and Royal Marines bearing lanterns. She searched the dock, then pointed to the two kegs.

"They must have been prisoners trying to escape." She sobbed and tried to get to her feet, even though she was nearly bare. Able held her down. "They forced them back into the kegs and drowned them!"

She closed her eyes against the awful screech of crowbar against wood as the nails gave way and the lids popped off. She heard gasps from hard men who probably weren't surprised by much of anything, and covered her face with her hands as if to blot out the sight in her mind. She felt John Mark burrowing close to her, and knew he was seeing what she couldn't.

"Would you be able to identify the workers?" Walter Cornwall asked. "I'll haul them in."

"That would be an exercise in futility," said a Royal Marine with gold epaulets. He said it with some finality, giving Meridee ample proof – as if she needed any – that the fate of Frenchmen in a prison hulk or murdered on a dock was of no concern to Englishmen. "The rascals that work on this dock should probably all be transported themselves." He smiled, and it wasn't a pleasant sight. "But frankly, madam, I do not mind if two more Frenchmen are taken out of the conflict."

"They were held down in those kegs like...like rats and drowned," Meridee said. "It was cruel beyond belief."

"You have said it, Mrs. Six: rats."

The lieutenant looked at his men and shrugged his shoulders, which made Meridee feel more vulnerable than even the fact that she was nearly naked and wrapped in a blanket.

He bowed to her, and she felt Able stiffen at the condescension. "When you know something of war, madam, then we will talk."

"Able, take John Mark and me home," she said.

Walter Cornwall must have found a cart from somewhere. No. She was tired, so tired, and unable to stop shivering. It was Sir B's town carriage.

"How did he know I needed him?" she asked her husband, as he carried her to the vehicle.

"When Betsy raised the alarm, we knew what to do," he said, then buried his face in her neck. "Meri, you came so close. In God's name, what kept you alive?"

She put her fingers in his damp curls, thinking of the times his hair was wet with sweat from making love with her. There would be more days and nights like that, for which she was grateful beyond all reason.

"You did, and Ben, and someone else." She tugged on his hair. "Able, don't laugh. Euclid." He laughed.

# — Chapter Twenty —

To Able's infinite relief, Nathan Laing, one of Haslar's young surgeons, was knocking on his front door when the carriage pulled up to their home. Right behind him was a familiar, smaller figure: Davey Ten, who carried the surgeon's satchel.

Laing hurried down the steps and climbed inside the carriage, not wasting a moment.

"She's so cold, Nathan, and she won't stop shivering," Able said. "Davey, lend John Mark a hand, will you?"

It was then that he noticed Piers, the silent child from the block pulley factory, the one Meri knew she was also feeding with John Mark's greatly expanded lunch pail. He cowered close to John, his eyes huge in his face, silent, but with a silence that spoke of hard times and tribulation the equal of any old eyes in the fleet, maybe even Able's own eyes.

"Master, he showed up at the water kegs, maybe even before I did," John said. "Should I take him back to the factory?"

"Where is he sleeping?" Able asked, diverted momentarily from his wife's needs. "Do you know anything about him?"

John shook his head. "He doesn't talk." He glanced at the smaller boy and put his arm around him. Obviously John had no intention of sending Piers back, if that was even his name. Able had his doubts. "He did show me where he sleeps."

"I'm almost afraid to ask."

"It's a pile of old rags under a staircase that no one uses," John said. His sigh said more than words could, except words that Able understood completely. "Master, we were better off in the workhouse."

"Then he's not going back to the factory until he goes with you after morning classes tomorrow," Able said decisively. "We can add a cot to the room you share with Nick."

John nodded. "I don't know how to tell him that, but I think he'll follow me inside."

"You *are* a leader, John."

"Am I?" John asked, gratified.

"Most certainly. Get along inside now, and hold the door open for me."

"Able?"

With all the love and worry in his heart probably showing on his face, Able looked down at the dear woman he held, and he saw her fear.

"I hurt everywhere."

The surgeon crouched there in the carriage. "We'll get you to bed and warm you up. You won't hurt so much," he assured her, then spoke to Able in a low voice. "She must be rubbed down until she protests."

At his words, Meri nodded, closed her eyes and forgot to breathe. Laing gave her a shake and then another, more urgent one. "Mrs. Six! Breathe handsomely now." He climbed out of the carriage and gestured to Davey. "The ammonia," he ordered.

Davey found the brown bottle. Not waiting for instructions, the boy opened it and held it under Meri's nose. She opened her eyes in surprise and started breathing again.

"Inside. Now," the surgeon ordered. "Fast as you can, Master Six."

Able darted from the carriage, running past John Mark, who held the door open, shouldering aside Mrs. Perry and taking the stairs two at a time. Meri was no burden.

"Towels!" the surgeon shouted to Mrs. Perry over his shoulder, then, "Heat some dry rice in bags, if you have it. If not, find something else." He looked around. "These boys are underfoot."

His heart grateful, Able saw Betsy come forward and pull John Mark into her arms. Without hesitating, she reached out to the little ghost from the factory who crowded close to the Gunwharf Rat.

Free to concentrate on Meri, Able sat her down on their bed. Her eyes opened when she heard Ben crying. "He needs me."

"Not now, Mrs. Six," the surgeon said, which only made Meri narrow her eyes and fix him with a slow-burning stare. "Well, well, you must come first," he added lamely.

"You're not a father, are you, Surgeon?" Able asked as he yanked off Meri's sodden chemise. "Ben's going to be the carrot on this stick. Hand me a towel and stand back."

He had seen this trauma before, a cold body slowly turning to ice because the innards weren't warm enough to resist. He and the surgeon dragged Meri to her feet and held her upright. He started to rub Meri's front vigorously, even as she protested and cried for Ben.

"You'll get him once you're warm, Meridee Bonfort Six," he told her in his sternest voice. "And you will breathe deeper, damn it." She gave him such a hurt look at all three names, and the tears welled in her eyes. "I mean it. *Breathe!*" He didn't want to use his master-in-a-typhoon voice, but he wasn't sure how much she could hear.

The surgeon took the other towel and began rubbing Meri's back.

"You're hurting me!" she shrieked. "Both of you!"

"I don't care!" Able yelled back. "I've seen cold men die, Meridee Six, and you're not going to do that while I'm standing this watch!"

"What watch?" she blubbered, even as she tried to breathe deep.

"The marriage watch, you silly twat," he growled at her, which only made her more angry. Perfect. She was breathing deep out of her mouth now, ready to hurl any number of invectives in his direction, if her tired, oxygen-starved brain could think of any. He rubbed harder, trying to convince her blood to circulate.

He caught the surgeon's eye. "Anything else we should do?" he said quietly.

"Not yet," Laing said. "Do you see the finger marks on her waist? They were ready to use her sorely."

"There are times when I hate Portsmouth. Good girl, Meri. Keep breathing."

He hated to make her cry and rage and plead for her son, but her brain was clearing and she could form coherent sentences now. Hopefully when she felt more like herself, she would forget some of the names she called him. He doubted she would forgive "twat."

Held upright between two men as they bullied and pummeled her cold body, she opened her eyes finally. She took low and slow breaths, her chest rising and falling regularly now, even though she continued to shiver. The surgeon stopped toweling her and rested his ear against her naked back, listening.

"Better. Better," he said. "She's still too cold. Master Six, take off your clothes and get in bed."

Able didn't hesitate. He stripped and climbed in bed, holding out his arms for Meri. The surgeon helped her to bed and maneuvered her against him until they were back to front. Able held his wife close, his arms and legs around her, his hands pressed against her middle.

"Here you are."

Mrs. Perry held out towel-wrapped bags of rice, heated on the Rumford. The surgeon pressed them against Meri's stomach and nether parts. He spread the last one against her feet, and pulled bed covers over the two of them.

"I want my baby," Meri whispered. "Oh, please. I've been ever so good."

Able couldn't help his tears. "You have, my love. Mrs. Perry, get that squalling baby in here. We'll find a way."

Foggy, dull, shivering, she reached for her son when Mrs. Perry brought him to her. Able helped her tuck Ben against her arm and guided her nipple toward his mouth. Famished, Ben latched on and Meri closed her eyes, her relief nearly palpable.

The surgeon sat next to her on the bed, eyes alert, breathing along with her, which touched Able's heart. He wondered if the doctor was even aware. Surgeon Laing rested the back of his fingers against the pulse in her neck, held still a moment, then nodded. "Not so thready," he said. "I'll be much happier when she stops shivering."

"That's my job," Able said.

Laing nodded. "Mine, too. I'm going to sit here as long as I feel like it, with no argument from you." "No, sir," Able said. He looked up at Mrs. Perry, who loomed over them all, her expression unreadable, which worried him. In all the many years he had known his late carpenter's wife, he had felt healthy fear at her expressions. Her face registered nothing now. Able reached across Meridee and held out his hand to Mrs. Perry.

She grasped it and sat down on the bed, too, tears on her cheeks. "John Mark told me what happened."

"How is he?" Meri asked, which startled Able. She sounded nearly normal, except her voice shook from the trembles.

"Sad mostly, mum, and fearful. Blaming himself because he ran for your help, and terrible things happened to you," their housekeeper said.

"Bring him in here," Meri said.

"No, Meri. You need to rest and..."

"Durable Six, don't you deny me my Gunwharf Rat," she said in no uncertain terms. "Mrs. Perry, bring him in here. He has to know I am alive and determined to stay that way."

If he weren't practically stuck to his shivering wife, Able would have gone to his knees in gratitude. This was the practical, kind and devoted woman coming back to him from the edge of the grave. Even in the passion and fever of their wildest coupling, he had never felt so much bone of her bone and flesh of her flesh. *I am the world's luckiest bastard,* he thought.

"Absolutely," he said. "Bring in John Mark."

"I'd better move out of the way," Surgeon Laing said when John Mark, his eyes so anxious, stood in the doorway as if fearful to come closer. "It's fine, lad. You sit here where I am. I'll find a spot by the fireplace."

John came closer. Meridee patted the space the surgeon had vacated. She rested her hand on his arm. "I think the surgeon should look at your head, my dear," she said. "That man gave you quite a blow, didn't he?"

"Mam..."

Even though the room was bathed in shadow, Able saw the pain in the little boy's eyes. He was afraid to come closer, certain it was his fault that the dearest, kindest woman in the world lay so still now.

"John, in no way are you responsible for any of this," Able said. "Sit there by Mam. She needs to know you are all right."

Never one to disobey authority, John did as he was told, which gave Meri opportunity to put her hand on his neck and draw him into her wonderful orbit. When she did, he leaned against her hip and sobbed. Meri brushed his hair from his face, even though he was tidy. She touched his face over and over and crooned to him until his tears stopped. Able smiled, thinking of the many times his wife had caressed his face until his wildly active mind was calm.

When she spoke, her voice was firm. "Now, John, you did the right thing to run for me. We tried to keep a monstrous wrong from happening and we failed. But we tried, and I am not really the worse for wear. Turn your head a little toward the light. Surgeon?"

Surgeon Laing may not be a father yet, but his education had grown exponentially that evening, Able reasoned. He came to Meri's side and peered down at the boy, clucking his tongue. "You were right fierce in your defense of Mrs. Six," he said. "This cut might need a suture or two. Come to the kitchen with me, and we'll consider the matter in better light." He put his hand against Meri's neck again. "Much, much better, Mrs. Six! I foresee a complete recovery. You have quite a champion in this lad."

"I am ever grateful," she said, fully alert. "John, if you hadn't jumped on that man's back, I never would have had time to get out my scissors, and where would we be?"

Oh, perfect. John Mark, the quiet, tan-skinned boy who knew something of turmoil, kissed Meri's cheek. "I wish we could have done better, Mam."

"So do I, but we tried. That counts for a great deal. Go tend to your wound. Dear me, will this leave a scar, Surgeon?"

"I believe it will. You're not even in the fleet yet, John, and already with a battle wound." The surgeon clapped his hand on John's shoulder. "Lad, you'll be the envy of St. Brendan's."

He motioned Able follow him into the hall. He sent John ahead. "Keep a good eye on her all night, which will probably mean staying awake, because she could stop breathing. I'll sleep in the sitting room. Sing out if you need me."

"Aye, aye. Masterful job there, Surgeon Laing," Able said. "Why do I think he's going to get a stitch or two, whether he needs one or not?"

"A surgeon can't be too careful," Laing countered. "He can brag about it, and no harm is done." He chuckled. "I believe I promised Hippocrates I would do no harm."

"You, sir, will go far in the fleet."

Laing turned serious. "Watch her carefully." He laughed out loud then. "And for the Lord's sake, Master Six, put on some clothes!"

# — Chapter Twenty-one —

A ble watched his wife all night. He burped Ben and put him to sleep in the cradle Mrs. Perry brought up from the cellar, now that his son had graduated to a larger crib in the next room.

"She needs to know he's near as her fingertips," he explained to Mrs. Perry, after he pulled on a nightshirt and made a quick trip downstairs after son and wife slept. "Well, Mister Mark, it appears that you needed a ship's surgeon."

John touched the impressive bandage that probably went above and beyond the call of duty, if Surgeon Lang's smile was any indication.

"It's a true battle scar," Laing said. "He didn't even flinch when I sutured him."

Able looked around the warm kitchen, where Nick and Davey chatted by the fireplace, catching up on matters, now that the older Davey was apprenticed to Haslar's apothecary, but still considered himself a Gunwharf Rat. The little ghost from the block pulley factory had seated himself in front of a steaming bowl of fish stew, but his eyes were on a mound of petit fours left, so Mrs. Perry told them, by their baker down the street. In that navy way no one understood but everyone accepted, Ezekiel Bartleby had gotten wind of the trouble on the docks. Able helped himself to a petit fours.

"Sit yourself down, Nathan Laing, and have some cod stew. No one makes it better than Mrs. Perry."

"You'll get no argument from me." The surgeon sat down and motioned to an empty chair. "Join me?"

"I'll take a tote upstairs," Able said, unwilling to be gone long. "Mrs. Perry, will you and Betsy please set up that extra cot in the lads' room? We'll put our silent visitor in there. Also, are there any clothes that would fit him? It seems to me that Stephen Hoyt had outgrown some that he left behind."

"Consider it done, sir," Mrs. Perry said as she filled a mug with soup and stuck in some bread to soak.

He was heading for the stairs, when he heard a knock. Balancing the food in one hand, he opened the door on Constable Cornwall.

"Just checking," the constable said. "A nightshirt, sir?"

"It's my home," Able replied, with as much dignity as he could manage.

In a few sentences, Able brought him up to date, thanking him again for his prompt help with Mrs. Six. He told the constable to go into the kitchen for bread and stew and maybe petit fours, if they hadn't been entirely devoured.

"I am full of petit fours," the constable said, and followed that statement with a surprising smile, surprising because Able couldn't think of a time Walter Cornwall had ever smiled. It threw the years off him by the handful. "Who should stop me on my way here but Ezekiel Barnaby? He claims we are all heroes." The smile left his face. "I only wish we were."

"You were right where we needed you," Able said simply.

"The credit goes to Betsy MacGregor," he said, but there was no overlooking his blush at praise. Able thought perhaps constables didn't get as much commendation as they deserved. "Poor girl. She's still afraid of me, but that didn't stop her at Landport."

"You absolutely terrified her, at first meeting by the ash cans," Able said.

"I know, and it's bothered me this year and more," Walter said. "It took a lot of courage for her to run to Landport and ask for me, but Mrs. Six told her to."

"Courage seems to be our coin of the realm, eh, constable?" Able said, wanting to put him at his ease, and wishing Meri were there, because she was better at that.

"I suppose it is," he said. His expression lightened when he heard Mrs. Perry and the maid leave the kitchen, carrying a cot between then. "I'll help with that, Mrs. Perry, if you'll let me."

Able watched the constable took the cot from both women and shoulder it. Mrs. Perry led the way, but Walter hung back for a moment. Able felt as though he were eavesdropping on a personal moment, but where was he to go, standing there holding a mug and bread?

"Miss MacGregor, thank you for what you did," Walter said. "I...I know I frighten you. I wish I didn't."

His words were simple, forthright and honest, much like the man himself. Able tried not to watch, but he wanted to know how she would react. He could put it down to research. Moments like this were to be studied.

He knew Betsy to be just as forthright and honest, much like her twin, serving the fleet in the Mediterranean. She did not disappoint.

"Maybe it is time I stopped fearing you," Betsy said. "You were only doing your duty that night." She looked away and smiled, something she did occasionally that Able found charming. "Truth to tell, I *was* digging in an ash can for food, and I *had* run away from a workhouse." Again, that endearing look-away half smile. "And what's more, you know it, Constable Cornwall, think on."

Walter made a small gesture with his hand. "I've been there, too, miss. Over and done?"

"Aye, sir."

"It's Walter," he said. He hurried after Mrs. Perry with the cot perched on his shoulder as though it weighed nothing.

Betsy looked down at the sheets and pillow in her hands, smiling at them in that way Meri sometimes did when she had secrets. *Well, well,* Able thought.

Then it was upstairs himself, ready to spend the night standing his own watch over his wife. He lay down beside her, relieved that her shivering had nearly stopped. She woke up in tears twice before morning, but he was awake and ready, standing a personal watch that went far deeper than any watch on any quarterdeck on any ship on any ocean.

Surgeon Laing came upstairs twice in the night to assess his patient, listen to her lungs and rest his hand gently on her abdomen, feeling for those deep shivers that had wracked her body. The second time he had smiled, and told Able he was going home to his own bed. "You have the matter well in hand, Master Six," he whispered, as he darkened his slatted lamp and left their bedchamber. God bless the Royal Navy's surgeons.

By morning, Able had questions, but not questions for Meri, who had come upon the whole wretched scene after John Mark had run home to enlist her aid. He knew the lad was observant. He also knew the whole experience had jolted him and he might not want to remember. All Able could do was ask John Mark just what had alerted him to the water kegs in the first place.

First, he changed Ben's sodden diaper and talked to his son, which woke up Meri. She sat up and stretched, which made her wince a little. Still naked, she looked down at her breasts and shook her head. "That dreadful man grabbed my dress by the collar and jerked down my bodice," she said, and Able heard all the rage. "Look, he scratched me."

She pulled back the covers next, looked between her legs and started to cry. "Someone else put his hands on me down there. I have bruises."

Able set Ben down at the foot of their bed and took his wife in his arms. "It's nothing that won't fade and disappear," he murmured.

She burrowed close. "Will I stop *thinking* about it?"

"In time," he said. "In time. You're safe and you're mine, and you're not going near the docks again for anything."

"No, I am not, except..." She held her arms up as he lowered her nightgown on her. "What if one of our Gunwharf Rats needs me and you are not around? John is only eleven, after all."

"I have some ideas on the matter. Perhaps he could use a bodyguard."

"Thanks, love." She took Ben from him and unbuttoned her nightgown. "And where will you find such a commodity?"

"St. Brendan's has its share of workhouse toughs, Meri." He kissed her cheek. "I'll send Mrs. Perry up with breakfast for you, after which you will remain a lady of leisure today and stay in bed. That was Surgeon Laing's last stipulation before he raised anchor at three seventeen this morning and went home."

"I'll be bored," she said, in that mutinous tone of voice that reassured him as nothing else could that his Meri was going to be fine, and soon.

"That I doubt. You will be resting. Behave yourself, wife."

He looked in the room that John Mark, Nick and now little Piers shared, but it was empty. He found everyone at a breakfast that Mrs. Perry must have confused with a holiday. When he asked what the occasion was for veritable mounds of food, she glared at him.

"I felt like it, Master Six," she declared, reminding him that Mrs. Six may have been called Mam, but Mrs. Perry claimed the menus.

Nick and John had finished, but Piers continued to eat steadily, packing away eggs and cakes and sausage. Able joined him, reminded of ragged children at the docks of any port in any country, on the prowl for food. "Piers?" he asked.

Nothing. "That's not your name, is it?" Able asked. "I think you don't speak English."

As he ate, he observed the child, still dressed in yesterday's rags, his yellow-orange smock grimy and smelling like something worn too long. There was faint writing on the back of the shirt. Able leaned back, wondering why he hadn't noticed that sooner. He saw what looked vaguely like a T and an O, and understood. Better not say anything yet, though.

"John, let's you and me walk toward Building Twelve."

"But I don't go until after morning classes," he said. He tried to keep his voice steady, but Able heard the fear.

"Lad, it's Saturday. Just a little stroll. I know it must frighten you, but I'll be with you." John nodded. "I don't think Piers will stay here if I am not here, too."

"That's fine. I have an idea. We'll stop first at St. Brendan's and see if we can convince Smitty to join us."

John gasped. "*Smitty?* He's ferocious."

"I know. Think what an excellent bodyguard he will make. I believe I can convince Headmaster Croker to let him join our little excursion this morning. Let's go find out."

While both boys waited on the stone bench that probably had seen its fair share of recalcitrant monks and worried lads through a few centuries, Able told Thaddeus everything that had happened yesterday. He saw all the dismay on the headmaster's face, and the anger at foul treatment that went far beyond any punishment of French prisoners.

"There's something havey-cavey about all of this," Able concluded. "I can't figure out what it is yet, but I have my suspicions. First, though, I mean to employ Smitty as a bodyguard to escort John Mark to and from the block pulley factory every afternoon."

"Smitty? I pity anyone who tries to interfere with him," Thaddeus said promptly. "I can pay him well, but he's a thug and a blackguard and..."

"...and he excels in seamanship," Able added smoothly. "You should see him when he takes the helm of the *Jolly Roger*." Oh, he could do this. "I need a thug."

He thought of that gray morning in early autumn when the rough-looking boy who claimed to be only twelve was found curled up at St. Brendan's front door. "I want to be a sailor," he had announced to Able and Headmaster Croker. "My name's Smitty and that's all I'm going to say."

So it was. Even Headmaster Croker knew this enigmatic lad was not a baited bear to poke.

Smitty had no objection to this early-morning duty, even though it was Saturday and the Gunwharf Rats had permission to sleep until eight of the clock.

"After noon mess, and after class at four, you will escort John Mark to and from Building Twelve near Gunwharf," Able said as the four of them walked past the bakery and slowed down. "A shilling a week."

Smitty nodded. He wasn't much for conversation.

John Mark must have had a sixth sense about Ezekiel Bartleby, who spotted them and joined them on the street. He looked over his shoulder at his shop. "Can't let my ball and chain see this, but here you are. A man has to keep up his strength."

The factory ghost's eyes widened when the baker pressed a macaron in his hand. Even Smitty was suitably impressed with the macaron.

Able reassured Ezekiel Bartleby that Mrs. Six was going to be fine, but she had been frightened.

"Master, if I ever see your wife running down the street like a crazy person, I will stop her," he told Able, after doling out the rest of the macarons.

"You can try," Able said. "We'll pass by here again in a while. If you had some petit fours, Mrs. Six would probably consume them all. I'll pay, of course."

"You can try," the baker said in turn, and went back into his shop.

The wharf where the water hoys docked was deserted. The barrels had been stacked neatly, everything in order, waiting for the requisition to fill them and sail out to the prison hulks in the harbor.

Able sat down on the bench by the kegs. He knew John Mark didn't want to stop there at all, but he patted the spot beside him. Even little whoever-he-was looked around, uneasy. Only Smitty seemed unconcerned, but he hadn't been there yesterday.

Able couldn't help himself. He looked into the water, remembering every terrifying moment of leaping in, groping in the darkening water as the light faded, desperate to find his wife. It might have been seconds ago that he flailed about and grabbed handfuls of her hair. He wondered that she hadn't complained about a sore scalp this morning.

*Stop it*, he told his brain. He turned to John and put his arm around the boy, who melted into his side as though he belonged there. Perhaps he did.

"What do you remember about yesterday right here?"

"I don't want to remember," John whispered.

"I know, but you must. We have to understand what happened," Able said, feeling like a perfect churl to ask. "Please try. Why did you even stop here? It's not directly on your path."

Silence for a long moment. He knew John Mark was thinking, because he knew St. Brendan boys obeyed orders.

"They were laughing," he said finally. "I wondered what was so funny."

"What were they laughing at?"

The lad started to cry. Able held him closer, then gave him his handkerchief.

John blew his nose. He took a deep breath. "They were teasing a man in a yellow shirt who tried to climb out of the keg." He stared in the direction of the harbor, barely visible through the tall masts of other ships docked close in. "He was from the hulks, wasn't he?"

"Aye. He…they… must have been trying to escape."

"The dock men… held him down and took out another prisoner from the second keg." He turned his face into Able's shirt. "Then they started to fill the keg and I ran for Mam."

Able held him tight. The rain began, softly at first, then a harder cold rain, reminding Portsmouth that March wasn't through yet. "Do you remember anything else, some small detail that might not even seem important to you?"

Again, the silence. John was a deliberate boy, a thoughtful one. He blew his nose, then wiped his eyes with a clean corner. He sat up suddenly and Able held his breath.

"Do you know what was odd?"

"Tell me."

"Out of all those kegs, the man with the water hose knew right where to go to find the other man and pull him out. He didn't hesitate."

*So that's how it was,* Able thought. He turned his attention to Smitty, because he knew, unlike Headmaster Croker, just how shrewd a workhouse boy could be. "What does that tell you, Smitty?" he asked.

"There must be a mark of some sort on the keg," he said.

"Two kegs, and they were nailed down last night by dockworkers, and then pried open by the Royal Marines. Find them."

Smitty wasted not a moment, walking to the tall kegs, running his hands along each rim. A wooden lid leaned against each keg. Halfway down the row he stopped and angled out one keg, and then another. "These."

Able came closer. He set the lids with their nails still in place on one keg and then the other. The other kegs had only a few nail holes. These two had many, irregularly placed, enough to keep a desperate man inside from forcing them open. "Help me move these out farther," he ordered.

Smitty slid one out while John Mark steadied it. Able walked around the keg and stopped. "John, did you bring along your little sketch pad?" he asked.

"Always, master."

"Copy that, please. And the one on the other keg."

The boy bent to the task, then held up his tablet. "It's a C and a P," he said.

Master, mechanist in training, and formidable thug, they looked at each other. Smitty spoke first. "The water hose man knew which kegs held the men inside, didn't he, Master Six?"

For all his toughness, Smitty sounded suddenly as young as he really was. He even moved a little closer to Able.

"I believe you have it. That's what I wanted to know. Thank you, gentlemen. Smitty, you and John can start back to St. Brendan's."

"Aye, aye, sir."

Able collared the little factory ghost when he started to follow. He knelt down to be on eye level with the plainly terrified boy. *"Parlez-vous français?"*

The lad couldn't look at him. Able gently put his fingers under the child's chin and raised his head. *"Bien? Comprenez-vous?"*

The waif nodded, his voice barely audible. *"Oui, de parle français."* He sobbed, then quickly put his hand to his mouth. *"Vas-tu me tuer?"*

*Break my heart, child,* Able thought in utter anguish. "No, I am not going to kill you," he said softly in French. "Let's go home."

He knew the child could run away if he let go of him, but he let go anyway. To his supreme gratitude, the boy didn't run. He took a few steps and Able saw the T and O more clearly on his shirt, mostly faded out, unless viewed at the right angle. Transport Office. All prisoners wore such shirts, courtesy of the British government, even little prisoners, apparently. They walked behind Smitty and John, and as they walked, the French prisoner of war put his hand in Able's.

"I wish I knew what is going on," Able said in English. He watched the harbor. Seven prison hulks. "I wish I knew. Any advice, Euclid? No?"

# — Chapter Twenty-two —

## PRISON HULK HMS CAPTIVITY

Seriously, how could a man numbered One Dash Eighty-Seven make himself small on a prison hulk? Jean realized that his survival depended on Ianthe Faulke saying nothing about his presence in the steward's pantry. He also realized that he trusted her not a whit.

*Calm, calm,* he told himself twenty times that day, and the next. Maybe the men in the kegs were able to slip away from the dock, because the hoy had come in late and the dock was shrouded in shadow. Or perhaps the man who knew where they were – the other end of the conspiracy – had an argument with his wife and remained behind to patch up the quarrel. Quite possibly this conspirator had taken ill and lay at death's door. By evening Jean allowed himself to breathe. He was a generally optimistic man.

Two days later, when Jean began to breathe easier, his optimism vanished. They had assembled on their deck for the tedious roll call before breakfast of watery oats. He answered when his turn came, already bracing himself against the slime of oats sliding down a throat that in good times savored buttery brioche, poached pears, café au lait, and perhaps two eggs.

He hadn't slept well last night, not that he ever did, but some nights were better than others. He imagined the distress of drowning in a keg of water and finally just lay there swinging in his hammock, hopeful that Ianthe Faulke had said nothing.

The buzz started quietly, and seemed to pass from row to row: "Did you hear?" "Can it be?" "Drowned in the keg?" "You heard this from the damned Englishmen swinging aboard the fresh kegs this morning?"

Jean held his breath. Perhaps it was some other prison hulk, and not the *Captivity*. Alas, no. Why was there always someone who seemed to know a little more than the others? Hiding behind a taller man in the line in front of him, Jean watched Claude Pascal move from row to row, whisper a little and move on. Jean knew he was watching the origin of the dreadful story, and it sickened him.

By the time roll call ended, the story had fleshed itself into a narrative of two men held down in the kegs and nearly drowned, then nailed into the water-filled kegs. Oddly, there was another story of a woman rushing up with a small boy in some sort of uniform. A brawl followed, with the woman knocked into the water.

And then this from the man in the next row, who made no effort to hide his horror: "Someone claims there was a little boy dressed in a yellow shirt like ours who ran up with the uniformed lad."

"Pierre Deschamps," another prisoner whispered. "Little Pierre? The child who fled in the first water keg? What about the gunner Remillard who escaped in the other keg with him?"

Several of the prisoners clustered around Claude Pascal, since he was their self-proclaimed leader and the man who did his best to smooth over their wretchedness.

Upon later reflection, Jean knew this was the moment when he should have denounced Claude Pascal. He could have stood on a table and declared in ringing tones that this man they thought as their sympathetic friend had begun his vile career of picking them off one by one for money. Pascal was going to dictate how and when they arranged escapes, which would always be fouled - or at least enough of them to keep suspicion away from Claude's sorry carcass – so Captain Faulke could get the credit, and Claude the money.

He said nothing. *Wise of you*, the cowardly side of his brain told him. *It's every prisoner for himself.* Jean knew he had a better side to his character, so he waited for that side to chide the cowardly side. Nothing.

He slumped against the bulkhead, aghast at himself, acutely aware as never before that he was no better than the coward Rene Caillou, who drew himself into a ball and shuddered and shook through each day, screaming when anyone approached him. No better than the *rafalés*, who darted around naked, insane and disgusting.

"*Mes amis*, hear me," Claude Pascal was saying. "We had better lay low for a few more weeks."

A subdued lot now, the other prisoners looked at each other and nodded.

"We'll never give up, because we are Frenchman and devoted to the cause of liberty, equality and fraternity," that scum Pascal said. "We must simply be more cautious."

Every inch the righteous leader, Pascal looked around. Jean shrank back against the bulkhead. To his horror, the leader and traitor without parallel stared at Jean Hubert. He continued his surveillance finally, as if taking his own roll call of their bravery or their cowardice. "Listen, all of you: there may be traitors in our midst. We must be very careful. If you hear of any escape plots, let me know."

*No, no, tell anyone but Claude Pascal*, Jean wanted to scream. He remained silent, moving closer to a pile of oily rags, trying to conceal himself, uncertain and afraid. "I am next," he whispered softly.

He stayed where he was, as his fellow prisoners talked among themselves, looking over their shoulders as if wondering who they could trust. "Thank God for Claude Pascal," Jean heard. "He will get to the bottom of this." "He will keep us safe."

Under the oily rags now, Jean forced himself to think rationally. He had no idea if Ianthe Faulke had told her father he had been in the steward's cubby when the two scoundrels plotted ruin for the men in the water kegs. Possibly she had said nothing. He shifted uneasily, not able to convince his mind that Ianthe could be trusted even slightly.

*I have to leave somehow*, he thought, and could have cried with the futility of such a statement in such a place. The only people who got off the hulks easily were the dead.

Strength in numbers, or hiding in solitude? As foul as breakfast was, his stomach overruled solitude and he joined his fellow prisoners in the line. The food went down easier than he would have predicted, until he realized that slimy oats were the least of his problem.

Instead of snatching the opportunity to paint in the few moments of sunlight allowed in through the iron grating of the porthole by his hammock, Jean stayed in the shadows, watching for Pascal. Perhaps he was already in Captain Faulke's quarters, finding out that Jean Hubert – prisoner, painter, and eavesdropper – had overheard their earlier conversation. Perhaps they were waiting for him to knock on the door to Faulke's quarters, sketchbook and paints in hand, to begin this morning's lesson? It was time, after all.

What could he do? His mind a jumble, Jean took the usual precaution of taking his modest leather pouch of money from under his pillow and putting it around his neck. His hands shook as he picked up the leather satchel containing his painting supplies. One deep breath and another took him to the guard at the top of the narrow companionway leading to the deck.

The guard barely gave him a glance as he motioned Jean toward the little alcove where he had been given permission to store those clean clothes that Madame Faulke had insisted upon. Nerves practically humming, he changed clothes and climbed the last flight to the deck.

He took his usual deep breath. The air was still foul, but so much better than the air belowdecks. He stood for a moment gazing on a gray day, one of many endured in England. He noticed the usual guards, none of them interested in him because they were used to seeing him on deck. Two played cards; a third scratched himself and stared out to sea, probably wondering why fate had sentenced him to service on a prison hulk.

Not a religious man, Jean nevertheless crossed himself to see the pile of dead bodies underneath a tarpaulin, ready to go ashore for burial in a mass grave somewhere. They were the lucky ones, liberated from prison and surely in a better world, if one believed in God, which he didn't. Still, he had crossed himself.

In the afternoon, a vessel would come alongside the *Captivity*. Practiced by now in harvesting the dead, seamen would snare hooks in the tarp grommets and swing the bodies all at once onto the cutter's deck. They would go down the line of hulks, adding corpses to end up in a mass grave somewhere. All over France, wives, daughters and mothers would spend the rest of their lives wondering what had happened to their men. *C'est la guerre.*

What happened next would never have happened if Jean Hubert had given the matter careful consideration. He was not a man to rush into anything, but this was a bold idea requiring instant action and little thought.

He took another look around and strolled toward the corpses under the tarp. He quickly lowered his satchel over the railing, sank down and crawled under the tarp.

Some bodies were still loose, some in rigor, but all were cold to his inadvertent touch. The unmistakable, unforgettable odor of decay filled his nostrils and lodged in his brain. Resisting the simultaneous urge to vomit, and shriek and evacuate his bowels, Jean sidled underneath the closest corpse, a skeleton of a fellow who perhaps even last year said *adieu* to his family as he sailed to glory and plunder.

To his horror, the body seemed to move. Jean peered closer into the gloom of the tarp. No, the man did not live, but he was covered with lice that moved about, because this was their haven, too. He felt the little beasts crawl in his hair and ears, and wondered why he had done this impulsive thing.

He listened, alert for any sign that someone had seen him and heard nothing. What he did hear disturbed him in the extreme. Some of the bodies were giving off gas, especially the corpse under him. Even Jean's slightest move seemed to press on some organ or other that hadn't quite finished dying.

Alive one day, dead the next. *C'est la mort.* Jean closed his eyes, decided he wasn't an atheist after all, and commended himself to God.

# — Chapter Twenty-three —

M eridee hadn't exactly pushed him from the house, but she had assured Able in forceful tones that she was fine now, and he *had* promised the Gunwharf Rats an afternoon's sailing to the Isle of Wight in the *Jolly Roger*.

"It's Saturday and you sail," she reminded him.

She had sweetened the pot considerably with a kiss, and the promise that yes, tonight would be no exception to their midnight swimming lesson in the stone inlet.

What a darling she was. The second night after her near drowning, Meri had informed him after their lodgers were in bed and Ben asleep that he was to accompany her to that stone basin and continue the swimming lessons abandoned last year when she was carrying their baby.

She had sobbed into his shoulder when he led her into the basin, and not from the cold. She hung onto him like grim death until her great well of courage filled to the top and she let go, leaning back and pushing her stomach up and legs out until she floated. He could not have been prouder of her. She did require a wheedling talk to turn onto her stomach and float, but it was a short talk. She hung onto the rope they had stretched around the edge of the basin and kicked her feet. Her triumphant grin told him everything he already knew about his wife.

Tonight after he returned with his crew from their weekly seamanship sail, he would see if she could coordinate her arms and legs and actually swim. All signs indicated such an outcome. He was a good teacher, and she was a determined pupil.

Other Rats were already waiting at the wharf when he, Nick and John showed up that morning at the berth where resided Sir B's yacht *Jolly Roger*. Everyone knew what to do, so they were soon in the harbor, heading toward the Isle of Wight with a spanking wind and following seas.

He watched his boys, mindful that John wasn't much of a sailor and prone to mal de mer. He had included Smitty as a reward for escorting John and Pierre to the block factory all week, and because he knew the lad was fearless. In fact, Able plucked one idea from the constantly generating pot that was his brain and approached the boy as they sailed.

"Mister Smitty, I need your help," he said, speaking loud because of the wind.

"Aye, sir." Smitty did not take his eyes from current duty, which was conning the helm. He pointed. "Beg pardon, sir, but what sort of flag is that?"

Able looked where he pointed. "That's the death flag," he said. "That cutter you're looking at is a death boat. The hulks collect the dead for the week and take them ashore to a mass grave."

"Beg pardon, sir, but don't they feed the prisoners?"

"They don't feed them enough." Might as well tell all. "And if you're ever captured, they won't feed *you* much either. At least, that was my experience."

Boy regarded master. Able knew Smitty understood. He also knew that Smitty wasn't as deferential as some of his students, making Able wonder if the boy had ever seen the inside of a workhouse. "But we're pretty good at doing without, aren't we, Master Six?" he said.

"None better. I have an assignment I'd like you to consider. I've observed your skills and you impress me."

"Thank you, master," Smitty replied, his face lighting up with his kind words. Able also knew how many compliments ever came to a poor child, workhouse bastard or not.

"Trinity House, and by extension, the Admiralty, has advised me to use the Gunwharf Rats to form a harbor surveillance crew," Able said. "More of a midnight watch."

"Beg pardon, master, but don't the Royal Marines already do that?"

"They do, and so do the Landport Gate constables occasionally. I'll admit to you that I did wonder about effective use of St. Brendan's lads in such a venture, but lately, I own to some uneasiness about the hulks."

Another thought pounded in. "Now that I consider it, we at St. Brendan's have perhaps the best viewpoint of the hulks." Able warmed to the idea. "Think of it strategically. We're on a quiet, seldom-traveled street and there is just enough bend in the lay of the land to make us obscure."

Able considered little Pierre, who had somehow showed up out of nowhere. "Think of the valuable work the block pulley factory will do when it is running. A mischief-maker could slow down the entire Royal Navy by destroying it. Or the ropeworks. And think how easy the naval stores could be set ablaze: one match to turpentine or pitch and *bam*! We're vulnerable on the docks."

"You would like us to watch the hulks exclusively, sir?"

"I would, for I do not believe anyone else is doing that. Maybe two Rats for First Watch, to be relieved by another two Rats for the Middle Watch, and two more for the Morning Watch. Six Rats each night. What do you think?"

Smitty's expression changed from doubt to interest. Able saw the pride that someone like Master Six wanted his opinion, and next, the duty and how to organize it. Perfect. The Royal Navy needed all the Smittys St. Brendan's could train.

"Organize it quietly. Let me know in a day or two what you have arranged."

"Aye, sir," Smitty said. "I can do this."

"I know you can. It's for the good of the fleet, and perhaps the entire Royal Navy." Was that going too far? Able wondered. No, it wasn't, he decided. True, these were lads of nine years to thirteen or so. He could sweeten the pot. "I do know this: the crews standing the watch will, in all likelihood, have sandwiches. The grog will be well watered down, or I will get in such trouble with Mrs. Six."

Smitty laughed out loud, then looked around, as if wondering who had laughed.

"You can laugh," Able said quietly, then couldn't resist. "Seriously, Mrs. Six may not appear so, but she is a tough'un."

Smitty smiled broadly at that. "You'll have your watch, Master Six."

The winds were fair and the sun actually shone, after the gloom of a long winter. In moments like this, Able found himself wishing that the deck underneath his feet was far out to sea, with nothing in sight except albatross and whales. At least the wind blew from land, which meant the stink of the hulks was headed away from them, as they skimmed across the water on Sir B's wonderful yacht.

Then he thought of his students who needed him right here at St. Brendan's, and his wife and son, who needed him even more. Or maybe *he* needed them more. He had not a doubt in his mind that Meri could manage a household quite well for a sailing master gone more than he was home, except that he didn't want to sleep in any bed that didn't have Meri in it, not even for a plum assignment at sea. And yet...and yet. The sea called to him faintly like the voices in his brain, Euclid's chief among them, but Newton's and Galileo's and now and then jolly Van Leuvenhoek's. William Harvey was usually too much of a grouch to say much.

"Master Six! Please look! Tots thinks I am crazy."

Able snapped to attention as John Mark held up the class telescope. Tottenham, a student in the older class, was laughing and twirling his finger around his ear. A frosty glance from Able ended that, but the boy still looked amused.

"Aw, sir, John claims he saw someone slide off that cutter. And we know how seasick he gets. Maybe he's hallucinating."

"I saw something, I did!" John said, his voice anxious. "Please, sir, take a look."

Able took the telescope and balanced his way carefully to the other side of the yacht. "Back the sails, Smitty," he said as he wrapped his arm around a sheet. "Where away, John? Point."

John Mark pointed and Able aimed the 'scope in that direction. He relaxed his eye and closed the unnecessary one, moving the 'scope to the death boat, where he saw a black tarp and an arm and leg angled out, stiff in rigor mortis. *Lord help us*, he thought. *Surely they aren't dumping the bodies in the harbor.*

"Maybe a corpse fell overboard," Tots said.

"Seems unlikely," Able replied. "Are you certain, John?"

"Sir, I am," came the firm reply.

After a lightning-fast determination of wind and water motion, Able carefully glassing the surface of the water between the death boat and the harbor. He held his breath to make certain he was not bobbing with the yacht. John Mark was right. A figure swam toward them, making poor progress.

"You're right, John," he said softly, almost as though he feared the death boat crew might be listening. The cutter carrying the week's corpses from the hulks lumbered on toward the still-distant wharf, apparently unmindful that it had lost someone quick from among the dead.

He made a rapid decision, one he hoped he wouldn't regret, mainly because Meri's struggle in the water was still fresh in his ever-active brain. "Smitty," he called over his shoulder. "Someone is in the water at two points off the larboard bow. I mean to shield him with the *Jolly Roger*. Take us between the death boat and the swimmer. Can you do it? If not, I'll take the helm."

"I can do it, sir." Smitty called to his classmates. "Watch the sails, Rats. I'll tell you what to do."

A few precise commands, and the yacht wore ship and sliced through the water toward the cutter. Able removed his shoes and his uniform, his eyes on the swimmer, who had stopped and was leaning back, looking upward.

"Handsomely now, Smitty," Able called. "He's almost done for."

With enough skill to make any sailing master on any Royal Navy warship beam with pride, Smitty took the *Jolly Roger* between the death boat and the swimmer. They came close enough to see bodies under the tarp because the wind had picked up and ruffled the canvas.

"Luff the sails, Smitty," Able said. "I'm going in. Steady as she goes, please."

Able slid over the larboard side of the yacht, gasping from the frigid water. He looked back, relieved to see that no one from the death boat could tell what he was doing. Using an underhand motion, Nick slid a ring buoy in his direction, with two lads at the ready on the rope to pull them in.

Able approached the swimmer carefully and spoke in French. "I'm going to reach across you and pull you toward me. Don't struggle, because I have no qualms about letting you drown, if you resist."

"I'm trying to escape!" the man replied in French. "How can you be French? What alchemy is this?"

"I'm English, you idiot. Don't argue," Able said, with some asperity.

"In that case," the man said in excellent English. "Good God, I am cold."

*What in the world have we here?* Able asked himself as he took the man into the same position he had used to carry his wife only a few days ago.

Damn, it was cold. Able swam them toward the ring buoy and looped his arm through the blessed little thing. "Haul away, lads," he called, but quietly.

They hauled. Able tightened his grip on the exhausted man as the Rats towed them to the *Jolly Roger*. "You're no corpse," he said in French, thinking that perhaps idle conversation wasn't out of the question. "You're a prisoner?"

"These two long years," the man said. His voice was faint and his breathing labored. "I could not manage one more moment."

"I was a prisoner once of the damned French," Able said. "Jesus God, it's cold. Did you really think you would make it to shore?"

No answer. Able slapped the man's head.

"I am alive," he said distinctly. "Don't do that."

"Just making certain. Why should I not turn you over to the authorities?"

"I cannot think of a single reason except humanity."

They had reached the yacht. Able held up the prisoner's arms and the boys hauled him to the deck. "Cover him with something," Able said, as John and Nick dragged him up and over the railing. "Anything."

Other of the crew grabbed Able. Nick took two blankets from the quarters below deck, draping one over the man who lay silent, his eyes closed, and handing the other to Able, who wrapped it around himself and sat down cross-legged by the prisoner.

"Smitty, take us back to the wharf. No. Take us to the stone basin instead. We can tie up there for now. You and you, turn him on his side and start rubbing him. I had better get dressed."

Able took off his soaked small clothes and dried himself with the blanket. He put on his uniform and his shoes and watched the Rats at work.

*Is this our spy?* he asked himself, as the prisoner shivered and moaned. *If he is, he is truly inept.*

# — Chapter Twenty-four —

Like the mariner he obviously was, even if he had come from nowhere he would state, Smitty brought the *Jolly Roger* neatly to the stone basin in the rear of St. Brendan the Navigator School. The yacht was far too large to gain admittance to the basin, but there was a small berth and iron rings outside. Soon the vessel was tied fast.

The sun was still too high in the sky for his next move, so Able helped the boys carry the Frenchman below deck to the snug cabin. "Shut up and stay here," he ordered, feeling no particular animosity, but wanting the prisoner quiet because he didn't need any more competition to the rousing clamor going on in his brain. "Topside, lads, smartly now."

He gathered his boys close to him on deck, speaking softly. "When it is full dark, we are going to help this man to my house. I am going to summon Sir B and ask his advice. Until then, you will watch him." He took his time gazing into each earnest face. "There are moments in your naval career when you must say absolutely nothing of what has transpired. This is one of those moments. Need I say more?"

Head shakes all around on serious faces. "Good. Smitty, here is my knife. Go below. If he makes any move toward you, kill him."

"Aye, sir," Smitty said as he took the knife. No question, no comment, no hesitation. Smitty had the makings of an admiral. That would never happen, of course, but even better would Smitty as a valued first mate. The boy went below without a backward glance.

Able put his hand on the other upperclassman. "Remain here on deck, Tots. I will return soon with blankets and food for the prisoner. Don't allow anyone else on the *Jolly Roger*. There's a cudgel here somewhere. Use it if need be."

"Aye, Master Six."

Able squeezed out his smallclothes, dumped them into the now-empty canvas bag of food that Meri always insisted upon and slung it over his shoulder. "Nick and John, come with me."

Silently they hurried to the most wonderful house in England. Both boys sighed when they crossed the threshold. "I always feel better here, too," he said. "Let's see if we can find Mrs. Six. Ah, here she is, mending our stockings. What a brave woman."

Nick chuckled. He and John moved quickly into the sitting room, Able right behind, after he indicated that Mrs. Perry follow them. The housekeeper set down the folded laundry without a question.

"This is a delegation," Meri said after he kissed her cheek and the boys sat down. "Am I in trouble?"

She immediately became serious as he told her what had happened on the water, and who was now under the watchful eye of the Gunwharf Rats. He knew what she would say and she didn't fail him.

"Poor man. He needs dry clothes. Able, is he your size?"

"He's not so tall and decidedly thinner. Any thoughts?"

"Jamie MacGregor left his outgrown clothes behind with Betsy on his last visit in port," Mrs. Perry said. "I'll go ask her, and heat up some water for the pig."

"Beef stew is on the hob. Should I get a tin ready?" Meri asked. "I have bread and petit fours, too."

"Oh, Mam, not too many of the petit fours, please," Nick said. "He's a prisoner, after all."

"Gluttony is one of the seven deadly sins, but I see your point, Nick," she said, then smiled. "A little mercy is a good thing, but we'll limit him to two." She left the room.

Able thought John Mark might question him, and he was not disappointed. "May I ask? Sir, what do you plan to do with him?"

"You may always ask," Able said. He reached in his pocket for a coin. "Hail a hackney and go to number Twenty-five Jasper Road. Tell Sir B what has happened and ask him to come here after dark. Tell him you will take dinner with him."

John's eyes widened with the responsibility but Able saw no reticence. "Aye, sir."

He took the coin. Able half-expected him to ask where to hail a hackney, because he knew John had never attempted what he had just been told to do. The boy saluted smartly and hurried on his errand. *Good lad*, Able thought.

"And me, sir?" Nick Bonfort asked.

What for Nick? In seconds, Able recalled Meri's conversations of the past few days, sorting through them, and arriving at the perfect duty immediately. After putting Ben to bed two nights ago, Meri had speculated on various ways to draw Grace Croker more into Sir B's orbit.

"Go to Miss Croker. We will spare the headmaster, because he is still not well. Tell her to come here after dark, as we need her advice."

"If she asks me questions?"

"Tell her it's for the good of the navy, and you have your orders."

He could have laughed out loud at Nick's doubtful expression. "She has a way of wanting to know everything all at once."

Able had never heard a better description of the efficient, intelligent Miss Croker. "She does, but you are under my orders, Nick. Then come back and eat your dinner."

"Aye, sir."

Able went in search of Meridee, who was scooping beef stew into a tin. "What are you thinking, Able?" she asked, which made him laugh and slap her fanny. "Oh, you know what I mean," she said, pinking up and looking as luscious as the petit fours on the table. "Silly genius, why do I tolerate you?"

"A question for the ages, Mrs. Six! I am thinking this could be our spy that Trinity House warned us about," he said. "I am certain he will never tell us the truth or at least the whole truth. I am also thinking about next Tuesday's algebra lesson, and what must happen in the next few months to put William Pitt back in power. Which of those to you want?"

She threw her arms around him, and he was happy to hold her. "I want the one where you tell me you love me."

"That's so easy," he said, and kissed her soundly. "I love you. Give me a challenge, wife."

"Oh, you," she said in that gruff voice he liked so well. As he watched, she found a basket for the food and added a towel. Mrs. Perry came out of the storeroom with some of Jamie MacGregor's clothes he had outgrown on his last voyage, and held them up to her generous waist.

"What do you think, sir?" she asked.

"Mrs. Perry, he kissed me when I asked him that same thing," Meri teased.

"Actually, I was about to say that they won't fit you, Mrs. Perry, but I value my life."

The African housekeeper gave him a formidable look that took Able back to earlier days when she had sailed with her carpenter-husband on Able's second ship, under the command of Sir B. He held up his hands in surrender.

"Mrs. Perry, those trousers will do, and that shirt. Oddly enough, he is wearing regular clothing, well cut, and not convict garb. That might be our first question to him."

"Who is he?"

"That I doubt he will divulge. Mrs. Perry, let's see what we find out."

Carrying their goods and trying to look inconspicuous, the three of them strolled beyond the stone basin to the *Jolly Roger*. Tots greeted them by touching a wicked-looking marling spike to his hat.

"Anyone come nosing around?"

"Just a cat and two dogs, sir," Tots replied. "I sent them on their way."

"Excellent. Mrs. Perry, perhaps you could give this good fellow a petit fours."

She could and did. Able moved in front of Meridee and she followed him down the narrow companionway to the cabin, her hand on his shoulder, because the stairs were steep.

There sat Smitty in the hammock, leisurely pushing off with his foot and swinging in the small space. The Frenchman's eyes were closed, but the half smile on his face looked like nothing more than relief. If he was a spy, he certainly was serene about it.

The man's nose began to twitch like a dog's when he smelled the stew Meri carried. "If I open my eyes, is this a dream?" he said in excellent English.

"Not at all," Meri said. "I would advise you to not gobble it down, though."

Able watched in appreciation as the man opened his eyes and just gazed at Meridee Six for a long moment, as if he could not imagine the good fortune of food *and* a pretty woman at the same time. Under his appreciative scrutiny, Meri stepped back until she touched Able's body. He put a reassuring hand on her shoulder.

"Meri, let me introduce this ogler to you," Able said, "or at least I would if I knew his name. Sir?"

The prisoner paused a moment, as if wondering the wisdom of giving his true name, then gave a Gallic shrug. "Jean Hubert, *madame*, at your service. Lieutenant, that is, of the late sloop of war *Calais*, captured near Saint Domingue."

"Meri, may I introduce Lieutenant Jean Hubert to you? Lieutenant, this is my wife, Mrs. Six. I am Sailing Master Able Six, currently assigned as a professor of nearly everything at St. Brendan to Navigator School."

Lieutenant Hubert's eyes grew small as he smiled. "Charmed, Madame Six and Master Six." He took a deep breath. "I know I am showing the worst kind of manners, but you said there was food in that tin…"

All business now, Meri opened the tin and poured its contents into the cup she had brought. "Careful, it's hot," she warned as she handed it to Hubert. "Here is a spoon and bread."

Able doubted the starving man heard a word she said. The stew was too hot, so he dipped the bread in and sucked it, pausing only to wipe the tears from his eyes.

"I…I have more at the house, lieutenant," Meri said, then turned her face into Able's sleeve, because she was tenderhearted.

Able heard Mrs. Perry sniff, but he knew better than to glance at the big woman. He had seen her around shipwrecked sailors before – French, English or Dutch, it never mattered.

"Did he say anything to you?" he asked Smitty.

"No, sir. Of course, I was tapping the knife in my hand. Sir, do I look formidable?"

"A little. Consider it an asset."

"He looked at me and said '*C'est formidable*,'" Smitty said. "I think it was the knife, Master Six."

"You do have a bit of an air about you, Smitty," Able said. "I knew you were the man for the job."

He turned his attention to the prisoner, who was just accepting the two petit fours from Meri with a bow. Trust the French, once they were not on the sorry side of starvation, to pay attention to the ladies. How he managed to look in control of his situation – a blanket wrapped around him, and his lips nearly blue with cold – was one of the mysteries of life. The occasion called for some plain speaking, but not with Meri and Mrs. Perry within earshot.

"Meri, you and Mrs. Perry may return home. I'll see to this fellow."

"Is he coming home with you?"

"That will depend entirely on what I learn from him in the next few minutes, and if I believe anything he tells me." That was plain enough, and entirely for the lieutenant's ears.

Meri seemed to understand his game. She put the empty tin in the basket and handed the towel to Lieutenant Hubert. "We'll eat at six," she said, and blew Able a kiss.

Now it was Smitty, Lieutenant Hubert, Able and Tots, who came below when Able called him.

"Now, sir, strip and dry off and see if these clothes will fit," Able said.

"With an audience?" Hubert asked.

"Absolutely. I might even ask you to spread your cheeks. If you're going to cross the street with me to the house where my wife and baby sleep, there will be nothing on your person except, well, your person."

"Fair enough." Hubert removed his shirt, revealing ribs ready to poke out of his sides, and a back well-acquainted with a lash. Once naked, he turned around and spread his cheeks, which struck Able as more of a taunt than a wish to comply. The man *was* a Frenchman, after all. Able made no comment, even though Smitty was hard put not to laugh.

Jamie's old trousers went on easily, if too short. So was the shirt, but at least he was decent. Able draped a blanket around him.

"I'll repeat an earlier question: why should I not summon the marines and turn you in?" Able asked, when the lieutenant was dressed, barefoot still.

The prisoner opened his mouth to speak when they heard the noise of feet overhead. Tots went to the companionway and came down with little Pierre carrying a pair of Able's old slippers.

The boy dropped the slippers and turned as ghostly white as the spectre Able still considered him: a quiet lad who said nothing and tagged after John Mark. Able looked at the lieutenant. He saw every emotion cross Hubert's face, starting with amazement and ending with relief of a profound nature.

"Pierre Deschamps," the prisoner said and held out his arms. "Master Six, he was my powder monkey on the *Calais*."

The boy tumbled into them, sobbing in French, "Lieutenant Hubert, he abandoned me!"

*What is this?* Able thought, wishing he could hear more of what they were saying. Hubert had immediately whispered to Pierre, and they spoke softly, urgently.

To turn them in or not? Able had nothing of a concrete nature on which to base his next move, nothing beyond a certain instinct that every seaman in any navy seemed to share. Enemy he might be, Lieutenant Hubert also looked after his men, even the little ones.

Whether this would prove to be a blessing or a dreadful mistake, Able had no idea. None of the characters who roamed about in his brain seemed to have any idea, either, or at least they weren't divulging it. Trust genius to fail you when you need it.

Better *appear* decisive, at least. "Smitty and Tots, return the *Jolly Roger* to her berth. Can you do that without embarrassing St. Brendan's?"

"Aye, aye, sir!"

Able smiled to himself, knowing what he had asked. It was their first independent command, taking the *Jolly Roger* from her *ad hoc* mooring by the stone basin to her regular slip near the Gunwharf, the distance of one quarter mile. From Smitty's serious expression, it might have been from Portsmouth to the Scillies through rough Channel chop.

"See that you do it handsomely and to St. Brendan's credit. Report across the street when you are done. There are more petit fours."

When the boys hurried above deck, Able formally motioned his prisoner toward the companionway.

"What have you decided?" his prisoner asked.

"I trust you not at all, Lieutenant Hubert, but I do value the opinion of a little boy, who seems happy to see you," he said. "You're coming home with me. Whether I regret this bit of generosity on my part is up to you."

# — Chapter Twenty-five —

To pretend to feel alert and stout-hearted or let down his guard? That was Jean Hubert's question; he had no answers. All he wanted was more warm food, and a bed with sheets and blankets. Mrs. Six seemed to be a soft-hearted lady. Having her on his side would do him no harm. The question of whether leaning on Able would earn him more sympathy entered his mind and left it quickly, when he realized he really did need the sailing master's help to stand upright.

Jean was rewarded with a tender glance from Master Able's wife who stood in the open door across the street. His delight in his continuing power over the weaker sex turned to sackcloth and ashes when he saw the master's frosty expression. *I think I cannot fool this one*, he thought, chagrined that he had even tried.

He would not even attempt to solicit sympathy from the African woman, who appeared completely capable of thrashing him and feeling no regret. And the big lad, the one with such broad shoulders? Where in the world did a boys' school find a hound of hell like that?

It was a worthy question and he did want an answer. He leaned on Master Able's arm as they slowly crossed the street. "Tell me, sir: if I had moved toward...toward...Smitty is it?... would he really have killed me?"

"Aye, lieutenant. I gave him an order."

*I shouldn't have asked*, Jean thought. Suddenly he knew, somewhere deep in his brain, that no matter how long this conflict raged, the British were going to win. There seemed to be no shortage of young men like Smitty.

"How old is he?" Jean asked as Able helped him up the first steps toward a pleasant stone house with empty window boxes waiting for spring.

"He is twelve."

Jean wondered why he felt this need for conversation with his captor, except that the man had an engaging quality about him, despite his frosty glare. "Twelve? I would have thought him older."

"The workhouse will do that," Master Six replied, leaving Jean to wonder just what sort of school St. Brendan's was, and whether he had been wise in impulsively striking out for shore from under a pile of corpses.

Perhaps he had been hasty in thinking himself capable. The mere sight of four more steps up to the house's front door exhausted him. "I don't think I can," he murmured.

"*We* can," Master Six replied. "Smitty?"

Hands under his arms, they lifted him right up the steps and into the house, with Mrs. Six holding the door open.

"I don't know why I thought that hard," Jean said, then promptly fainted.

When he came around, he was lying in a bed with sheets and blankets, just as he had dreamed of for the past year and a half. Sitting on one side was Mrs. Six, this time holding a sleeping baby. Standing on his other side was a tall, thin woman with intense-looking eyes and an expression suggesting she had no love for the French.

"I'll get Sir B," she told Mrs. Six, who nodded.

"Where am I?" Jean asked.

"You're in my home." Mrs. Six smiled as if she had knowledge he would never possess. "We share it with students we call our little boarders – two lads from St. Brendan's, across the street."

"St. Brendan's, St. Brendan's," he said, almost afraid to look around for the menacing Smitty. "Your husband mentioned a school for boys. What…what sort of school is it?" He couldn't resist smiling back, because Mrs. Six seemed so genuinely interested. "Smitty fair terrifies me."

"They are lads like my husband, in this case being trained for service with the fleet," she began. "Well, sort of like my husband. No one is quite like him. Like him, though, they were raised in workhouses. They are England's cast-offs, her by-blows, her unwanted."

No fool he, Jean had already noticed the glances between Master and Mrs. Six. Able Six certainly wasn't unwanted.

"Trained as what?"

"Sailing masters, mainly, but we are discovering they have other talents. One of our boys is now an apothecary's apprentice at Haslar," she explained. "That is the royal naval hospital. Three are at sea already, apprenticed to sailing masters and acquitting themselves well."

She turned her attention to the open door and her expression lightened. Jean knew without even looking that her husband stood there. The connection between the two was palpable. "Able, he's alert. Should I leave you and Sir B with him?"

"No. Stay here. You know I value your opinion."

Mrs. Six took a seat closer to the fire. She put her baby to her shoulder and settled herself. The man he already knew as Able Six came in, followed by a man in a wheeled chair, pushed by what must be his valet, a pale fellow with deep-set eyes that wore a look of worry, for some reason. *Do you think I can leap up and smite you?* Jean thought, wondering at the expression. His next thought surprised him. *I do believe you are French. We Frenchmen have a look, don't we?*

The tall, thin woman returned and sat beside Mrs. Six. Her glance went to the man in the wheeled chair and lingered there, telling Jean even more about this singular collection of humanity crowded into a fairly small room.

He closed his eyes for a moment, wondering who everyone was, wondering how much truth to tell. There was no fear in the room, except what he seemed to see in the eyes of the valet. Ah well, he was merely a servant and of no particular account.

To his surprise, the young lodgers, as Mrs. Six called them, crowded in at the door, Smitty among them. Working his way closer was Pierre Deschamps. Jean thought of the times his powder monkey had wormed his way into shipboard meetings on the *Calais*, simply because he was small and blended in.

Since Pierre was watching him, Jean shook his head slightly, hoping to ward him off from any possible comment or exclamation. To his dismay, Smitty seemed to intercept the admonition, too. The boy's eyes darted from one to the other. *Blast and damn*, Jean thought.

To his relief, the tall woman shooed the boys from the door, only to see them replaced by the African behemoth in turban and matching apron. He didn't think the tall woman would shoo her away, and she didn't.

Master Six began with no preamble. "Monsieur Hubert, what are we to make of you?"

Interesting. Jean had expected the man in the wheeled chair to preside. He seemed to be the aristocrat among the bunch, but no, this was Able Six's house, and he was in charge. How *did* the wind blow in this house and with these people? He had better figure it out. Perhaps sticking to the truth as closely as he could might be advisable. Master Six's eyes had a restless quality to them, as if they searched for more than the average man even suspected.

"I am who I said I was," he began. "Lieutenant Jean Hubert, late of the sloop of war *Calais*, captured off Saint Domingue by the frigate *Venture*. I cannot recall the captain's name."

"Edward Bartlett," Master Six informed him, "dead these five weeks after a sharp engagement near Gibraltar. Don't try to look sympathetic."

*Good Lord, who is this man?* Jean asked himself, startled. "I shan't."

"Why were you wearing citizen's clothing?"

Master Six did have a relentless air about him. Jean saw no need to lie about the matter. "I had been instructed to give drawing lessons to the daughter of Captain Tobias Faulke, who commands the *Captivity*. Mrs. Faulke didn't care for prisoner garb."

"Nicety in a hulk? How singular," the man in the wheelchair said. "By the way, I am Captain Sir Belvedere St. Anthony." He rationed out a smile. "I am called Sir B, in most circles."

He seemed kind enough, without Master Six's edgy ways. "Sir B, who are you in this gathering of mortals?"

The man smiled at Jean's small witticism, then quickly set him straight. "I am another mortal who can return you to the hulk, if I don't like you."

"Wretched place, full of disease, lice, rats, and starvation rations," Jean said quickly, not willing to waste Sir B's time, now that he had made himself perfectly clear. "I was crossing the deck to instruct Ianthe Faulke in her daily art lesson. The weekly pile of dead men lay on the deck and no one was paying attention. I slid among them on a whim and here I am."

Mrs. Six was obviously the room's softest touch. He saw real sympathy on her face. He glanced at the tall lady and saw a studied, neutral expression. The African woman looked ready to toss him out the window.

"Art?" Master Six asked. Jean heard all the skepticism. "So you say." He went to the door, leaned out, spoke a few words, then leaned back in with a tablet and pencil. "Prove it."

"You don't believe me?" Jean asked, suddenly tired and sore and hungry.

"I don't. I subscribe to Admiral Nelson's philosophy. I hate the French as I would the devil. Draw something."

What to sketch? Jean knew the lovely rolling hills above Rive Loire well, and the high-cliff Normandy beaches were close to his home. He looked and found his subject, because he was not a stupid man, merely a desperate one. Mrs. Six was the ideal subject. She wasn't watching him, which made it better. She had leaned forward, her attention on her baby, who waved his arms around. *Madonna of Ratty Portsmouth*, he thought as he sketched. She was perfect, all serenity and loveliness, and by God, he knew he could snare Master Six with his effort.

*Play your hand well, Jean Hubert*, he told himself as he handed the completed sketch to Master Six.

The sailing master saw right through him. He gave the sketch a perfunctory glance, flipped a page in the table and handed it back. "Draw me a sloop of war, you master manipulator."

Properly chastened, Jean drew, resolving never to attempt fooling this man again. Well, no more than he had to. He drew the clean lines of the *Calais*, remembering sunny days in the Caribbean, pliant women on shore, flowers in bloom no matter the season. He lay back and stared at the ceiling, utterly spent.

"Your ship?"

"My ship."

Master Six put the tablet in Sir B's lap. They spoke quietly. He turned to the previous page, and the invalid smiled, showing the drawing to the tall lady.

"Your English is excellent, by the way," Sir B said. "Don't you agree, Able."

"Aye, Sir B. I also suspect he is an opportunist, probably in any language."

"Able, really." Mrs. Six said.

"I never trust a Frenchman, my dear." He held out his hands for their child, and put the tablet in her lap when she handed over the baby. "He thought to appeal to my emotions."

"I do that all the time," she said, which made everyone laugh, clearing the air. "What a lovely drawing, Mr. Hubert. May I keep it?"

"It is yours, Madame Six. Shame on me for playing on anyone's sympathies, but I do not wish to return to the prison hulk. May I be of service here somehow?"

"We're considering it," Sir B said. "Excuse us. Gervaise? Wheel me into the hall."

"Stay here, Smitty," Master Six said. Still carrying his baby, he followed Sir B and the tall woman. He closed the door. Jean was not surprised in the least to see that Pierre had remained behind, crouched in the corner. Smitty seated himself so he could observe everyone.

Jean had questions. "Madame Six, who is that tall lady?"

"I should have introduced you," Mrs. Six said, as calmly as if this were a sitting room, and not part of a tribunal deciding his slender chance to remain here. "That is Miss Croker, the sister of St. Brendan's headmaster. She teaches beginning mathematics now, English grammar and log writing, general medical treatment, and whatever she thinks future leaders in the fleet should know."

Well and good. "The man in the chair?"

"He is a hero of Aboukir Bay – perhaps you know it as the Battle of the Nile. He is a good and true friend of St. Brendan's. He also has amazing connections."

"And your husband?"

"He is a genius," she said simply. "Don't ever try to fool him."

That was plainly said. Perhaps Mrs. Six was as tough as the others in the room, the ones deciding his fate right now. For the first time in his life, he found himself silenced by a woman.

The door opened and in came his tribunal. Sir B indicated for his valet to wheel him closer to the bed.

"Because you are an officer and prisoner, and with the consent of the Admiralty, I have the power to grant you a parole," he began. "With your pledge to remain on the premises of St. Brendan's, unless we ordain otherwise, we would use you to teach French and art, particularly art of a maritime or mechanical nature. We will watch you closely. At the first hint of trouble, you will be returned to the *Captivity*. Able?"

"You'll be paid for your services," Master Six said. "You will lodge here in my home. We have one extra bedchamber, the one where two of our St. Brendan's lads lived last year. What do you think?"

Jean nodded. Was it even possible that he was going to be allowed to sit out the war in safety? Had his fortunes finally turned? *"Mais oui,"* he said, relieved not to have to brave another encounter with Claude Pascal or Captain Faulke, who were probably scouring the hulk right now for him.

"Sir B will make the legal arrangements," Master Six continued. "I trust you won't mind sharing your room?"

"Solitude is always nice," Jean ventured.

"I agree," Master Six said, sounding most amiable. He looked over his shoulder and gestured. "However, I do not trust you. Smitty, would you like to become a lodger here?"

*Good God*, Jean thought, with a combination of resignation, rue, chagrin, and grudging respect for the tall, curly-haired man who hated the French as he would the devil.

"I would like that above all, Master Six," the boy thug said. "I have never been a sound sleeper. You'll be in safe hands."

"Precisely," Master Six said, as he returned the baby to his wife. "And now, Meri, I think our new lodgers would both like something more to eat, while Mrs. Perry makes up that other bed."

*I have been played by a master*, Jean thought in dismay.

# — Chapter Twenty-Six —

J ean found it easy enough to tell Mrs. Six a bit more of the truth, when she and a pretty
redhead returned to the room with a tray of food. Mrs. Six told Smitty to go below
with Betsy to eat.

She walked Jean's new and unwanted roommate to the door. Smitty stood there a
moment.

"Yes, Smitty?" she asked.

Master Six's enforcer looked suddenly young and precisely twelve years old, to Jean's
eyes. "I've wanted to live here," he said in a rush. "We all do."

"I wish I had room for all of you," the lady said. "When you finish your meal, fetch
your belongings and bring them back. You are welcome here."

Smitty grinned, and Jean saw all the genuine pleasure. It had been years, but he
remembered his home, and Maman and Papa. Those were simple times, before Maman
died, Papa married a dragon, and France plunged into the Terror. *And now I am here in an
English seaport, because I dove into a pile of corpses. Life is strange.*

Still Smitty hesitated. "Should I leave you, Mrs. Six?"

"I will be fine. Go eat before your food is cold. Sir B and Miss Croker are staying for
dinner, too, so mind your manners."

"That's the hard part about living here, isn't it?" he asked, and Mrs. Six laughed
out loud.

As Jean watched the little scene with growing appreciation, Mrs. Six planted a kiss
on Smitty's cheek – Smitty the enforcer – and pulled him close for a second.

"Smitty, think what you can learn by listening to such august company," she said.
"There will be dessert."

No thug now, Smitty beamed at his benefactress and clattered down the stairs,
spurred on, no doubt, by dessert. And look, there was dessert on Jean's tray.

"Madame Six, you have achieved excellence in the management of boys," he said,
then tucked into the food in front of him.

"I treat them kindly, and have never been disappointed."

*Madame, have you any idea how charming you are?* he thought. Jean felt every care in his
life slide away, if only for a moment. Pleasant smells – except for him – filled his nostrils.
True, the food was English, but why quibble? The mattress was soft, and he was warm
enough for the first time in the long winter. No one argued or babbled or shrieked

or raged. True, he had lost all his art supplies, but he knew there would be more. He doubted that St. Brendan's boys would be as sly as Ianthe Faulke. He closed his eyes, happy to blot out her petulant face.

"Pierre, have you been here all this time? Oh, I do wish you understood English."

He opened his eyes to see Pierre standing close to the bed, giving him a worried look that made Jean sigh inside. *I don't want to think of war at all*, he told himself, then felt ashamed because after all, Pierre was his powder monkey and he was *Capitain* Hubert to the little fellow.

"He is so quiet that I sometimes forget where he is," Meri said.

*You learn that in a prison hulk*, Jean thought.

She sat Pierre down and wiped off her fork. "Here you are, Pierre. I can eat later. I know I can trust you two, so I will go below. I wish you understood me."

"You may eat the kind lady's food," Jean said in French.

Silent as usual, Pierre ate with no hesitation.

"Wait, please," Jean said as Madame Six picked up her son and turned to the door. "Let me tell you why I speak English."

"Does it matter, really?" she asked.

It did matter all of a sudden. He, Jean Hubert – adept liar, scrounger, meddler, because life in a prison hulk had made him that way – wanted to tell as much truth as he could.

"Please."

"Very well." Up went the baby to her shoulder as she gave Jean her full attention.

"My mother died when I was about Pierre's age," he began. "Papa owned a hotel in Cherbourg near the beach." He smiled at the memory; couldn't help himself. "Papa had visions of grandeur. Much of our trade was English visitors – this was before the Reign of Terror, of course – and he knew we should all learn English." He shuddered elaborately. "He found a perfect dragon of an Englishwoman and she became our teacher."

"A dragon?"

"Poor Papa." Jean described the terror they all felt when Papa married Millicent Nash, and how she became a tyrant, forcing English down their throats, and turning preening, grandiose Papa into a meek little fellow who let her run the hotel as she wanted.

"I'm so sorry," Mrs. Six said, and he knew she meant it. "But…but… at least you learned English." It was her turn to chuckle. "Able says my destiny is to be forever trying to make the best of a wretched situation."

"That is hardly a crime."

"No, it isn't. He teases me a lot…" She stopped and her face reddened.

"Come now, Mrs. Six, how bad can this be?" Why did he want to know more about the Sixes?

Again, that little laugh. "He teases me, then he turns around, bends over and tells me I can thrash him, if I feel like it."

They laughed together, which made Pierre look up in surprise, startled at a pleasantry.

"I envy you your good fortune, *madame*," Jean said simply, then steered the conversation back to its logical course. "Of my siblings, I alone had the epiphany, in the midst of our linguistic misery, that if I paid attention, I would learn a valuable skill. So it has proved. Anyway, it has landed me here, because I speak English and taught art, in English, to a scheming child."

"I had no idea that the hulk's officers were allowed to keep their families on board."

"Some do, some don't." He had said enough about Ianthe Faulke. Just thinking of her reminded him too forcefully of Captain Faulke. "That is my story."

"What happened to your father? Your brothers and sisters?"

Should he tell her? Why not? Nothing was normal about his situation. "Two brothers, one sister. Papa dropped dead one day and Madame Millicent turned us out. My older sister was already married. She died on the guillotine. My older brothers? One is dead, the other in Canada somewhere. That is what war can do. I ran away to sea."

"So did my husband," Madame Six said. "One too many beatings in the workhouse."

He stared at her in amazement. "Your...your husband was a workhouse child, too?"

She nodded. "The sixth illegitimate baby born in 1775, and Durable because he was found naked in February in Scotland. And that is *his* story. Perhaps we have both told enough truth for now, Monsieur Hubert."

She looked at Pierre and gestured for him to pick up his dishes. "Would you please tell him to follow me with his dishes? He has kitchen duties."

"I can and will. Would you allow Pierre to come back up here for a brief time? I was his captain on the *Calais* and I would like to know how he is faring."

"Certainly. I have no fear leaving you by yourself, sir," she said. "You are a gentleman and you have given your parole, or will, as soon as Sir B arranges it."

He had no intention of leaping out a window and escaping, when she closed the door. "You have it, Madame Six."

After she left, he considered the matter. Even if he *had* wanted to escape, she had declared him a gentleman and bound him to St. Brendan's, wherever that would lead. In this time of revolution, world war, and stomach-churning turmoil, there were worse fates than a parole to teach at a boys' school.

He dozed while waiting for Pierre to return, content to enjoy the half-sleep that comes with a full belly and no one after him for punishment or worse. The hulks in the harbor seemed worlds away.

"Capitain? Capitain?"

Pierre stood beside his bed. Taking a page from Madame Six's book, Jean sat up, held open his arms, and allowed Pierre to tumble into his embrace. The lad wasn't more than ten, and this was no time for naval discipline.

"Pierre, what happened to you?" he asked, when the boy wiped his eyes on the sheet. "We learned that the keg escape had been successful, but heard nothing more. Tell me."

He allowed the child a moment to compose himself, but no reminder of duty could wipe away the fright in the child's eyes.

"It went as we had planned, Capitain Hubert," he said. "Gunner Remillard crawled out of his keg and pried the lid from mine. He helped me out and...and he ran away!"

Jean saw all the fright of a child finding himself in a strange place where no one spoke his language and everyone was an enemy. "Just left you there? Abandoned you?"

Pierre nodded as his tears fell. "I didn't know what to do or where to go, sir, and I was hungry."

"Go on. You're here, so your fortunes must have changed."

"They did after a while, sir. It was raining, so I found a building with a side door unlocked. I hid under the stairs. There was a pile of rags."

*Who runs off and leaves a child like that?* Jean asked himself. *I thought Remillard was a better man.*

"And then?" he asked gently.

"I heard workers in the morning. I went upstairs and everywhere there was sawdust and boards. I found a broom and started sweeping." He said the last with quiet pride.

"I'd say you were resourceful," Jean said.

"I was only doing what you used to tell us on the *Calais*, sir."

"*Moi?*"

"*Certainement, capitain.*" Pierre chuckled, the bleakness of his expression gone. "Don't you recall how you stalked the deck, ordering us to find something to do when we had finished our work? 'There is always something else,' you said."

"So I did," Jean replied, surprised how easily his days commanding a ship of France had retreated from his mind. Or maybe it wasn't a surprise. Looming over every victory, large or small, was the shame of capture. Who wants to remember that?

The little boy seated on his bed didn't need to know how beaten down his captain was. Better to preserve some dignity, after all. "They let you stay? No one asked any questions?"

"No. They really did need someone to sweep," he said with the kind of shrug no Englishman could imitate. "They shared their lunches with me, and gave me a blanket. I don't think they knew or maybe cared where I slept, as long as I was there in the morning to sweep. I met John Mark, and then Madame and *Professeur* Six came once, I suppose to find out what they do there."

"Is it a factory?"

"Oui!" Pierre exclaimed, his eyes bright. "They are getting ready to make metal block pulleys. You know, we have wooden ones."

Jean knew block pulleys. What ship moved across the waters without them?

"It's a wonderful place! Soon they will turn out enough pulleys for every ship in England." Pierre laughed. "Maybe ours, too, if we could steal the building."

"And ship it home," Jean joked in turn.

Pierre's face fell. "Should I be sweeping in a building making something that will cause hardship for *la belle France?*"

"We won't worry about it now," Jean told him. He indicated the glass and empty desert plate. "Return these to the kitchen. And now you sleep here?"

"*Oui,* since I ran with John Mark when the dock men were drowning those men from the *Captivity,*" Pierre said. He shivered. From his expression, he had shouldered responsibilities too large for a child's shoulders. "I sleep below, off the kitchen. In the mornings, I help Betsy with whatever she needs, then I walk with John Mark after luncheon to the block factory. Smitty escorts us, because Maman...*pardonnez moi...*

Madame Six… wants us to be safe." He thought a moment, perhaps grappling with an idea bigger than he had considered before. "Is that what mothers do?"

"It is, lad," Jean said, remembering the sweetness of his own mother.

After Pierre left, Jean lay back again, exhausted. He had nearly drifted off when Pierre returned. "I thought you were below for the night," he said.

*O dieu, what a look in your eyes,* Jean thought in sudden alarm. "What is the matter?"

His expression apprehensive, where it had been cheerful enough when he left, Pierre handed Jean a small piece of paper, scarcely larger than a postage stamp, but creased and folded many times.

Silently, Jean unfolded the tiny paper, squinting close to read the words. *Watch for a citizen who will make the wharf blossom with orange flowers,* he read. It made no sense. Maybe he was tired. "I don't understand." He held it out to Pierre, who backed away. "Where did you get this?"

Biting his lip, Pierre rubbed his upper arm. He took a deep breath, came close again and whispered, as though the room was full of eavesdroppers. "The valet of the crippled man."

"Yes, I think Master Six said he was French. Gervaise?"

"*Oui,*" Pierre said, his voice even softer. "He grabbed me by the arm in the hall, made me take the paper, and ordered me to ask you, 'Are you the one?'" He rubbed his arm. "He wasn't very nice."

"The one what?"

They looked at each other and shrugged. Pierre spoke first. "Sir, I am going to sit on the stairs until I am certain that Gervaise has left with the one-legged man."

"Do that."

He read the tiny note again after Pierre let himself out of the room. Orange blossoms? A wharf? It made no sense.

Jean pulled the coverlets to his neck and stared at the ceiling. *You are going to sign the parole, teach at this school and sit out the war,* he reminded his brain.

Blast and damn, why did other side of his brain, the uncomfortable side, warn him that he might be in the middle of something bigger than he intended? *I should have left that pile of dead men alone,* he thought, and swallowed the note.

# — Chapter Twenty-seven —

If Grace Croker was happy, everyone at St. Brendan's was happy, or so Able had quickly divined last year when she began her tenure as an unpaid instructor at St. Brendan's. Now she was paid, thanks to the generosity of Trinity House, and she seemed to find a colleague in the French prisoner.

True, the man had signed a parole. True also, he had some skills as a teacher. True again, once he had food and better clothing, he was a handsome fellow, if thin. Able would not have thought Grace Croker, self-admitted spinster, to be susceptible to a handsome face. She said she was thirty-five, after all.

He had broached the matter to his wise wife a week later, as they were preparing for bed. She plopped down on the bed and stared at him. "Durable Six, why would you ever think that because a woman is thirty-five that she doesn't admire a handsome man?"

"I don't know," he had to admit. "She *has* told me several times she is a confirmed spinster."

Meri patted the bed and he sat down. To his surprise and delight, she turned his face toward her with both hands, put her lips close to his, and said, "My love, just because a woman says something like that, don't think for a minute she means it."

*It is so easy to kiss you*, he thought as he did precisely that. All the ideas scrambling about in his head slid away as he pulled her down with him and had his way. Or maybe it was her way. He neither knew nor cared.

After a massively pleasant interlude, he helped her hunt for her disappearing nightgown, then continued his line of thought as she put it on and cuddled close. "You have also told me that our Grace Croker is in love with Sir B."

His wife kindly spelled out the difference between admiring a handsome face, and feeling something special for the man she loved. He took the natural step.

"Are you admitting that you don't mind ogling a handsome bloke?"

Meri made herself comfortable. "Certainly," she said, with no embarrassment. "Don't tell me you've never admired a pretty face and well-turned ankle besides mine?"

In his usual split second recall, he considered other women he had bedded in earlier years, and shook his head. None of them held a candle to Meridee Six. And since their wedding? No one looked as good to him as his wife, not even a fleeting glimpse.

"At the risk of having you call me a great prevaricator, no. Should I be embarrassed?" he asked her.

His wife rose up on her elbow. "Able, you're the rarest man in the world," she said softly.

"You already knew that," he replied, touched. Any other woman would have run screaming into the night at his weirdness. Meri had embraced it.

The next day, Able added that thought about his wife to the many in his brain as he crossed the street with the usual little lodgers and Jean Hubert, who looked particularly natty in his washed and pressed shirt and trousers. The French did have a certain flair with clothing, Able had to admit.

After their initial wariness, and after Able and Headmaster Croker had explained the nature of a parole, St. Brendan's students took to Jean Hubert's casual approach to education. To an older boy's belligerent comment, "Why do we need to know how to draw anyway?" Jean had a ready answer.

"I asked him, 'Suppose you, as first mate, are sending a boat of marines to take a seaport?'" he told Grace and Able in the few minutes they carved out during lunch each day when they sat together. "'If you can draw some terrain and buildings, does this improve their chances?' He seemed to think it might, and we continued," Jean said, and returned to his sandwich. "I like this teaching."

Nothing seemed to disturb him, but then, Able reasoned, how could anything greatly perturb a man who had suffered incarceration on a prison hulk, or spent the better part of a day hiding under dead bodies?

Smitty began escorting John Mark to the block pulley factory, with Pierre the little ghost tagging along to continue his sweeping. The lad hurried from class at the end of each day to escort them home. He did it with no complaint, and Able relaxed, knowing he could depend on the boy who looked villainous, but who, Able was coming to realize, had a heart of oak.

Able asked Smitty to be alert for shady characters, which made Smitty smile. "Master, pardon me, but you and I know that everyone on the Portsmouth docks looks shady."

Able couldn't help laughing. "Well, then, extra shady." He took a second to ruffle through the files in his mind. "Consider this: John Mark told me that Mrs. Six took her embroidery scissors to her attacker's face. Time may pass, but it will leave a scar."

"Aye, sir. I will try to find the shadiest one of all."

After dinner at the end of the week, Smitty took Able aside to show him the roster he had drawn up of lads to stand the watch behind St. Brendan's, along the sea wall. "Sir, perhaps two younger lads can take the First Watch, and two upperclassmen the Middle Watch, which requires more discipline to stay awake. What should I do about the Morning Watch?"

"That's a puzzle. How can lads make breakfast and early class, if they're standing that morning watch?" Able looked at the paper, neatly organized into columns. "Well done, Smitty."

"Monsieur Hubert helped me with this part last night before lights out," Smitty said. He smiled one of his rare smiles and pointed to the leaping dolphins at the top of the roster. "He drew this one and I drew the others."

"Those Frenchies have a certain élan we will never possess," Able said in grudging approval. "I see your difficulty with the Morning Watch. I'll think about it." He tapped the paper. "Good work, Smitty. I'm impressed."

"No, you can't praise the lads too much," he told his wife that afternoon. "I complimented Smitty and he practically wiggled like a puppy. Smitty. My thug."

"Stop calling him that," she said. "He's a dear boy."

"Aye, aye, sir!"

Smitty solved the problem of that early-morning watch. On Saturday when Able and that week's particular yacht crew returned to St. Brendan's, Meridee met him at the door, and pulled him to the kitchen.

"Able, Smitty has the perfect early morning watch!" She handed him a biscuit topped with crunchy things, which told him where she had been. Ezekiel Bartleby always insisted that she drop by the bakery on Saturdays for leftovers, even though all parties concerned knew they weren't left over from the week, but were newly baked. It was everyone's little fiction.

"Explain yourself, but do it sitting here," he told her, pointing to his lap.

"So you can drop crumbs on me?" she teased. "Earlier in the week, Ezekiel told me that the student with the scar and the intense eyes – who but Smitty? – dropped by and showed him the roster. Swore him to secrecy. 'I know bakers get up really early,' he told Ezekiel. 'I know you used to serve in the fleet. Could you stand the morning watch if I get someone to trade off with you?'"

"That's good thinking," Able said, and reached around Meri for another crunchy-topped thing. "He agreed?"

"Couldn't agree fast enough, Smitty told me. Once a sailor, always a sailor. When I dropped by the bakery this afternoon for our completely fresh stale pastries, he told me not only would he stand the watch, but Mrs. Bartleby would take turns with him so the bakery would not suffer."

He wasn't often surprised by events, but this one floored him. "His ball and chain? I'm not even aware of her real name."

"Emily," she said promptly. "I met her yesterday for the first time."

"Why in the world...."

He watched his wife as her eyes filled with tears. "Able, she came out of the back room and told me herself that she wants to fight Boney, too. Dared me to argue about it." She sniffed back her tears. "And guess who else wants to fight Boney?"

"Not you on that watch," he said in what he hoped was a firm, husbandly tone. Hoped. He had discovered in the past year that even a genius is sometimes baffled by the fairer – not weaker – sex.

"No, I'm fighting Boney right here," she assured him. "Mrs. Perry will take a turn." She straightened his neck cloth. "She hates Boney, too. Said her husband would still be alive, if not for the war. He could have left the sea when he started feeling rheumatic, and taken his carpenter skills to a healthier place in England, but for the Corsican Tyrant."

"She's right." He kissed her cheek. "Anything else that I don't know?"

"That seems unlikely in the extreme," she said and leaned against his chest for a peaceful moment.

The room was empty. He kissed her hair. "Tell me something I don't know. Double dare you."

To his utter delight, she whispered in his ear. The tickle of her lips set his nerves humming. He whispered back, "I thought perhaps you liked that, but I, um, fell asleep too soon to inquire. Shall we add that to our amorous repertoire?"

"Most definitely," she whispered. "Tonight."

# — Chapter Twenty-eight —

The Gunwharf Rats began standing the watch on Monday, after a super-secret meeting in a room in St. Brendan's cellar, with everyone crowded together to hear Headmaster Croker discuss the matter.

Able looked around the room at the serious faces of his students, every one intent, involved and committed. What a room it was. He hadn't known of its existence, but the headmaster seemed to know his building from attic to cellar. He also had an unexpected flair for a solemn occasion in a secret place.

Thaddeus asked Jean Hubert to attend. The Frenchman stood beside Grace, his expression serious. Ezekiel and Emily Bartleby were there, as was Mrs. Perry. Ezekiel had entrusted the bakery to Meridee, Ben, and Nick Bonfort, who became the instant envy of his peers, surrounded as he would be by bread, tarts, and éclairs.

The surprise was Walter Cornwall, who slipped in before Able closed the door. "Sir B's orders," was all he said as he stood against the door.

Headmaster Croker held up Smitty's roster, copied onto smaller sheets, but with the playful dolphins still cavorting over a most serious schedule. "This is Smitty's work and I applaud him for it. Smitty, hand these 'round."

When everyone had a roster, the headmaster went over the schedule. "All I ask is that you simply stand the watch," he said. "Others are watching, too, but we feel the need here, and we do have an excellent view of the hulks, one the others don't quite have." He rationed out a smile. "I think our long-ago monks, perhaps St. Brendan himself, saw the need for vigilance, not only from sin, but also from European adventuring."

As the headmaster looked at each student again, Able felt his heart swell. He knew his workhouse students' origins, challenges and turmoil. *No one wanted me*, he thought. *No one wanted you, either, but here we are, standing the watch for England.*

"I want you to walk behind St. Brendan's, along the sea wall that faces the harbor," Headmaster Croker explained. "Train your telescopes on the hulks every ten steps or so, and also the water." He seemed to study their expressions. "I see by your faces that you wonder why." He gestured to Jean Hubert. "People have a way of slipping off hulks. Monsieur Hubert has given his parole, so we need not worry about him."

"What a burden of honesty you bear, Jean," Able whispered to the Frenchman. His comment earned him a hard stare, followed by a wry expression that made Grace Croker put her hand to her mouth, her eyes merry.

"Please, sir, if I may: What are we looking for?" asked one of the younger lads.

"People who would find ways to ruin us," the headmaster said. "I can't be more specific. Watch for people or things going on that don't seem to fit."

"Thank'ee, sir."

"You are most welcome, Whitticombe." Headmaster Croker clapped his hands. "Very well, let us go to class, and tonight, let that watch commence."

It began quietly, as all good watches should begin, this one sweeter than most because Meridee and Mrs. Perry made sure the eight p.m. to midnight lads were well-fortified with grog mild enough for Able's careful wife, and bread and butter sandwiches the size and thickness of Spanish roof tiles.

Betsy made certain the midnight through four a.m. crew received the same treatment, then retired to bed. Ezekiel and Emily Bartleby left a note stating they were standing the four a.m. to eight a.m. watch, and placed it on top of a dozen of Meri's favorite rout cakes, the ones with lemon and sugar icing.

In the morning, Able checked the tablet with the date, time, and room for comments. He chuckled to see that the midnight to four a.m. watch had observed a couple "doing something fishy by the stone basin," with the added comment, "Don't tell Mrs. Six."

"If that's the worst thing they see, huzzah," he said as he initialed the page and turned to the next one.

And the next one and the next one. The week passed with nothing happening, which was precisely what Able wanted. He laughed one morning to read Walter Cornwall's pithy comment about that same amorous couple, in all likelihood. "I sent them on their way with threats," he wrote. "Mrs. Perry thought it was funny."

He shook his head over Mrs. Perry paired with the formidable constable from Landport Gate, wondering how that would work, but was wise enough not to ask Mrs. Perry. He had been the recipient of her fixed stare years earlier during his days in the fleet, and didn't relish her censure.

What did amuse him was the housekeeper's willingness to include Walter in breakfast, after coming off that morning watch. He became a regular, fitting in well with the lodgers because he never minded answering the boys' questions about his employment, or his own early years in a Cornish workhouse.

Meri pointed out to Able one morning as she was dressing that Betsy seemed not so shy around Walter anymore. "Mrs. Perry told me that yesterday morning Betsy was awake and served Mr. Bartleby and Walter sandwiches."

"What am I to infer from that?" Able asked. "Isn't she a little young to be anyone's interest? I know for a fact that her twin is just fourteen." He buttoned up the back of Meri's dress, putting cold fingers on her bare skin until she yelped.

"Mercy on us, Durable Six, does blood not circulate in your appendages?" she asked.

"You know it does. I still say she is too young for anyone's attentions," he replied, not meaning to raise his voice but thinking of young girls in workhouses who were preyed upon by house masters who should have known better. He closed his eyes, relieved when Meri covered them with her warmer hand.

"Shh, shh, no fears, love," she soothed. "Mrs. Perry and I have matters in hand." She moved her hand and kissed him. "Here is something Betsy told me yesterday. I've been trying to find a moment of privacy to pass it on to you."

"Such moments are hard to come by, aren't they?" he said, sorry he had raised his voice. "Should I worry?"

"Not at all." Meri sat him down and tied the neck cloth he had slung around his neck. "Sit still. You're worse than Ben trying to wriggle out of his nappie." She applied herself to his neck cloth. "She told me that when Jamie was being considered for St. Brendan's, he lied about his age to Headmaster Croker, who had told workhouse masters that the school wanted lads between eight and twelve, the better to train them. He said he was twelve. Betsy said they are now sixteen, not fourteen." She stepped back to survey the results. "My word, but you are a handsome man."

"Meri, there are days when you are certifiable," he countered. "Sixteen now? He was fourteen then and passed for twelve?" He thought a moment. "He did seem tall for twelve, I'll admit."

"She told me that in his last letter, Jamie said the matter preyed on his conscience."

He considered her comment, in light of Walter's interest. "Should I give Constable Cornwall an avuncular talk and tell him to mind his manners?"

"Let's see: you are twenty-seven now and Walter is a few years younger. I don't think so."

"I'm relieved," he said dryly. "Give me a theorem any day."

"You know, Able, we might someday be the parents of daughters," she told him. "Think about *that*."

He closed his eyes and groaned. "Meri, this parenting business is not for the faint of heart, is it?"

*I really should become better adept at divining what makes people do what they do*, Able thought during spare moments in the day, when he wasn't teaching, or coaching students in the dismantling and reassembly of a sextant.

With his older students, he balanced on a raft in the stone basin behind St. Brendan's, the better to simulate the difficulties of taking a reading to determine longitude, that bugaboo of maritime navigation until recent years. He knew what he was doing and could explain it in his sleep, which allowed him the luxury of considering what it was that attracted a male to a female. Or vice versa, although he doubted Betsy had made the first advance toward as prepossessing a fellow as a Portsmouth constable.

He was still considering the matter hours later when he sat with Meri, Grace and Jean, on their way to dinner at Sir B's in Grace's carriage. Betsy had been left in charge of Ben, stuffed to his gills and tugging at his eyelashes, ripe for bed.

While carrying on normal dialog with the other occupants of the carriage, he thought about Grace and Sir B. If the dinner grew boring, he knew he could entertain himself trying to figure that one out and still carry on as superficial a conversation as any dinner required. He had long ago learned that a discussion of the weather did not require a detailed analysis of wind velocity and temperature.

He had another aim, one that had occupied his mind since the sextant class. As the boys had practiced, Able had looked up at St. Brendan's to see Jean Hubert standing at the second floor window, sketchpad in hand. He was drawing something in the harbor, but what? *Any day now, I will become as suspicious as billy-be-damned,* he thought. *Soon I won't be fit for company.*

He resolved not to consider the matter, as they greeted Sir B in his dining room, a dignified room, but not a pretentious one, and not so large that they all felt a little silly, a small party of five – six if you count Gervaise – strung out awkwardly in the middle of twelve chairs. The table had been set companionably close to Sir B, who was already seated at the head.

It was the usual excellent meal, but one more in tune with the navy, beginning with common barley broth soup, served in any wardroom from the Arctic to the Antipodes. It was followed by a crisp rack of lamb and then coq au vin, possibly an odd juxtaposition, unless one considered that the early stages of any voyage meant there might be lambs baaing and chickens clucking in the hold, waiting to be eaten sooner rather than later in the officers mess. Able could have eaten more of the polenta, because it was cooked as he had first devoured it in a grog shop in Malta, fried crisp with cheese from Parma or Reggio sprinkled on top – crunchy, flavorful and something never found in a Scottish workhouse. He could happily eat polenta all day. The meal ended with Meri's favorite Voluptuous Little Pies, and fruit and nuts.

Halfway through the meal, Able noticed Gervaise staring intently at Jean Hubert, as if expecting something from him. *What have we here,* he thought. He noticed something else – Grace, her eyes soft, gazing at Sir B. *And what have we here? Meri is so right.*

# — Chapter Twenty-nine —

M ight as well play this out. Might as well test Mr. Pitt's earlier suspicions. Able knew Sir B had better sense than to dismiss the two ladies to a sitting room while the gentlemen talked. When the table was cleared and a new cloth laid down, Sir B directed Grace to pour the tea.

Now or never. "Sir B, John Mark wanted you to see his illustration, to a half-inch scale, of the scoring machine at the block pulley factory," Able said. He took John's careful drawings from his inside uniform coat pocket and spread them on the table. "Jean, have you seen these?"

"No, but they're certainly wonderful," the Frenchman said, giving them a cursory inspection. "Who is helping the lad? I know my art class hasn't begun to approach this level of sophistication."

"Simon Goodrich, or possibly Henry Maudslay," Able said, "when he has time to drop by. John Mark said Mr. Goodrich has asked him to illustrate all the machines. I think the factory is about to begin production."

While Sir B and the ladies contemplated the illustrations, drawn by a gifted student, Able looked at Jean Hubert, who had turned his attention to the loose skin around his fingernail. It would have been hard to imagine a man less concerned with strategically sensitive drawings.

*Jean, you ninny, Napoleon could use these illustrations to manufacture his own metal block pulleys,* Able thought. *Aren't you even slightly interested?*

He wasn't, to be sure. Able glanced at Gervaise, who usually stood behind Sir B's chair, ready to serve him in an instant. The valet had edged closer to Jean Hubert, but his eyes were on the drawings, his mouth open.

Silent, doing nothing to attract anyone's attention, Able watched as the valet moved slowly closer to the prisoner, who suddenly scooted his chair nearer to Able. That he was obviously trying to avoid Gervaise struck Able like a brick thrown into his brain. This was not a man seeking to connect with a fellow Frenchman. This was someone trying to get away.

*I can oblige you,* Able thought. He stood up and offered his closer chair to Jean, who accepted it with relief in his eyes and a nod of gratitude. This placed him next to Meri, who gave Able a questioning look. He shook his head slightly and she returned her attention to the drawings, her face a study in blandness.

Even closer to the drawings, Jean still showed no interest in them. All he had wanted to do was get away from Gervaise. *What in the world is going on?* Able asked himself. *Any idea, Euclid? Galileo? Sometimes you gentlemen are completely useless to me.*

Out of the corner of his eye, Able watched Gervaise return to his usual position behind Sir B. In one of his usual lightning-fast blinks, Able noticed one thing that seemed to play out as if in the slow movement of a bad dream. For the tiniest moment, stretched out in the odd way that his brain sometimes functioned, Able saw vast unease on the valet's face.

Able didn't have to wrack his brain even the slightest to remember William Pitt's breakfast observation in London that the disgusting Captain Ogilvie had palmed something off onto Gervaise during the ungodly business outside Trinity House. Able's face grew hot just thinking about the humiliating experience.

Time to end this evening. Time to go home and think. How good an actor was he? More to the point, how good was Meridee? Why not find out?

"Sir B, you'll have to excuse me, but my sweet wife is starting to nod off," he said, hoping he sounded urbane and totally doubting it. "What with starting this evening watch at St. Brendan's, we're all keeping unusual hours."

The quizzical expression on Gervaise's face was all the reward Able needed. The valet had no idea about the additional level of observation. Able thought he could make something of this.

"Gervaise, you look surprised," he said. "Aye, we've decided to have the Gunwharf Rats stand a harbor watch."

"Whatever for, sir?" the valet asked, then stepped back. "Beg pardon, Sir B," he said. "I am speaking out of turn."

Sir B waved his hand casually. "No matter, Gervaise. Able, explain it to him. Anything to defeat Boney, eh, Gervaise? I know how you émigres loathe and despise the man."

"We decided the boys could use the experience before watches get thrust upon them in the fleet," Able said, and watched Gervaise relax visibly, standing there behind his employer's chair. "No more than that."

"I hope you don't plan to do it too long," Sir B said with a chuckle. "You'll wear out the lads and they will wish themselves back in the workhouse."

"No, they won't, sir," Able contradicted quickly. "But never fear. Our own Smitty has created an admirable schedule that spreads out the duty so no one suffers." He glanced at Meri, blessed darling of his, who caught his eye and yawned precisely on cue.

Sir B couldn't help but notice. He patted Meri's cheek. "Go on home, you dears," he said. "It's late. It's just that I enjoy your company," he said simply.

"And we, yours," Meri said.

The captain kissed her hand. Able heard Grace Croker's quiet sigh. *My word but life is complicated in the ordinary world*, he thought.

"You'll have to tell me more about this watch," Sir B said as Gervaise wheeled him toward the entrance, his guests beside him.

"I'll be pleased to, sir," Able replied.

They made curious progress to the door, with Meri close to Able on one side and Jean Hubert crowding him on the other. Grace may have noticed Jean's eagerness to get away, but she said nothing. She confined herself to chatting with Sir B in that teasing, casual way of theirs, the sort of conversation that came from years of friendship. For a split second Able almost envied them. He had no idea if the few friends he had made in the Dumfries workhouse were even alive.

The bigger issue now was getting Jean out of the house without Gervaise coming close. Jean took care of it. He opened the front door before the butler even had a chance and darted out. "I'll alert the coachman," he said over his shoulder, and was gone.

"I would have done that," said the footman, sounding wounded.

"He does like to be of assistance," Meri told the servant. She gave him her smile that continued to captivate men of all ages, from little boys in the lower grades, to the husband standing beside her, his hand on her waist. "Sir B, let me know if you would like some rout cakes from Ezekiel Bartleby's bakery. He asked about you only yesterday."

*Oh, Meri, you're a wonder,* Able thought, as they left the house and moved down the front steps, talking about pastry. Meri waved goodbye to Sir B and blew him a kiss. Gervaise had no choice but to close the door.

Meri waited for him with Grace until Jean returned from the stable. "What was that?" she whispered.

"Later," he said. "I'm not done."

Smart woman. She nodded and stood with him the few minutes it took before the Croker carriage came around the corner and stopped in front of Sir B's row house. With a flourish – his expression settled now and cheerful – Jean helped Grace into the carriage and Meri next.

"How forgetful of me," Able said suddenly. "Go on without me. I left my umbrella inside."

"We can wait," Grace said. "It's rather a long walk."

Meri leaned close to Grace. "Sometimes Able likes a long walk to clear his mind. We'll go on."

"So true," he said with a rueful shake of his head. "I'll wander home soon."

Before the carriage pulled away from the curb, he bounded up the steps and opened the door without knocking. The hall was empty, but he called out for Sir B. Gervaise came to the door of the captain's bookroom, his expression neutral, the perfect valet.

"Gervaise, I forgot my umbrella. Would you please look for it? I might have left it in the sitting room."

*Do you doubt me?* Able thought, watching skepticism work its way quickly across the valet's face and vanish. "Just please look," he said in his sailing master voice, not loud, but commanding.

"Very well, sir." Gervaise started down the hall, taking one backward glance.

Able went into the bookroom and locked the door behind him. Sir B looked up from the desk, surprised. "What in the world, Able…" he began.

"Not now," Able said, equally commanding. "I need to talk to you and Gervaise cannot overhear us."

He had never spoken to his captain and mentor in that tone of voice, but it carried the day.

"Very well," Sir B said and closed the ledger. "Unlock the door or Gervaise will be even more suspicious than he already is. I'll fob him off."

Able did as he was asked. He heard Gervaise's footsteps and sat down in the chair by Sir B's desk, leaning back, his arms behind his head.

"Sir, I can't find your umbrella," Gervaise said most carefully.

"I'm too young to be this forgetful," Able replied. "Well, damn me. Now I have a long walk."

"I can summon a hackney with no trouble," the valet told him.

"So can Able," Sir B said. "I'm glad he's here, actually, because I have a small matter to discuss." He coughed into his hand. "I'm still hearing rumblings about the mysterious disappearance of Master Blake last year."

"Good God, don't tell me identifying parts of him are starting to show up at low tide," Able said, happy to play along. Blake's parts had long gone to a dubious reward.

"Nothing that drastic," Sir B said with a languid wave of his hand. "Gervaise, go upstairs and prepare my bed. I'll give you a halloo when I need your help."

"Very well, Sir B." He bowed and left the room. Able thought his back looked a little stiff, his shoulders higher than normal.

"I've offended him," Able said. "How suspicious will he be?"

Sir B waved his hand again. "No matter. I'll just shake my head over the whole business and blame it on a careless bastard who has no manners whatsoever, even though his wife tries so hard."

Able laughed and the captain joined him. Still laughing, Able locked the door and pulled his chair close to Sir B. "I won't take long, but you need to know what I saw tonight."

"Tell me." Sir B said, his casual air gone, his eyes steely.

"Am I right? I don't know," Able began. "Gervaise kept trying to move closer to Jean. He had such a look in his eyes! And when I pulled out John Mark's illustrations from the block pulley factory, I thought Gervaise was going to crane his neck right out of his shoulders."

"I didn't notice," the captain said.

"I watched Jean, too. He wasn't even slightly interested in the drawings." Able sat back. "What can you tell me about Gervaise?"

A long silence passed between them, captain and sailing apprentice again, sitting in a frigate wardroom, years apart in age, miles away in social station, galaxies separated in brain power. Their glances never wavered. Sir B finally leaned back, too, breaking the spell.

"What are you thinking, Able? Tell me the whole thing."

"I am thinking that if Gervaise isn't a spy, he's been alerted by someone to watch for one, and he thinks it's Jean Hubert."

"And?"

"Jean Hubert is either a greater actor than Edmund Keene, or he is precisely who he claims to be."

"Which is?"

"A prisoner, a bit indolent, apolitical, who wants to sit out this war without too much strain to himself," Able said. "And there is this – Gervaise seemed equally interested in the Rats standing the watch at St. Brendan's."

Sir B nodded slowly. "You're doing what Trinity House mandated."

"Precisely. We're adding another layer of protection." Able moved closer until his knees pressed against Sir B's chair. "Sir, were you aware that Captain Ogilvie handed Gervaise something during that…that humiliating altercation outside of Trinity House."

"No. Captain Ogilvie?" Sir B sighed and rubbed his eyes. He made a visible effort to collect himself and squared his thin shoulders. "Gervaise is the son of Henri Françoise and Madeleine Turenne of Toulouse. He was an estate manager to the Duc d'Orleans, who had extensive properties in that Languedoc region and elsewhere. When things went from bad to worse after the storming of the Bastille …what, fourteen years ago… Henri and Madeleine escaped to England with Gervaise, a boy of eight. They settled in Kent." He sighed again. "They had also managed some of my French property."

"*You* had French holdings?" Able interrupted.

"The less said about that the better," Sir B replied, in that sharp voice Able hadn't heard in years. "Had, had, mind you!" He chuckled, but Able heard no mirth. "I put Henri Turenne to work managing my Kent estates, and Gervaise came to work for me when…" Another sigh. Able knew this was hard for a proud man. "When I needed him."

More silence. Able heard footsteps in the hall again, quiet ones this time. He gestured to the door and shook his head. He took a pen and paper from the desk and wrote, *Perhaps we should keep an eye on Gervaise.* Eyes troubled, Sir B nodded. Able listened. The footsteps receded.

Something else needed to be said. Something else he had noticed, brought to his attention a few days ago by his wife. He doubted Sir B would appreciate this bit of impertinence.

"I noticed something else tonight at dinner," he said at last.

"What *now?*"

Able knew that tone of voice from years at sea with his mentor. Sir B was not a happy man. Able gave the matter his usual nano-second consideration, which included the fact that he had a signed contract at St. Brendan's that even Sir B couldn't touch, if what he was about to say irritated him enough to request his resignation.

"Sir, Gervaise wasn't the only person watching someone." How to say this? Able suddenly wished Meri were sitting beside him, her hand on his knee. "Sir, are you aware how Grace watches you?"

Sir B's hand went to his eyes again. He said nothing. Able plunged on.

"Meri remarked on that to me, how she seems to lighten up when you come into a room. I…I…watched her tonight. She does."

Sir B slammed his hand on the desk, making the inkwell bounce. "What am I supposed to do about that?" he shouted in his quarterdeck voice, one he hadn't used since the splinter cut off his leg at Aboukir Bay.

Able stood up. He unlocked the door. "That is for you to decide, sir."

He left the bookroom and stood in the hallway, distressed with himself. Tears came to his eyes, as he heard his beloved mentor weep. To go back in? To leave? Why had he poked about in what seemed to be a harder subject than he thought? And where was Meri when he needed her?

# — Chapter Thirty —

Hoping she wasn't wrong, Meri opened Sir B's front door. She held out her hand to Able who stood so indecisive in the foyer. He followed her from the house on Jasper Street where nothing felt well or right. Meri took her husband's arm, leaning close as they stood together on the top step of Sir B's house. Merciful darkness covered the bleak look that had shocked her when she opened the door.

He seemed surprised to see her, surprised that she would wait, since she had no idea how long he would be. "It's cold out here, Meri," he said as they started down the sidewalk. "See here, I thought you left with Grace and Jean. How long were you planning to wait for me?"

"Until you were done. I changed my mind about leaving."

He put his arm around her and they walked down the front steps. "It's a hard thing to tell a man that his trusted valet might not be who he thinks he is."

What could she say to that? He seemed to be in no hurry, and truth to tell, she had long ago begun to cherish every quiet moment with this man she adored.

"I hate war," he said finally. He didn't stop walking, but he turned slightly and looked back at Number 25 Jasper Street. "It nearly killed a good man." He managed a mirthless laugh. "It hasn't done me any harm. Thanks to death I was able to advance my career at a rapid pace."

"Don't, Able." She couldn't help herself.

"It's true." He chuckled again, but she heard the humor this time and relaxed a little. "I do have to give credit to the damnable Treaty of Amiens, without which I never would have met you. Meridee, keep loving me. I ask no more."

She stopped and grabbed him everywhere she could reach, holding him closer than a common streetwalker because she knew he needed her. He sighed and let her. When his breathing slowed, she let go. They continued arm in arm down the dark street that sloped toward the harbor.

He spoke in a normal tone of voice, all business. "Gervaise Turenne showed an altogether too great interest in John Mark's drawings tonight. I know you noticed how he tried to edge close to Jean Hubert."

"...and how Jean kept moving closer to you," she finished. "Are we to assume that Gervaise is a spy and he somehow thinks Jean Hubert is, too?"

"It might be a deeper game, Meri. Sir B said he would make some discreet inquiries through Trinity House to find out a little about our young émigré. As for Jean…well, we will continue to watch him."

She considered that. "There's more."

"You know me. I had the nerve to point out to my captain, mentor and superior that Grace Croker appears to take a serious interest in him." He stopped. "I made a hash of it. Left the man angry at me and in tears."

"She cares," Meridee said, with a shake of her head. "I wish I had good advice. One difficulty might be that they know each other too well."

"How can that be a deficit?" Able asked, and he seemed genuinely puzzled, which always surprised her, because he knew everything. Almost everything.

How to explain something to her amazing husband? "It's like this: after years and years of acquaintance, some people take old friends for granted." She wondered how he would take *this* additional information. "Married couples have been known to do that."

She nearly laughed out loud to see the shocked look on his face, at that bit of news. Her next instinct was to sniff back tears, because she knew he would never take her for granted. *How* she was sure, she couldn't have said, except that this living, breathing extraordinary human she had married wasn't constituted that way. Whether he knew it or not, the odd clicks, whirls and turns of his mind occasionally worked in her favor, too.

"You didn't know me at all," he said, sounding so mystified. "Would your mother have been horrified?"

"Hard to say. My brother-in-law was horrified, if you will recall," she said, knowing what would follow.

"Recall? Oh, Meri." He cleared his throat. "I can still see him waving around that chicken leg! 'I vow, if your sister did not need your help so much, I would send you packing, too, Meridee.' And so on."

He even had the inflection and tone right, and the chicken-leg waggle, which made her giggle. "Able, please never change," she said.

"I doubt I could," he replied, and she felt the weight of those words, too. "Seriously, Meri, what can we do for them?" He looked down at the sidewalk. "Sadly, if it happens, this marriage would be no meeting of robust participants. He is so frail. I wonder…well, you know what I wonder."

"Would they be able to satisfy each other in marital ways?" she asked gently, wondering where she found the courage for *that* commentary. One didn't speak of such things. "Would she weary of the attempt? Would he die too young? Would neither of them make the other happy, no matter how much money they have, or how good their intentions? It's a tangled web."

They walked in silence, arms around each other's waists now, Able certainly as confident as she was that such a dilemma would never be their challenge.

"He's missing a leg," she said. "It's not the end of the world."

"But they're both afraid to do anything or say anything to each other, because such matters aren't bandied about in typical discussions." He chuckled. "We're even having a hard time right now, and look at us – quite married and with a child."

"It will take something drastic, I think," Meridee predicted.

A hackney came by, probably in the command of a jehu on his way home after a hard day. Able stepped into the street and raised his hand. "As much as I love a good stroll with you, wife, discussing embarrassing matters, it's late and we're a long way from St. Brendan's," he said over his shoulder, then beckoned to her when the conveyance stopped. "Up you go."

"Where, please?" the man asked, rubbing the sleep from his eyes.

"Kindly take us to St. Brendan's on Saint's Way," Able said.

Meridee had no objection to the ride, enjoying the chance to relax in capable arms. Able was in good enough humor by the time the jehu informed his horse in a quiet voice that this was the place. He took Able's coin with a smile and tip of his hat, and they were again alone on the street.

"Let's walk along the sea wall. It's the tail end of the First Watch, which should be Nick Bonfort and Smitty tonight," he said, and offered his arm. "The sea wall is a little slippery, Mrs. Six."

"I'll hold on extra tight, Mr. Six," she told him.

He shook with silent amusement. "Do you ever laugh at your – my – preposterous last name?"

"Now and then, Durable," she joked, getting into the humor of the moment.

"I could petition to have it changed," he told her as they strolled along in no hurry, because they could see their home across the street.

"Never change our name," she said firmly. "I like it."

"So do I. Now. It took a while."

He helped her down the few steps to the narrow walkway between the stone basin and the small copse that opened onto the harbor. The night was clear and cold, because winter seemed in no hurry to leave the scene, even though it was late April.

"Where are they?" she whispered. "I can't see them."

"Stand here. We'll wait for them."

When her eyes accustomed themselves to the real darkness, she saw the outline of the hulks, filled with French prisoners. For most of her young life, she had been exhorted from pulpit and hearth to hate the French. All she felt right now was deep sympathy.

The sight reminded her of something else. She patted her husband's sleeve. "Able, last week, I came here one afternoon because I had left my extra towel by the stone basin. I looked up at St. Brendan's and I saw Jean standing at his classroom window, sketching. Why he would he do that?"

"It seems unlikely he would want a keepsake drawing of his miserable life there," Able said. "I'm within my rights to ask to examine his sketchpad."

"Not yet. Here they are!"

Meridee watched two dark figures materialize out of the gloom, Nick and Smitty, one short, the other tall. Before they advanced, Smitty called out in a gruff voice that lacked very little to be considered intimidating. "The password, please."

"I have no idea," Able said. "I doubt it is Sine, Cosine and Tangent."

The watchman became a boy again. "Master Six! We...well, I...thought a password would be a good idea. You know, perhaps detect a French accent."

"I applaud your good sense," Able said, and Meridee heard not a quaver in his voice. "Do you set a password at the beginning of the watch?"

They were close enough to see now. Nick flashed his charming smile, reminding Meridee, if she needed reminding, how young they were. "Aye, Master." Nick glanced at Smitty. "Should we tell them?"

The older boy nodded. "They're not the enemy, Nick. Go ahead, since you picked the password tonight."

"Spotted Dick, because I like Spotted Dick," Nick said.

"Mine would have been Polenta," Able replied, again in utter seriousness. "Have you seen anything out of the ordinary tonight?"

"Just you two," Nick replied, which made Meridee laugh softly. "It's usually cats and dogs and a drunk now and then. Maybe a couple up to mischief. Pardon me, Mam."

"Tedious work, isn't it?" Able commented.

"Aye, sir," Smitty replied. "But we might see something unusual, mightn't we? That's why we stand the watch."

"As you were, men, and good thinking."

The Gunwharf Rats walked past them, taking turn to train their telescope on the harbor, wait a moment, then walk on, taking turns.

It was a pleasant stroll past the stone basin, which Meridee looked at with more fondness than trepidation now. Only last Tuesday night she had swum across the basin, accompanied by her husband's applause. Able made certain that the watch stayed away for the little-enough time he was teaching her to swim. The Rats walked along the edge of land past the row of houses next to St. Brendan's, until swimming lessons ended.

"Do we need to keep practicing?" she asked. "I can swim now."

"I recommend it. In summer, I'll take you out alone in the yacht to the Isle of Wight. You can practice in deep water there," he informed her.

"I'll agree to anything, because it's hard enough getting a spare minute alone with you," she joked.

"You obviously have no plans to take me for granted."

"Heavens, no!"

Why she suddenly remembered an occurrence more than a month ago, Meridee couldn't have said. Perhaps the sky was this dark. Maybe the moon shone just the way it did now.

"Able, I need to tell you something I probably should have mentioned weeks back," she began, wondering if this was a silly notion.

He was still in a teasing mood. "Should I worry?"

When she remained silent, he looked closer at her. The moon was only half full. Able took hold of her chin and gently turned her face toward the faint light. "Your expression tells me yes."

She nodded. "Able, if I told you I saw blinking lights coming from one of the hulks, what would you think?"

# — Chapter Thirty-one —

"I would think we had better sit down," he said, his voice urgent. "Right here at the basin. Up you get."

He lifted her up to the lip of the stone basin, and sat beside her, their legs dangling. "What did you see? When was it?"

"If I were you, I could tell you exactly when it was, what time, and precisely, well, everything," she said with some vexation. "I wish I could."

"Don't ever envy me, Meri," he said seriously. "It's more curse than blessing. Tell me what you recall. That's enough. Just…take your time."

She took her time, lulled by the gentle way he stroked her arm. She watched the moon, sending her mind back three weeks, then four weeks. "I suppose I am remembering right now is because the moon was precisely as it is now, or close."

"That would make it on or about March 16. A Thursday," he said.

"How do you do that?"

He shrugged.

"Ben had some wind on his stomach that night," she said, after rolling her eyes at him and knowing he couldn't see them in the dark. Or maybe he could. She had no idea. "I didn't want him to wake you, so I walked across the hall with him into the empty bedchamber where Smitty and Jean Hubert are now lodged."

"Which overlooks the harbor."

"Yes. I saw flashes of light coming from one of the hulks."

"Do you know, can you recall, watching from port to starboard in the line, which one?"

"The first, I think."

"The *Captivity*. Go on. Do you remember the flash pattern?"

"I…I'm not certain," she told him. "I wish I could…."

"Do this: Think of everything about that time with Ben – what he smelled like, how you felt, anything. Relax your mind."

She closed her eyes and visualized out loud the totally unremarkable evening: She had eaten something with onions, and they did not agree with Ben Six, who cried and scrunched his legs close to his belly. *No more onions, baby, I promise,* she remembered saying to him as she walked across the hall.

"What else? What else? Relax. You walked around the room, consoling your son, apologizing to him. You looked out the window."

"I saw two flashes – little pinpoints – a pause, two more flashes, a pause, and then one. That was all."

"Two pause two pause one."

"Yes. What was it?"

"I don't know, except that it was likely the end of a message," Able said. "I wonder who it was intended for? That was a month ago." He shook his head. "On a Thursday. Did you stay at the window?"

"Yes. I rubbed Ben's back. He finally let go with a monumental explosion worthy of you, well my goodness, after *you* eat onions. No more onions for either of us!"

He laughed, got off the rim of the stone basin, and helped her down. "Other than *that*, Meridee Six, do you remember anything else?"

"No, sir! That was all Ben needed. He fell asleep in my arms and I returned him to his crib."

"Master Six."

Able grabbed Meridee and put her behind him as a caped figure came out of the gloom. "No closer," he said.

The figure held up both hands. "I didn't mean to startle you, Master Six. It's me, Walter Cornwall."

Behind Able, Meridee sighed with relief and leaned against his back. All the talk of spies and looming trouble had her nerves on edge. Someone should admonish the constable against startling honest folk. She reconsidered. He was probably doing his job, and seriously, how many honest folk could one expect to see so close to midnight on a Portsmouth dock?

He came closer, all cape and tall hat, his walk purposeful. He patted a cudgel in his hand.

"I'll admit you startled me, Walter. Is this part of your beat, too, even on nights when you're not scheduled for our Gunwharf Rat watch?"

Walter removed his hat, which eliminated some of the intimidation. Even with his hat off, the constable was still a man to be reckoned with, unless Meridee reminded herself of the times she had seen him eating hot bread in Mrs. Perry's kitchen while Betsy hovered by to refill his mug with cider. Or that time she had hurried home from an overlong visit with Grace Croker and found Walter patiently walking up and down with noisy Ben, who was demanding a meal.

Before she had thanked him and whisked her baby away to the solitude of her own room, Meridee had asked Walter where he acquired his skill with babies, since she knew he was a single man.

"I have a daughter," he told her. "Right now she is in the care of a draper's wife on my street. My wife is dead."

He had said nothing more, only quietly left. A glance at Betsy's expression had been Meridee's first inkling that something was happening in the Six kitchen that went beyond meal preparation and cajoling small lodgers to wash dishes and dry them. She hadn't mentioned the matter to Able, who had more on his prodigious mind than an acquaintance possibly turning into something sweeter.

"Walter, you must burn the candle at both ends," Able said, as the constable fell into step beside them.

"I sleep fast," he replied, which made Meridee chuckle. He gestured toward the harbor with his cudgel, a wicked-looking weapon that probably knocked heads and separated fights in Portsmouth's infamous grog shops and gaming hells. "Them ships. I don't trust'um, especially not after what happened to you, miss."

She shivered. Able tightened his arm about her. "Did you watch the hulks before we started our own Rat watch?"

"Aye, sir."

"See any flashing lights?"

"Now and then, but they seemed to be signaling 'tween ships, so I paid it no mind," he replied. "Should I have?"

"I don't know."

The constable patted his cudgel. "As for tonight, I was scaring off a couple up to no good, down in the trees once, so my attention was elsewhere. Sorry, mum, but that's the business here."

"A couple, eh?" Able said. "The Rats mentioned that once or twice. The same couple, do you think?"

"Able, really," Meridee murmured.

"Aye, really," he replied, with a touch of asperity. "How close did you get to them? Close enough for a look?"

*My goodness, Able,* she thought. *You're embarrassing me. You're no voyeur.*

"A man and a women, or two men? What do you remember?"

*I'm going to sink into the ground with mortification,* Meridee thought, aghast at her husband.

When she felt brave enough to look up, Able and Walter were regarding each other thoughtfully.

They had almost circled the stone basin. Meridee could see their house now. "Would…would you like to come inside, Constable Cornwall?" she asked, at a loss over this midnight social situation. There were times when Durable Six was too blunt. Maybe she needed a cudgel.

The constable laughed at that. "Aw, mum, it's too late for a visit." He looked into the distance. "Now that I think of it, there was something odd about the matter."

"Which was…"

"The couple. It was dark, of course – the moon was a bit like this one – but they looked older to me than the usual randy sprites I run into at the docks."

"How could you tell? You said there was only a moon like this one."

They stood on the curb facing their home. In sudden alarm, Meridee looked at the second story windows, and sighed with relief to see no lights of any kind. Everyone slept.

Walter Cornwall stood facing the other way, looking toward the harbor. As much as she could see his face, he seemed to be remembering, much as she had remembered only a short time ago, herself.

"They moved slow, like older people," Walter said, then shook his head. "That's all I remember." He was silent a moment. "Come to think of it, this happened twice. The second time, there was a third man. Or person. I'm beginning to wonder what I saw at all."

"Take your time. Was there a discernible pattern?"

The constable took his time, much as she had carefully considered the midnight she had walked up and down in the empty room crooning to a baby with a complaint.

"That month – well, last month – it was one night, then nothing, and then the next night," he said finally. "Aye, that was it."

"While you were scaring them off, did you think to look at the hulks?"

"No. Sorry, sir." Walter Cornwall was not slow. Meridee watched him nod slowly, his mind obviously engaged. "Were they waiting for a signal?"

"I wish I knew."

Walter walked them to their front steps. "When are you usually on duty at Landport Gate?" Able asked, his hand on the doorknob.

"Lately it's mornings to nightfall, six days a week," he said.

"So you do this walkabout on your free time, when you should be sleeping?" Able asked.

"Guilty as charged," Walter said. "I don't take my job lightly, sir, and besides, I care about the Gunwharf Rats and you gentry morts and coves."

"That's hardly me," Able replied, amused.

*Who else do you care about?* Meridee wanted to ask, but she had a good idea.

Able opened the door, ready to usher Meridee inside. "Oh, no," she said. "I want to hear this."

Her husband closed the door. "You probably should. Walter, if I were to talk to Headmaster Croker and Sir B, and we chatted with your magistrate at Landport and he approved, would you object to focusing all your attention here for now? You know, not just that Morning Watch you share with the Bartlebys and Mrs. Perry?"

Meridee could see the humor in the constable's eyes. "I'm reet fond of Mrs. Perry. I'd miss her in that Morning Watch."

They all laughed quietly, hopeful the ever-watchful housekeeper wasn't standing somewhere in the hall.

"In particular, would you watch that copse all night next Tuesday and Thursday? We have a waning moon and I have a theory."

# — Chapter Thirty-two —

Some theory. Able knew it was a sieve he was trying to fill with seawater, a drop out for each drop in. Instead of coming to bed, he stayed downstairs in the sitting room and thought, never an easy process, because there was always so much to think about. He sometimes wished it were possible to get the geniuses who traipsed so blithely through his mind into a big argument and take their quarrel elsewhere, leaving him alone.

From Newton to Copernicus, everyone always wanted something. Perhaps when Ben was a toddler in leading strings and confident that yes, he did rule the house, Able would have developed the patience attributed to Job, since he had to placate the sometimes-childish minds in his head.

"Gentlemen, unless you have a solution for me, let me be," he said finally, after looking around to assure himself that Meri was asleep upstairs, and the formidable Mrs. Perry ditto.

What he hadn't been prepared for was the super-silent opening of the front door. Just as quietly he rose from his chair and walked into the hall. To his amazement, he confronted Jean Hubert, shoes in hand.

Neither man said a word. *I will stare you down*, Able thought.

Jean looked away finally, a muscle working in his cheek, his eyes dark with disappointment.

"You have broken your parole," Able said, feeling no triumph, no disgust, only sorrow, because he liked the affable Frenchman. "I must return you to the prison hulk. Jean Hubert, why?"

Jean said not a word. Slowly he sank to his knees and pressed his forehead against the rug. "Please, no," he said in a voice far removed from his usual cheerful one. "I will die there. You don't know."

This was no time to even think of leniency, but as he watched Jean prostrate himself on the floor, Able wavered. He knew that no matter what excuse the man offered, he dared never truly trust Jean Hubert again. How could he? Why should he? He also knew this humiliating scene was another of the millions of bits of information to replay over and over in his head, one more messy development to further cloud his decidedly odd path through life. He couldn't explain it to anyone, maybe not even Meri. Certainly not to this man.

"Why did you leave my house? Give me the truth, if it is in you," he said finally and sat down again. "And for God's sake, get off the floor. I am no Turkish potentate. Sit in Meri's chair."

Jean did as ordered, sagging into the other wingback chair pulled close to his own, her mending in a basket between them. "It's not the first time," he said, then rested his head in his hands.

Able sniffed the air between them, smelling tobacco and grog. He sniffed again, breathing in the faint odor of newsprint. He also noticed that the Frenchman wore the clothes he had been found nearly drowning in, the shirt and trousers supposedly given to him by the wife of Captain Faulke, so their daughter would not see him in prison garb. Able wondered if that story was true. He wondered about everything now.

"You've been in a grog shop," he accused. "Meeting someone we might like to know about?"

"No."

"That's it? No?"

"Do you wish me to invent someone, perhaps a spy, possibly that servant of Sir B's, the one who gives me the chills? You want a story?" he said, his voice rising. To Able's ears, Jean Hubert sounded exasperated and weary.

"Stop it. Mostly I don't want you to wake up anyone. What were you doing?"

"You won't believe me," Jean said, with more than a touch of petulance.

"Probably not, but do enlighten me, Lieutenant Hubert."

"Have you ever been a prisoner?"

"Aye, in one of your prisons. What a horrible place, but I learned French."

"No one ever dangled a parole in front of you?"

"*Me?* Certainly not. A bastard and not even a sailing master then? I'm no gentleman officer. I escaped when I could, down a sewer drain and into the ocean." Able considered the matter. "If you have been coming and going, why do you keep coming back here?"

"Because I gave my parole and I meant it," Jean said. He held up his hand and chopped down suddenly. "I did! I am an officer and a gentleman." He leaned forward. "Here's what else I am: I am a man who liked to leave a house, walk down a street, and into a grog shop, where I order ale, even though nothing on this damp island approximates the wine shops I know in La Havre and Cherbourg. I sit in the back and watch not particularly sober men play darts, which makes me laugh. I read a newspaper and then I walk back here."

"That's all?"

Jean spread his hands in that Gallic way. "That's all. I do it because I'm free for an evening. I'm not begging anyone's permission to go here or there, and no one tells me what to do or denies me. So simple. I hate this life."

"In our defense, we treat you well at St. Brendan's," Able said. "And how is it that Smitty doesn't hear you leave? I had thought…"

"Able, as fierce as he looks, he's a child," Jean reminded him. "He sleeps soundly and I am never gone long."

Able sat back. *You need this man*, a genius in his brain told him. Well, hell, it was Rene Descartes, another Frenchman. And wouldn't you know it, here was another Frog, handsome, well-dressed and looking slightly bewildered. *Mon Dieu*, it was poor, newly arrived Antoine-Laurent Lavoisier, his head atop his neck again, the brilliant chemist who ran afoul of the Reign of Terror. Oh, and this tears it! Blaise Pascale, you too? And there he was, clamoring and speaking loud French with the other two, all the while waving about his Treatise of the Arithmetical Triangle, so Lavoisier had to duck. *Damn you, Blaise, but I love that treatise*, Able thought with dismay. He closed his eyes and surrendered to the Frenchmen in his brain.

"Jean, I can't trust you now," he said quietly, once his inter-cranial Frenchmen bowed and left the stage, triumphant and probably heading toward champagne. "I need you here in the school. If…if you want to leave for a drink, just…" He looked away in frustration.

"I won't do it again."

Able nodded and rested his chin on his hand, staring into the distance. Jean rose and went to the door. Able stopped him.

"Tell me one thing," he insisted. "I don't know if it will be the truth, but I have to try."

There was no overlooking the unease on Jean's face. He nodded.

"If there comes a time when you have information you know I need, would you tell me?"

Silence, and then a slight nod from Lieutenant Hubert. He left the room. Able didn't even hear him on the stairs. God, but the man was silent. In his own ill humor, he wondered if Jean had learned to pad about so quietly to escape from his liaisons with other men's wives. He was, after all, French, with his own reputation. Or maybe he was merely cautious. War can do that to a person.

Able slept badly the rest of the night, tossing and turning until Meri actually growled at him, which made him laugh and hold her close until they found something to do that relieved part of his distress. He was tired in the morning, but at least consoled. He knew he would never tell Meri what had happened in the sitting room when he was trying to think.

The other matter called for an immediate convocation of all the Gunwharf Rats, and so he told Headmaster Croker. "Sir B, as well?" he asked.

"Yes, please, but no Gervaise. Send Smitty for Walter Cornwall, too. They can pick up Sir B. And not Jean Hubert this time," Able told him. "He is to remain in his classroom." *I cannot trust him*, he thought, *but I daren't tell the headmaster*.

The headmaster gave him a quizzical look, but said nothing. "A summons in one hour?" was all he asked. "No Frenchmen."

"Aye, sir. That's how it is. I'll ask Meri if she can convince the Bartlebys and Mrs. Perry to join us, while she stays in the bakery."

They met in the cellar, crowded together, everyone intent and alert. Speaking as quickly as he could, Able told them his suspicions about the hulks and advanced his puny theory.

"This may be folly on my part, but I'll take the risk. Constable Cornwall has run across a couple in that little copse by the stone basin, waiting for something or someone.

He and some of you rats commented that it must be an amorous tryst. I'm not convinced. There may have been another man there, too. We are not certain."

He had everyone's attention, but the doubts circled in his brain like sharks eyeing a starving man on a life raft. He took a deep breath. "These people, whoever they are, seem to be waiting for some sort of person or sign, on or about the middle of each of the past two months. I wish I could tell you more, but we must be vigilant next Tuesday and Thursday nights in particular."

It was vague; he knew it was vague; he knew he could do nothing about the vagueness. "That's all." He gestured to Sir B. "Sir, were you able to make arrangements for Constable Cornwall's service?"

"Done and done," Sir B said cheerfully. "Headmaster Croker, may he have suitable lodging here at St. Brendan's?"

"It can easily be arranged. Thank you, Constable," the headmaster said.

As he listened and chafed, the last piece slid into place in Able's mind. How strange he hadn't considered it sooner. He raised his hand like a schoolboy. "Headmaster?"

"Master Six?"

"Our little Pierre was part of an escape. We know that. He has told us with no hesitation that his fellow escapee in the water kegs was a gunner named Remillard, but that Remillard got away. Left Pierre alone, in fact."

He took a deep breath because he still didn't like to think about Meri's brush with death on the wharf where the water kegs were stored, and the murder — what else could he call it? — of two more would-be escapees.

"We know there was a failed escape attempt in the water kegs. I know the constables and Royal Marines have been watching carefully and seen nothing else. We Rats alone witnessed Jean Hubert's escape." Another deep breath. "I suspect that Jean's escape was entirely spontaneous and had nothing to do with the others." *Pray God I am right*, he thought. "I think there will be another attempt before next week, perhaps on Tuesday or Thursday. Something is being planned right here under our noses. We daren't overlook the fact that the man who came with Pierre was a gunner, used to working with explosives."

Able let that sink in, hoping at least some of it was true. He, Master Durable Six, who knew everything, didn't know what was going to happen.

"Preserve your silence on this, Rats," he said quietly. "As you were. Return to class."

# — Chapter Thirty-three —

Sir B remained in the cellar with Walter Cornwall, his expression grim. Able felt discomfort settle on him like a soggy blanket as he remembered last night's unhappy parting from the man he valued and revered above all others. *I have to clear the air,* he told himself, *but how? As much as I value you, Walter Cornwall, please leave.*

Possibly Able wasn't the only penitent seeking redemption. He had witnessed Captain St. Anthony heaping coals of indignation on other offenders in the fleet. Which was it this time? Did the captain want to apologize as much as Able did, or was he planning to push back harder?

Sir B cleared his throat. "Walter, will you help our headmaster up the stairs? He may argue that he is strong enough, but I would differ, eh, Thaddeus?"

"Damn you, Belvedere," the headmaster said with perfect equanimity, which made the constable stare from one man to the other. "No fears, Walter. I know this rascal very well." His expression become more philosophical. "As it happens, confound him, Sir B is right. I could use an arm to lean on. Besides that, I need to show you to your room here at St. Brendan's. We're a bit Spartan, but the mattresses give in all the right places."

"Aye, Headmaster. And you, Sir B?" Walter asked. "Should I return for you?"

"I will be fine." Sir B. gave a languid wave of his hand that took in Able, the damp stones and the beams overhead. "Able will see to me. If he needs help, he can collar a student."

"Sir B, thank'ee for your confidence in me," Walter said, "and the increase in pay. I didn't expect that."

"Take it from me, lad: We often don't expect what we sometimes deserve."

*That cuts in many directions,* Able thought, as he tried not to wince. Better stand here and take the coming rebuke like a man. God knows he had endured enough of those in his life. At least Meri loved him.

The cellar door closed behind the headmaster and the constable as they made their way slowly up the narrow stairs. Able sat beside his mentor - hopefully still his friend - and waited for him to speak.

He didn't wait long. Sir B, a dignified man who seldom touched others, grasped Able's arm. "Look me in the eyes, Able," he commanded. "I'm not upset with you. Well, not now," he said. "I would ask you the same question that drove you out of my house, but in a kinder tone, because your question has merit: 'What am I supposed to do about it?'"

"Talk to Grace, tell her you've finally realized that you love her, and ask her to marry you," Able said quickly. "Talk to her."

He braced himself, but Captain St. Anthony said nothing. Wordless, Sir B pulled back the elegant woven blanket of Turkish design that covered him and set it on the cellar's dirt floor. He looked down at himself. "You see before you two legs. One is quite fine and works well. The other one is gone far above mid-thigh. Now and then it hurts billy-be-damned awful, even the part that isn't there anymore. Your wife, I am certain, has told you about the time she helped me with that pain. What a woman she is, Able."

"I know," Able replied, finding his voice.

"If I were to remove my trousers, well, if I even could by myself – it isn't easy without Gervaise to assist – you would see a real mess of a scar, all puckered and wrinkled."

"I've seen amputations, sir."

"You've even performed a few, because your blinding knowledge was needed at critical times and you had no choice," Sir B said. "Ugly, aren't they?"

"Aye, sir. They are."

"Would you want Meridee to see you helpless and with such a scar?" Sir B asked, his voice toneless. He looked away and swallowed. "Would you want her to struggle to figure out how to make love to you, to decide which position works best? Would you? *Would you?*"

For once, Able's brain was completely silent, as if his busybody celestial mentors were hanging on his every word. They offered no advice for a change, and no one argued. The novelty of a silent brain beguiled Able almost more than the anguish of Sir B's question.

"It's a simple question," Sir B said, the relentless tone back in his voice. "Would you want her to stare in disgust or horror at your manly organ and the grotesque fact that it is now longer than one of your legs? No longer do you have proper proportion. You can't even stand up without help. You're a freak show worthy of Astley's Royal Amphitheatre. Would Meridee recoil in disgust and demand separate bedrooms?"

Able sat back and considered the question. This was no time for platitudes. He understood the society he currently inhabited, a more genteel one where people never discussed what they were discussing right now. He thought about Meri and her happy appreciation of his manly organ, and couldn't help smiling.

"How dare you smile."

"It's easy enough," Able said, deeply aware of his mentor's pain. Just a light touch here, or a humorous one? How about a little of both? "I've never seen your manly organ. What do *you* think? Mine is reasonably impressive." He couldn't help smiling again. "Meri, no expert, told me early in our marriage that it compares favorably to the bare naked Greek statues in one of her father's books. How about yours?"

Obviously Sir B hadn't expected a breezy comment. "Well, I..." He reached for the blanket and covered his legs. "Damn you, Able, is it not possible to have a serious conversation?"

"This *is* a serious conversation, Sir B. Pay attention to me." Good Lord, he had never spoken like this to his captain. "If my right leg, like yours, were torn off tomorrow, Meri would take care of me however I needed her help. She would cry, but she would adjust. She would let me heal, and then she would go right back to loving me. Of this I am certain."

"How can you possibly know that?" Sir B burst out.

"She loves me," Able said simply. "If something like that happened to *her*, I would do precisely the same thing, because we are lovers. I can't spell it out any plainer, Sir B."

"I suppose you cannot," the captain said reluctantly. "But I lack a leg!"

It was Able's turn to put his hand on his captain's arm. He gave it a little shake. "I'll tell you what you lack, Sir B. You lack courage."

There wasn't anything more to say. The men both sat back and looked at each other. Able watched a single tear roll down Captain Sir Belvedere St. Anthony's cheek. It was followed by another one, and another. Able did the only thing he knew to do. He took out his handkerchief and calmly wiped his captain's face. He kissed Sir B on the forehead, then went to the door.

"In fifteen minutes, I'll send down two of my students to help you up the stairs," he said. "Is your carriage out front?"

The captain nodded, unable to speak.

"They'll help you in, and Gervaise will take care of you when you're back in Jasper Street."

"And if I am not brave enough, Able?" Sir B said, his voice ragged with emotion.

"You will probably die, sir. That is the plain and simple of it. Plants need sunlight and water. Humans need love." He said it as kindly as he could; he knew he was right.

"What a thing to say," worked itself into his brain and made itself at home that afternoon. He decided he was a far better actor than he knew. As he taught with his usual panache, and led the afternoon's all-purpose class in climbing up and down the ratlines on the rigging and mast set up beside the stone basin, he heard his calm voice and his humor as if from a distance, even though his brain whirled.

High on the rigging himself, he saw faithful Smitty escorting John Mark and little Pierre from the inlet by the water hoys. He couldn't see Building Twelve, located as it was behind an identical brick structure that was an office building of some sort, considering all the ink-stained clerks and men with leather cases who regularly came and went. He knew what was going on in Twelve because of John's eagerness to describe each moving part of the block pulley factory, until Nick took him aside one night before bed. As Meri and Able tried not to howl with laughter, Nick informed his fellow Gunwharf Rat that not everyone was as excited about block pulleys as he was.

The memory of that carefully worded caution — for an eleven-year-old — still made him smile. If Nick did not find a place in the maritime world, the diplomatists at Foreign Office would welcome him.

His heart torn in so many ways at the moment, Able watched the two boys stop at Bartleby's Bakery and come out with a bag of some promised pastry that Meri had commissioned, or that Ezekiel and now Emily too had decided the Rats needed.

The smile left his face as he watched Jean Hubert leave St. Brendan's, cross the street and enter his own house, head down and melancholy about something, probably chafing that he had promised not to leave the house late at night. How sad that someone thought of the Six household as a prison, when it was the kindest, sweetest place in all England.

He thought of his own confinement for a year in a French prison, one with no parole and food so dreadful that the mere thought of eating was almost as unnerving as the food itself. In no way did it compare with Jean's treatment in the Six household except in one way: he was not free to leave, and neither was Jean Hubert. Stone walls or mere pledges given – who could say which was more irksome?

Meri knew he was agitated about something, but she carried on that evening with her usually calm competence, seeing that Smitty, Nick, John, and little shadow Pierre were busy with school work brought home, or reading, or in Pierre's case, sitting quietly and listening. His English was still rudimentary, but improving.

When Ben was fed and slumbering, the lodgers tucked in, and the last kitchen duties either finished or assigned for the morrow, he hurried Meri upstairs and babbled out what he had said to Sir B. She took it calmly, her eyes filled with sympathy for him, of all people, when it was Sir B who needed the help.

"You were plain spoken," she said after she returned from the washroom and put on her nightgown.

"Was I cruel?" he asked in anguish. "Was this something I should not have said? He looked positively stricken."

"Lie down, Able," Meri said, and patted the space beside her.

Muscles taut, tense and uncertain as never before, he did as she said. She held him close, humming, much as he had watched her croon to Ben when he was fretful. *I'm not an infant*, he wanted to tell her, but he couldn't, because he felt himself relax. His eyes grew heavy. She smelled sweetly of lavender, too.

"You said what needed to be said, my love," Meri told him as his eyes closed. "I can't imagine a harder conversation, but you did it."

She was rubbing his temples now and he could have groaned with pleasure. "Was I right, Meri?" he asked, eyes still closed.

"Completely. If you were wounded as grievously as Sir B, I would love you just as truly. Silly! Don't you know that? Well, of course you do, because you told Sir B as much."

He opened his eyes and regarded her. "What will you say if Grace Croker asks you?"

"I already did, dearest," she told him. "We both cried."

She moved closer and he opened his arms to pull her against his chest. "Oh, better. A tense and unhappy Able Six is not much of a cuddly husband, is he?"

He couldn't help laughing. "You're speaking to me as if I were a four-year-old," he protested, but not strenuously, because her touch and serenity had mellowed him. Her hand massaging his thigh didn't hurt, either.

"Here's the way I see it, Able," she said twenty minutes later, all business once more, after she had found her nightgown and before the cacophony in his brain resumed the usual chatter. "We have given both of them unwanted but necessary advice: Two proud people in love with each other, facing daunting challenges."

"Are you describing them or us?" he asked, eyes closed.

"That's an interesting comment. How did we overcome our trepidation?"

He thought about it for his usual brief second. "Simple. We talked to each other."

# — Chapter Thirty-four —

Nothing happened the following Tuesday, absolutely nothing. Able wondered if this was what it felt like to present a startling, controversial scientific paper to the Royal Society and have the fellows of that august organization hoot and whistle.

Thursday was different. In fact, everything changed on Thursday.

"Walter, I'm going to watch the copse with you tonight," he told the constable, who had become a willing dinner guest in the Six household. They were standing on the front steps, Able with his hands behind his back, and Walter calmly finishing the last of his cheroot. "You know that is a bad habit," Able said.

For all his noticeable stature and intimidating demeanor, Walter was a mild fellow. He looked down at Able, who was not short, either. "Master Six, would it comfort you to know you are not the first person in this household to tell me that?"

*Who? Mrs. Perry?* Able nearly blurted out, then he heard Meri's voice in his head, far more welcome than his assortment of polymaths: *Able, Betsy asked me so sweetly if Constable Cornwall could eat here occasionally.*

"Pay attention to Betsy," he said with a smile, relishing the blushing confusion of a man who probably hadn't blushed in years, if ever.

The constable's professional demeanor returned almost immediately, then to Able's surprise, disappeared, replaced by a shy smile that turned his lived-in face surprisingly sweet.

"Aye, sir." Walter hesitated, and Able waited for whatever additional surprise this ordinarily serious fellow was about the spring on him. "Master Six, I know Betsy MacGregor gets half days on Sundays."

"Aye, she does," Able agreed, feeling suddenly parental. "She's scrupulous about telling us her plans, I might add. She lets us know where she is going, and when she'll be back."

"Good. Portsmouth's not a place to roam, is it?"

"It's different for men, isn't it? I roamed to a few grogshops and gambling hells in my day," Able replied.

"You, sir?" Walter stared at him in amazement.

"Constable, I'm only twenty-seven and I haven't always been married," Able protested, feeling like old Ancient of Days, himself. Come to think of it, he had noticed one or two gray hairs just this morning. They were easy to pluck, without a word to Meri.

"Beg pardon, sir," Walter said quickly. "I didn't mean…." He stopped himself, perhaps wisely seeing the value in not digging a deeper hole. "Sir, this Sunday, may I escort Betsy to the draper's house, where my daughter Jennie lives? I'd like the two of them to meet." His professionalism was replaced by a look of such a serious nature that Able wondered if the constable thought Betsy must petition Master Six for permission.

*So this formidable man thinks he needs my permission?* Able asked himself. *I'll let him keep thinking that.* "Aye, you may, Walter. How old is Jennie?"

"Almost three, sir, and a bright child she is." A small sigh and the way he squared his shoulders told Able everything about tough times in the Cornwall household that meant someone else had to tend his daughter. "I've told Betsy about her."

"Then they had probably better meet, hadn't they?" Able said, wondering how he would feel when Ben worked up the courage some distant day to make such a request.

They stayed on the steps as the sun went down, discussing the news of the docks and another attempt at an escape by water kegs foiled successfully, or so the captain of marines had informed Sir B.

"I hear the prisoner set up a fearful racket, screaming and protesting and digging in his heels. He tried to leap into the water," Walter said. "He's in the brig now, but will be returned to Captain Faulke on the *Captivity* in the morning."

"Jean Hubert's hulk," Able said. "Only one prisoner? I thought that two was the pattern."

"That was the report," Walter replied, with a shake of his head. He chuckled. "Four or five prisoners could have escaped, sir, what with all the racket and commotion focused on that one noisy Frog! Empty kegs knocked over and rolling around, noise, and confusion. Some of the kegs even ended up bobbing about in the water."

*And that's what happened,* Able thought suddenly. How simple would it be, in such confusion, to slide out of one of those kegs rolling about, swim under the dock and wait until everyone left? There could be half a dozen prisoners on the loose. Or one.

Able motioned Walter closer and whispered his suspicions. The constable listened, his face perfectly neutral, just the kind of expression Able needed to see.

"Do you think this unknown escapee or escapees has met up with the others?" Walter asked.

"Hard to tell. I wonder… could that older couple in the copse be waiting for him or them?"

They were both silent, considering the possibilities. Walter spoke first. "The old couple in the copse – I have seen them on those evenings after that time when the moon is in the proper position. You know, when Mrs. Six saw the flashes of light, and when the Rats noticed them, too."

"I wonder… are they waiting for someone else from the hulks to show up, as part of whatever it is they are planning here?" Able asked, speaking his thoughts out loud, happy to share them with a constable willing to consider something hypothetical, rare enough in any organization, or so Able had noted through the years.

Walter built on the thought, his eyes filled with the same enthusiasm that Able recognized in himself. "They wait, and when no one arrives, they leave. I have to wonder who they are waiting for, and how many times the plans have been scotched. Or have prospered."

They looked at each other and nodded at the same time. "I'm going to be closer to the copse tonight," Walter said. "It will be dark in two hours."

"I'm coming with you," Able added. "And let me suggest this: If we do find the escapee that may or may not exist" – they both grinned – "let's just watch. One of us can follow them, and we will watch the hulks for a signal."

"How will we interpret the signal?"

"My conversational French is excellent, but I do not know about signaling," Able admitted. "If I had a few minutes with a French signaling manual…" He shook his head. "But I don't, and proper signals go fast."

"We don't need that, Master Six," Walter said. He pointed up to the second floor. "We have Jean Hubert, don't we? He captained a ship. He must know French signaling. He gave us his parole, didn't he?"

*God help us*, Able thought, as the bottom dropped out of his stomach. *I can't trust him.*

The sick feeling deepened as Able knew he had not done his duty when he caught Jean breaking his parole. He was now complicit and subject to navy discipline. He felt the sweat break out on his forehead and he felt his dinner rising in his throat.

"Master Six, are you well?" Walter asked, his expression anxious.

Able shook his head. He leaned over the iron railing that defined the modest porch and vomited.

"Master Able! I'll get Mrs. Six."

*No, not her*, he wanted to say, but he was too busy throwing up on the bushes that were just starting their spring bloom. He waved Walter away, but the constable was already inside the house and calling for Mrs. Six.

By the time Meri came running, her eyes full of alarm, Able sat with his knees up and his forehead resting against them. If a sea monster had suddenly risen from the harbor and swallowed him, he would have considered it a great kindness. How could he face the dearest person in his life and tell her he had committed treason? A man didn't ignore the breaking of parole.

And his damnable brain took over, scrolling back to an incident in this very harbor. He was not yet a sailing master. Their hold was full, the ballast carefully arranged, everything trim and ready as they waited for the wind and tide. They were stopped the next morning by the melancholy sight of a man hanging from the yardarm of a small craft. The naked corpse bobbed and swayed with the current. The body was striped front and back with lashes from a cat o'nine. Around its neck hung the sign, *This wretch gave comfort to the enemy.*

Around the harbor it went, bobbing and dancing, condemned forever by his mates and his country. Able's captain, a harder man than most, had assembled everyone on deck to witness. Captain Dales had leaned over the railing of the poop deck and stared at them. "So shall ye end your life if you smooth the way for a Frenchman!" Able had nightmares for weeks.

He had another one now, a worse one where *he* was bobbing and dancing on the end of the rope, with Meri and Ben forced to share the same fate. "Oh God no," he muttered.

"Able, please," his wife said, kneeling by him. "What is the matter? Shall I send Betsy for a surgeon?"

He shook his head, beyond words grateful to see her alive, considering how vivid his vision or whatever one called a nightmare from which there was no awakening. He spoke with great effort. "Walter, help me inside. I have something to tell you both, and it can't wait."

# — Chapter Thirty-five —

"Meri, I don't know what to do."

"Not know what to do? Able, what is the matter?" she asked. She and Walter helped her husband into the kitchen, where he sat down with a plop and covered his face with his hands.

"Able, what in the world..."

She had left Ben in his high chair, and there he sat, waving about pudgy arms and demanding more food. Betsy hurried from the pantry, ready to take over and concentrate on the little tyrant who ruled the Six household, no matter what. "Thank you, dear."

"No mind at all, mam," Betsy said calmly. "Ben, you are going to gut-founder some day and won't you be surprised."

Able looked up, the bleakness still there, but also the admiring glance of a father. "Better listen to Betsy MacGregor, son," he said, then leaned back, his expression now that peculiar blankness Meridee remembered from last year, when everything become too much for a relentless mind that never stopped spinning.

*This is different*, she thought, as she steeled herself for whatever troubled him. *This has the look of ruin about it.*

"The Rats are reading and finishing their ciphers in the dining room," she said, striving for serenity. "Go into the sitting room with Walter. Mrs. Perry will look out for the boys."

"Where is Jean?" Able asked, as he rose.

"In his room, I believe."

"Are you certain?"

*Is that it?* she asked herself, and felt the beginning of fear. "He went upstairs, so that is my surmise."

Mrs. Perry took one look at her and asked no questions when she told the woman to see to the Gunwharf Rats. The big woman with the bigger heart took her hand and held it close.

Meridee rested her head on Mrs. Perry's bosom. "I don't know what the problem is," she said.

"You are not alone here," Mrs. Perry said. She squeezed Meridee's hand and gave her a little push toward the door. The little push turned into a friendly pat on her shoulder. "Never think otherwise."

Able looked no better. She closed the door to the sitting room quietly, but she startled him anyway. She sat beside her husband, her heart breaking when he moved away from her. "None of that, Able," she said firmly, and reached for his hand. "Tell us what has happened."

A whole series of events poured out of him, from Jean's disappearance and return that late night, to the unknown couple in the copse, to the potential escape, and ending with, "I was duty-bound to surrender Jean immediately to the captain of the marine guard when he broke his parole. I did not. If I ask Jean now…if I demand that he come with us and tell us what those signals mean – if there are signals – can I trust him? How badly have I compromised any chance of success in determining what is going on and how soon will it happen?"

Meridee raised Able's hand to her lips and kissed it. The act brought tears to his eyes. Matter-of-fact, she took a handkerchief from her sleeve and wiped his eyes. She turned to Walter, who had sat silent through the entire, agonized narrative, his gaze inscrutable. She knew she was looking at a man of the law. Better ask him.

"What do you think, Walter?" she asked, looking for kindness in a face she knew to be stern and duty-bound, as well. What she saw made her nearly sigh with relief.

"I think we don't know enough to worry either way," Walter said, in his deliberate manner. He settled back in his chair, which somehow gave Able permission to do the same. "Look at it this way, sir: If you had done your duty and he had been returned to the hulk, there would be no opportunity now to, uh, press him a bit, would there?"

"I suppose not," Able said, sounding more normal, to Meridee's relief.

He seemed to make up his mind, returning to the decisive man she knew. "I have suspected there is more to Jean Hubert's story than he has told us." He made a self-deprecating gesture. "I cannot really tell you how I know that, but I do. Let us find out whether this will help us or hinder us, shall we?"

He released her hand and stood up. "I'll bring him downstairs, tell him everything we know, and assure him we will return him to the *Captivity* if he does not help us." He looked at Walter. "Let us take him to the copse, if he chooses to cooperate."

"And if he doesn't?" Walter asked.

"He goes back to the hulk."

Able left the room. Meridee looked at her hands in her lap, wishing they did not tremble, and wishing the war to be suddenly over, wishing she could run away with her baby and her husband to someplace without war or tumult. She felt the constable's eyes on her and she looked up. "There is a lot at stake, isn't there?"

He nodded. "Our nation?" The tone of his voice made the idea sound foreign to him, and she understood. "When has England cared about us?"

"I do," Meridee said simply.

He bowed to her, surprisingly graceful. "I hope Jean Hubert sees what is at stake for all of us." He cleared his throat, and sounded less certain. "I shouldn't waste your time with this now."

When he hesitated, Meridee pushed aside her concerns for her husband and focused on a young man in love. "Tell me what is troubling you."

"It's not important," Walter said. "I mean, here we are, talking about war and tumult."

"It's important to *you*, Walter Cornwall. Tell me."

He took a deep breath. "Do you think Betsy's brother will like me? I mean, he remembers me as the ogre who tried to scare his twin to death and back into a workhouse. I was doing my job."

"He will like you, Walter," she said, her voice soft. "People change. How much, depends on them."

"Why am I concerned about such a small thing, when France is threatening us?" he asked, his surprise evident, and perhaps his dismay to discover he was not the tough constable he had always seemed.

"It's not a small thing. It's everything to you," she said. She heard steps on the stairs. The door opened, and there stood Able and Jean Hubert. Trailing along behind was Pierre Deschamps, quiet boy who blended into the background.

She wanted to smile at them, to reassure them, but she could not, because the fear on Jean's face was bested only by the apprehension on her husband's. And there was Pierre, visibly shaking.

*This will never do*, she thought, and beckoned to Pierre, who glanced at Jean for what, she did not know: permission? Seeing nothing except fear, the little fellow sidled toward her and soon pressed against her side. She put her arm around him, grateful she could soothe someone.

"Sit down, both of you," Meridee said, when no one seemed inclined to move. "There on the sofa." They either would or they wouldn't. She had no power to command anyone.

They did as she said, Jean trying to distance himself from Able on the small sofa. He stared straight ahead, his face blank, as if this summons had leeched all the color and life out of his normally expressive face. What on earth had Able said to him?

No one spoke. Meridee glanced at Walter, who managed a miniscule shrug but remained silent. It wasn't his home, and he probably felt the Six's sitting room not his place to interrogate anyone. Maybe he was weighing the relative seniority of an instructor at a boys' school to that of a constable.

The silence grew heavier as each second passed. Was anyone beside her even breathing? Meridee shifted in her chair, caught her husband's eye, and suddenly realized the genius behind the silence. Deeply appreciative of Able, she folded her hands in her lap and waited.

"I don't know anything and I haven't done anything," Jean Hubert said at last. It came out in a rush, as if all his pent-up nerves were trying to shoulder their way through a mental door at the same time.

Another long, long wait. It was as if Able Six had all the time in the world, even as dusk settled on Portsmouth and Meridee knew he and Walter needed to be in place in the copse before anyone arrived. Or perhaps the game had changed, becoming much deeper than she had anticipated.

Silent and watchful, Able turned his attention to Pierre, leaning forward, eyes intent, as if ready to spring. Meridee felt her blood start to run in chunks, even though she knew this man better than anyone else on earth. He was beginning to frighten her.

Suddenly Pierre buried his face in her apron and started to wail. Meridee rested her hand on his back, and he wailed harder.

"He doesn't know anything," Jean said, angry now. "Leave him alone."

"I have neither said nor done anything to either of you," Able said. "I thought we would sit here for a while." He looked at Walter. "How much time do we have?"

Walter was a quick study. "All the time in the world, Master Six." He yawned and put his hands behind his head.

More silence. The air seemed to hum with it. When Meridee didn't think she could manage another moment, and goodness knows, *she* had nothing to hide, Able spoke in his most affable voice, the one full of kindness, with just the smallest touch of deference and apology. He didn't use it often. In fact, the last time she recalled, was when he was trying to impress her brother-in-law, during their admittedly curious courtship.

"Something is afoot in the harbor," he said calmly. "It will probably happen soon. And you both know nothing? Jean, translate for Pierre, please."

Jean spoke in a low voice to the lad who still had not raised his face from Meridee's apron. Pierre shook his head.

"Jean?"

The prisoner shook his head, too. "I am who I said I was, a prisoner who wishes to sit out the war in a safe place."

"Oh, really?" Able asked, so affable.

"Yes, really," Jean replied, his voice firm.

*I don't think he knows anything*, Meridee thought. *I wish he did, because something is going to happen.*

Able stood up. He went to the window and looked out at the darkening sky. When he turned around, Meridee held her breath. She knew that implacable expression. She had seen it directed at Master Blake, fish food and long gone.

"When whatever it is happens, I will personally take you both back to the *Captivity* and turn you over to Captain Faulke. Depend upon it." He smiled at Walter now, who looked as calm as Able. "Let's lodge these two in your gaol until such time, shall we?"

"Aye, sir. An excellent idea," Walter said, all business now. He stood up, looming over them all, intimidating.

"No. Don't." Jean stood up, too.

"But you don't know anything," Able said, rounding on him.

"I don't!" Jean shouted.

"I don't believe you!" Able shouted back. Meridee put her hands over Pierre's ears, as he tried to burrow through her apron and into the sofa.

Jean turned toward the door, but there was nowhere to go. Walter stood there, his stance wide, immovable.

Able changed his tone to the reasonable one Meridee and all the Gunwharf Rats were used to. All signs point to something about to happen here on our docks, here in England, my home. The place where my wife and son are safe. You, sir, are far from home. We are your enemy and we will stop you."

"Stop what?" Jean asked, and there was no overlooking the panic in his voice. "I don't *know* anything. I am who I said I was, nothing more."

"Then what about the note Gervaise Turenne gave you?" Able asked.

"He didn't...I never..."

"Have it your way, Jean. I will miss you teaching French and art, and providing captivating commentary about this and that."

Able shrugged and squatted beside Meridee's chair, where Pierre was silent now. He spoke in French to the child, the quiet one, the one no one ever noticed, and then in English.

"Pierre, someone gave you a note for Jean Hubert. Don't deny it because I have no qualms about hanging you, too."

"You're a beast!" Jean raged.

"I am an Englishman," Able snapped. "This is war and you know it. Come sir, if you would spare this lad. The note, *s'il vous plaît*."

# — Chapter Thirty-six —

*J*ust don't look at Meri, Able thought. *If looks could skewer, you'd be sleeping on this sofa until 1900, at least.*

It was a mere bluff. Mr. Pitt had witnessed a note between the rude Captain Ogilvie and Gervaise Turenne. Someone must have received the note, or so Able reasoned. And hadn't Jean been terrified of Gervaise at Sir B's dinner? If not to Jean, then who but Pierre Deschamps?

There were times when any man could be forgiven for hating his job, but surprisingly, this wasn't one of them. He would have to talk with someone – Sir B? William Pitt? – about this strange emotion that filled him. All his life he had known he was a workhouse bastard with an odd brain. His luck had turned, but he always knew the workhouse waited to pounce, should he fail.

That feeling was gone, replaced by something that felt like love of country, but did he even have a country? He had never felt like a son of Scotland, not even a bastard son. True, he had the brogue, but he could turn it off at will. If not a son of Scotland, than of England? Hardly. He felt even fewer ties to the land that had employed him since the age of nine, and which had ridden roughshod over Scotland, where he was born. Where did one's loyalties lie? With his dead mother? His likely foreign father?

He had assumed that the Royal Navy constituted his strongest tie, and then St. Brendan the Navigator School. As he stood there, ready to work ill on a child and a lieutenant, now prisoner, in the French navy, it struck Durable Six that his most enduring allegiance was to his wife and son. By extension, anyone who tried to hamper their security would bring down ruin upon themselves.

Perhaps someday, if this cruel war faltered and the tide ran strong for England, he might consider himself a true son of the British Isles. Until that happened, he would devote himself to protecting the people dearest to him, his wife and son most assuredly, and the Gunwharf Rats. Maybe he could explain this to Meridee some evening, if it was just the two of them. Until then, there were more pressing matters.

"Sit down, Jean," he ordered, his voice conversational again, but with that edge of authority he had cultivated from years at sea. It no longer felt like a cloak he was allowed to wear now and then. It belonged to him.

Jean sat. Their eyes met. *Don't hate me too long,* Able thought, *but if you must, you must. I need information.*

"Do you still have the note?" he asked quietly. "I must have it."

"I ate it."

"I would have done the same thing. What did it say?"

The test. Would this be the truth? *Please God*, Able prayed. *Please God, I will know the difference.*

"As a prisoner of war, I do not have to divulge anything that might give aid and comfort to the enemy," Jean said. He smiled, and Able saw the playfulness that everyone at St. Brendan's enjoyed. *"Je remercie le Siegneur* that eating my words has never given me indigestion."

"Unless that note is as long as Newton's three laws of motion, I doubt you have forgotten it," Able said, perfectly in control, confident. Curiously, he noticed that the spectral crowd of onlookers that he seemed to share his brain with were silent, even the French among them.

"There was a commotion at the water hoy dock this afternoon," Able continued. "Kegs were overturned, men were milling about and yelling. Walter told me it sounded a little staged, but it's a surmise. A prisoner was captured and led away, but we think there was another man. Or men."

"No one saw him? Maybe, Master Six, you are grasping at straws," Jean said.

*Come, come,* Able thought, weary of this. *You have no cards to play.* The time to feint and jab had passed. There was work to do this evening.

"Take the boy, Walter," he ordered, turning around and gazing out the window to the harbor and the hulks, still visible but fading in the approaching twilight. "We'll hang him and return Lieutenant Jean Hubert to the *Captivity*."

He could have sighed with relief when Jean stood beside him, looking out the window, his face calm resigned. He spoke, but quietly. "'Watch for a citizen who will make the wharf blossom with orange flowers.' That was the note, damn you, Master Six." He turned to Pierre, who was firmly in the constable's grasp, and spoke softly to him in French. The boy relaxed, although his eyes lost none of their wariness.

"Pierre gave me the note, which had been handed to him by Gervaise Turenne, Sir B's valet. Gervaise wrapped it in a slightly larger paper with the words, 'Are you the one?'" Jean explained, his eyes on Able. "I have no idea what that means. None."

"What a puzzle this is. Ben is calling my name, but I don't want to miss a minute of this."

Meri was the last person Able thought would interrupt, but she had done precisely that. He opened his mouth to say someone he knew he would regret, but had the good sense to close it, words unsaid. Maybe it was that overly sweet look she sent his way. He knew her well enough to trust that whatever she had in mind was probably to his benefit.

What do you propose, Meri?" he asked, instead of the curt statement that would have fried his chances for peace at home for an indeterminate period.

"If I am discreet, would you gentleman mind if I fetch my son?" Meridee went to the door and opened it. "And look, here are Nick, John and Smitty, just as eager as I am to know what is going on."

Able watched in growing appreciation for his wife's adroit defusing of a situation so fraught that the air seemed to hum. "I have no objection to the lads or my hungry son. Any of you? She is an expert with a blanket."

Jean made a courtly gesture with his hand and Walter tried not to smile.

"I'll be right back," Meri said. "The boys want to listen." She spoke to Jean alone. "You're their French and art instructor and they value you, Lieutenant Hubert. I doubt you would care to disappoint them."

"I believe I would not," he replied.

Able heard something thoughtful in his tone, now that the anger was gone.

He gestured to his students. "Sit down and no talking, Rats." He spoke to Pierre in French and the little shadow joined the boys, sitting cross-legged with them by the unlit fireplace.

Meri returned with their squalling son, worked some magic behind a blanket, and soon all was silent, except for Ben's enthusiastic little suck. The sound, so homely and vulnerable, seemed to reinforce everything Able felt about why he was defending England. He didn't particularly care what happened to addled-now-and-then King George, because there was always someone to succeed him. He did care greatly about the woman and the baby.

She looked up and nodded. "Please go ahead with this. If I am to keep this straight, Gervaise slipped a confusing note to a Frenchman, our own Jean Hubert, who I think has no idea what is going on, either. Am I right, Jean?"

"Precisely so, Madame Six," Jean said. He was silent a long moment, obviously weighing something in his mind, perhaps – to Able's skeptical mind – trying to decide how much more truth to tell. The calm look returned, telling Able that the prisoner of war had made up his mind, whatever he had decided.

"I can agree not to hang Pierre," Able said, trying to overlook the gasps from his Gunwharf Rats. "But I will return you both to the hulk, Jean, unless I hear a compelling argument why that isn't a good idea. If harm is coming to Portsmouth and by extension to my family, I won't rest until I know. Sit down with me. Tell me."

"If I am returned to the *Captivity*, I will be killed," Jean said with no hesitation. He shrugged. "I know that news will not cut up any Englishman's peace for long, except you need to know this, something I learned because I was in the wrong place at the wrong time: Both Captain Faulke and a prisoner ringleader are in league somehow to do damage at the wharf."

"Rats, this doesn't leave the room," Able snapped. "Swear to God."

The boys murmured and moved closer together. Meri's mouth opened in surprise. Able could have sworn even Ben stopped sucking, but that couldn't be.

"I sincerely want to believe this," Able said.

"Then do, please," the courtly Jean Hubert replied. "I was Ianthe Faulke's art instructor on board the *Captivity*. I happened to overhear her father and a Frenchman plotting ruin for men trying to escape in the water kegs."

"Why would either man do this?" Walter asked.

"Constable, as near as I can divine, the captain is paying the prisoner – one Claude Pascal, damn him – for escape information. Captain Faulke takes the information to someone in authority here in Portsmouth. The culprit is captured on the dock and Faulke, damn him, gets the credit." Jean turned to Able. "Tell me, Master Six, what kind of officers are put in charge of prison hulks?"

*I wish I could say this surprises me*, Able thought. He saw Meri's dismay and Walter's. "You can guess, Jean. What kind of seaman is put in charge of a vessel that does not move?"

"Someone with no patronage, or someone with no skill," Jean said promptly, almost as if it were a recitation. "We have similar mariners."

"Which is Captain Faulke?" Able asked. "You have suffered the fruits of his leadership."

This answer came with more thought, as though it had occupied Jean's mind for a long while. "I know he has money, because a lot of it has gone into the pocket of Claude Pascal," Jean said. "I suspect he has an ambitious wife. Perhaps it is her money. Capitain Faulke wants to move up, and what better way than buying the credit that comes his way because a scoundrel Frenchman wants to move up, too?"

"And how do you explain Claude Pascal?" Walter Cornwall asked.

"An ambitious man who cares not a whit for his country," came Jean's prompt reply. "He is selling out potential escapees for money." He couldn't help a shudder and it didn't look theatrical. "Blood money of the worst kind."

It was a family joke now, but certainly true, that Able could not tie a neck cloth to save his soul. He also had difficulty doing simple arithmetic, so much so that Meri took over that task when the butcher and the coalman disputed his payment of their accounts. He never minded Meri's good-natured teasing because he knew better than anyone that his brain was a peculiar one.

What it was extremely good at was looking beyond the obvious and entertaining other thoughts. He had one now, with no way to test the theory except to let some of the unraveling mystery play out.

"There is another level to this chicanery," Able said.

"It's bad enough as is," Walter reminded him.

"Most assuredly, Constable Cornwall," Able said, certain of himself. "I suspect it is even worse. Follow me here: Some of the escapes have succeeded and some have not, as far as we know. I have to wonder if Monsieur Pascal is playing an even deeper game. Nick? Do you see where I am going with this?"

Nick pinked up when heads swiveled his way, but he did not falter. "Um, I hate to think about it, but is it possible that Claude Pascal is burning his candle at both ends?"

"Why would you think that?" Able asked, knowing down to the decimal point how many times this sitting room had already turned into a classroom.

"Probability," Nick said. He ticked off his fingers. "Claude Pascal likes money. He wants more. Let us assume...."

"...always dangerous..." Able interrupted.

"For the sake of the argument," Nick continued, after a sunny smile in Able's direction that disarmed the sailing master.

"Let us assume, then, that he's not a totally bad fellow and also has some feelings about his country. Maybe there is someone higher up instructing him to do us damage on the wharf." Nick frowned. "I wouldn't do that, not even for money."

"Then you, Mister Bonfort, are better than most of us," Jean Hubert said.

"Continue the thought, Nick," Able encouraged, after a frown at Jean, who shrugged.

"Well, he satisfies Captain Faulke's ambition by letting some of the escapees get caught and sent back, giving the captain the credit," Nick explained. "He also lets some of them go through, the ones that are meant to do damage, and not just run away, once they are free of the hulk."

"And which is Lieutenant Hubert?" Able asked.

"I think he just wanted to get away," Nick said, with a charitable glance in Jean's direction. "He's sort of trapped in the middle."

"Didn't Pierre mention a gunner named Remillard?" Smitty asked.

"Bravo Smitty, he did. How much damage could such a man do? Remember, he got away," Able said.

Smitty whistled. "This whole city is a factory for war against the French."

Able looked around the room. With the exception of Ben, who slumbered now, he saw thoughtful expressions.

"Rats, how do we prove a hypothesis?"

"Master Able, we test it," John Mark declared.

# — Chapter Thirty-seven —

Able doubted he would ever make such a strange request of the Gunwharf Rats, assembled again in the cellar, but where could he do better? Or so he told Meri as dusk deepened and he returned home to change into black trousers and sweater.

"I told them I needed two lads expert at the art of skulking," he told her. "Two hands went up immediately."

"Where else but our school?" she joked.

"Where, indeed? I told them I needed two Rats for dangerous work, if, mind you, if the older couple is in the copse again and if – oh, that damnable word – the man who escaped shows up. I want them to follow the three of them. We need to know where they live. I have my suspicions."

"Should I worry about you?"

She kept her voice light, but he knew it was a show. "No more than you would for any bit of skullduggery involving dangerous characters from our avowed enemy." He grabbed her tight until she squeaked. "I know something about skulking, myself," he assured her. "Jean, Walter and I will watch."

"Can you trust him?"

"Oh, I think Walter's a good'un." He smiled when she rolled her eyes at him. "I have to trust Jean," he told her seriously. "I have to. Invite Grace over to keep you company."

"Have you said anything to Sir B?"

"No and I won't until I have something more concrete to tell him about Gervaise. Kiss me quick. I'm off to an adventure."

She didn't kiss him quick; she kissed him slow. "Hold that thought," he told her, and added a dagger to his waistband. He opened the knock on the door and ushered in two Rats from the older class. "Whitticombe and Tots, you both know Mrs. Six."

Meri curtsied back when they bowed to her in that way of twelve-year-olds not used to the niceties, and gave her husband a questioning glance.

"These lads were recommended by Smitty, who will patrol the outside of our house. Whitticombe and Tottenham will be based in our sitting room, but circulate inside the house during the course of the evening," Able explained. "Because we do not entirely know what game is afoot, we will be prepared here, won't we, lads?"

"Aye sir!" they chorused. Able ushered them into the sitting room.

"You don't think I will break their concentration if we offer them hot bread and grog, do you?" she asked, walking arm in arm with him to the front door.

"It certainly wouldn't have broken mine, at their age," Able declared frankly. "Don't go outside, Meri. See you topside."

He kissed her hand. She held tight a moment, then let him go.

The sun was down and the air brisk as he joined Jean Hubert and Walter Cornwall by the stone basin. Without a word between them, they blended into the line of trees and sat close together. Silent, they watched the water darken and lights begin to twinkle here and there along the curve of the great harbor. The tide was out and the smell strong enough to counteract the usual odor of hemp and tar, two of Able's favorite odors before he met Meridee Bonfort, with her lavender talcum and personal fragrance. She teased him that he smelled like brine and soap. He smiled in the dark, thinking of the little things that made up a marriage. Even in this time of uncertainty and national emergency, he had found love.

He glanced at Jean Hubert, who sat between him and Walter Cornwall, and owned to some uneasiness to compel a man to betray his country and threaten the life of a child. Still, if this Claude Pascal was willfully sending other Frenchmen to their deaths, then he should be stopped.

They sat in silence for an hour as Able's misgivings grew. The two Rats assigned to the First Watch were due to begin their four-hour circuit of that small section of the harbor that fronted St. Brendan's and the row of houses close by.

Oh, doubt, you devil! Possibly no one had escaped from the water hoy dock at noon. Maybe the old couple that sat by the water's edge really enjoyed a moment together and nothing more. Perhaps Gervaise Turenne liked to pass on cryptic notes to scare the bejabbers out of people.

Or perhaps everything was true. Able held his breath as he heard footsteps on the walkway by the sea wall. The three of them seemed to stop breathing simultaneously as three people left the walkway and moved toward the water. They were silent, too, but sure of step as they passed within a few feet of the dark-cloaked men waiting there. No one hesitated. The three figures seated themselves close to the water's edge, one of them seeming to perch on a low-hanging limb, the other two on the ground. The indistinct shapes were as motionless as the three men watching them.

Able heard the sound of a match striking a stone, and then smelled tobacco smoke. Nothing, nothing, and then he heard another match and saw three brief flashes from a signal lamp as the little door opened and closed three times.

*Now we watch*, he thought. He heard the trio speaking to each other in low tones. Jean tensed. "My countrymen," he whispered to Able in French, or maybe to himself. *Please don't move, Jean, please don't do anything*, Able thought, as he put his hand to his dagger. *I don't want to kill you.*

One minute passed, then three more, the seconds ticking past in Able's brain. At three minutes and thirty-five seconds, he heard the splash of an oar and the creak of the oar locks as a dark craft pulled to the shore and a man stepped off. He gave the boat a shove with his foot and it continued bobbing down the shoreline.

The Frenchmen didn't waste a moment in climbing out of the copse. Able smelled Tobacco Man again, and then someone damp with the odor of low tide clinging to him. Able sighed, vindicated. Someone had gone into the harbor, probably at the water hoy dock, and swum away, and here he was, smelling of foul low tide. A third fragrance caught his attention, and made him sad.

Gervaise Turenne was no dandy. He was a valet, probably not the career his émigré parents of comfortable means would have chosen for him, but who has a choice in the middle of an all-consuming revolution? An otherwise unexceptionable fellow, as suited a servant, Gervaise did like his vetyver cologne. Able breathed it now.

They turned to watch. As the Gunwharf Rat First Watch passed the four men crouched by the sea wall, they waited, then rose once the watch passed and hurried to the empty street. Able, Jean and Walter rose, too, moving steadily toward the sea wall.

After a moment in quiet conference, the man who smelled of vetyver left the other three, turning back to whisper in a loud voice, "I trust this is all you require of me."

More conversation, then, "*Merde,*" from Vetyver Man, who angrily stalked toward the street.

"Follow him," Able said to Walter. "I think he will hail a hackney on the corner by the bakery. Don't lose him."

Able waited until the remaining trio continued toward the street, confident that his Gunwharf skulkers were enveloped in their own darkness and ready to follow them.

"What do we do?" Jean whispered.

"We wait right here," Able told him.

"Why?"

"You'll see." *I hope,* Able told himself.

*"I could have devised a better plan." "I seriously doubt it, you thief of ideas."*

Able closed his eyes, and resisted a curse of his own. This was no time for Isaac Newton and Gottfried Leibnitz to start bickering in his brain. *Euclid, deal with those two ninnies,* he thought, and tried to ignore them.

He breathed easier when he heard the nearly silent patter of bare feet coming closer. "Down here, lads," he said, rising slightly above the sea wall. "What did you learn?"

He knew Lark and Wren to be sober-minded lads with a talent for skulking. From the same workhouse in Norfolk, they had been named as babies by a workhouse master who enjoyed birding in his spare time. Able and Grace had had a quiet laugh about the matter last year when the boys joined the upper grades. Grace had remarked in her droll way that they should be grateful they weren't named Albatross and Titmouse.

Not usually demonstrative (no workhouse boy ever cared to call attention to himself), they nearly jumped up and down in their excitement. "Steady, my fellows," he cautioned. "Well?"

"Just two doors south of St. Brendan's," Wren said. "Two doors! That's where the old lady and her invalid son live. We help them sometimes."

"You have, I know," Able said. They had moved in last summer, and lived as quiet as you please, just the two of them. Maybe. "Thank you for your help tonight."

"Should we stay and watch some more?" Lark asked, ripe for more adventure.

"No, lads. You've done what I asked, and done it well. Thank you."

They grinned and started for St. Brendan's. "If you skulk along the wall and cross the street so no one sees you, I think you will find hot bread and grog in my quarters," Able told them. "It's three knocks and the password is 'Ben loves his papa.'"

They laughed and darted toward the street, then remembered to skulk.

"And that is the secret to leadership," Jean commented as the boys skulked away. "Food from Madame Six?"

"Aye. Think of the lessons you are learning here," Able said. "Two doors down."

"A good view of the hulks."

"Prime. Now, lieutenant, let us skulk a bit ourselves and move toward the house in question. I want to see what happens next."

"Aren't we going to summon the watch?"

"And tell them what? If what happens next is what I suspect, I will need your skills. The Royal Navy may be far ahead in daytime flag signals…"

"You only wish," Jean muttered.

"I heard that," Able said with a smile. "We are not so good in night signals yet. That is what I am waiting for, and what I would like you to translate for me."

"And if I chose not to?"

"Back to the hulk."

"And if I give you the wrong information on purpose?"

Able shrugged, hoping he looking more casual than he felt at that looming possibility. "I will look like a horse's ass, something bad will happen to me and those I love, but you will still go back to the hulk."

"Very well. Let us watch," Jean said promptly, needing no time to consider his options, apparently.

There was no cover from the trees, but they hunkered down by the sea wall. It might have been May in some warmer, more congenial place in the world, but here in Portsmouth the wind blew raw. At least the tide was running now, and the stink of mud and dead things was abating.

"Does Cherbourg stink so bad when the tide is out?" he asked his partner.

"Get captured and you can find out for yourself."

With a smile, Able watched the dark house. An hour passed, and another forty-seven minutes. There it was. "Jean, what does it say?" *And tell me the truth*, he prayed silently.

Jean was silent, then, "'I am here. What comes next?'"

They both turned and watched the hulks. Another wait and then little pin pricks of light, not coming from the main deck, but from the gun deck. *I'll wager Captain Faulke has no idea what is going on below him*, Able thought, and felt a great anger rise in him.

"And?" Able prompted, when the hulk was dark again.

Jean scratched his head. "'Bâtiment douze. Floréal Buglosse.' I don't understand."

"I do," Able said slowly, as the French words reeled through his brain in record time. "Building Twelve, May Seventeenth." He understood. *Remillard, the first escapee, is a gunner. He knows powder. Perhaps the new arrival has another target.*

"Whoever is in the Grundy's house is going to blow up the block pulley factory, Building Twelve, on May Seventeenth," he said. "Why did your country change to that ridiculous revolutionary calendar? It slowed me down."

"Not noticeably," Jean said dryly. "We have five days. Rather, *you* have five days."

"We will be in London tomorrow night, as will *you*."

"Me?" Jean exclaimed. "Am I not enough of a traitor to my country right now?"

"If what you say is true about a rascal belowdecks who is killing his own, I rather think you are somewhat of a hero," Able assured him.

"'Somewhat of a hero,'" Jean echoed. "Who would have thought it?"

# — Chapter Thirty-eight —

They were in London the following evening by midnight, travel-stained, hungry and tired. Sir B nearly shook from exhaustion, and Able's eyes felt like burning coals in his head. Grace managed to look tidy and Jean kept his own council, staring into the dark night. Able had no idea how well Gervaise traveled. He was sitting in the coachman's box because there was no room inside for him, too.

There would have been room, except that Meri made a surprising request. Before he left, Meri had held him close, caressing his face. "Please, please don't get over tired," she begged. "You know how I worry." The tears spilled onto her cheeks.

"All I know is we must hurry," he told her. He nodded his thanks when Mrs. Perry, her face militant, handed him a large canvas bag with food. He knew better than to refuse it and didn't wish to, anyway.

To his surprise, Meri had turned to Grace, who had come over to sit with her during the evening's skullduggery. "Grace, you must go, too."

"Oh, but…"

"Excellent idea," said Able, who needed no nudging from any of his possibly imaginary friends. He understood completely.

"I am thinking that Gervaise might be occupied with other matters, once they reach London and Trinity House," Meri said. "Sir B will need some comfort, and you are in a good position to provide it."

"Meridee, that would be highly improper," Grace scolded, but Able didn't hear too much real dismay. "I could not possibly tend to Sir B. His needs require a valet, and there is Gervaise. I can't imagine he will be too busy to do his duty by his employer."

"I can," his wife said serenely.

"I second the motion," Able said. "Grace, now's the time."

He knew he wielded no Royal Navy authority over women, especially one as formidable as Grace Croker. He used his voice of command, without increasing the decibels to an uncomfortable level, and gave her that narrowed-eye look that had never failed him.

"Very well," Grace said, her face decidedly more rosy than usual. "I believe you two are nearly certifiable." She turned on her heel and left the sitting room, pausing in the doorway to say that she was going to fetch a traveling bonnet and warmer pelisse. Perhaps a nightgown.

"What will come of all this?" Meri asked him as he pressed her to him again.

"Nothing right now, but when I get back, I hope you will create a monumental diversion of some sort so I can have my way with you."

"Able! You are hopeless of remedy! I mean with Sir B and Grace. And the conspirators, and whatever else you are up to." She had pinked up nicely, as well.

"I have no idea what will happen. That is rare. I don't like it."

And he didn't. Theirs was a solemn ride to London, one that involved changing horses, snatching food at inns when Mrs. Perry's ran out, and pounding over indifferent roads toward Trinity House. He doubted anyone slept, although little was said. To his sleepy satisfaction he did notice that Grace had put her hand in Sir B's.

He placed all his dependence on the post rider that Sir B had sent galloping ahead of them, carrying a message to William Pitt, prime minister again since only last week, and still warden of Trinity House. With good horses and any luck, the Brethren would be assembled by the time their slower conveyance arrived.

There was time for solitary thinking. Able understood the message Gervaise had worked so hard to pass to Jean Hubert, that non-existent spy. Could they trick the actual spies into playing out a broader hand? *I believe we can*, he thought.

And so it was after dark on the next day that the carriage pulled to a stop in front of Trinity House and shook out its frazzled, slightly smelly occupants. Grace Croker still appeared tidy, although there were dark circles under her eyes.

Sir B looked like warmed-up death, except for the slight smile on his face, put there, Able reckoned, by the fact that Grace still held his hand. He had placed the blanket over their hands, and seemed content to let the kind lady lean against his shoulder, too.

Sir B winced when, cold and shivering from his day and a half sitting next to the better-dressed coachman, Gervaise lifted him from the carriage and set him in the wheeled chair Able had removed from the cubby at the back of the carriage and set up. The two of them lifted the chair up the entrance steps, where the front door was open and the same porter stood. He was slightly less formal in robe and nightshirt, with uncombed, cowlicky hair sticking up, but no less cheerful.

"Come in, come in!" he said as he rubbed his eyes. He noticed Grace and bowed. "Just the one of you this time?"

"Just one. I promise to be silent," she said.

Only two lamps burned in the entrance hall. The porter gestured for Able and Gervaise to help Sir B up the stairs.

"What? You again? God's wounds."

All the humiliating memories came back at that voice. Able turned around to see Captain Ogilvie standing behind him. He couldn't help that his hands curled into fists. He felt more embarrassment because the odious man noticed, too, if that's what his mocking expression revealed.

"Come with me, Master Six," he demanded.

"I am here on urgent business," Able replied, unwilling to go anywhere with the man who didn't want him there in the first place. "You have already made your opinion of me amply evident, and I don't need another lesson."

"Will you let me accompany you, Master Six?"

He knew the voice. Another man stepped out of the shadows, William Pitt, who had only in the last few days, after careful and clever maneuvering, returned to his position as prime minister of a wartime England.

"Well, I…" Able looked at his friends, who had already started up the stairs. Grace had hung back to watch him, concern writ large on her face.

She started down the steps, fire in her eyes, when the prime minister spoke again. "He's in good hands, Grace," Pitt said. "No worries, please. We will join you quite soon. Come, Able. Over here."

Ogilvie held the door open. Able swallowed, wondering if he was going to see Meri and Ben again, wondering if this was his last day on the planet, hating the thought that he had underestimated Captain Ogilvie, who must be more than a mere bully.

"What have I done wrong, sir?" he asked Pitt, unnerved as never before.

"Not a thing. You are owed an explanation, though. Do have a seat and trust me when I tell you this is not a Star Chamber."

Able sat at a small table. Pitt and Ogilvie joined him, the captain with glasses and what looked like madeira from the sideboard. He poured three drinks and handed them around. Able eyed his with some wariness, which made Captain Ogilvie roll his eyes.

"Master Six, unless I have suddenly developed amazing sleight of hand skills – and I assure you I have not – no one is here to poison you. Are you always this suspicious?"

"Only when my last view of you was an angry man kicking my ribs," he replied.

"Ah, yes, regrettable display of temper," William Pitt said. He tossed off his drink and pushed his glass over for a refill. Ogilvie obliged. "I almost believed him, myself."

Able looked from one to the other, his lively brain strangely silent. Suddenly, a cosmic hand tweaked his head with thumb and forefinger and he sat back. "I believe I have been diddled," he said, and knocked back his drink.

"Let me tell you why," the captain said, all snark and innuendo gone from his voice. "I have been following a tip Trinity House received from a source that will remain anonymous. I have been observing Henri and Madeline Turenne, that respectable émigré couple now currently residing in New Romney, Kent." He pulled out a timepiece and examined it studiously. "Or they were. Quite possibly they are on their way to Portsmouth, courtesy of a Royal Marine escort."

"What are you saying?"

"My sources tell me that in the past six months, the Turennes have been visited by, shall we say, questionable characters of French origin," Ogilvie said. "New Romney is marshy country to be sure – my late wife would never have wanted to live there – but it's so close to France."

Able let that sink in. Pitt obligingly poured him another drink.

"I followed one of those visitors – a really unsavory-looking bloke, and uh, convinced him to relinquish a note I had observed Monsieur Turenne handing him before he left."

"Skulking in the bushes, sir?" Able asked, curious to know, but still not ready to forgive him for his rough treatment.

"I skulk for Trinity House," Ogilvie said simply. "That is all I will own to. The only thing that stubborn man would admit was that Gervaise had agreed to involve himself. He also admitted he was determined to cause more mischief, all for the glory of France. He would say no more, no matter how much persuasion we attempted."

"Do I want to know what happened to him?"

"No, you do not," Ogilvie replied in a kindly voice. He turned his attention to the prime minister. "That was when we at Trinity House felt it wise to inform you, Mr. Pitt. You know the rest."

"Except this: why not tell Addington?" Pitt asked. "He was prime minister until a week ago."

"It didn't seem to us that he would be in power much longer, begging your pardon, sir," Ogilvie replied, all complacence.

"You decided to palm *that* note onto Gervaise and see what he would do with it," Able said. "And that was why you Trinity Brothers specifically asked my Gunwharf Rats to patrol at St. Brendan's."

Ogilvie gave a little bow from the waist up. "We have other uh, well, let us call them agents, watching the rest of the waterfront. There have been rumors about the hulks."

"And you made a big show of humiliating me why, precisely?" Able asked, still feeling no particular charity toward the round but solid fellow who sat next to him.

"To put Gervaise off his guard," Ogilvie said promptly. "I slipped him that note when everyone was trying to help you and your sweet wife and paying him no attention. I do hope Mrs. Six will accept my apology. Oh, I also included my own note with the planted missive, taken off that poor dead man."

"What poor..." Able stopped. "Oh, aye. The one who didn't have any more information for you."

"Alas, no," Ogilvie said with a sorrowful shake of his head. "In the note from me, which I am certain Gervaise has long since relocated to a safer place – perhaps the fireplace – I told him to be alert for a Frenchman to get in touch with him, and hand off that note when he found him."

"He really terrified Jean Hubert, when the note came his way, via a little boy," Able said.

No one said anything, although Captain Ogilvie gave Able several inquiring looks. "Do you have something to add, Master Six?" he finally asked quite politely, a far cry from the angry, fire-breathing man who had made Able's life a misery that afternoon at Trinity House.

"I am curious about something," Able said. "Did you keep Sir B in the dark about Gervaise?"

"We felt it best," Mr. Pitt said.

"He'll take this hard. Gervaise has been his lifeline for several years now," Able said. "I wish this could end differently."

"So do I," Mr. Pitt said. "War doesn't play favorites."

"Is there more?" Captain Ogilvie asked briskly, leaving Able to wonder if he ever had a sympathetic thought for anyone.

"Quite a lot, actually," Able said. "I suggest we go upstairs now, where others can hear it."

"After you, Master Six," Ogilvie said with a little bow as he stood up.

"Oh, no, after you, sir," Able said, equally affable.

William Pitt uttered a most un-ministerial snort and led the way up the stairs to the assembly room. The three men were joined by four beefy-looking Royal Marines, who planted themselves outside the door.

*Gervaise, I feel a little sorry for you, but only a little,* Able thought as he followed the prime minister into the room, where ten Elder Brethren sat. He glanced at Sir B's valet, who stood in his usual place behind the captain at the table. The young man appeared calm, either innocent, or a spy who had no idea what was heading his way.

*I wish it were the former,* Able told himself, as his attention turned to his former captain and mentor. Sir B rested his cheek on his palm, weary of body and soon to be sick of soul. *One man will miss you.*

Grace Croker sat quietly next to Jean Hubert in an out-of-the-way corner, her eyes on Sir B. Able saw the love and uncertainty.

William Pitt gestured to a chair toward the end of the U-shaped circle. "Master Six? As you can see, we are not all assembled this late night, but we have enough, should any business need our approval. Please seat yourself here." The prime minister directed his attention to the other side of the U, where Sir B sat.

"Captain St. Anthony, you requested this meeting. I received the message three hours ago from a muddy post rider," the prime minster said. "Would you care to tell us what is going on down there in Portsmouth? Your dispatch was brief and unsettling."

"We have knowledge of possible misadventure toward the Royal Navy's new block pulley factory, which is scheduled to begin production in a week," Sir B said. He nodded in Able's direction. "Master Six can tell you everything we know."

All eyes turned in Able's direction. He braced himself for his usual workhouse doubts and fears to crowd in, but they didn't. His brain was calm and silent, too. Oddly, he could almost smell Meri's lavender talcum powder. He was in charge.

In a quiet voice he told the Brethren of prison escapees found in empty water kegs, and others drowned by dockworkers. He told of his wife's near disaster at the dock, and the courage of his Gunwharf Rats as they stood the watch as directed. He indicated Jean Hubert, who sat close to Grace Croker, his eyes troubled.

"My St. Brendan yacht crew and I rescued that man when he slipped from under a pile of corpses being taken off the prison hulks in our harbor." He heard the gasps and low murmurs. "Sirs, it is possible to be that desperate. We at St. Brendan the Navigator School granted him a parole to teach…"

"Good God, man, he is probably your spy!" one of the Brethren declared.

"Then what better outcome than to watch him and see what he planned to do?" Able quickly countered. He saw Gervaise lean forward, intent, then glance at the closed door. "If we had sent him back to the hulk, what would we know of his possible target?"

"Perhaps," the Brother grudgingly admitted, although plainly he was not convinced.

"We decided that Lieutenant Jean Hubert, late commander of the sloop of war *Calais*, merely wants to lie low and stay out of trouble," Able said. "He's no coward, I assure you, but he has no interest in the fight. In fact, without his assistance, we would not be here tonight with our own accusations and solution to a serious matter about to happen on May 17."

He gestured to Jean. "Lieutenant Hubert, let us stand together and tell these men what you know is happening on board the HMS *Captivity*, one of the prison hulks." Able looked around the table as he rose to his feet. The light was low, but he saw determination on the face of each man committed to this fight to the death between France and England. "You won't like what he tells you, but I beg you, believe him. Jean?"

# — Chapter Thirty-nine —

G race Croker patted Jean's hand. "Will they believe me?" he whispered to her.
"I do," she said quietly. "Able does."

Jean stood up and walked with what he hoped was confidence toward the strangely shaped table. No one looked friendly except Able. He decided to direct his remarks to the sailing master who had saved his life and had faith in him.

"Sir, all I ever wanted to do was sail my sloop in the service of France and harry your frigates," he began. "We were captured near Saint Domingue and forced to strike our colors. We ended up in HMS *Captivity* in Portsmouth Harbor."

"Let me mention here that the *Captivity* is captained by Tobias Faulke," Sir B said. He coughed politely. "Some of us remember him as the poor unfortunate who ran his ship aground in broad daylight near Falmouth."

Polite chuckles. They remembered.

*And here I am, about to betray a countryman, who, granted, is a nasty piece of work,* Jean thought. *Try as anyone might, word has ways of getting back home. I will never be allowed in France again.*

"Jean?" Able prompted.

He nodded. "It is an ugly thing to betray a man." He glanced involuntarily at Gervaise Turenne, and watched him flinch. "But I must tell you of Claude Pascal now." Another glance at Gervaise showed him a man greatly, supremely relieved. He had plainly never heard of Pascal. Jean reached in his coat pocket and took out a handful of drawings, which he handed to Able. "Master Six, please share these with the men here."

He waited while Able smoothed his little drawings, stacked them neatly and sent them on their way, pencil sketches he had made of naked, giggling, insane *rafalés;* men slumped against the bulkhead with eyes sunk deep; a prisoner dumping a chamber pot from an iron-barred porthole; a starving man turning away from an empty soup pot.

"I stood at my classroom window, stared into the harbor at the hulks and drew these from memory," he said, as the drawings circulated. "There is a ship's carpenter name of Claude Pascal, at least he claims he is a ship's carpenter, but he is vague about which ship. He wormed his way into our confidence and anointed himself our liaison with your Captain Faulke," he continued, trying and failing to keep the emotion from his voice.

"If he is so troublesome to you, why did you and your fellow prisoners allow him any power?" asked one well-fed Brother.

172

Jean bit back the comment he wanted to make, something about over-stuffed men sitting in a comfortable room having no concept of life aboard a British prison ship. He settled for, "Sir, one becomes amazingly apathetic on a diet of gruel and little else. It plays with the mind. Hope becomes practically an aphrodisiac."

The inquisitor sat back, not happy, but at least silent.

"Claude Pascal held councils with us, and took our puny complaints to Faulke." He couldn't help the tears in his eyes. "Sometimes the result was better treatment for a day or two, but it was never much."

"You are prisoners," someone said. "What can you expect?"

"Obviously little," Jean snapped, then reconsidered. He bowed in the direction of the questioner. "We are still men who love our country as you love yours, sir," Jean replied. He gestured toward the sketches making their way slowly from hand to hand. "I am an artist, as you can plainly see."

"And a good one," another Brother said. Jean heard the admiration, and it warmed him as nothing else could. Now to the hard part.

"Claude Pascal began arranging escapes from our hulk. He made sure we funneled all our attempts through him, because he said he didn't want the matter to get out of hand and arouse too many suspicions on deck." Oh, this was difficult. "So he claimed. What he didn't tell us was that he was in league with Captain Faulke."

He closed his eyes when the Brethren, nearly as one, shouted him down, their fists raised. He bowed his head and stood there in silence, feeling more alone than he had felt in years. Funny that he would think of the cheerful faces of the Gunwharf Rats in his classroom, some of them good artists, others painfully bad, but then, it wasn't given to every human to know what to do with a pen. But they tried. The thought of being returned to another hulk and away from the youthful camaraderie he had come to cherish at St. Brendan hurt worse than no food, no bedding, no letters, no hope.

"Come, come gentlemen," he heard. "We need to hear this man."

"Mr. Pitt, will you insist that we believe him?" came a sneering question.

"I insist that you listen with an open mind, even as I am doing," came the quiet but forceful response.

Jean took heart when Able moved closer beside him. Then suddenly Grace was there, too, crooking her arm through his.

"We teach with Jean Hubert," Grace said, speaking distinctly, her chin up. "We believe him. As Englishmen, please give him your attention." She looked around as Jean admired her right down to his stockings. "This is a long and weary war, and I doubt we are near the end of it. If it leeches out all your humanity, what good will we be when it is over? Jean?"

"I was ordered to provide art lessons for Captain Faulke's daughter, Ianthe," Jean said. "I did not want to, until I was informed by the captain that when I finished each lesson, I would be allowed to eat a regular meal in the little pantry off the dining room. And so I taught her. I was hungry."

Jean took a deep breath and another. Grace tightened her grip on him. "One day I was finishing my luncheon in the pantry, when Captain Faulke and Claude Pascal came into the dining room and closed the door."

"How did you know who it was?" asked Captain Ogilvie.

"Sir, it was the captain's quarters, and Claude speaks with a lisp and a Bretonese accent. Claude distinctly told the captain that there would be an escape, the second one, in empty water kegs. He told him when the escape would be made."

He nodded to Able. "I do not have Master Six's total recall of all conversations, but I can never forget what Claude said. 'This, Captain, is your chance to alert the shore authorities and have those two men apprehended.'"

"What did Faulke say to that?" Mr. Pitt asked.

"He laughed and said it was perfect," Jean told them. He tried to hide his bitterness, but he couldn't. "He said most distinctly, 'Three or four more of these escape attempts that I can alert the navy to, sir, might give me my own liberation from this damned scow.'"

Jean heard the low murmur around him and continued. "I heard coins change hands."

Everyone was silent, listening. "That's when it occurred to me that there was a deeper game going on, one that I do not believe Captain Faulke is aware of."

"Well? Well?" someone asked, and not patiently, when Jean could not speak.

"Lieutenant Hubert?" Mr. Pitt inquired more gently.

"I strongly suspect that Claude Pascal had been planted in the hulk by someone much higher up. Think of it," he said, warming to the subject. "Most of us had come from one ship or other, and we knew each other in that way of navy men. You know what I mean, sirs."

He looked around and saw nods. They understood the fellowship of the fleet.

"Claude didn't seem to know anyone. One day he was in our midst, with his encouraging words, and plans for escape, and, oh, I cannot continue."

*I have betrayed my own country*, Jean thought. *All I ever wanted was peace. God forgive me, if la belle France cannot.*

"We won't know until the ringleaders in that house near St. Brendan's are convinced to talk, but it appears that there are spies on the *Captivity*, with the sole aim of working us ill in Portsmouth, and using the hulk to do it," Able explained, filling in the gap that Jean could not speak of. "Think of the ropewalk, the naval stores, the lumber. Jean?"

"Captain Faulke and Claude Pascal finally left," Jean said, resuming the narrative. "I waited a while to make sure it was safe, and opened the door on Ianthe Faulke, my little student, and sly. I…I don't know if she told her father I had been listening, but I would not doubt it. At the first opportunity, I jumped ship in that pile of dead bodies." He bowed and gestured to Able.

The sailing master picked up the story, his own voice hardening when he told of his wife's encounter with the murderers on the dock who knew full well which kegs contained the men trying to escape, and who drowned them as one little boy and Mrs. Six tried to stop them. "They attempted to interfere with my darling wife, then threw her in the water to drown. Thank God I arrived in time."

"My boys and I helm Sir B's yacht in the sound," Able continued, after a moment to gather himself together. Jean could only envy the steely resolve in his voice. "We discovered Jean Hubert nearly dead and rescued him. We told Sir B and our headmaster, of course. They agreed to grant Lieutenant Hubert a parole if he would teach at St. Brendan's."

"What do you teach?" Mr. Pitt asked.

"French, because it is a useful thing for any man in the fleet to know, as this war grinds on," Jean said promptly. "I also teach art, which has evolved into basic mapmaking and charting." He smiled at Able. "Courses have a way of changing to suit the needs, don't they, Able?"

"Aye, they do. Your story now or mine, Jean? Me? We found ourselves at Sir B's house one memorable night, and the next part of this mischief-making equation came to light."

Master Six took his own deep breath, and told of the night he watched Gervaise Turenne attempt to sidle close to Jean Hubert, as if seeking information.

Jean turned to watch Gervaise grow pale. The valet wiped sudden sweat from his face and backed away from Sir B, who stared at his servant in shocked silence, his eyes full of hurt. He turned toward the door.

Captain Ogilvie leaped to his feet and grabbed the valet, who struggled briefly, then sank into a chair and began to weep. Jean flinched to hear the awful sound in the suddenly silent room. The door opened and the Royal Marines stood there at port arms.

"Brothers, some of you know that I and other agents like me have been watching various émigrés living near the Channel." Ogilvie clamped his hand on the valet's shoulder and shook him into silence. "We intercepted a message with this unfortunate valet's name on it, after a nasty piece of work left the Turenne house in Kent." He leaned closer and spoke into Gervaise's face. "Your own parents, fool! What do you say to that?"

Gervaise shrieked and tried to struggle out from under Ogilvie's grasp, but the stronger man forced his face against the table.

"Stop it, I say!" Sir B commanded. "Maybe you see the need for force, and sir, I still dispute how you treated Master Six last February, but must you be a brute, too? Wheel me closer, Able, if you will."

The sailing master did as requested, until the captain sat next to his terrified servant. "Why, Gervaise, why?" he asked quietly. With some effort he took a handkerchief from his pocket and gave it to his valet. "Blow your nose. It's not the end of the world."

"Not yet, anyway," growled Ogilvie, and got a fierce stare from Sir B for his pains.

"Why?" the invalid captain asked again. "Tell me. Tell all of us. What were you trying to do?"

Gervaise blew his nose. He raised his head, but he could not look in his employer's eyes. Jean felt a pang that Gervaise could look nowhere, because he was surrounded by the enemy, even as he, Lieutenant Jean Hubert, was.

"Tell us now," Sir B said, and the steel returned to his voice. Jean had to wonder what the man had been like commanding a quarterdeck during a battle. Able could probably tell him stories.

"It was Sophie Deladier," Gervaise said, "my friend. You remember?"

"I do, lad. You told me Sophie was accused of Royalist leanings, and you asked me if there was anything I could do to spirit her out of France." Sir B shook his head. "I told you I could do nothing. It was true." He sighed heavily. "And you tried to take matters into your own hands, didn't you?"

Gervaise nodded. He took a moment to compose himself. "I was informed by someone my parents knew that if I would pass on a note to a French prisoner there in Portsmouth who would make himself known to me, I could help Sophie." He looked at Jean, who felt his heart break, as he thought of all the thousands of innocent people accused, briefly tried, and sent to the guillotine. The glorious revolution had cannibalized itself and Napoleon was the result. "He said that was all I would have to do. Jean Hubert was an escaped prisoner. God help me, I assumed he was the man to receive my note." He gave Jean a look that seemed to ask, *Why weren't you the man I was supposed to find?*

"It's never that easy, is it?" Mr. Pitt asked, speaking more to himself than the others, or so it seemed to Jean.

"What else could I do?" Gervaise asked the room at large. Jean saw no sympathy on any face; he expected none.

"You could have talked to me when it happened," Sir B said, his voice so gentle, all the sorrow evident. "I trusted you."

Gervaise returned to the sodden handkerchief, weeping for himself, for Sophie, and for his parents. Jean wanted to wail to the heavens as he thought of the prisoners in the hulk, plotting their pitiful escapes and not knowing that Claude Pascal, their own leader, was cannibalizing them, too. Was this convulsing birth of a nation worth so much pain? He turned away to collect himself.

"Guards, take this man away," Mr. Pitt said.

Gervaise threw himself on his knees. "I never meant to cause harm! Please believe me!"

His expression troubled, the prime minister gestured to the guards, who lifted up the sobbing valet. "We cannot countenance anything that threatens the security of our nation, Gervaise Turenne. You have loosed something worse on us, which we must now stop." He spoke to Captain Ogilvie. "Have his parents been apprehended?"

"Aye, Mr. Pitt. They're being escorted to Portsmouth now."

"We meant no harm!" Gervaise kept repeating, until the doors closed. His voice became fainter until he was out of hearing.

Exhausted, Jean sank into a chair. Grace made her way to Sir B's side and held his hand. Mr. Pitt shook his head.

"Jean wanted nothing to do with Gervaise Turenne," Able continued. "He mentioned the matter to me later. Why didn't you tell me sooner?"

Jean managed a little bow and didn't hide his smile. "Able, I am still a Frenchman and officially your enemy. I wanted to see how this played out. Surely you cannot blame me for that?"

"I suppose I cannot," Able replied, with a smile of his own. "I have been a prisoner of the French. I know what you are saying."

"I've been there, too," said a Brethren. Jean strained to hear a friendlier tone, and found it.

"Sirs, please believe me, but Captain Faulke is no better a captain than I am a spy," Jean said. "I am convinced that Claude Pascal is playing a deep game, intent upon causing havoc in your primary port. To his everlasting damnation, Claude tosses Faulke a bone now and then when he authorizes escapes that are going to be intercepted by you English. Without telling Faulke, Pascal arranges other escapes that are truly the work of spies."

More confident, Jean let that bit of nastiness sink in. His sketches had made their way around the table. He picked them up and held them to his chest. "The desperate prisoners, I among them, were none the wiser."

Calmly, Able continued the narrative, up to the intercepted signals from the hulk, probably the work of Claude Pascal, belowdecks. "Sirs, we know what they are going to do and when," he concluded. "The plan is to blow up the block pulley factory on May 17. That is why we have come here to lay out this plot for you."

"You know where the escapees and spies are?" Mr. Pitt asked.

"We do," Able said, and Jean heard the pride in his voice. "My Gunwharf Rats are even now keeping their eye on the house, along with a particularly effective constable with the Landport Gate station."

"They should all be arrested at once," said one of the Elder Brothers, "and that reprehensible Captain Faulke and Pascal captured. Now!"

The sailing master raised his hand. "Brothers, I have a better idea. Hear me out." He bowed to the prime minister. "It's a good plan, because we must be vigilant to quash additional mischief."

# — Chapter Forty —

It *was* a good plan, the serviceable kind to get a dirty job done. Able knew it startled the Brothers at first, but they agreed, even Captain Ogilvie. To be fair, especially Captain Ogilvie, Able decided next morning, after he and the others had snatched some sleep in Grace Croker's townhouse. Ogilvie did like a bold stroke, and the plan was a bold stroke squared. The man nearly chortled at the whole thing, and insisted upon helping.

"I'd rather never see Ogilvie again, but we probably need his good will," Able admitted to Jean as they lounged in Grace Croker's sitting room, everyone tired, but still too alert to sleep. "He said he will follow us to Portsmouth."

Captain Sir Belvedere St. Anthony did not join in the discussion, but sat with his head bowed, his sorrow bared for all to see. He was past caring, never a good place for a proud man to dwell.

"Sir B, what do you think will happen to Gervaise?" Grace asked. She was never one to gild a lily. "His parents, too, I suppose."

Sir B raised bleak eyes to hers, which made the proper Grace take his hand and rest it against her cheek. "I hate this war," he said.

"If it is any consolation, we all do," Able said, thinking of a peaceful life teaching a generation of Gunwharf Rats and watching his children growing up far removed from workhouses and the ugliness he knew and could do little about.

"What will I do without Gervaise?" Sir B asked. "I can't...I need someone."

Able winced at the plaintive words of a proud man humbled to the dust because he could barely wipe his ass without assistance. He thought of all the ways Sir B had mentored him when he was a mere seaman on his second frigate, sailing into battle against the French. His debt to the hero of Aboukir Bay was unpayable, and he could do nothing to make it right.

Thank God Grace was made of sterner stuff than a helpless genius. "I have arranged for Junius Bolt – my steward from Kent – to assist you tonight and afterwards, if you wish," she said. "He's waiting upstairs in my best guest room. And there's this: he had a misspent youth with the fleet in earlier days."

If she thought that would cajole Sir B into a smile, she failed. Able gave her credit for trying.

"What I *wish* is to go to my own house. I do have one here in London," he grumbled, unwilling to be dependent upon anyone, even though he knew he was.

"Not tonight, dear friend," Grace said, neatly overruling him. "It's too late and your servants are a lazy lot."

Able wanted to laugh, but he knew better. *Sir B, it would serve you right to marry this forthright lady,* he thought.

"They are not lazy!" Sir B insisted, until his innate honesty reasserted itself. "Possibly they are. Very well, Gracie, have your way with me."

"You haven't called me Gracie since I was eight or nine," Grace said.

"You haven't provoked me as much as you are provoking me right now," he retorted.

She laughed and pushed his chair into the hall, where two marines lifted him up the stairs.

"That is a woman I would never care to cross," Jean remarked.

"Few of us do," Able agreed.

"You realize, of course, that they are the perfect couple," Jean said. He yawned. "Imagine the lively fights, the sparring, the wit, the kindness…" He sighed. "And how will that ever happen?"

"Divine intervention," Able said. He rose and stretched. "You and I are sharing a bed. I hope you do not snore."

"No more than you do, *probablement, mon ami.* Good night."

When Grace returned, Able still wondered how he was going to tell Meri his part in the upcoming punitive action. Grace sat beside him on the sofa, then did something so unexpected that he knew he would always admire this prickly, intelligent, forthright woman. She leaned her head against his shoulder.

He put his arm around her. "What's the matter, Grace?" he asked, feeling not even slightly out of place now. He knew when a woman needed something. Meri had trained him well, bless her darling heart.

"Sir B is lying in bed and the tears are running down his face," she said, not without difficulty of her own. "Junius informed me. The poor old fellow is standing in the hall and wringing his hands. What am I to do?"

"Tell Junius you will handle the matter, go to Sir B and curl up next to him," Able said with no hesitation. "On top of the covers or between them is of no consequence to me. I recommend between them. It might be May, but your house is chilly."

"Able, you're serious?" She sounded hopeful.

"Never more so. Your house *is* chilly."

She thumped him as he deserved. "How does Meridee tolerate you?"

"Quite well, actually. Ben is proof, if you need any verification."

"Oh, you! The servants will talk about me."

"Why should you care if they do?" He kissed her cheek and stood up. "For all we know, they are wagering in the servants' hall that you will do precisely that!" He yawned. "G'night, Grace."

Jean was already asleep and snoring lightly by the time Able shucked his clothes and crawled in bed. He lay there, listening, and soon heard the door to the guest room next to his open and close quietly. *Good for you,* he thought. He told Euclid and whoever else was screeching in his head to shut down. It took a moment, but they must have known he meant business. He slept.

They returned to Portsmouth the way they had left it, traveling fast, changing horses, and snatching food when possible. He observed Sir B and saw a quiet man, but not a melancholy one. Whatever Grace Croker had done must have stuffed the heart back into his body. Junius Bolt also accompanied them, so they were crammed close together in the post chaise, Junius riding inside because he was too old to face the rain with the coachman.

Jean volunteered to sit on the box with John Coachman, but Grace disagreed. "See here, I will sit next to you, Sir B. You will put your arm around me and we will manage splendidly."

They arrived in Portsmouth the following afternoon in a rain squall. Able could barely make out the hulks in their straight line. He panicked for a tiny moment when he couldn't see Building Twelve, but there it was, one more nondescript structure in rows of identical brick buildings. He patted his pocket for the Prime Minister's signed and sealed documents for St. Brendan's, the Royal Marines and the Landport constabulary to work together in silence, for the good of a nation at war.

He handed the packet to Junius Bolt when the post chaise stopped at Jasper Street. "Guard this with your life," he said.

Grace's old retainer could not have been more delighted. He grasped the documents with their official seals and tags and put them to his heart. "The future of England is safe with me," he declared in ringing tones that made Sir B grin like he used to.

"Spoken like an old salt, Junius," Sir B said. "What unfortunate ship did you serve on?"

"The *Agamemnon*, Captain St. Anthony," he said promptly. "I was invaluable to the good of the fleet."

"A cook?"

Junius beamed at him. "Ta best."

"Our first stop in the morning will be the Marine barracks," Sir B said, after Able and Jean helped him from the post chaise and Junius arranged the blanket around him. "And then it is noon in Headmaster Croker's quarters?"

"Precisely," Able said. "We will have our chosen Gunwharf Rats present."

Sir B took Able's hand and Jean's as well. "Today is May 15," he said, as serious now as on any fleet action. "Two days, my friends." He looked toward the post chaise and blew a kiss to Grace Croker. She was properly red-faced when Able told the driver that St. Brendan's was next and he and Jean sat down again.

Grace assured him that Jean could escort her up the steps of St. Brendan's and the two of them could explain the plan to her brother. "You need to speak to Meri," she told him. "I wish you luck."

He made a face at her words, and she kissed his cheek. "I spent a very good night with Belvedere," she whispered.

"Jean, give me a minute with this lady," Able said.

With a private, French sort of smile, Jean bounded from the post chaise. Able moved to Grace's side of the muddy vehicle. "Well, madam, on top of the covers or between them?" he asked, hoping she never repeated his commentary to Meri, who would be aghast at her husband.

"You, sir, are a nosy man," she said, but he heard the affection in her voice. "Between them. My house *was* a little cold."

He turned slightly to face her. How much did he dare ask? "Did you learn anything new?"

She sat so silent, contemplative almost, which wasn't Grace Croker, not really. She was quick of mind and action, decisive. There she sat. She looked him directly in the eyes. "Dear, dear friend, I learned that I am brave enough."

With a bow to a brave lady, Able went up his own front steps across the street. While he and Grace were gone, Headmaster Croker must have set his lads to work and plenty of it, because Nick, John and Smitty barely looked up when he came into the house and walked by the dining room.

"Meri!" he called. "I'm home."

She came out of the kitchen, wiping her hands on her apron, eyes worried, hair frizzy from the heat of the Rumford range. He had seldom seen her more beautiful.

He folded her in his arms. "We must talk."

She darted into the kitchen and came back without her apron. She took his hand and led him upstairs, her face serious and determined. How did she already know that it wasn't going to be a conversation she enjoyed? How marvelous was woman.

He looked in Ben's room, touched to see his son sleeping on his stomach, his little bottom pooched high. *I love this boy of mine*, he thought. *Please God, let everything go smoothly.* He couldn't have said with any accuracy whether he meant the conversation with his wife, or the events in two days' time.

"You're tired," she said. "Lie down and tell me what I don't want to hear."

He told her. She cried and protested. He held her close until her tears stopped, but she didn't give up.

"Surely someone else can go with Jean to the *Captivity* besides you," she said, her arms tight around him.

"No one here speaks French as well as I do, Meri," he explained again. "I can't in Christian conscience send Jean into that hulk alone. We have to snatch Claude Pascal before he disappears among eight hundred men, or before any of the prisoners know what is going on."

He pulled the blanket at the foot of their bed over both of them, cocooning them together in their own world, a place far better than any other world here or in his inventive mind.

She cried again and he didn't argue with her tears or try to reason with her. He held his handkerchief to her nose when she had subsided into hiccups and she blew. She wasn't stiff in his arms, a woman unwilling to forgive him for taking his life into danger.

"You need a bath, Able," she said finally. "When was the last time?"

Relieved, he could have cried. "It was a fast trip. There wasn't time to change my linen."

"I can tell. Were you eating onions, too?"

She sniffed and he grinned over the top of her head so she couldn't see, even though the enveloping blanket made their nest dark. "Husband, the boys are busy in the dining room, and Mrs. Perry is at the market, probably terrifying the fishmongers. No one is using the laundry room, and there is hot water on the range."

"Only if you scrub my back, Meri."

"Certainly I will," she said, sounding a little indignant. "What sort of wife do you think I am?"

She couldn't keep up the banter, but her tears were fewer this time. They still broke his heart.

# — Chapter Forty-one —

M ere hours later, Headmaster Croker ushered the major of the Royal Marines
barracks, Walter Cornwall representing Landport Gate, Captain Angus Ogilvie,
Jean Hubert and Able Six into his sitting room. Looking as serious as the others, Nick,
John Mark, Smitty, Lark and Wren sat on the floor. Simon Goodrich was already seated,
but he offered his chair to a little man with pince-nez perched on his long nose, and the
look of a clerk.

*I am getting so proficient at explaining the plan*, Able thought, as he stood to one side until
everyone was seated and Thaddeus Croker nodded to him.

Deeply mindful of the minutes and seconds sweeping by, Able explained the crisis as
economically as he could: the conspirators, the plot to blow up Building Twelve (which
made Simon Goodrich wince and say something best not repeated), the devilment being
planned aboard the prison hulk *Captivity* (the Marine commandant narrowed his eyes at
that one), and the remedy, designed to confuse the ringleader on the hulk and flush out
the perpetrators.

"That brings me to you," Able said, addressing the little man. "Mr. Markham, is it?
Navy gunners are going to place charges in your building and blow it up."

The little man's mouth made a perfect O. The spectacles fell off his nose. Nick
caught them and handed them back. "M...mm...my building? Good God, sir, but this is
highly irregular. Does Admiralty *know* what you are doing? 'Pon my word."

Able had to look away when the major's lips started to twitch. Sir B managed a
discreet cough. *Stern navy face*, Able told himself.

"Aye, sir, Admiralty knows. So does Trinity House. The actual target of the French
conspirators is Building Twelve, directly behind you, the block pulley factory."

"I know what is behind me, and it is dashed noisy," Mr. Markham retorted. He tried
to put his spectacles back on upside down, to the amusement of the Gunwharf Rats.
They sobered instantly when Able gave them his sailing master stare.

"That factory, noisy and all, is vital to the war effort, which is why the French are
planning to blow it up on the evening of May 17," Able explained. "The conspiracy
is being directed from aboard the *Captivity*, that first hulk in line in the harbor. When
Building Eleven blows instead, they won't be able to tell the difference from that distance."

"Dash it all, why don't you just nab the conspirators on the hulk and avoid the drama?" Mr. Markham asked, and it was a good question. "My building will remain standing," he added pointedly.

"Sir, there are three hundred prisoners on each level of the hulk. If the ringleader even suspects what we know, he will blend in with the others and we will not find him," Able said. "We also suspect he has been planted by Napoleon to create havoc on our port and destroy other valuable resources. And consider this: We are not entirely certain just how many conspirators there are on land right now. Your building has to go. The conspirators must think they are successful, and we hope, overplay their hand."

"One more thing, Mr. Markham," Sir B said. "Jean Hubert and Able Six will be in place in that hold, watching for the conspirator to answer a signal which he will see from the conspirators' house on shore, when Building Eleven explodes. If he has another signal to send to that house, we need to know it. Then they will pounce and nab him. Your contribution, sir, is of vital importance to the war effort."

"So is paperwork, sir," the little man said stubbornly. "What will become of my folders and files?"

"Starting tomorrow, you and your office workers will box them and move them directly behind you to Building Twelve," Able told him.

"I have room in my building," Simon Goodrich assured Mr. Markham. "You will move the boxes at random tomorrow and Thursday, in case anyone is watching us. A box here, a box there, until the job is done."

"It is for the good of the nation," Thaddeus Croker reminded him gently. "We can replace your desks and chairs."

"I wish it could be otherwise, sir, but these are the facts," Able added, wondering what the stubborn fellow would do if suddenly confronted by Mrs. Perry in full pugnacious mode. The idea was tempting. "And there is this: Absolutely none of your clerks or office boys must be told anything beyond that the paperwork must be relocated to Building Twelve. They must vacate at the usual hour of six of the clock."

The head clerk nodded as Able's words sank in, but he did not go gently. "You realize, sirs, that the records and bills of lading will be all jumbled about. We will not know if ten dozen pairs of woolen stockings were delivered to Plymouth or Chatham. Watch caps will probably wind up in… in God help us Scotland, and who will know what to do with them there?"

"It's a weighty business," Able said. "Ye cannot depend upon the Scots, but this is war, sir, not watch caps." Sir B coughed louder.

"Mr. Markham, one of my Marines will escort you back to Building Eleven," the major said. "You may call upon him and other Marines with him to help you pack your invoices and bills of lading. Come with me."

Mr. Markham left, probably destined to worry himself sick about those watch caps misplaced and trousers headed toward some other remote outpost of empire.

"Napoleon calls us a nation of shopkeepers, or so I have been told," Headmaster Croker commented. "What next, Able?"

"Jean Hubert will instruct Nick Bonfort in the signal he is to send from inside the house to the *Captivity*, after the explosion in Building Eleven," Able said. "As for the house, I have asked Smitty, Wren and Lark, who will be assisted by Ezekiel Bartleby, to help the Marines and constables. I need stout lads, because we don't really know how many conspirators are in there."

"It's dangerous work," the headmaster said. "Are you Gunwharf Rats ready?"

"Aye, sir," they chorused, with so much enthusiasm that Able wondered if he was training men for the fleet, or pirates for the Spanish Main.

"And John Mark? What will he do?"

"Headmaster, he and a few of the other Rats and constables will remain by the sea wall and watch if anyone from the hulks strikes out for shore," Able said. "Captain Ogilvie, will you accompany Jean and me and the Marines in the apprehension of Captain Faulke?"

"Capital!" he declared, rubbing his hands together. "I know a variety of ways to encourage his cooperation."

*I'll wager you do*, Able thought with some distaste. "I'll leave it to you and the major to deal with a traitor."

"Meanwhile, Grace and I will carry on teaching, right here at St. Brendan's," Thaddeus said. He bowed to Sir B. "We can use your help, Captain St. Anthony."

"I never sparkled at mathematics, but by God, I can tie any knot known to a sailor." Sir B looked around the crowded room, assuming command in his effortless way that Able could only envy and never duplicate. "I trust I need not remind you that this is a matter of grave national importance and you must say nothing to anyone. Do I have your word on it? Good."

"And that is that, Meri," Able told his wife that night, after the boys were finally in bed, and Jean probably pacing back and forth in the room he shared with Smitty. "How about a cuddle? Meri?"

He held her as she tried not to weep, taking great breaths. "Better now?" he asked gently. She nodded, unable to speak.

"I know it's dangerous," he told her as he rubbed her back. "I am counting on total confusion belowdecks."

She nodded and burrowed closer to his chest like the wounded cat set upon by rat terriers that he had snatched up from a back alley, during a port of call in Tangier, where helpless animals had few friends.

"Meri, I'll come back to you in one piece. I promise," he told her.

"If you don't, I will die," she whispered.

"I didn't marry a woman that helpless," he told her. "I married a resourceful, lovely lady who will always take care of those she loves."

"Just words, Able," she said, and she sounded so weary. With a pang, he knew it was the closest she had ever come in their short married life to turning away from him.

He held her until she fell asleep, thinking of lonely Isaac Newton, who had never known the love of a woman. He did not know about Euclid. Copernicus had been chastised by two bishops because of his over-fondness for his housekeeper. He thought of sad Lavoisier, the newest polymath to join the odd fraternity in his brain, moping about because his Marie-Anne, wife and lab partner, cried for him from the distance of a France in turmoil.

He could try to explain to Meri that he had to play out this chancy hand to the end, but he doubted she would understand. She was as bright a female as he could have hoped for, but she was a wife and a mother first.

When he knew she slept, he pulled on his dressing gown and walked to Ben's little room. He stood over his son's crib and watched the simplicity of a baby sighing and settling himself deeper into sleep, not a care anywhere because his mother always had a meal for him, and people changed his nappies.

Able closed the door quietly, then walked downstairs, unhappy with himself, suddenly uncertain about the day after tomorrow. He knew enough about fleet actions to know they never went as planned. He could tell Meri that he and Jean would get into the hold and nab Claude Pascal before he saw them, but she was a woman and practical. Who was he fooling? He knew crafty men like Claude Pascal were unaccountable in their conduct.

"Master Six, you're going to wear out the carpet."

He turned around, surprised to see Mrs. Perry standing in the sitting room doorway, looking more enormous than usual in her blue and white-striped nightgown that looked like mattress ticking.

He knew she had seen fleet actions because she sailed with her carpenter husband. Granted it was irregular, but the officers in the wardroom had even joked behind their captain's back that he wasn't brave enough to tell her no.

"Meri is so unhappy with me," he said simply.

He sat down and she sat beside him, crowding him on the sofa. He wondered what she would do if he leaned against her shoulder. She decided the issue, pulling him close. Able closed his eyes and savored the softness of her bosom. Not for the first time, he asked himself what kind of mother she would have been, she who rough-mothered half the sailors on each of her husband's frigates.

He thought of the mother he had known only briefly, as she gave birth to him and died, leaving him to face alone the hardness of life. He couldn't cry over her loss, really. Rational thought, something he was full of, assured him it was impossible to miss someone he never knew. But he knew Meri Six, knew everything about her, and loved her past all understanding.

"The last person in the world I ever want to injure is my wife, and here I am, doing precisely that. Mrs. Perry, Napoleon is the puppet master of Europe. He jiggles our strings and we dance to his tune."

"It won't last forever," she assured him.

"My sole aim is to survive the next two days," he said. "I don't care about forever. Just two days."

"Mrs. Perry, I wondered where he went. Hand him over to me."

Able's brain politely informed him that an hour and ten minutes had passed. He opened his eyes to see his wife crouched beside the sofa.

"He's not much," his big housekeeper told her, which made Meri laugh.

"I know, but I love him."

"Then here he is, Mrs. Six. Take him upstairs and put him to bed."

# — Chapter Forty-two —

May 16 passed in a merciful blur. After a morning's classwork where he taught by rote and his students paid only polite attention, Able escorted John Mark to his usual afternoon assignment at the block pulley factory.

Even the effervescent little fellow was strangely sober. "Is it always like this before a fleet action?" he asked, as they passed the water hoy inlet that still sent Able's stomach down to his shoes and back up again, as he remembered everything.

"No. We don't usually have the luxury of planning ahead," he said, as he asked himself which was harder, the plan that never went quite as expected, or the spontaneous battle they made up as they went along. "Hard to say which is worse, though."

He noticed with satisfaction that Mr. Markham had tapped into an unexpected vein for the dramatic in his bean counter's heart. He and John watched as the clerks, dressed as ordinary dockworkers now, carried out papers and invoices in boxes labeled screws, nuts and bolts. They went in twos and threes, waited a while, then crossed the alley randomly, always carrying something.

Simon Goodrich's artificers had already covered the windows facing the back of Building Eleven with heavy boards, but from the inside. "I am certain the glass will go when the powder ignites, but this will save my machinery," he said. He gestured with his head toward the corner of the building, where two drunks sprawled. "Those worthless layabouts are Royal Marines, dressed rather more casually. They'll deal with any suspicious characters who might wander into the alley between now and then."

Simon turned to John Mark, whose eyes were wide with the adventure of it all. "Never a dull moment, eh, laddie?" he said, and rested his hand on John's head. He took it off quickly. "Oops, there. My wife says I shouldn't do that if my hands are oily, as they usually are."

"I don't mind," John said, an honest fellow. "I really don't."

"He doesn't, either," Able said as they watched John walk down the corridor to the room where he copied machine parts. "My wife tells me that workhouse boys need a good touch now and then, no matter how long they have been away from that grind. And look, here is his shadow."

They watched Pierre Deschamps sidle past them, worry in his eyes, until he came up to John, who took his hand and walked into Simon's office.

"I know you have plans at St. Brendan's for John," Simon said. He paused, as if he didn't know how to say what was on his mind. Able had noticed that the artificers at the block pulley factory were long on mechanical skills but short on conversation.

Maybe he could help this young man who obviously had something on his mind.

"Aye, we do, but we at St. Brendan's have already discovered that some lads are better suited elsewhere than at sea."

"I have something more in mind, beyond the fact that John Mark does have the makings of a mechanical artificer."

Simon took a deep breath, and looked around. Able wondered how private this conversation needed to be. They were in the middle of a block pulley factory after all, probably not a place for someone to bare his soul.

The artificer spoke softly, and Able leaned closer. Too many years of cannonading had worked on his hearing. "My wife has been unable to carry a baby to term." He shook his head. "Eight difficult years. Honestly, Master Six, she is hungry to have a child or two about the place, and I wondered…"

Able swallowed the great lump in his throat, thinking of all the children in his workhouse, their faces pressed to the windows, whenever they knew couples were coming by to take a look at them. He felt his heart grow light, freed, at least for the moment, from the awful burden of the action coming tomorrow. Another thought traipsed through his mind of little flowers that sometimes grew on kitchen middens or dung heaps. Only last night, after Meri got him back to bed and loved him, she had whispered into his chest. "I will never lose hope," she had said. "Please don't give me a reason to."

He looked in Simon's eyes and saw the hope and kindness and a certain resolve evident on the face of every man on the Portsmouth docks. From stevedore to harbormaster to factory builder, they were engaged in a great enterprise, one that could decide the fate of nations, and they knew it. But in all this worry and bustle and commotion, hope still flourished.

He put his hand on Simon's shoulder. "Come 'round and see us after we have got through our trying time tomorrow. Bring your wife to my house, too. We'll see what John Mark has to say about your proposal." He smiled. "The one you're a little shy to admit."

"Am I whistling in the wind?" Simon asked. "I won't take Lydia anywhere unless I have some assurance that her heart won't be broken again."

"You're not whistling in the wind," Able told him. "I'm glad you told me this. And now, sir, to work."

"One more thing, Able."

"Aye?"

"Lydia and I are both Methodists. I've been told that there isn't anything you don't know, but are you aware that John Mark was also referred to in the book of Acts as John, and other times simply as Mark?"

Able smiled inwardly at the earnest look on Simon's face. He thought he knew where the artificer was going with this, and it touched his heart.

"Master Six, John Mark needs a last name, because it isn't Mark," Simon said in a rush, his face red. "I want it to be Goodrich."

"I believe you are right," Able managed to say. "Come to my house later, both of you. We have to leave this in John Mark's hands, but I know he worships you and Mr. Maudslay's amazing block pulleys."

Simon's smile could have lit the darkest room. "We're praying for the success of your action tomorrow night."

"Thank you. I've never been much of a believing man," Able said as he dabbed at his eyes. "All science argues against it. And yet…yes, please pray for us."

The morning of May 17 dawned clear and cool, with a little chop on the water. Meri had not let him out of bed, clicking the lock and taking off her nightgown. She laughed when he shrieked "help" in a tiny voice, as he had done the morning after their Devonshire wedding. It was their little joke.

When she was sleeping again, he dressed quietly, unlocked the door, laughed silently about that lock and key, and padded down the hall for a look at Ben, who kindly slumbered, too. He tapped softly on Jean's door, then opened it.

The lieutenant sat on his bed, fully dressed, a pad in his lap and pencil in hand. Smitty slept. Able noticed that the boy's thumbs were curled inside his fingers, the way Ben slept.

"I'll get him up," Jean whispered. "One hour in the headmaster's office?"

"Aye. What are you writing?"

Jean shrugged. "My sister is dead. I have a brother somewhere in Canada with a fur company. Do you think a letter addressed to Christophe Alain Hubert, North West Company, Canada, will get to him? It's a big country."

"Probably. Eventually. Leave it with Meri."

"Have you written a letter?"

Able shook his head. He could never tell anyone that he had pressed his heart to Meri's heart last night and this morning, as close to his wife as humanly possible, legs and arms twined together. What could he possibly say? "Should I?" he asked.

"You should."

Able nodded. "One hour, across the street."

He tapped on John Mark and Nick's door, stirring them awake with less effort than usual because they knew what day it was, and what was coming toward them. He had seen serious youngsters aboard many a ship, mere children slapped on the rump in hammocks or dumped out, if the bosun was more unkind than most. He had had been turned out that way, himself.

"One hour, lads, then over to Headmaster Croker's office," he said. "We're reviewing everything one more time."

He did as Jean directed, writing a note to Meri in the sitting room, knowing how fearsomely inadequate it was, how little it expressed the depths of his heart. She already knew where their modest money was banked, and where whatever documents either of them deemed important were stashed. They had already discussed what she would do and where she and Ben would go, should matters fall out in a way neither of them wanted. He had encouraged her to marry again, because every boy needed a father, every wife a husband. He didn't mean it, and she understood. Meri could follow her heart however she chose.

He wondered if he had left her with child. A daughter would be nice, maybe named Mary after his mother, who had tried so hard to make sure he had some chance at life. Benjamin and Mary, dear ones. He knew they would be in excellent hands because his wife was everything he had ever hoped for. More time would be nice. *Time, time, bend some time for me, Newton,* he thought in exquisite agony. *Give the universe a wave of your magic wand and speed time to end this war. Do it for me.*

Miserable beyond words, he sat back in his chair at Meri's writing desk and demanded that the people in his brain give him all possible help. He had never asked them for much. He had made no demands. His life had conditioned him to expect nothing. Most days he didn't even want the voices.

"Do this for me now," he whispered. "If you cannot guide me and keep me safe somehow, help the others. Help my wife."

His brain was strangely silent. He heard kitchen noises, the murmur of voices from the Rats' room, the sound of Meri's bare feet going down the hall to Ben's room, his son the tyrant indignant that he was wet and hungry. To his delight he also heard the beguiling sound of the ocean in the middle of the Pacific, and suddenly, a grand chorus of singers doing celestial justice to Mozart's final Requiem in D Minor.

When the last chorus faded, he signed his name, folded the paper, wrote *Meri, Meri, joy of my heart,* and tucked it in the desk where she could find it someday.

The day was cool, so he pulled on his boat cloak, centered his bicorn, and left his home.

He shouldn't have looked back, but he did, hopeful. She did not fail him. Meri stood at their son's window, Ben in her arms, her hair untidy because he had run his fingers through it even more than usual. He loved the feel of her hair.

He lifted his bicorn to her, and she waved and blew him a kiss. She pressed her hand against the glass and he raised his in imitation. He could almost feel the warmth of her palm against his, even from across the street.

*God keep you, Meri.*

# — Chapter Forty-three —

Dusk started the great engine of battle.

The day began with an assembly in St. Brendan's cellar of what Sir B used to call "all the moveable parts," with the Gunwharf Rats selected for this fleet action on land suitably sober and wide-eyed.

Looking burned to the socket, but with the old zeal and resolve evident to Able, Captain Sir Belvedere St. Anthony went over the entire plan. Wisely, he began by complimenting a beaming Mr. Markham on the efficient way his clerks had vacated their office in Building Eleven with dispatch and order.

'Pon my word, sir, I do believe we all enjoyed this bit of derring-do," the accountant said, practically rubbing his hands together in glee. "We clerks don't often have such fun."

Able was grateful he stood in a dim cellar, so Mr. Markham couldn't see his smile. Sir B managed himself with real aplomb. "We of the Royal Navy could not conduct this punitive action without your excellent cooperation. King and country thank you."

From his expression of sublime satisfaction, apparently that was all the praise required for the senior clerk to forget the disturbance to his typically dull day of ledgers and numbers, and the upcoming loss by fire of what office furniture couldn't be hauled out discreetly. Mr. Markham pounded his heart with clenched fist. "We are honored to play our small part in ridding the world of the Corsican monster," he declared.

"Well, yes, er..."

Even Sir B couldn't withstand that. Able saved him by stepping forward and with a perfectly straight face ordering, "St. Brendan students, three cheers for the accountants!"

The three cheers were administered with great enthusiasm, giving Sir B and the normally stuffy major of the Royal Marines, Portsmouth, time to recover. Headmaster Croker held up remarkably well. Politely dismissed then, Mr. Markham went his way rejoicing, a happy and patriotic man.

No fool by any means, Able had put Walter Cornwall in charge of the sortie to surround and seize the house where the lantern signals had originated. The constable's initial reluctance to speak "in front of me betters" vanished nearly at once, because he was thoughtful, careful and knew what to do.

*Good show, Walter*, Able thought with admiration, as the constable described how the Marines, Gunwharf Rats and other constables would cover front and back doors, then rush in, pistols ready, and swords drawn. "Go in swinging and shouting," Walter advised. "I've been impressed how useful that is in discomfiting everyone." Perhaps Walter had been bitten by the educationist's bug, because he turned to Smitty next. "What do we do then?"

"Gag'um and bind'um," St. Brendan's talented sailor-in-the-making with the look of a street thug said. He patted Nick Bonfort's head. "Then we make sure Nick can send a message to the hulk."

"And?" Walter asked.

"If there is a response, we all take down the flash sequences so there is no error," Wren said. Lark nodded.

Able next yielded the floor to the gunner's mate, Royal Marine Artillery, who described the powder laid down in those first floor rooms – the upper floors had been used for storage since the reign of Charles II – and how it would all be touched off at nineteen hundred hours with a long lead, one hour after the clerks left Building Eleven and right after the conspirators' house was secured.

"Sor, we'll 'av ta fire brigade close as can be, so nuffink spreads," he assured the rest of them. "Flash, bang, smoke and fire."

"Now then, John Mark, Whitticombe and Tots, you'll be stationed at the sea wall to watch if anyone comes ashore from the hulks," Able said.

"And if they do, sir?" John asked. "We're not very big."

"I forget that now and then," Able said, which had the desired effect of straightening the lad's posture and putting a proud smile on his face. "Major, can you spare some marines for sea wall duty?"

He could and made a few notes on his tablet, and proved he was a father, too, by adding, "They'll be back-up in case these capable-looking lads need a little more dash. One or two is all we need. I have confidence in St. Brendan's."

*I, too,* Able thought, as the Gunwharf Rats filed upstairs toward their morning class with Miss Croker, who had no intention of letting a major naval action stop her from nouns, adjectives and adverbs.

The major hung back for a moment to assure Able there would be more like six Marines close to the sea wall. "The lads don't need to know that, but we'll feel better, eh?"

"Yes, major, we will," Able said.

Nick and Jean remained in the cellar for another lesson. Yesterday, on Jean's direction, Simon Goodrich's best artificer had fashioned a rough approximation of a French signal lamp.

"We don't know if there is a coded signal to be sent when what they think is Building Twelve goes boom," Jean said as he lit the paraffin in the small metal cup. "I'd show you how to send *Mission accompli. Quoi de suite?*"

"Which is, sir, if I may ask?"

*Mission accomplished. What now?* Able thought as Jean told Nick. *What now, indeed?* Thoughtful, worried, tense and calm in turn, he helped the last marine in the cellar lift Sir B's wheeled chair up the narrow cellar steps, where he saw, to his relief, Grace's old retainer waiting there for his new charge. Sir B whispered to Able, "He's a bit of a bull dog, is old Junius. We're rubbing along famously."

And then it was time to wander, because he couldn't help himself. First down to the kitchen, where the cooks were stirring a great pot of burgoo. Able had already told the Rats that was to be their noon meal – well-sugared oats. "It's what we men eat before a fleet action," he had told them yesterday. "After we're served, Cookie douses the galley fire to keep the frigate safe as we sail into action. You'll get apples around four o'clock and maybe grog the way Mrs. Six fixes it. That's it until the action is over."

"Why, Master Six?" Lark had asked. While there were no stout students at St. Brendan's, Lark had discovered the pleasure of food, once he came here and learned how good it felt to be full.

"I want everyone in his fighting trim," Able said.

The cooks knew what to do, and politely chased him out. Grace was teaching. Nick and Jean were practicing. Because one of the old salts from the dockyard was taking Able's place in the classroom this morning, prodding the lads to dismantle and reassemble a sextant, Able found himself oddly non-essential. He thought about going home, but he had left Meri cheerful enough, and he would only pace the floor and worry until shadows lengthened.

He walked to Building Eleven, where the clerks had been replaced by Royal Marines dressed in sober black suits, sitting at the desks and looking busy, should someone walk by and take a too-great interest. A corporal showed him the trail of powder and piles of rags doused with coal oil and more powder. "We'll get out and fire it, and you'll hear a respectable bang, Master Six," the man said with some relish. "Just a day at t'office."

The other fake clerks laughed and sent him on his way, too. He paced the Gunwharf, where cannon were stored when fighting ships were placed in ordinary. The cannon were gone now, laid down aboard frigates and ships of the line that sailed and fought in all the oceans of the world. Again, he felt that tug and pull, as relentless as a tide, that whispered to him, "Come to sea again, Master Six. You know you miss us."

"I would miss my wife and child more," he said out loud, then looked around, hoping he was alone.

As it turned out, he wasn't alone. He looked and there was Meridee, cloaked and bonneted, a most proper lady who had thrown in her lot with a common bastard.

"What in the world brings you here?" he asked when she came closer, reached up to kiss his cheek and took his arm.

"Sir B stopped by the house on his way home and told me you were pacing about, most melancholy. Ben is sleeping and Betsy and Mrs. Perry are standing guard."

She put her hand to her mouth, and her eyes shone with mischief. By God he loved to see her that way, her eyes turning into little blue chips. "And do you know what?"

"Better tell me." She didn't know he had watched Walter Cornwall cross the street with real purpose on his face, heading to the Six house, a man on a mission.

"I peeked in the kitchen to tell Betsy I was going out for a walk, and what did I see but Constable Cornwall giving her such a kiss! I backed out before they saw me, because who wants to interrupt that?"

"Not I."

He turned and they strolled to one of the dry docks, where a swarm of workers were patching a great hole in the side of a seriously wounded frigate, back from one of the many nameless ship to ship encounters in the Mediterranean. It was noisy work, but he didn't have anything to say. It was enough to feel Meri close to him and know she loved him.

"I was thinking this morning…" They had moved away from the dry dock and were walking toward the quiet street where they lived. He felt his face heat up, which made him wonder about man and woman and marriage. He had been married long enough to know there wasn't anything he hadn't done with this woman that should raise a blush now.

"About what, my love?" she prompted.

"I was hoping perhaps you were with child again, and if it is a girl, you would name her Mary, after my mother," he said.

He knew precisely what his words would do to her, and they did. She leaned into his arm and tears filled her eyes. "Able, don't," she whispered. "This sounds like a last will and testament. You are *not* going to die tonight."

"We have no way of knowing that, wife," he told her.

"*We* will eventually have a daughter and *we* will name her Mary," she said, and he marveled at the ferocity of her words. "I'm worried enough without your worries, too."

"I know. Forgive me."

"You've done everything you can. You've probably even rehearsed what to do when everyone goes wrong," she told him. "Aha! I thought you had. Do you know what you need?"

He chuckled, which made her turn rosy. Was Meridee Six always going to be a modest thing? Probably.

"Able, do men ever *not* think about women?"

"I doubt it."

She tugged him into Ezekiel Bartleby's bakery. "This was what I had in mind."

He winked at Ezekiel beaming behind the counter and watched as Meri looked though the biscuits and eclairs and settled on petit fours, her favorite. She selected a dozen, paid for them over the baker's protests, and took Able outside to sit on the bench in the sun and eat them. Each one was sugary heaven. He ate more than he should have, but she was laughing and talking and he was, too, almost as if there was no war, no danger, no threat. For a brief moment they were a couple with nothing to do but eat and discuss those mundane bits of nothing that constituted marriage.

He knew what time it was. The clock in his head never failed him. He fell silent, then, "Go home, my love. I'm to meet Jean and Captain Ogilvie at the Marine Wharf in twenty minutes."

She nodded. She wetted her handkerchief with her tongue and wiped the sugar from around his lips. "Can't have you looking like a schoolboy, can I? What would people think?"

He gave her a businesslike kiss, because it seemed to suit her mood, then followed it with a better one that suited his, and as it so happened, theirs. He turned her about to face their home at the end of the block, and he walked the other way toward the Marine Wharf.

He told himself to forget her and Ben, and he did, as he and Jean changed into prisoner garb: too short trousers and orange-yellow shirts with TO inked on the back for Transport Office. Shoes came off. They debated manacles and decided on loosely tied rope, so they could slip out easily when the moment came.

Daggers secured under loose shirts, Jean with a cudgel up his sleeve he found somewhere, they sat down between their marine guard, with Captain Ogilvie aft in the cutter.

"What time is it, Able?" Jean asked.

"It wants twenty minutes of seven," he replied. "Nineteen now."

"How do you do that?"

"Don't ask."

They came alongside the *Captivity*, and the bosun piped them aboard. God, but the ship stunk. *I am getting soft*, Able thought, remembering other ships at sea and their overall stench. Prison hulks were different, it appeared. Despair has an odor.

All pomp and power, Captain Ogilvie demanded to see Captain Faulke. He held out Mr. Markham's best bit of forgery: Two notarized chits for one Jean Hubert, late of the *Calais*, escapee, and Solide Six, late of the *Bon Dieu*, escapee.

His eyes on the much sharper-looking marine guard that accompanied Captain Ogilvie, the *Captivity*'s corporal took the chits, saluted and scurried below deck.

"Seven minutes," Able said under his breath. "Let us hope Captain Faulke isn't constipated and sitting in the head. Ah, no, here he is," he finished in French.

Captain Faulke probably had too much power in his little kingdom of misery and suffering, Able decided, especially when he started to argue with Captain Ogilvie about being disturbed at his dinner.

He was starting to wave his arms about, and order Captain Ogilvie to just leave the damned escapees when Building Eleven blew. The night sky lit up with one bright orange ball of fire, and another. The sound hurt Able's ears.

*There you are, Monsieur Spymaster, whoever you are*, he thought, with a combination of relief and satisfaction. *Orange flowers to blossom on the wharf, even if it is the wrong building.*

Since everyone's attention on deck was riveted to the shore, Able and Jean both slipped out of their rope ties. Captain Ogilvie nodded to his sergeant, who smoothly stuffed a gag in Captain Faulke's mouth while his corporal roped him tight.

The *Captivity*'s guards had rushed to the railing, gesturing and jabbering. They didn't even notice when two more of Ogilvie's Marines looped another rope around Faulke's pudgy legs and neatly lowered him over the side to the remaining Marines in the cutter bobbing below.

Not losing a moment, Jean ran to the companionway that led to the hold. Able followed, alert, wondering when the hulk's guards would notice their pathetic captain was gone. Maybe they wouldn't notice at all, and assume he had gone back to his quarters, protesting done and his dinner waiting.

At the companionway, Jean turned suddenly and shoved Able back. "I'm doing this alone," he said. "You don't know what Claude Pascal looks like and I do."

"You need help," Able replied, and pushed against the Frenchman. "We're wasting time."

"Trust me," Jean said.

*Do I?* Able asked himself in instant alarm. His doubt must have registered on his face. Without a word, Jean Hubert, lieutenant and man who had given his parole as a gentleman, smashed his cudgel against Able's temple. Even the voices in his brain stopped, stunned, as he dropped to the deck.

# — Chapter Forty-four —

*He will never forgive me,* Jean thought, as he ran down the too-familiar steps into the hold, where his former friends and shipmates had all crammed close to the portholes on the side closest to the still-distant docks. He didn't care. He didn't want to be part of a sober-looking delegation who had to tell Meridee Six that her man was dead and their son fatherless.

*Bien sûr, I will probably be dead, too,* Jean reminded himself. If he couldn't extricate Claude Pascal, protected by his collection of thugs who bullied the weaker prisoners, he could at least get close enough to stab the man before they murdered him in turn. Able didn't need a fate like that.

He had forgotten the dim fug of the hold, the air murky and barely breathable. The stench made his eyes water. *How did I live here for nearly two years,* he asked himself in dismay. *And how are my countrymen managing?*

"Don't think these things," he muttered under his breath. He lowered his cudgel and edged closer to the crowd of prisoners, grateful now for the vile fog, because he stood out from them, well-fed and healthy, his hair thick again and nicely trimmed, because Mrs. Perry was a surprising barber.

The way the deck slanted, he knew all eight hundred prisoners on all three levels were watching the spectacular blaze from their tiny portholes with the iron bars.

"Jean? Lieutenant Hubert? *Est-ce vous?*"

He turned around slowly, fearing that his enterprise was about to end before it began. Maybe he shouldn't have clubbed Able Six. His sigh of relief was heartfelt and unheard, thanks to the chatter of voices by the portholes. Jacques Rien crouched close to him, Jacques, his signalman.

"*Oui, c'est moi.*"

Jacques looked worse than before, his hair nearly all fallen out from malnutrition except for a few straggly clumps, his arms skeletal. He had the same grin, though, if minus a few more teeth. The fire still burned within.

"Claude said you were dead, but I thought you must have escaped."

"And you need to come with me," Jean whispered. "I have an idea you would prove yourself useful."

"To the English? Sorry, Jean, but no."

"To a boys' school. Follow me if you want, but don't hinder me now. We have to relieve the world of Claude Pascal," Jean said.

Two pats on his back and a little push forward told him that Jacques was no enemy, no matter what he decided to do about Jean's impulsive offer. *And if Able ever forgives me for what I just did to him*, he thought.

It wasn't hard to move closer and closer. Jean had more strength than most of the unfortunate wraiths chattering excitedly and he shouldered them aside easily. He heard snatches of conversation, as the prisoners wondered what this might mean for them. Had Napoleon landed French troops on England's shores? Was the end of their endless captivity near?

With Jacques Rien behind him, Jean finally stood next to Claude Pascal, traitor to his own and in league with the captain now trussed neatly and waiting in a Royal Navy cutter on the hulk's starboard side. And was he more? Had his deeper game included terrorism in English seaports? If that was so, should he, Jean Hubert, Frenchman, stop Pascal?

Suddenly undecided, he watched the shore, squinting to see the house two doors down from St. Brendan's. Hopeful and fearful, too, he wondered if Walter Cornwall and the Marines had followed through and cleaned out the nest of conspirators so Nick Bonfort, small Gunwharf Rat with a mighty heart, could send his message.

And there it was: "Mission accomplished. What now?" Jean held his breath. A godless man, he prayed to the Omnipotent Almighty that there was no code and Pascal would not be suspicious.

"*Ah bien*," Pascal said. He laughed, and flashed his own returning signal as Jean tightened his grip on his cudgel.

But wait. Look. Could it be? From another house two or three doors from the conspirators' den came another signal. Shocked, Jean watched, then leaned back to inquire of his own signalman, the faithful Jacques Rien. "What do you read?" he asked.

"Drydock Two on what day?" Jacques whispered.

Claude Pascal flashed an answering signal as Jean the atheist prayed again that Nick and the other boys were alert enough to write down these flashes, too. Good God, how many plants were there along the shore? With or without Claude Pascal in tow, he had to get out of the hold alive to alert Able. Jean scanned the shoreline and to his relief saw no more pinpoints of answering light from land-based signals.

He had to act. If he survived, there would be time later to ask himself when he had turned from his own revolutionary cause to the British, and their response to Napoleon's determination to rule the world for France. He knew there was no woman involved, and no guarantees for himself. As he wavered, Jean Hubert remembered the kindness of his rescue. He remembered his friends and little students, who had already labored their young lives under more handicaps than ever burdened him. He was a man of the world. When the war finally exhausted itself, he would get on. Maybe someday he could return to France. If not, he would manage.

"Jacques, I am going to club Pascal and grab him. Do or do not help me, but do not hinder me," he whispered. "I am still your commander and that is an order."

He didn't wait for an answer. The fire in Building Eleven had died down and the men cramming the few portholes were starting to drift back to their hammocks. So much enthusiasm had exhausted them.

In silence, he slammed the cudgel against that demon Pascal's head and grabbed him around the neck when he screamed and struggled.

*Oh hurry, hurry*, he told himself as he started dragging Pascal toward the companionway. His bare feet slipped on the deck, slimy with human waste from prisoners with not enough strength to get to the foul buckets, but he stood up and forged ahead in the semi darkness.

The man was no lightweight. Jean knew Pascal had been eating better, if not at Captain Faulk's table, then someplace where starving prisoners couldn't see him. Pascal clawed at Jean's arm, and tried to regain his footing.

"Oh, no you don't," Jacques Rien exclaimed. The signalman snatched the cudgel from Jean's hand and slammed it down on Pascal's knee, with a satisfying crunch. "You have troubled us enough."

As the two of them dragged the screaming Claude Pascal to the companionway, Pascal's thugs and toadies muscled their way through the crowd of prisoners staring as if mesmerized by the odd scene before them. Starvation had rendered them slow of thought and they milled helplessly.

Jean's head jerked back as fingers in his hair yanked hard and threw him sideways. He clung to Pascal, trying to turn him to use him as a shield against the kicks and blows that rained down on him now. With a moan, he heard the faithful Jacques Rien give way.

*If I cannot drag you, Pascal, I will kill you*, Jean thought, even as he felt a rib crack and the knife drop from his hand.

Sudden sounds of many men in the companionway. Yells and good round English curses. Flashes of light and the smell of gunpowder. Thank merciful heaven that the fingers clawing at his hair let go. He slumped to the deck as others grabbed Pascal. He tried to reach for Jacques Rien, but someone stepped on his arm.

"Oh, beg pardon, you rascal."

It was Able Six, cutlass in one hand and a bloody bandage around his head. The Marine guard had cleared a path in the hold, with Captain Ogilvie shouting in desperately bad French to the now-cowed prisoners, who scrambled to get far away from this unwanted interference, and *qui sait?* Maybe his dreadful French.

"Captain Ogilvie needs my French class in the worst way," Jean said in French to Able, who laughed and helped him up, putting his free arm around Jean's waist.

Jean swayed but managed to stand by grabbing at the stair railing. They watched as two Marines trussed up Claude Pascal as handily as they had tied Captain Faulke, and rushed the cursing, spitting conspirator up the stairs.

"And what about this man?" Captain Ogilvie toed the silent and crumpled form of Jacques Rien. "Friend or foe of yours, Hubert?"

"Friend. Does he live?"

Ogilvie bent down and placed his hand on the signalman's heart. "He lives and by God he stinks."

"Then pick him up and bring him along, too, *s'il vous plâit*," Jean said. "If he decides to cooperate, he may prove of more assistance to your cause than I ever could. He is a signalman."

"And if he does not?" Ogilvie asked, obviously not a man with much of a heart.

"We will think of something else, sir," Able said firmly.

And that was that. Jean took a last look around the hold, in tears to leave behind brothers in arms. He was still a man with no choice. To stay here would be to die at the hands of disgruntled prisoners, or to perish from starvation and evil treatment, not trusted by the French prisoners or their British captors.

And true to the heart of scavengers and desperate men, someone in the hold would find surely Pascal's golden horde of English coins from Captain Faulke and figure it out. It was the best Jean could do because a man has to live, no matter how, during a long war.

He and Able helped each other up the companionway. The deck was cleared and tidy. The *Captivity*'s Marines were already under the firm hand of Ogilvie's sergeant of Royal Marines. "There will be another captain on board tomorrow," Ogilvie said as he put a steadying hand on Able. "Mrs. Faulke and her daughter have been informed and are packing."

Jean remembered. "You need to know this right away. When Pascal was responding to what we know was Nick Bonfort's signal, I saw other signals from another house two or three doors down from the conspirators' den."

"Merciful heaven!" Able exclaimed. "Captain Ogilvie, we need to head for shore handsomely now."

Moments later they pulled away from the *Captivity*. Captain Faulke sobbed and gargled behind his gag, and from the smell, must have filled his trousers. Trussed and silenced as well, Claude Pascal glared at the men around him, looking longest at Jean Hubert, who glared back with peace in his heart that no more French prisoners would be sacrificed to further Faulke's aim for a better berth for himself, and Pascal's plans for money, land and a fat wife. In the scope of the conflict now playing out on a broad canvas, it wasn't much, and would certainly never land in the history books. It was enough to know that justice of some sort had prevailed.

Captain Ogilvie's hastily scribbled note, put in the hands of the fastest runner on the cutter once it docked, was quickly in the hands of the major of Marines. A few crisp orders, and twelve men set off at once to clear out the houses closest to the known conspirator house.

Jacques Rien regained consciousness soon enough to find himself in the capable hands of a Haslar surgeon and his aide, Davey Ten, who grinned at Able Six, then frowned to see the bandage.

"I'm fine, Davey," Able assured him. "Nothing wrong with me that a good scolding from Mrs. Six won't cure."

"Mam does that, doesn't she?" Davey asked.

"No surer sign that all of us Gunwharf Rats are loved," Able said. "Go tend with your surgeon now. We'll talk soon enough."

Captain Ogilvie promptly vetoed any suggestion that Jean and Able walk back to St. Brendan's. Once arriving there, he also vetoed Able's request to continue down the row to the fourth house, where Marines had lined up six more conspirators. "I'll keep Lieutenant Hubert with me," the enigmatic Trinity Man said. "We might be needing a translator, eh, Jean?"

"*Certainmente, capitain,*" Jean said. "All you Englishmen think you need to do for a Frenchman to understand English is to speak louder and slower. *Zut alors,* I hear them now!"

He craned his neck painfully to look back down the quiet street, where Gunwharf Rats poured from St. Brendan's and the Six house across the street. Mrs. Perry and the Bartlebys stood close by, ever protective. Was that Walter Cornwall holding little Betsy MacGregor so tight? Meridee Six had already wrapped her arms around her husband, the most fortunate Able Six, even if he was a bastard and too smart for anyone's own good.

Jean Hubert – artist, adventurer, prisoner, seaman, and now man without a country – smiled in the dark. He knew he would come about soon enough, whether the war lasted another ten months or ten years.

# — Chapter Forty-five —

Classes were suspended at St. Brendan's the next day because no one could think about scholarship, not after such a night. Just as well; Able's head ached abominably where his friend Jean Hubert had clubbed him. The pain was rendered more bearable because Mrs. Six cuddled close to him, cried a bit, scolded, but cuddled more.

He felt well enough to at least sit up in bed – Jean's wallop had necessitated a few stitches – but he had made no objection to wallowing about in the comfort of his bedroom, Meri close by with Ben, and various friends trouping through to fill him in on the continuing saga.

John Mark came bouncing in first, holding up his bandaged arm, nearly beside himself with excitement. "Master Six, imagine this! I thought we who were left by the sea wall were going to languish into oblivion..."

Able laughed out loud. "John, you could never languish into oblivion. Tell me, were you wounded in a fleet action? Is there going to be a respectable scar?"

"I hope so," the little fellow declared, as Meri turned away to laugh. "Seriously, Mam, would you want to be stuck at the sea wall where *nothing* was happening?"

"I am certain I would not," she said. "You found adventure?"

"Gor, did we ever! Captain Ogilvie directed us to help surround and take the other house two doors down from the first one. I was tripped on the stairs by a real scoundrel with a dagger! Whack, whack, five sutures. Isn't that simply famous?"

Able held up a placating hand. "John, you need to learn something about the ladies." He reconsidered quickly, because he dearly loved to tease Mrs. Six. "Well, perhaps not. They like to see those scars, too, but only after they have healed." *I will never tell anyone how much Mrs. Six likes that scar on my knee,* he reminded himself. A wink in the general direction of his wife made her blush, because she knew him pretty well, scars and all.

Ahem, moving right along. "John Mark, you will be the envy of nations tomorrow when school resumes," Able assured him. "Just don't pick at your scar and infect it."

"No, Master Six. Davey Ten already told me how to take care of it." His eyes grew wide again. "Davey even stitched me!"

Later that afternoon, Ben was dozing between Able's legs on his bed when Nick Bonfort came in, quieter and more serious, because that was Nick. Jean Hubert, sporting his own bandage, leaned against the doorframe, regarded Nick with some pride.

"Come closer, Nick," Able said. "In fact, you can sit with me. Ben is gone to another world right now and you won't wake him."

"Is this one of those times when I can call you Da?" Nick asked.

"It is," Able told him, and swallowed down the lump in his throat. "I hear from Smitty and all concerned that you were calm in the face of real danger in that house."

"Da, I wish we could have saved Mrs. Grundy and her son," he said, his face clouding over, because Nick was a tender child.

"That is war," Able said. Smitty had stopped by earlier to tell him that the conspirators had killed the old woman and her feeble-minded son that morning, to prevent any interference, in preparation to leave the house and destroy Building Twelve at dusk.

"Sir, they did a bad thing," Smitty said, showing his own tender side. "They duped the old dear into thinking they were harmless dockworkers and paid her rent, then killed them when they weren't needed."

"We live in desperate and trying times, Smitty," Able told him simply.

But here was Nick, leaning close, happy for Able's arm around him. "I flashed the message and got the answer." He looked back at Jean in the doorway. "Master Hubert was able to read that second message."

"*Oui*. Dry Dock Two was to be the target in two days, the same night as the ropewalk, which was Nick's message. Everything is better guarded, as of this morning. The Marines are even now searching all the houses along this stretch of shoreline. We owe a debt to Nick. Everyone is saying so."

Nick nodded and Able both heard and felt his sigh of satisfaction. "Nick, might you want to learn more about signaling? We of the Royal Navy have a great flag system." He gestured to Jean. "Perhaps you might ask your friend Jacques Rien if he could teach your night time system. How is Rien feeling?"

"Better. We will have to see if he will help us. I am not certain. Perhaps when he is eating better and regains his strength, he might be willing." He shrugged. "Come, Nick. Let your sailing master sleep." He laughed. "I knocked him on the head pretty hard. I don't think his brains fell out, but we can't take any chances."

After the door closed, Able leaned back and admired his son, sleeping so peacefully, safe and secure in his baby world because the Royal Navy's wooden walls and iron men were standing the watch. His peculiar specters had been remarkably silent today. Maybe they were thinking twice about continuing their relentless reign in his head, since it could prove dangerous, even in a boys' school. *Will I miss you?* Able asked himself, and thought that he might. Time would tell.

Sir B arrived with Grace, his face troubled. *Uh oh. Bad news about Gervaise*, Able thought, and felt his own regret. "What have you heard?" was enough to launch Sir B into telling what he knew, and it wasn't pretty.

Able noticed but made no comment as he watched Grace hold Sir B's hand, as he said the Turennes were currently guests in the Royal Marines brig right there in Portsmouth, near the dock. "I don't know what will happen," he said, with a shake of his head. "Henri Turenne claims they were forced to carry notes by someone they would not name. I asked if I could visit Gervaise, but he sent me a note that he was too ashamed to see me." Another shake of the head, followed what looked like an absent-minded raising of Grace's hand to his lips for a kiss. It was hard to tell with Sir B.

Hours later, Meri helped Able to his feet and assisted him as he dressed for dinner. "I know you were thinking about that scar on your knee," she accused, which made him tickle her in a spot he knew she liked, since she was bending so close. "Stop that! Someone will see you. You are hopeless of remedy and a sailor such as parish priests warn about over the pulpit."

"Aye, Admiral Six, and who is knocking now? Our bedroom has turned into a regular scuttlebutt."

"Hold still while I attempt this neck cloth," she ordered. "It's Walter Cornwall and he wants a word with both of us."

"I think we know what is coming," Able said. "Should I tease him a little?"

"Don't you dare. He is terrified."

He was. Constable Cornwall nearly shook as he stood at attention in their bedroom, Able lounging in his stockinged feet with Meri proper beside him.

In a clear voice, he declared his love for Betsy MacGregor, and yes, she is young, but she loves me too, and already loves my little daughter, and please, sir and madam, I will treat her ever so well and furnish all her wants and needs. All in one prodigious breath.

He calmed down then, and delivered this piece of excellent news. "The powers that be have already announced a willingness to reserve all houses along the shoreline for families of constables." He took a deep breath, almost as if he didn't believe his well-earned and sudden good fortune. "Captain Ogilvie has already promised me the house two doors down that we raided yesterday, which now has no owners." Another breath, one more confident. "Please, Mr. and Mrs. Six, your consent."

It was a remarkable outpouring from a self-contained, organized fellow who had served his own harsh apprentice in a Cornish workhouse. *So this is what it will feel like when someone someday asks for the hand of a future daughter of mine,* Able thought, beguiled by the notion. He glanced at Meri.

"What say you, Mrs. Six?"

"I am completely in favor, although I will miss Betsy MacGregor's cheerful help," Meri said, not sounding even slightly sad. "She'll be two doors down and mistress of her own household." Then the tears came, and Able hugged her. "I'm fair delighted!"

"They're like this," Able assured Walter as he patted Meri's back. "You'll come to understand."

"I already do, Master Six," the constable said. "I had a wife once, remember?"

"Aye, you did."

"I've missed this, tears and all."

He gave Able a small salute and with a smile on his face hurried down the stairs. Able crossed his fingers that Mrs. Perry would not threaten him.

Walter was still in the kitchen later when Able made his way downstairs, leaning on Meri's arm, not because he felt particularly infirm, but because he knew it made her happy to help him.

Nick and John Mark had already set the table, which meant Meri had to abandon him in the sitting room holding Ben while she dashed around and put the forks and spoons where they really belonged. Consequently, it was John and Nick who answered the doorbell and ushered in the dinner guests, come to celebrate a successful naval operation.

They ran out of chairs, so the invited Rats scurried across the street for more chairs and a small table. Mr. and Mrs. Simon Goodrich brought along a surprise guest of their own, Henry Maudslay himself, who apologized profusely for invading their premises uninvited. "I am in town because the factory begins official operation tomorrow and I want to see it," he explained.

Captain Ogilvie strolled in with Headmaster Croker, followed by Grace Croker and Sir B, ably pushed by Junius Bolt. Mr. and Mrs. Bartleby, all apology and feeling uncertain in such august company, furnished an assortment of éclairs and profiteroles and found an especially warm welcome. Walter Cornwall blushed and protested, but Betsy herself sat him beside Jean Hubert and dared him to move. Able could tell already that this would be a wonderfully successful marriage.

They were mashed together tighter than whelks in a basket. Sitting at the head of his table, Able looked around in real pleasure. He cocked his head, delighted to hear the mentors and polymaths in his brain applauding politely. He already knew they were a hard lot to impress.

Even Euclid and Copernicus fell silent when there was a knock on the door, and an awestruck Betsy ushered in William Pitt himself, prime minister, Trinity House Warden, and man with a message. Able happily yielded his seat at the head of the table and joined Meri at the foot, sharing her chair.

Dinner was a sailor's delight, beginning with tried-and-true lobscouse, succeeded by sea-pie, rounded off with whipped syllabub, and chased down with éclairs and profiteroles and smuggled sherry from Mr. Pitt himself. The food went around until everything was consumed except the pattern on the china. Rum formed the toast, not watered down this time, but dark and aromatic, because every man at the table, old and young alike, knew that rum was for heroes. Able laughed inside to see Meri watching her Gunwharf Rats' consumption, anyway.

They looked to Able for a toast. Flattered, he yielded to the prime minister of England, seated in his house at his table – the wonder of it all.

William Pitt rose and nodded deferentially to Able, who smiled back. "There are so many we could toast this evening," he said. "I will limit myself, because it would not do for you to see your prime minister shot in the neck and staggering blind."

He grew serious after the laughter died down and raised his glass. "A hearty toast to the Gunwharf Rats and St. Brendan the Navigator School," he said. "Your creation was a brilliant stroke, for which we thank Headmaster Croker. You former workhouse lads have earned the confidence of a grateful nation. This will be a long war and your best effort is needed for king and country. To you, future masters."

*Don't cry*, Able told himself as he raised his glass. *Don't cry. What do you think of that, Euclid?*

Following other toasts, the guests gradually took their leave. The Goodriches hung back to ask Able and Meri if they could stroll to the sea wall with John Mark and Pierre Deschamps. "We'd like to ask them something," Simon said.

"As you wish," Able told them. "I think you'll be pleased with their answer."

"We have room in our house," Mrs. Goodrich said, her eyes hopeful.

"What's more important, you have room in your heart," Able replied.

William Pitt was next, bowing to Meri and shaking Able's hand. He looked toward the door, where an impatient Captain Ogilvie waited with no good grace. "If that man were not so useful to Trinity House and this nation, I vow I would order him to Canada on permanent assignment," Pitt told them.

"He does seem eager to leave," Meri said.

"You would be, too, madam, if you had just been informed that Claude Pascal has been allowed to escape," Pitt said, in that droll way of his.

Meri gasped. "What?" Able exclaimed, certain he had not heard correctly. Maybe Jean had struck him harder than he thought.

"We at Trinity thought it best to allow Pascal to escape. He will be followed to the ends of the earth, I don't doubt, by Captain Ogilvie," Pitt said. "If anyone can turn up details about a truly evil man and his other plans, Angus can. Come now, Able Six! You of all people should understand the right man for the right event."

"I suppose I should," he murmured. "Captain *Ogilvie?*"

"If you want to thwart a spy, set a bloodhound on his trail. Go lie down, Able. You look a little fine drawn," the prime minister said. He glanced toward the door to the sitting room, where Sir B and Grace appeared to be engaged in a lively discussion. "Those two," Pitt said, then brightened. "Do something about them, Able. That's an order from your prime minister. Good night."

He took his leave, walking by himself because Captain Ogilvie had already hurried ahead. As Able stood in the doorway, watching England's prime minister make his way casually down the street, swinging his walking stick like the *bon vivant* he wasn't, Able noticed a man in the shadows. Alert, he clapped his hand to his hip and could have groaned aloud. Why did he never have even a pea shooter handy when he needed one?

There was no call for drastic measures. Captain Ogilvie stood in the shadows. Able knew the time was long gone when he should fear the man, but the hairs on his neck rose, anyway.

"Sir, I hear you are soon to be on the trail of Claude Pascal," he said as Ogilvie came closer.

"Aye, Master Six. I am Trinity House's dogsbody. Now you know."

"Surely there is some glamor with the drudgery," Able said cautiously.

"Precious little. I have the happy task of seeing if Monsieur Pascal will lead us to other rascals, who will disappear when *I* find them." He rubbed his hands together, obviously a man who liked his employment.

What could Able say to that? He took a long look at Angus Ogilvie, seeing this time a spy catcher, all bluster, common, vulgar, and someone with a remarkable facility to blend into his surroundings.

"I waited in private to tell you something about the men we routed from that second house," Ogilvie said. "One of them had a nasty scar. Looks like someone dragged a pair of embroidery scissors down his ugly face. You'll be pleased to know it appeared infected. Obviously not all the men on the dock that night were English."

"How did you find out about…" Able stopped. Captain Ogilvie seemed to know everything. Best not to question it. "Where did you take him? I have a score to settle with a man so eager to do my wife great mischief."

Captain Ogilvie shook his head with something almost approaching regret, but not quite, not if the gleam in his eyes meant anything. "Poor man. He met with an awful accident between the house and the brig."

"I'm almost afraid to ask."

"Wise of you," the spy catcher answered smoothly. "Let us say he will never trouble your wife, or anyone else's wife, again. That one gave me real satisfaction!" He doffed his hat. "And now, master, I had better hurry after Monsieur Pascal. I'll see you again when you least expect it."

*Of that I have no doubt,* Able thought. He watched Ogilvie do his own saunter down the street. He swore he was watching him closely, but the man seemed to vanish beyond a street lamp.

Thoughtful, Able closed the door. Meri stood by the stairs. He took her hand and steered her toward the sitting room. "Well, my bountiful wench, I've been given an order by William Pitt. Follow my lead here."

He spoke to Junius Bolt, who stood respectfully by the door. The old retainer laughed softly and moved away. Without a word, Able wheeled Sir B into the sitting room, lifted the protesting man from his chair and sat him on the sofa.

Quick to follow, Meri directed her friend, the prickly Miss Croker, to the same sofa and sat her down.

When Meri joined him at the door, Able issued his final order of the day, this time to his captain, friend, and proud, stubborn man.

"William Pitt ordered me to do something about you two. I'm closing the door. Talk to each other. It's that simple. I'll lock this door if I have to. Good night."

Silence on the other side of the door, then laughter from the two old friends inside. Then soft conversation, suggesting to Able that a great deal was going on. He extended his arm to his wife, who tucked herself close.

"I have a headache, but it won't last forever," he confided. "Classes resume tomorrow and the war continues. What can we do about that?"

"Weather on handsomely," she said.

"Spoken like a perfect sailing master's wife. My dear, let us go to bed so this nice couple can propose to each other."

They looked in on Ben as usual, and found him sound asleep. "This is why we fight, Meri."

"Thank you for saying *we,*" she told him.

"It's your fight, too," he acknowledged, which meant she kissed his cheek.

"Don't be long, my love." She went into their room. He paused a moment, then tapped lightly on Jean Hubert's door. The Frenchman came into the hall. "Smitty is asleep," he said in a low voice. "I really should apologize for hitting you so hard. I have to know something: do you trust me now?"

"Completely," Able said without a qualm.

"That's all I need." It was said quietly, but with deep feeling.

"I trust you so much that tomorrow, if matters settle out with John Mark and Pierre as I think they will, I'll move Smitty in with Nick Bonfort, and you can have your own room."

"Would you trust me to walk along the sea wall if I feel like it, and maybe go to that tavern to watch Englishmen play darts while drunk?"

Able laughed. "If you must."

"*Oui bien sûr*. I enjoy laughing at drunk Englishmen."

"Very well, friend. Good night."

# — Chapter Forty-six —

"Gracie, you realize, of course, that my damned wretch of a sailing master genius is expecting me to propose to you."

"I know. Cheeky of him, isn't it?"

Grace sidled closer to Sir B's right side, the side with the leg mostly gone, attempting serenity, when she wanted to straddle the man, shake him by his shoulders, plant a kiss on his lips and propose to him.

Her brother always said she was too impetuous, and that was the reason no one had ever asked for her hand, but she knew better. She sat back, a smile on her face because no one was going anywhere, and remembered the times in their youth when she had whipped Belvedere St. Anthony at whist. Horrified, Mama had ordered her to lose gracefully, if she ever expected to get a husband, but it wasn't in Grace to do any such thing, not with someone who played poorly and cheated, too.

"Why, pray tell, are you favoring me with that daffy smile?" Sir B asked.

"I was merely thinking of all the times I have trounced you at whist, dear Belvedere," she said, digging it in because she knew how he disliked his first name. ("Blamed idiot name inflicted on me by parents of unsound mind," he had joked with her years earlier.)

He chuckled and put his arm around her. "Go ahead and beat me soundly once more, Penelope Mehitabel Grace Croker," he told her, remembering how *she* hated her first two names. "I know you're better at whist than I am. Billiards, too, as I recall."

She rewarded him by leaning her head against his shoulder. How to proceed? Able Six expected them to talk and settle the matter, but this was no ordinary man, no ordinary circumstance.

"I could beat you in a foot race," he said finally. "I remember several such instances." He took a deep breath and another. "I could not do that now."

"No, you could not," she said, not hanging back for a single moment, as an ordinary lady would, because every word mattered. "See here, Sir B, we are a little old for foot races."

*Who first? All I stand to lose is my happiness,* Grace thought. *If I am rebuffed, I still have all my wealth. Thaddeus would still want me to teach here. Meridee will be my friend. I'll have my Gunwharf Rats.* She cleared her throat and doubted that sailing against an enemy fleet could be more terrifying than this.

"Did you ever think I would fall in love with you?" she asked, her voice soft. "I did, you know, even though you and Thaddeus teased me for years, and I knew all the pretty young ladies fluttered around. I even read those boring *Naval Chronicles* to see where in the world your ship was. When rumors of battle reached us in Mayfair, I worried. So many times I nearly wrote to you, but that would have been too forward. I wanted to, though. Believe me I did, but years passed."

His arm stayed around her, which gave her hope. He remained silent. She plunged on. "I convinced everyone, perhaps you as well, that I was perfectly happy to remain a spinster. I had money, my own town house and landau. My less than happily married friends assured me I was better off, and thank goodness I didn't need a man to provide the money, home and prominence they needed."

She heard a little sound from deep in his throat. He tightened his grip on her.

"I suppose I would have muddled along pretty well, if Thaddeus hadn't begged me to teach here at St. Brendan's," she continued, speaking more quickly now. She would be done soon enough. What more was there to say, after all? "I had pretty nearly convinced myself that I was fine, at least, until I found myself in your orbit again. And then wouldn't you know it, I found myself watching the Sixes and envying them for their courage in loving each other. There they were, neither of them with more than pennies to rub together, but so happy. I wanted that for myself. There. I admit it."

"Then find a man with all his parts, Gracie," he said finally.

If he had called her Grace instead of Gracie, she would have stood up and left the room. But he called her Gracie and hope can twine about a slender thread.

"I don't happen to love a man with all his parts," she argued. "What are you going to do about that?"

Silently, he pulled back the throw covering his legs. He took her hand and placed it on the small portion of his remaining leg. "I don't stand well, if at all. Sometimes the stump hurts. You'd have to hand me a urinal, and help me sit on the chair in my room with the lid that raises up. All that aside, I haven't felt strong since Aboukir Bay. I doubt I will live long, Gracie. Is that what you truly want for yourself? Work of an embarrassing nature? Early widowhood? The bleakness of a sickroom? Think hard."

Calmly, she thought about what he had said, waiting for disgust or sorrow or worry to change her mind. All she felt was relief and joy, because she knew she could win this. Maybe she didn't even need words.

Silently, she took the throw and pulled it over both of them, settling the end around her hip and putting her feet on his hassock next to his foot.

"I still love you," she said, her heart light. "You won't mind if I call you Sir B, because I already do. And when we have a son, we'll find a better name than Belvedere, which I'll agree sounds vaguely silly. I'm partial to Daniel, or maybe Edward. I will negotiate about Penelope, however, as long as we don't rope it to Mehitabel."

She tipped her head toward his, her hand across his chest now. "I'm brave enough," she whispered in his ear.

"Able told me not so long ago that all I lacked was courage," he said finally. "He was right."

"How fortunate that I have courage to spare," she said. "I rather enjoyed that recent night in my townhouse, sharing a bed with you because you were sad, even though you snore and mutter in your sleep." She patted his chest. "You haven't said how you feel about me, and I'd like to know, especially since I've been so brazen."

He settled in more comfortably next to her. "You'll think this odd, indeed, but since that night we took John Mark to Astley's Amphitheatre, I've been thinking how much fun it would be to take a child of my own there, and a wife. You, in particular."

Grace gasped in pure delight and started to laugh. Sir B joined in, until he kissed her into silence.

"Would it amaze you to know I had the very same thought at Astley's?" she said minutes later. "You, in particular."

"Then we are wasting time," he told her.

She heard the voice of command again, the sound of a man with his mind made up. She knew no amount of gloss could disguise what was lost, but she heard no hesitation. He was right; they *were* wasting time.

"I can't get down on one knee and propose, as a gentleman should," he said, sounding not even slightly apologetic, the old Sir B returning, the tease and the childhood friend who never minded a lively argument now and then, and who didn't object when she beat him at whist. "I love you, though. Grace Croker, will you marry this battered sea dog, who has seen better days?"

"I will," she said promptly. "Sir B, your better days are just beginning."

"And yours?"

"Aye, aye, you lovely man," she said softly.

They kissed again, found it better than the time before, and kissed once more. Sir B was starting to sound breathless, and Grace knew her hair was untidy.

"You realize we are behaving like twenty-year-olds," she said, trying to pat the pins back in her chignon. "What do we do now?"

"My house or yours?" Sir B asked. "There aren't any extra chambers here at the Sixes, and I personally would not care to face your brother's butler across the street in the monastery."

"I wouldn't, either," Grace agreed. "He's a perfect beast. Do you think Able locked this door?"

"Unlikely. He's no fool." He patted his waistcoat, with its silver fob and dangling bosun's pipe. "Your man Junius gave this to me to summon him."

He took out the silver pipe, put it to his lips and piped five rapid high notes.

"Which is…" Grace asked, fascinated by this man.

"The Hail. Junius Bolt, if he is worth his salt, will open that door," he told her. "Gracie, better get out from under this blanket with me. Some decorum is in order, even though you are going home with me tonight. My carriage should be out front."

She did as he said, wishing her hair was neat and organized. Junius opened the door, followed by Able Six. She stood up, wishing for dignity.

"Sir B and I would like to go to 25 Jasper Street," she said, and laughed when Able staggered back in mock amazement. "Oh, go to bed, Able! You're a nuisance, at times."

He managed an elegant bow. "After Junius and I get my captain into his carriage," he said. "Stand aside, Grace. Follow us."

She did as he said, a smile on her face as Able picked up his commander and carried him down the hall. Meridee sat on the steps leading to the chambers upstairs and blew Grace a kiss.

"I've never been a matron of honor," Meridee hinted. "Should I be getting a new dress?"

"Give me your measurements tomorrow," Grace said as she followed her beloved Sir B, pushing the empty wheeled chair. "I have a cunning modiste in London and you will look lovely in primrose. She sews on short notice."

# — Epilog —

## LATE SUMMER - 1804

A visit to Portsmouth from Jamie MacGregor was turning into a pleasant summer ritual. Last year Jamie's frigate had landed in dry dock for necessary repair. This time he had come to Portsmouth in a sloop of war with a midshipman and a young gentlemen, taking a transfer to the *Halcyon*, a thirty-eight commanded by Captain David Pettibone.

"You should find yourself on the receiving end of prize money, if the stories I hear about Pettibone are true," Able told his former student as they walked by the sea wall. "Even better, Sailing Master Marchbank will teach you everything else you need to know. You will be a mate to the master soon enough."

"Do you know everyone in the fleet, sir?"

"Pretty nearly." Able felt that tug again, especially standing with someone who smelled like brine. The odor was fading from his own uniforms, and he wasn't sure he liked that.

Theirs was a longer walk than usual. Jamie had the inclination, and Able the time. He had sent Smitty with an eager crew of Rats into the sound in Sir B's *Jolly Roger*. Meri had taken young Ben to meet his aunt, uncle and cousins in Pomfrey. They were coming home tonight, and he was eager to see them. Mrs. Perry was presiding in the kitchen, ruling supreme. Jean Hubert had convinced Jacques Rien to accept a parole. It was half four and they were coaching a select class of lads, Nick prominent among them, in learning night signaling.

He smiled to himself as they walked in silence. John Mark Goodrich made a point to drop by the house at least once a week. He still attended morning classes at St. Brendan's, but his afternoons were increasingly taken up with mechanics in the block pulley factory, which was churning out a steady supply of pulleys for the fleet. Pierre Goodrich's English was improving, but Lydia Goodrich still worried about his shyness.

"Jamie, your sister was hoping you wouldn't be upset with her because she did not wait for your return to port before marrying a very worthy fellow," he said, which made Jamie laugh and shake his head.

"Since we never know when we'll raise Portsmouth, I wouldn't have expected her to wait," he said. He turned serious then, and apologetic. "Sir, we should have told you we

214

were older than we said. Our workhouse master specifically stated twelve year olds was the outer limit, and I knew I wanted to be here."

"No apology necessary. I know something about ambition and a burning desire to put the workhouse behind, no matter how. Where away the *Halcyon*, Jamie? Can you tell me, or are your orders a secret?"

"I think we can trust you," Jamie teased, with that same endearing camaraderie they had fallen into, now that one of St. Brendan's first graduates was slowly and steadily advancing in the fleet. "We're heading into the Pacific on what Captain Pettibone calls a fishing trip."

"Then prize money for sure, lad."

"Sir, is there anything I should know about going around the Horn?"

"Don't try the deck without a rope around your waist and pay attention to your sailing master," Able said promptly, remembering in vivid, instant detail every single trip around the Horn from the age of nine on. "You'll probably learn a whole host of new curses, too."

"Is that even possible?"

They laughed together. They stopped on the walk by the sea wall, and Able described the events of last May. "Trinity House and the Navy Board each sent the school letters of commendation for service rendered. They're hanging in our assembly room across the street. Be a proud Gunwharf Rat, Jamie."

"Aye, sir, I am."

He said it with quiet pride. They looked at the hulks in the harbor, still wretched places for prisoners, but less so, with more care and attention from the Transport Office and frequent inspections from the Navy Board. Able had served on two inspections. While conditions were by no means perfect, at least they weren't quite so soul sapping.

He pointed to the iron cage swinging by the Gunwharf, final resting place of Captain Tobias Faulke, late of the hulk *Captivity* and unlamented. "He was flayed within an inch of his life, then hauled up a yardarm and hanged. A placard announcing *Traitor* was nailed to his chest and he was paraded naked past all the ships," Able said.

"That's hard to watch."

"Aye, it was, Jamie. He went into that iron cage and there he remains, a warning to all." He peered closer. "Look like he's been reduced to bones."

"I hear there was a French conspirator involved," Jamie commented. "Or maybe that's just scuttlebutt."

"I'll tell you this, but it's between you and me: Claude Pascal is being followed by a Trinity House thug with surprising abilities. Already I think Captain Ogilvie has silenced several conspirators in other ports."

"And how is Sir B? Betsy mentioned him in a letter that caught up with me at Gibraltar, but the paper was waterlogged, and the ink had run."

"He married Grace Croker," Able said and laughed. "I hear from Nick and some of the other Rats that she is much more pleasant to her students when they struggle with log writing in class." He nudged Jamie. "Not your favorite skill, if memory serves me."

Jamie made a face. "Memory always serves you, Master Six, but my handwriting has improved. It was either that or walk the plank, my old sailing master told me."

"Jackie Smithers would say that." He could tell Jamie more about the St. Anthonys, but forthright Grace was surprisingly shy about informing the world she was increasing, according to Meri. Well, it would be obvious eventually.

Back at the house, Jamie politely declined an invitation to dinner. "I'm to eat two doors down from St. Brendan's," the future sailing master said. "Betsy's so proud of her cookery and her very own sitting room."

"As she should be. We've all come a long way, Mister MacGregor. Stop by tomorrow when Mrs. Six is home. She'll want to say hello."

The evening was too fine to go inside. Able sat down on his front steps, content to look across the street to St. Brendan's. On Monday he would take his next batch of youngsters to the stone basin to strip to their smalls and practice floating.

He had his own news for Meri. It wasn't something he could put in a letter. When they were comfortable in the sitting room, Ben asleep and her feet in his lap as he massaged them, he could tell her about his own visit to Trinity House, and the invitation to come aboard as a Younger Brother. The request came from Captain Rose, who had followed William Pitt as warden, now that Pitt was too busy.

Able had accepted with surprise and real pleasure, looking forward to occasional visits to London for meetings, as long as Meri and Ben could come along and stay in Lady Grace St. Anthony's townhouse, which even Sir B agreed was nicer than his own. There were still times when Able needed his wife's bolstering faith and love, those times when he felt like a child of the workhouse. Thankfully, those moments were spaced farther and farther apart, maybe shooed away by his nosy specters, or by his own will and destiny.

The other matter touched his mind and heart. Captain Rose had taken him up another flight of stairs to a series of offices, and opened a door.

"I want you to see something," he said as he lit a lamp. "We don't use all these rooms. A few weeks ago, we were doing some inventory and I noticed this."

He held the lamp up to illuminate a small painting in an exquisite gilt frame that reminded Able of similar frames he had admired in a Cádiz shop. His mind flew back to that hot afternoon in 1795 when he stood there, tempted to buy a frame, and put someone's portrait in it, to pretend he belonged in a family. The moment had passed and besides, the frame was too dear for his pocketbook.

"Look closely."

Able shut down the little scene in his mind and gave the picture his full attention. He stepped back in amazement.

"That's what I thought, too," Captain Rose said.

"Who…who is this?"

"I'm not certain. There was a time some years ago, as you know, when Spain was not warring with us. A naval delegation from Cádiz visited Trinity House, wanting to tour the dry docks at Portsmouth, and lighthouses." He tapped the picture. "The name on the back says Francisco Jesus Domingo y Guzman, Conde de Quintanar. That's all I know."

"I look like him."

"No doubt."

"Maybe it's the curly hair and the straight nose. Spaniards do have a look," Able said.

"They do," Captain Rose agreed. He blew out the lamp and indicated the door. "I wanted you to see it. You may form your own opinion."

He knew Meri would be pleased at his Younger Brother status, but he knew she would be more interested in the picture. *Meri, where are you? I really don't care to have you out of my sight and it has been thirteen days, seven hours, thirty-six minutes and fifteen sixteen seventeen.... Stop it, brain.*

Maybe if he stared up the street past the bakery, he could will the post chaise into sight. Meri had argued about a post chaise versus the mail coach and he ignored her. Their funds were modest, but he decreed such a luxury for a wonderful woman who should have more of life's finer things, except that she loved a sailor.

Ah. The post chaise turned the corner, carrying the two dearest people in his universe – sorry, Euclid – coming home. Coming home to him.

# — About the author —

Bryner Photography

A well-known veteran of the romance writing field, Carla Kelly is the author of forty-two novels and three non-fiction works, as well as numerous short stories and articles for various publications. She is the recipient of two RITA Awards from Romance Writers of America for Best Regency of the Year; two Spur Awards from Western Writers of America; three Whitney Awards, 2011, 2012, and 2014; and a Lifetime Achievement Award from Romantic Times.

Carla's interest in historical fiction is a byproduct of her lifelong study of history. She's held a variety of jobs, including public relations work for major hospitals and hospices, feature writer and columnist for a North Dakota daily newspaper, and ranger in the National Park Service (her favorite job) at Fort Laramie National Historic Site and Fort Union Trading Post National Historic Site. She has worked for the North Dakota Historical Society as a contract researcher.

Carla's interest in the Regency Period of England has moved well beyond the more-typical lords and ladies Regency romances. She feels more at home writing about ordinary people of that interesting era, in particular those involved in the Napoleonic Wars both on land and at sea. She feels equally at home writing about the 18th century inhabitants of the American Southwest, as reflected in The Spanish Brand Series, set in the royal colony of New Mexico in the 1780s. Other novels reflect her interest in the American West of the late nineteenth-early twentieth centuries, involving coal mining and ranching.

You can find Carla at www.CarlaKellyAuthor.com